"What are you doing?"

"Kissing you, unless you've got a problem with that."

In answer, she threaded her arms around his neck and tugged his head down lower. She wasn't short at five-foot-six, but he was still almost a foot taller.

Noah captured her mouth and found himself capsized on the wave of Kelsey's lips. He tasted her. Absorbed her. Her flavor. Her warmth. Her Kelsey-ness.

Engulfed. He was engulfed in the intimate experience of her soft, delicious lips. And he devoured her.

Or maybe she devoured him. It was hard to tell with so much heat.

Mouths open and searching, they shared one quivering breath under a network of hot wet kisses. She was as hungry for him as he was for her . . .

By Lori Wilde

LORI WILDE

THE *Christmas* DARE

A TWILIGHT, TEXAS NOVEL

AVONBOOKS

An Imprint of HarperCollinsPublishers

Excerpt from *To Tame a Wild Cowboy* copyright © 2019 by Laurie Vanzura.

First Avon Books mass market printing: November 2019
First Avon Books hardcover printing: October 2019

Print Edition ISBN: 978-0-06-246831-4
Digital Edition ISBN: 978-0-06-246832-1

Cover art by Larry Rostant
Cover photographs © Tancha/RonTech3000/Patryk Kosmider/
Dmitry Zimin/pictoplay/Shutterstock (six images)

FIRST EDITION

19 20 21 22 23 QGM 10 9 8 7 6 5 4 3 2 1

To Dixie-Lee Campbell, your big heart and kind spirit are an inspiration to those who know and love you. Shine on, you bright, sweet star.

CHAPTER 1

On a Christmas-scented Saturday morning in early December, Dallas's newly elected mayor, Filomena James, walked her only surviving daughter, Kelsey, down the pew-packed aisle of the lavishly decorated Highland Park United Methodist Church.

She slipped her arm through her daughter's, and off they went to the instrumental score of "Let Me Tell You About My Boat." Filomena had insisted on music hipper than "The Wedding March" for her child's big day.

Bucking the old guard.

That was how she won her mayoral seat. Filomena was innovative, clever, and resourceful. Never mind that Kelsey was a traditionalist. After all, Filomena was the one shelling out the big bucks for this shindig, and to quote her campaign buttons, *she* was the "rebel with a cause."

She'd insisted on the December wedding date, so as not to conflict with her mayoral bid. In mild protest, Kelsey put up a feeble fuss. Her daughter was not a fan of December in general or Christmas in particular. But as always, Filomena had prevailed.

"Lucky" for Kelsey, Mama knew best.

Everything was going as Filomena had planned. That is, until the groom hightailed it for the exit, elbows locked with his best man.

Fifteen minutes later, back in the bridal room of the church, Kelsey sat as calm as a statue, ankles crossed demurely, feet tucked underneath the bench, expression mild. Her waist-length hair twisted high in an elegant braided chignon. A bouquet of white roses and a crumpled, handwritten Dear Jane letter were lying in her lap.

Sounds of car doors slamming and hushed voices stirring gossip drifted in through the partially opened window.

The poor thing.

Do you think Kelsey suspected Clive was gay?

How does Filomena recover from this?

Exhaling deeply, Kelsey hid her smile as relief poured through her. Okay, sprinkle in a dab of sadness, a jigger of regret, and a dollop of I-do-not-want-to-face-my-mother, but other than that, Clive's abrupt adios hadn't peeled her back too far.

Hey, it wasn't the most embarrassing thing that had ever happened to her. She'd get through this.

Filomena paced. As if struck by a hundred flyswatters all slapping at once, her cheeks flushed scarlet. Black Joan Crawford eyebrows pulled into a hard V. "Do you have any idea how humiliated *I* am?" she howled.

"I'm sorry, Mother," Kelsey said by rote.

"This is your fault. If you'd slept with Clive, as I told you to, instead of sticking to that wait-until-the-wedding nonsense, *I* would not be on the hook for this nightmare."

"Yes, Mother. You're right. You're always right."

Filomena's scowl lessened. "Well, at least you admit it."

Kelsey's best friend, Tasha Williams, who'd been standing by the door, lifted the hem of her emerald green, charmeuse maid of honor dress and strode across the small room to toe off with the mayor-elect.

"Are you frigging kidding me?" Tasha's deep brown eyes narrowed and she planted her hands onto her hips, head bobbing as she spoke. "Kels got stood up, not *you*."

Yay, you. Grateful, Kelsey sent her friend a thank-you smile.

"The media will eat me for dinner over this." Through flinty eyes, Filomena's glower could wither houseplants to dust.

Uh-oh, Kelsey knew the look far too well. A clear signal to give her mother a Grand Canyon–sized berth.

"Have an inch of compassion, you witch." Tasha glared lasers at Filomena.

Proud that her bestie had not called her mother a "bitch" when she knew the word was searing the end of Tasha's tongue, Kelsey cleared her throat. Long ago, she'd learned not to throw emotional gasoline on her mother's fits of pique. Courting head-to-toe, third-degree burns was *not* her favorite pastime.

"What did you say to me?" A sharp, cutting tone curdled her mother's voice. Her icy stare could quell Katniss Everdeen.

Gulping, Tasha couldn't quite meet Filomena's eyes. "Just . . . just . . . have a heart, dammit. She's your daughter."

"Don't you lecture me, you little upstart." Filomena shoved her face in front of Tasha's nose.

In a soothing, even tone, Kelsey pressed her palms downward. "Mom, I'm fine here. Please, go do damage control. You'll find a way to turn this to your advantage. You're a master at spinning gold from straw."

"Excellent idea." With stiff-legged movements, Filomena shifted her attention off Tasha. Finger pinching the ruching at the waist of her snug-fitting mother-of-the-bride dress, she straightened herself, dusted off her shoulders, and stalked toward the door. "Clive's father owes me big-time."

Filomena's exit left Kelsey and Tasha exhaling simultaneously.

"Ah, gotta love how she turns every disaster into a political stepping stone," Tasha muttered.

"It's her superpower," Kelsey said.

"What's her kryptonite?"

Rereading Clive's scrawled letter, Kelsey didn't answer. Before Clive fled with Kevin, he'd pressed the note into the minister's hand.

> *Dear Kelsey,*
> *Shabby of me to ditch you this way, but please believe me when I say I wanted to marry you. You are the kindest, most loving person I've ever met and my deep affection for you has gotten me this far. But no more cowering in the closet, praying to turn into something I'm not. You deserve better. I deserve better. I've been a coward, and you were safe. Time to stop running. Kevin and I love each other. We have for a long time. Last night after the bachelor party . . . well . . . let's just say everything changed forever. Out there somewhere is the real love of your life. Please, cash in the honeymoon tickets and spoil yourself with a trip of your own.*
>
> *Best wishes,*
> *Your friend always, Clive*

Floating off the page, three words stood tall above the others, accusing her of her most glaring shortcoming.

You were safe.

Yes, she played it safe.

Without question.

Guilty as charged.

While Clive's betrayal stung, the loss and embarrassment didn't equal the pain of the truth. If she hadn't been playing it safe, going for the most accommodating, least challenging man around, she wouldn't have ended up here.

Once again, her mother was right, and this *was* her fault. To avoid a major war that she stood no chance of winning, Kelsey had kept her own wants and needs suppressed. Filomena pushed the union because Clive's father was Texas Supreme Court Justice Owen Patterson. Kelsey had meekly accepted the union.

Intelligent, witty, urbane, Clive was entertaining and erudite, and he always smelled fantastic. How easily she'd slipped into a tranquil relationship with him. When he'd told her that he was old-fashioned and wanted to wait until the wedding night before they had sex, she'd been charmed.

And it was a major red flag she'd blown right past.

"'Sweet' is code for boring," Tasha had warned when Kelsey broke the news that she and Clive weren't having sex. "Who buys a car without test driving it first?"

Now she understood why Clive avoided having sex with her. Not because she was special as he'd claimed. Nope, because he wasn't really interested. She was gullible and had taken him at his word.

What a dumbass. Wadding the letter in her fist, Kelsey tossed it into the wicker wastebasket.

"Good start." Tasha gave a gleeful grin. "Let's cash in those tickets and get this party started. You need a wild night with a hot guy. How long has it been since you've had sex?"

Well over eighteen months. Since long before she'd started dating Clive. "I don't know if I'm ready for that."

"Will you stop? You gotta get back out there. Time's a-wastin'." Tasha reached for her clutch purse, popped it open, and took out a fifth of Fireball whiskey. "I brought this for the wedding reception, but we need it *ASAP.*"

"Believe me." Kelsey held up a palm. "I'm mad at myself for letting things get this far. I should have stopped the wedding, but my mother started the steam-roller, and I just climbed aboard the way I always do."

"Reason enough to take a shot." Tasha chugged a mouthful of hooch, let loose with a satisfied burp, and pressed the whiskey into Kelsey's hand.

"I don't—"

"Drink," Tasha commanded.

"Good gravy, I'm not wrecked. I promise."

"But you *should* get wrecked. Get mad. Howl at the moon. Let loose." Tasha stuck her arms out at her sides as if she was an airplane. "Wing woman at your service. Never fear, Tasha is here."

Sighing, Kelsey wondered if her friend had a point. Who would judge her for getting drunk after being jilted at the altar?

With a toss of her head, she took a short swallow. The cinnamon-flavored whiskey burned and lit a warm liquid fire in the pit of her stomach.

"Take another," Tasha coached.

Opening her mouth to say no, three words flashed vivid neon in Kelsey's mind. *You were safe.*

Clive nailed it. Since her twin sister, Chelsea, drowned on Possum Kingdom Lake when they were ten, she'd been playing it safe. Honestly, even before then. "Safe" was her factory default setting. Chelsea's death only compounded her natural peacemaking tendency. No adventuresome twin around to balance her out.

With a snort, Kelsey took another drink. Longer this time, and she felt her insides unspool.

"Good girl." Tasha patted Kelsey's shoulder.

After the third shot, Kelsey felt warm and woozy and ten times better than she had half an hour ago.

"Okay, okay." With a worried expression, Tasha took the bottle away from her. "All things in moderation. I don't want to hold your hair while you puke before we ever get out of the church."

Snapping her fingers, Kelsey reached for the bottle. "Gimme, I'm done playing by the rules."

Ninja quick, Tasha hid the whiskey behind her back. "I've created a monster. I'll return it when we're in the limo."

"Bye-bye limo." Kelsey hiccupped. "Clive and Kevin took it."

"How do you know?"

"Peek at the curb."

Poking her head out the window, Tasha said, "Oh well. Uber here we come."

"Where are we going?"

"Wherever you want. In place of a honeymoon, we'll spend the next two weeks doing something wild and crazy. *Fun, fun, fun* are our buzzwords."

"Don't you have a job?"

Spinning her finger in the air helicopter-blade style, Tasha said, "I quit last week."

"Wait. What? Why?"

"Had a fight with my boss. He pinched my ass and I slapped his face, yada, yada, he wins."

"Oh Tash, I'm so sorry. Did you consult a lawyer?"

"No need. Handled it on social media." Buffing her knuckles against her shirt, Tasha grinned. "Since he owns his own business, he can't get fired, but you can bet he got a lot of angry comments and people saying they won't be using his catering company."

"Why didn't I know about this?" Kelsey asked as guilt gnawed. She'd been a shitty friend. "Why didn't you tell me?"

"Wedding prep and getting your mother elected mayor of Dallas kept you snowed. When did you have time for my drama?"

"What are friends for? I need to make it up to you."

"Then kick up your heels."

"Shouldn't you be scouting another job instead of holding my hand?"

"No worries. Already got a new one."

"When? Where?"

"You're looking at the new executive chef for La Fonda's, and I start the Monday after the New Year."

"That's awesome! I mean about the executive chef job, not getting your ass pinched. Congrats."

"Let's do this thing." With one palm raised in the air as if she was a waiter balancing a tray, Tasha pumped her hand. "Celebrate my new job and your freedom at the same time. We'll have an epic adventure."

"No doubt." She mulled over Tasha's proposition. Why not? Time to break out of her bubble.

"Where should we go? New Orleans? Eat gumbo, drink hurricanes, and get inked?" Tasha wriggled her eyebrows. "What do you think about me getting a spider tattoo on my neck?"

Wincing, Kelsey sucked in a breath through clenched teeth. "Hmm, Cajun food upsets my stomach."

"Vegas? Blow through our mad money, pick up male strippers?"

"Um, I want something more—"

"Kelsey-ish?"

Sedate was the word that had popped into her head. Sedate. Sedative. She'd been comatose too long. "Where would *you* prefer to go, Tasha? Whatever you decide, I'm good with it."

Tasha gave an exaggerated eye roll. "Girl, you got dumped on your wedding day, and I can find a party wherever I go, even in your white bread world."

She adored Tasha's spunkiness. Spunk was also the reason Filomena wasn't a big Tasha fan.

Five years earlier, Tasha and Kelsey had met when Kelsey was organizing a fundraiser during her mother's bid for a city council seat. In charge of hiring the caterers for the event at the Dallas Museum of Art, Kelsey had gone to interview Tasha's boss, Tony, the ass pincher, without knowing of course that he was the kind of person who sexually harassed his employees.

When Tasha popped a mini quiche into Kelsey's mouth, and it was the best damn thing she'd ever eaten, she'd hired the caterer on the spot, based solely on Tasha's cooking skills. After hitting it off, Kelsey stuck around to help Tasha clean up after the gala, and the rest belonged in the annals of BFF history.

"Wherever we go there must be scads of hot *straight* guys," Tasha said. "How does a dude ranch sound?"

"Good heavens, I have no idea how to ride a horse."

"Yeah, me neither."

"Wherever you want, I'll go."

"Don't make me pick. I always pick, this is for *you*. My mind is lassoed onto hot cowboys. Yum. Ropes, spurs, yeehaw."

"Let the sex stuff go, will you? I don't need to have sex."

"Oh, but you do! Great sex is exactly what you need."

"If my libido were a car on the freeway I'd putter along in the slow lane."

"Because you've never had *great* sex." Tasha chuckled. "And for eighteen months, you've been in a deep freeze. Ticktock, time to climb down from your ivory tower, Rapunzel, and reclaim your sexuality."

"I dunno . . ." Kelsey fiddled with the hem on the wedding gown that had cost as much as a new compact car. Could Filomena get a refund?

"C'mon, you gotta have hot fantasies." Tasha's voice took on a sultry quality. "What are they? A little BDM? Role playing? Booty call in scandalous places? A park bench, a pool, a carnival carousel?"

"A carousel?"

"Hey, it happens."

"Tasha, did you have sex on a carousel?"

Her friend smirked. "Maybe. Once. I'll never tell."

Lowering her eyelashes, Kelsey tossed the rose bouquet into the trash on top of Clive's crumpled letter.

You were safe.

"Quit playing coy and cough 'em up," Tasha said. "Name your fantasies. Scottish Highlander in a short kilt and no undies? Or a football player wearing those skin-tight pants? Fireman? Doctor? Construction worker?"

"The YMCA players . . ."

Tasha hee-hawed. "No more gay guys for you!"

"Hmm, there is *one* fantasy . . ." Kelsey mumbled.

"Just one?" Waving her hand, Tasha said, "Never mind, not judging. One is enough. What is it?"

Not what, *who.* "Forget it."

"Is he a real person?" Leaning in, Tasha's breath quickened. "A celebrity? Or . . ." Her voice dropped even lower. "Someone you've met in real life?"

Unbidden, Noah MacGregor's face popped into Kelsey's head.

In her mind's eye, Noah looked as he had the last time she'd seen him. Seventeen years old, the same age she'd been, and six-foot-five. Broad shoulders, narrow waist, lean hips. His muscular chest bare, hard abs taut. Her lipstick imprinted on his skin. Unsnapped, unzipped jeans.

Wild hair.

Wilder heart.

Rattled and rocked, her safe little world had tilted. Noah was so big, so tall, and he had a wicked glint in his eyes. An honest man, independent and sexy. One hot look from him had sent her heart scrambling.

That final night, they'd been making out on the dock at Camp Hope, a grief camp for children on Lake Twilight. That year they were both junior counselors, after having attended every summer since they were eleven as campers.

On the dock a blanket and candles and flowers. Courtesy of her romantic boyfriend.

Fever-pitch kisses.

They were ready to have sex—*finally*—when he'd jumped up, breathing hard. His angular mouth, which had tasted of peppermint and something darkly mysterious, was pressed into a wary line. Noah's thick

chocolate-colored locks curling around his ears and
his deep brown eyes enigmatic.

In her bikini, she'd blinked up at him, her mind a haze
of teenage lust and longing. "What's wrong?"

"Did you hear something?" Noah peered into the
shadows.

Propped up on her elbows, Kelsey cocked her head.
Heard the croak of bullfrogs and the splash of fish breaking the surface of the water as they jumped up to catch
bugs in the moonlight. "No."

Doubled fists, pricked ears, Noah remained standing, ready for a fight if one came his way. Prepared to
protect her.

Her pulse sprinted.

Proud and brave and strong, he looked as if he were
a hero from the cover of the romance novels that she
enjoyed reading.

She'd fallen deeper in love with him at that moment.
Head right over heels. Over banana splits at Rinky-Tink's
ice cream parlor the week before, they had shyly said the
words to each other. *I love you.* Then again when he'd
carved their names in the Sweetheart Tree in Sweetheart
Park near the Twilight town square. Several nights that
summer they'd sneaked off for trysts after their charges
were asleep.

They'd kissed and hugged and petted but hadn't yet
gone past third base. Tonight was the night. She was on
the pill. He brought a box of condoms. They were ready
and eager. Kelsey reached for him, grabbed hold of his
wrist, and tugged him to his knees. Their first time. Both
eager virgins who'd dreamed of this for weeks.

Souls wide open. Hearts overflowing. Bodies eager
and ready.

"Come . . ." she coaxed. "Don't worry, it's after midnight. Everyone is snug in their cabins."

Allowing her to draw him back beside her, Noah branded her with his mouth and covered her trembling body with his own.

Hot hands.

Electric touch.

Three-dimensional!

The night was sticky. Raw with heat and hunger. Calloused fingertips stroked velvet skin. The boards of the dock creaked and swayed beneath their movements as he untied her bikini top.

Footsteps.

Solid. Quick. Determined. Immediately, Kelsey recognized those footsteps.

Filomena!

From nowhere, her mother was on the dock beside them, grabbing a fistful of Kelsey's hair in her hand, and yanking her to her feet. Kelsey's bikini top flew into the lake.

Angry shouts.

Ugly accusations.

Threats.

Curses.

Regular life stuff with her mother when things didn't go Filomena's way.

Mom, dragging her to the car parked on the road. She must have driven up with the headlights off. How had her mother known they would be there? Blindsided by the realization that Filomena must have been keeping tabs by tracking her every move via her cell phone, Kelsey's fears ratcheted up into her throat.

A hard shove and Filomena stuffed Kelsey into the

car's backseat and shook an angry fist at Noah, who'd followed them. Warned him to stay away. Promised litigation and other dire consequences if he dared to contact Kelsey ever again.

"Noah!" Kelsey had cried as her mother hit the door locks to prevent him from opening the door and springing her free.

Pounding on the car window, Noah demanded her mother get out and have a rational conversation with him.

Stone-faced, Filomena started the car.

"I'll come for you," Noah yelled to Kelsey. "I'll find you, and we will be together. We won't let her win."

Kelsey clung to that flimsy promise. Took it to mean something. Fervent hopes. Girlish dreams.

"Over my dead body," Filomena yelled.

"Please Noah, just go," Kelsey had said, half-afraid her mother would run over him. "We were just a summer fling."

All the fight had drained out of him then, and he'd stood in the darkness, fists clenched, face gone pale, shaking from head to toe.

Sobbing and shivering, Kelsey sat nearly naked in the backseat of her mother's Cadillac as Filomena sped all the way back to Dallas.

And Kelsey never saw Noah again.

Years later, out of curiosity, Kelsey searched for Noah and found him on social media, learning that he was a successful point guard in the NBA and married to a drop-dead gorgeous model—something she'd have already known if she had any interest in basketball. She did not friend him. It was far too late to rekindle childhood flames.

Lost hopes.

Empty dreams.

Ancient history.

Soon afterward, she'd met Clive, and that was that. But now, here she was, dumped and half-drunk, with nothing to look forward to but her mother's predictable holiday harangue. Plenty of reasons to hate the holidays. This year, she had little choice but to review her life's mistakes.

Ho, ho, ho. Merry *freaking* Christmas.

CHAPTER 2

"C'mon." Tasha prodded Kelsey out of her deep thoughts. "Fess up. Who is he?"

"It's nothing."

"Nothing? Girl, you just got the dreamiest look on your face."

"Nobody worth mentioning."

"You lie."

"Seriously, it's no big deal." Kelsey rotated her shoulders, one up, one down. Then reversed them.

"Your seesaw shoulders give you away. Bumps will sprout on your tongue if you keep lying."

"This is just silly."

"The tongue thing or the fact you have a secret crush you've never told me about?" Tasha wagged her finger at Kelsey.

"The tongue bump thing *is* weird, but it's not what I'm talking about."

"It's something my granny used to say to stop me from fibbing. It never worked. Let's get back to the guy."

Kelsey stood up and ran a hand down the folds of her wedding gown. "I need to get out of this thing and back to reality."

"You were grinning like a fool just then," Tasha pressed. "Who is he? Don't hold out on me. I want all the deets."

Kelsey shook her head. "It's absurd."

"So? Who cares. It's a fantasy. Honestly, I'm glad you have one. I was starting to think there was something wrong with you."

"There's no point in talking about it." Kelsey snatched off her wedding veil and dropped it onto the floor.

"There is *one* point . . ."

"What's that?"

"This fantasy man makes you uncomfortable."

"Which is why I don't want to talk about him."

"And it's *exactly* the reason you should."

"It was long ago. I was a stupid teenager—"

"Omigawd." Tasha playfully slapped her mouth with her fingers. "It's that hot guy you told me about once? Your first love. The guy from grief camp. Oh, that is so cute. You're still pining over him."

Kelsey felt the hole in her heart that she'd thought long healed flop wide open. "I told you it was stupid. I'm not really carrying a torch for Noah, it's just that we never had closure."

"No, no. Not stupid at all. Who knows? Maybe you could rekindle?"

"He's married."

"Oh." Tasha twisted her mouth up, a sure sign she did not want to let this go. "You sure?"

"I found him on Instagram before I met Clive. He's got this perfect life. His wife is a gorgeous model, and he's playing in the NBA. They have a big house near the Riverwalk in San Antonio. He's probably got a kid or two by now."

"Wait, he's in the NBA and you haven't checked him out since you met Clive. It can't be that hard to find things out about him."

"I'm not an internet stalker."

"But you did look him up once."

"Out of simple curiosity."

"Curiosity is lust of the mind."

"*You're* quoting Hobbes to me?"

"I have no idea who this Hobbes person is. I saw the quote on a Facebook meme."

Were Tasha and the philosopher Thomas Hobbes correct? Did Kelsey secretly lust for Noah in her mind? Tingles rippled down her spine. Maybe all over her body too. But he was a married man.

"A lot can happen over a year and a half," Tasha said. "You got engaged to and dumped by a gay guy since then."

"Smart-ass." Kelsey chucked a box of tissues at Tasha, who ducked and laughed.

"Let's check him out. What's his name?" Tasha whipped out her cell phone.

"Noah MacGregor," Kelsey said, far too quickly. Shouldn't she be more circumspect?

"Wait. What? *The* Noah MacGregor? I don't even have to look him up. He was with the San Antonio Spurs but he got hurt."

"How do you know this?"

"How do you not? It was all over the news at the time."

"You know I don't follow sports. I thought you didn't either."

"Tag," Tasha said, referring to her ex-boyfriend, "was a big basketball fan."

"What happened to Noah?"

"He blew out his knee. He's not playing anymore. Apparently, the rehab was so grueling that he decided to cut his losses and call it quits."

Kelsey's stomach churned. She hated to think about Noah suffering a career-ending injury. She put a palm to her heart. "Oh no! That's awful."

Tasha opened a search engine in her phone. "Well lookee here."

"What is it?" Kelsey rushed across the room to peer over Tasha's shoulder at her cell phone screen and a picture of Noah MacGregor holding an arm over his face to ward off photographers. She could barely tell that it was him.

Tasha held the phone closer so that Kelsey could see the article. "The Mrs. divorced him after he got hurt."

"That bitch," Kelsey growled, incensed on Noah's behalf. What kind of woman left her man when he needed her most?

"Ooh lookatchew. Been hanging with me too long, Kels. My potty mouth is rubbing off." Tasha's laugh was big and hearty.

"Noah is a good man," Kelsey said, surprised by the fierceness inside her. "Or at least he was when I knew him."

"You're still hot for him," Tasha taunted in a singsong.

"I am not." The corner of Kelsey's right eye twitched. From somewhere outside the open window, holiday music played. "Winter Wonderland." The tune rubbed her like sandpaper. Christmas, bah humbug.

"No wonder you're not broken up over Clive running off with Kevin. You've still got it bad for Noah Mac-Gregor."

"Truth?" Kelsey said, massaging her twitching eye muscle with two fingers. "If Filomena hadn't had my arm clamped against her side, *I* might have been the one to cut and run away from this wedding. Clive did us both a favor."

"That's probably why your mother insisted on walking you down the aisle. Your dad would have let you cut and run."

"Maybe. More likely, it's just Filomena grinding Dad into the ground like always."

Tasha studied her up and down. "If you were having doubts, why didn't you call it off?"

"This makes me sound like a wimp, but I didn't want to deal with my mother."

Tasha tapped her chin with an index finger. "I get it. Filomena is pretty overwhelming."

"I don't know what's wrong with me." Kelsey's eye twitched harder. "I'm twenty-seven years old. You'd think I would have learned by now how to express my wants and needs and not let my mother influence me so much."

"It's not you." Tasha stuck her cell phone back into her purse. "It's her. Your mother is a raging control freak and life is much easier when you just go along with her. Go along to get along. In your position, most people would."

Filomena was a complicated woman, but she could be accommodating when it suited her, and Kelsey had made a career out of accommodating her. "But not you. Why am I so afraid of confrontation?"

"Don't be too hard on yourself. If it hadn't been for your twin sister's death and your parents getting divorced right after that, you'd have found your own way years ago. You're a late bloomer. So what? Nothing wrong with that. Focus on the good news. Your time is now."

Kelsey covered her face with her palm. "I'm pathetic."

"Hey, hey, that's my best friend you're beating up. Knock it off."

"You don't call this pathetic?" Kelsey swept her hand at the room, at the Dear Jane letter, at the discarded bouquet, and the half-empty bottle of Fireball whiskey.

"You are not pathetic. You're having an awful day. Look at it this way, Kels. This is your chance to finally break free. Do what *you* want for once."

But what did *she* want? Honestly, Kelsey had no idea. She'd adopted her mother's goals and dreams as her own. "I'm Filomena's campaign manager. I can't just leave her in the lurch."

"And the campaign is over."

"She's hiring me as her office manager when she takes office in January."

"Well, it's not January yet. Or you could quit." Tasha shrugged as if it were that easy.

Quit? Managing her mother's career was the only job she'd ever had, short of working as a camp counselor as a teenager. The idea was terrifying . . . and electrifying. "I've never done anything else."

"You have a degree in hospitality that you've never used. Why don't you go work for a hotel chain?"

"I graduated six years ago. I wouldn't know where to start. I'm not even sure I still want to be in hospitality."

"How about we try a trick I learned in acting class to help get under the skin of characters?"

"As if I'm not even inhabiting my own skin?" Kelsey asked.

"I didn't mean it like that, but you have been dancing to Filomena's tune so long, you stopped hearing your music."

"What's this technique?"

"It's the specific noun technique where you list the five specific nouns that identify a character's loves and five nouns that the character hates."

"Um, okay."

"Don't look at me like that. It's fun. I'll go first. I love Belgian chocolate, sixty-degree weather, Old Gringo cowboy boots, pepperoni pizza, and *Breaking Bad*. I hate foundation garments . . ." She paused to tug on her girdle. "People who chew with their mouths open, licorice, foreign subtitled movies, and sand between my toes. Your turn."

Feet to the fire? What did she love? Kelsey mused a moment. "I love hot tea, hotter bubble baths, good books, soft blankets, and random acts of kindness."

"Ahh, I see a pattern."

"Which is?"

"You yearn for a gentle world because you grew up in such a hostile environment."

Could that be true?

"Okay, now," Tasha said. "What do you hate? Say the first thing that rolls off the top of your head."

"I try not to hate. It's such a strong word."

"We'll soften it just for you. What do you dislike?"

Kelsey scratched her chin. "Getting stood up at the altar is no fun."

"Besides that. No one would like that. Be specific to you. Quick. Don't think. What ruffles Kelsey's feathers?"

"Um . . . um . . . parking tickets, phone solicitors, gum on the sidewalk, adhesive notepads that don't stick—"

"The noun thing isn't helping much. I'm switching gears here. What's on your bucket list?"

"What's on yours?"

"White water rafting in Maine, volcano boarding in Nicaragua, going to a nude beach, a hot air balloon ride in the Loire Valley, taking cooking classes in Tuscany, meeting Oprah Winfrey . . ."

"Those things are all very adventuresome and ambitious. I'm just more of a homebody."

"All right then, what kind of skills would you like to learn?"

Tasha was trying so hard to help, and Kelsey didn't want to let her down. "What's on your list?"

"I want to learn fencing, kickboxing, miming."

"You want to learn how to be a mime?"

"Yeah. Silly, I know. I'd probably flop big-time at that since I can't seem to keep my mouth shut, but you get the idea." Tasha pantomimed filling up a bucket and writing a list.

What *would* she put on a bucket list?

"Well?" Tasha prodded.

"I'd like to get over my fear of water that I've had since Chelsea died. Visit world-famous museums. Learn to love Christmas."

Geez, what a lame-o list.

Tasha didn't say as much, but the expression on her face gave her away. She too thought Kelsey's bucket list was lame. "Nothing else?"

"I've always wanted to take knitting lessons."

Tasha whacked her forehead with her palm. "Argh."

"I'm sorry. Filomena made fun of me too when I told her I'd like to learn how to knit and she called me fumble fingers."

"Do not apologize!" Tasha growled. "You like what you like. If knitting is your jam, knit up a storm. What else?"

"I don't know."

"How about having great sex? That should be on everyone's bucket list."

Have great sex.

Yes, she would like that. And Tasha was right, she'd never had great sex or even an orgasm with a partner for that matter. But how did she go about making that happen?

Kelsey sank her face in her hands. "That's too much to think about right now on top of everything else."

"Okay, baby steps. That works. First step." Tasha held up a finger. "Road trip."

"Filomena will have a fit if I take off now."

"So let her have a fit. You won't be here to listen. Free yourself, girlfriend. Find your passion. Grab life by the short and curlies and get on with it."

Butterfly wings of hope fluttered up her spine. "You really think I could?"

"I *know* so."

"What did I do to deserve a friend like you?" Kelsey whispered.

"It takes one to know one." Tasha hugged her hard. "Love you."

"Love you too!"

Tasha stepped back and pressed the Fireball whiskey into Kelsey's hand. "Have another shot and chill out. I'll go make a call and see if I can cash in your honeymoon tickets for a refund and I'll book us an awesome vacation destination."

"Where to?" Kelsey asked.

Tasha shook her head and gave her a you're-a-lost-cause grin. "How about I surprise you?"

Kelsey nibbled her bottom lip, felt her eye muscle quiver. "I don't know about that."

"Say yes for once. Would I steer you wrong?"

Maybe. Tasha was a great friend, but she could be impulsive.

"I've got your back, Kels. Never doubt it."

"And I've got yours."

Tasha winked and disappeared out the door.

Kelsey sank back down on the bench and knocked back another shot of whiskey. Enjoyed the burn this time and the warm swimmy feeling that went through her. She thought about what her mother would say if she walked back into the room at that moment, and quickly hid the bottle in the folds of her dress.

You're a grown-ass woman, and you got jilted on your wedding day. You can slam back whiskey if you want. She pulled the bottle out, took another swig.

Footsteps sounded in the hall.

She held tight to the bottle. Lifted her chin. Ready to do battle with her mother.

"Knock, knock," a deep male voice called, and knuckles rapped lightly against the door.

"Come in."

The door swung open to reveal her father. Accompanying him, of all people, was Lionel Berg. The incumbent mayor who'd lost the race to Filomena.

CHAPTER 3

*Meanwhile, seventy-five miles away
in Twilight, Texas . . .*

"I wouldn't mind having a Santa like you come down my chimney," teased Raylene, the receptionist for the *Rockabye* Boatel, as she reached for a glue stick to dab the backs of the snowflakes she'd cut out of construction paper.

The septuagenarian had been married for the past forty-five years to Earl Pringle, the love of her life. She was an outrageous flirt but didn't mean anything by it. In her day, she'd been a Dallas Cowboys cheerleader, and had once run a local bar called The Horny Toad Tavern until she'd retired and turned it over to her son, Earl Junior. Raylene's sassy nature and lively grin were why Noah MacGregor and his twin brother, Joel, had hired her. She'd applied for the job saying retirement just wasn't for her.

"What would Earl think of that?" Noah MacGregor drawled and winked down at Raylene from where he stood on the step stool in a Santa suit—fake beard, pillow-stuffed waist, and all. He was not the least bit offended. Raylene was just being Raylene, outrageous and unapologetic.

"Earl says he doesn't care where I get my appetite as long as I eat at home." Raylene handed snowflakes up for him to hang.

"You do know I'm young enough to be your grandson."

"And you know I don't rob cradles."

"Did this conversation just turn creepy?"

"Hey buddy, you're the hot one. You have to expect some mindless flirting." Raylene stepped back, set down the glue stick, cocked her head, and eyed his handiwork.

"How's it looking?"

"You know," she said, her voice turning wistful. "Your mother would be so proud of you. I hate that she's not here to see everything you've accomplished."

"Yeah, so accomplished," Noah muttered. "NBA burn-out my first year on the court as a Spur."

"Honey, you know how many people with big dreams never even played college ball, much less went pro? You're a hero in this town."

Noah did know. Despite his career-ending injury, and the blowup of his marriage, Noah had bounced back. While he would never play professional basketball again, he could walk without a limp, and he'd made enough money in the NBA to go into business with his twin brother, Joel. First they bought the *Brazos Queen* paddle wheel boat, hiring it out for weekend dinner cruises. Joel was in charge of that arm of the business. Then they'd added a seasonal scuba diving business, also selling diving equipment and merchandise out of their brother-in-law Jesse's motorcycle shop.

Last year Noah bought Christmas Island—a small island in the middle of Lake Twilight—and a second paddle wheel boat. He moored the vessel out by the island and turned the boat into a B&B. Called the *Rockabye* Boatel, it had been open three months and while the boatel did not yet turn a profit, Noah was confident that it was only a matter of time.

His life after the NBA had gone pretty well. Noah couldn't view the career-ending injury as anything other than a stroke of luck. His marriage wasn't built on a strong foundation, so if his injury had cost him a wife he realized that some things just weren't meant to be and the marriage would have ended anyway.

And Noah, whose life motto was "Don't worry, be happy," had been able to let go and let things be without any bitterness.

His ex, Melissa, had said that was bullshit, that he was just shallow and lacked ambition, and when the going got tough, Noah found something new and shiny to capture his interest, rather than put in the hard work required. But hey, she was the one who took up with another NBA player.

Noah's take? He had a knack for accepting life as it came and that teed Melissa off because social climbing was her thing. He really didn't care all that much about status or keeping up with the Joneses.

The *Rockabye* was his baby, and he loved running it as much as he'd loved playing basketball. In fact, Noah loved life. The only thing missing? A wife and kids. But he was in no hurry.

He wasn't the least bit worried about ending up alone. Life had a way of working itself out.

Right now, his biggest goal was to top the donation he'd made last year to a charity near and dear to his heart. Research to cure amyotrophic lateral sclerosis, commonly called Lou Gehrig's disease, the progressive neurodegenerative disease that had taken his mother's life when she was forty. Last year, through his involvement in various activities, he'd raised twenty thousand dollars. This year, he was shooting for twenty-five.

And part of achieving that goal involved winning the town Christmas decorating contest and the fifteen-hundred-dollar prize.

"We've got to get the gazebo finished if we have any hope of winning the Christmas competition," Raylene said, reading his mind. "All entries have to be completed by Monday afternoon for the first round of judging, and you submitted the gazebo as part of the decorating schematic, so you can't leave it off."

"It's that soon already?" Time did fly, and his biggest weakness was his organizational skills.

Or lack thereof. Good thing Raylene was pretty great at cracking the whip.

"Boy, you do live in a dream world." Raylene picked up the supplies that she'd used to make the snowflakes and scurried around the reception desk. She was dressed like an elf: green tights, a red dress with a short skirt, and a Christmas cap with a jingle bell on the end that jangled merrily when she walked. "If you were a water park ride, you'd be the lazy river."

"Everyone loves the lazy river." He chuckled.

Raylene shook her head. "Everyone pees in the lazy river."

"Is there subtext I'm not picking up on?" Noah scratched his head.

"Good thing you're so hot, and women come to you instead of you having to chase them out."

"What's that supposed to mean?"

"You're too comfortable with the status quo."

"What's wrong with that?"

"We don't grow inside our comfort zones."

"You've been hanging around with Sean too much."

"He does like to show off his navy SEAL tattoo. *Get Comfortable with Uncomfortable.*"

"Good thing I was never a SEAL, huh?"

"Pfft." Raylene waved a dismissive hand. "You would have washed out the first day."

"You're saying Sean is tougher than me?"

"Oh baby, by leaps and bounds."

"Should I be offended?"

"Yes, but you won't be because you're too lazy."

"Are you forgetting who signs your paycheck?"

Raylene patted his cheek. "We've got to get a move on and get this decorating finished. And I'm not climbing up on any ladders. Break a hip at my age, and it's . . ." She made cutting noises and pantomimed a slashing motion across her throat. "All over but the crying."

Noah, who was headed to the town square where he was playing Santa for the afternoon toy drive, said, "Get he-man Sean to finish the gazebo. By the way, I'll be out late tonight."

"You could do the outside lights tomorrow morning."

"Did you forget that tomorrow is the First Love Cookie Club's brunch?" he asked. "You're supposed to be there."

The First Love Cookie Club was a group of local women who got together every year to bake cookies for the troops overseas, sip wine, swap cookie recipes, and gossip in equal measure.

The cookie swaps had been such a success that over the years the club members had added more events to support local charities. The money raised from tomorrow's brunch would go to fund the Christmas Angel Tree project for underprivileged kids. This year, his oldest sister, Flynn, was the club president.

"I'm only going for the mimosas," Raylene said. "Why? Are you going too?"

"Flynn twisted my arm to make my famous eggs Benedict for fifty people," he said. "I must be nuts. I'll be up before dawn."

"Oh, quit your bellyaching. I know you love this town's Christmas crazies. And you love for people to admire your cooking. So get your lazy bones out of bed and blow the socks off those cookie club gals with your culinary skills."

Noah grinned. He did love cooking. Especially at Christmas. Then again, loving the holiday was practically obligatory for a man who lived on Christmas Island.

"About the gazebo—"

"Bug Sean."

"He'll say entering the competition was your idea, and you should do it."

Noah picked up his Santa toy sack, brimming with gifts, which was sitting beside the door. "He's my employee. Tell him to get on it."

Raylene snorted. "I'm not bossing around a former navy SEAL. You tell him to get on it."

"I don't get any respect," Noah grumbled good-naturedly.

"By the way, the light on the front porch lantern needs changing." Raylene reached under the counter for a box of energy-efficient lightbulbs and pushed them toward him. "Have at it, Santa baby."

"Remind me again why I don't fire you?"

Raylene grinned. "I add spice to your life."

"Oh yeah, that."

Chuckling, he swiped the lightbulbs off the counter and in full Santa regalia, toy sack slung over his shoulder, Noah strolled out onto the deck platform that anchored the *Rockabye* to Christmas Island. The sky was cozy gray, the gentle colors of a soft hug.

Two miles across the lake, barely visible from where he stood in the drizzly December mist, lay Camp Hope, the bereavement camp for children. His nostalgic mind drifted to his childhood sweetheart, Kelsey James.

He'd heard on the news that Filomena had been elected the mayor of Dallas and Kelsey was her campaign manager and engaged to the son of a Texas Supreme Court Justice. He wished her all the best and prayed she was as happy in her life as he was in his.

A familiar double punch of longing and regret hit his gut. He still remembered how she'd looked that night, wearing a bright blue bikini, stretched out on a blanket on the dock. Full moon shining a halo of light over her. Her blond hair was damp and adorably frizzy from the humidity. Her blue-eyed gaze hooked on him as he'd stepped from the shadows and onto the dock, his heart pounding wildly.

He'd been in love with her since they were eleven-year-olds at camp for the first time. But since the previous summer, she'd bloomed into a full-grown woman, all sweet curves and soft lines, and their friendship had grown into something much more.

Her beauty struck him dumb.

God, she'd been magnificent. Like the water itself. Cool, quiet, deep. But beneath the surface ran a current of dark mystery, and primal passion as yet unleashed. She was self-contained, unruffled, observant and at the same time sizzling, sexy, and sumptuous. He'd fallen hook, line, and sinker for that devastating fire-and-ice combo.

And if he and Kelsey had ever made full use of that blanket, no telling where they might have ended up. Hell, he'd tried. Shucking off his shirt, unsnapping his jeans, sinking to his knees beside her as she reached for his zipper. Their hungry mouths groping for each other.

Seventeen.

Both virgins. Both burning with need. Both still sitting on a helluva lot of grief. Kelsey missing her twin sister. Noah mourning his mother.

He'd often wondered in the ensuing years if that's what their attraction had been all about. Comfort. Solace. Bonding.

Then while they were in the middle of the most passionate kiss of his life, out of nowhere, Kelsey's mother had come storming onto the dock. She'd dragged her daughter from his arms, threatened to have him arrested for sexual assault, and whisked Kelsey back to Dallas.

Several times he'd tried to contact Kelsey, but his letters had been returned unopened, his cell phone and social media accounts had been blocked. And when he'd shown up at her house, Kelsey's mother met him at the door saying that Kelsey never wanted to see him again and if he didn't back off that she'd get his scholarship to the University of Texas revoked. He believed her.

Filomena was a scary woman.

So he'd walked away from Kelsey and his ridiculous teenage fantasies.

Oh well, the past was the past. He'd gotten over her. Moved on. Aced college. Immediately got drafted by the San Antonio Spurs farm team, met Melissa, got moved up to the NBA, got married, got injured, then got divorced and . . . well, now here he was. Right back in the town where he'd started. Life had come full circle.

Back in Dallas . . .

Overjoyed to see her father, Kelsey launched herself into his arms, not even caring that Lionel Berg watched.

"Daddy!"

Country club golf pro Theodore James was dressed in his ubiquitous Hawaiian shirt and khaki slacks and golf cleats. Smelling of coconut sunscreen, he wrapped his arms around his daughter and squeezed her tight.

Berg too looked as if he'd been out on the links, in golf knickers, argyle socks, and a tweed golfer's cap.

"I am so sorry about Clive," Theo said. "I suspected he batted for the other team, but I didn't know how to bring it up, and I learned a long time ago, you've got to let people be who they are."

"Thank you, but it wasn't your fault."

"Or yours either, kiddo. I know how you take things to heart." Her father cupped Kelsey's chin in his palm. He'd been more of a mother to her than Filomena was, but he'd let the woman push him around. Maybe there's where Kelsey had gotten her passive, peacemaking ways.

"Remember when you thought the divorce was your fault?"

"If I'd just been a better kid—"

"You were a perfect kid. You were never the problem. Not with our divorce or Clive's choices."

Kelsey massaged her temple. "I should have seen the signs. They were all there."

"Don't beat yourself up. It's all going to work out."

"I agree." Kelsey nodded. "There are better things ahead for both Clive and me. I'm just glad you're happy. How is Leah? Is she here?"

"Leah thought she better sit this one out," Theo said, referring to his much younger girlfriend who Kelsey adored but Filomena loathed. Leah was only seven years older than Kelsey. "And now, it's your turn to find *your* place in the world. Wait, is that Fireball?"

"Do you want some?"

"Does a bear . . . oh just give it." Her father laughed and reached for the whiskey and downed a fourth of what remained. "Sorry to be greedy, I'll be seeing your mother later."

Kelsey slid a glance over at Lionel Berg, who was waiting patiently with his hands clasped behind his back. "I'm sorry Mom banned you from the wedding."

"At least she said I could come to the reception."

"I tried to get her to let you walk me down the aisle," Kelsey said, anxiety yanking the muscle at her eye. "I should have stood up to her—"

"Kiddo." Her father rested his hand on her shoulder. "You don't have to explain your mother to me. I was married to her for fourteen miserable years."

"It wasn't fair to leave you out of the wedding." Ashamed, Kelsey ducked her head.

"I didn't miss anything," he said. "I'll give you away at the *real* wedding. When you find the guy *you* want to marry, not the one Filomena picked out for you."

Kelsey caught Lionel Berg's eye. "Excuse me, Mayor, I don't mean to be rude, but why are you here?"

"I know this is an inopportune time." Lionel Berg straightened, cleared his throat. "Please excuse me for interrupting and please accept my condolences regarding your wedding . . ."

Kelsey raised both palms. "Don't worry about that. How can I help you?"

Lionel Berg shot a look at Theo. "Your father is my golf instructor, and he's told me that you're still planning to work for your mother at City Hall."

"She's making me her office manager."

Berg held her gaze. "*That* would be a tremendous waste of your skills."

"What skills?"

"The way you got your mother elected? Her win was all due to you. You're an excellent mediator."

"You're downplaying my mother's charisma."

"Oh, Filomena has her initial charm, don't get me wrong," Lionel said. "But *you're* what holds that ship together."

"Which is why I'm going to work for her at City Hall."

"What if you had another option?" Berg widened his stance.

"Meaning?" Kelsey tilted her head, shot her dad a sidelong glance. Filomena often said Theo was an overgrown frat boy and right now he was looking the part. Vivid tan even in December, his garish shirt, golden chain necklace, straight white teeth and let's-party-down smile. What had he and the outgoing mayor cooked up behind her back?

"I'm planning on running for governor in the next election, and I want you to be my campaign manager." He named a starting salary commensurate for a top-tier campaign manager.

Kelsey's jaw dropped open. "You're not serious."

"I am dead serious."

Her mind churned because it was a phenomenal opportunity. "My mother would have a fit."

The second the words were out of her mouth, Kelsey felt a swamp of things.

One, the urgent need to usher Lionel Berg out of the room before her mother caught a whiff of what was going on.

Two, pique at her father for blindsiding her like this.

Three, a strange, waterlogged feeling as if she had been drowning in the middle of the ocean and someone had just thrown her a life preserver.

Four, a fluttering deep within her chest that tempted *what if, what if, what if?*

"So that's a solid no?" Berg asked.

"No, no." Her father waved his hands like he was trying to hail a taxi. "We've just taken Kelsey by surprise, she needs time to think."

"Dad, what is going on here?"

"Lionel needs a campaign manager, and you're a great one. You got him booted from office, after all," Theo said.

"Forgive my father," Kelsey said and grabbed Theo's elbow. "He has a tendency to get overly excited."

"But you don't." Berg's eyes glistened. "You have a knack for staying calm when those around you are losing their heads."

"I've never managed a campaign of that magnitude. It's beyond my skill set."

"You underestimate yourself. I've been watching you closely, Kelsey. You have what it takes to be a star."

"Why would you want me?" Kelsey said. "Other than to gig my mother? There are plenty of other campaign managers out there with far more experience."

"I hate to see your mother bring you down."

Kelsey settled her hands on her hips. "Because you care about me so much?"

"I want you on my team. I'd rather have you with me than against me."

Kelsey stared at him. "This has nothing to do with you being upset that my mother won the election?"

"I've got better things to do than cross swords with your mother." Berg shot her father a withering look. "I thought you said she'd jump at the chance."

"Jump might have been a strong word." Theo rubbed his jaw. "But we sprang this on her."

"*After* I just got stood up at the altar," Kelsey reminded him.

"I apologize for the bad timing," Berg said. "But I wanted to strike while the iron was hot."

"You mean catch me when I'm down?"

"Listen, coming here today was your father's idea." Berg raised his palms in a gesture of surrender. "Why don't I leave you my card, and you can let me know by the New Year whether this is an opportunity you want to take advantage of or not. Understand one thing, Kelsey. I want you for *you*. Not to upset your mother's apple-cart." Berg pulled his card from his pocket, pressed it into her hand, and left the room.

Theo took the last hit of Fireball.

"Did that actually just happen?" she asked her father.

He shrugged and had the decency to look sheepish. "Look, Berg has long admired your political savvy. He's asked me about you all the time. It's not so strange that he would ask you to be his campaign manager."

"How did you get here so fast? I got stood up less than an hour ago."

"We were playing golf at the course down the road."

"You were playing golf on my wedding day?"

"Near the church. I was coming to the reception. I had a suit in the car. What was I supposed to do? You let your mother ban me from your wedding."

Heat flushed up Kelsey's neck. He was right.

"Your cousin, Pamela, texted me what happened, and we came on over."

Pamela was her mother's older brother's daughter. She was a year younger than Kelsey and a bit of a busybody who enjoyed stirring up trouble. Out of self-preservation, Kelsey tended to avoid her, but Filomena insisted she invite her only first cousin to the wedding. She couldn't help but think that a bit of schadenfreude was behind Pamela's sudden chumminess with her father.

"So, you didn't come to console me?" Disappointment huddled her shoulders up to her ears.

"Of course, I did, Kelsey . . ." He paused.

"And?"

"I took a chance, okay? Maybe it's blowing up in my face, but dammit Kelsey, I had to try."

"Try what, Dad?" A snail of wariness crawled through her.

"To pry you from your mother's grip. She's got her hooks into you so deep, and until you can put some distance between the two of you, I don't think you'll ever be able to see exactly how much you allow her to control you."

"Oh, Dad," she said.

Nothing had changed. Her parents were still using her as a tug-of-war toy. Theo was mad that Filomena had banned him from the wedding and he was using Berg to even the score. "Can't you see how you're doing the very same thing?"

CHAPTER 4

"Was that Mayor Berg I saw with Theo?" Tasha bounced into the room and glanced over her shoulder in the direction she'd just come.

"It was." Kelsey plopped onto the bench again.

"Why was he here?"

"To offer me a job."

"Huh?" Tasha sank down beside Kelsey. "Doing what?"

"Managing his campaign. He's running for governor."

"No shit!"

"It wasn't a real offer. Just something my dad cooked up to get back at my mom." Kelsey waved a dismissive hand.

"Same old yo-yo, huh?"

Kelsey sighed again. "I should be used to it by now."

"How do you know the offer isn't real? You shouldn't sell yourself short. You are a damn fine campaign manager."

"I have a feeling that both of them just want to get a dig in at my mom."

"There *is* a long line of people who want to do that," Tasha mumbled.

"What's that?"

"Never mind."

"I know my mother can be difficult, but I can manage her. She needs *someone* in her corner."

"Forget Filomena for now. Let's stay focused on what's important."

"Which is?"

"A two-week, set-Kelsey-free, nonstop par-*tay*!" Grinning, Tasha held up her cell phone. "Got it all right here. I found the perfect spot. A getaway tailored to fit *you*."

"So somewhere quiet? Fireplace? Snow? Lots of books? No electronics? No crowds?"

Tasha rolled her eyes. "Lordie, you are such a comfort kitty. You hate to stretch and grow."

"That's not true. I read all the time."

"You read *waaay* too much. If I didn't keep pushing you to have fun, you'd spend ninety percent of your free time in a bubble bath with a novel."

"And what is wrong with that?"

"Comfort kitty."

"Put that on a T-shirt for me. I'd wear it . . . proudly."

"Of course, you would." Tasha made a time-out sign with her hands. "Here's the deal. No books allowed on this trip."

"Aww, I thought you wanted me to have a good time."

"You will. Trust me."

"Please don't tell me it's Disney World." Kelsey winced. "I can't handle that much happy holiday cheer."

"Hells to the no on that mess. I'm up for *adult* entertainment."

"Not Vegas!" Kelsey tried not to whine. She loved her friend, but Tasha could be a force of nature.

"I'm not gonna tell you where. It's a surprise."

"Please tell me it's not Christmas themed."

"It's December, Kels." Tasha lowered her chin and her eyelashes and gave Kelsey her patented get-on-board-with-the-program stare. "*Everything* is Christmas themed."

Kelsey gnawed a thumbnail. "I'm not sure I want to do this."

"Too bad." Tasha lifted her shoulders and dropped them hard. "Girlfriend, you need to step up your game. It's already done."

"I don't *have* to go."

"What are you going to do? Hang around the house and mope?"

"I could get started on the mayor's agenda for the new year."

"Seriously?"

"What?"

Tasha shook her head and clicked her tongue. "You don't even realize that you've given up your own life in favor of your mother, do you?"

"I haven't," Kelsey denied.

"Okay, name the last thing you did that was totally all about you."

Kelsey blinked. When was the last time she'd done something just for herself? "Um . . . um . . ."

"Can't think of anything, can you?"

"I read—"

Tasha held up a stop sign palm. "Books do not count."

It was a bit frightening to realize that she couldn't come up with a single thing she'd done in the last few years that didn't revolve around her mother's career. Even her engagement was part of Mom's plan.

"I hang out with you. Mom doesn't like that."

"It's a huge responsibility being your only window into the outside world," Tasha quipped.

"You make it sound like I'm a prisoner."

"If the shoe fits and all that . . ."

"I like being her campaign manager," Kelsey argued, ignoring the knot forming in her stomach.

"Do you? Do you really?"

"Well, Mom can be a handful, but I enjoy the work. I'm great at organizing and keeping things running smoothly. There's really nothing else I'd rather be doing."

"How do you know? You've never done anything else."

"I was a camp counselor once."

"That doesn't count. You were a teenager."

"I got paid." Kelsey lifted her chin. "That makes it a real job."

"Semantics. Admit it. You're scared of change."

"I wouldn't say *scared*."

"Terrified?"

"Reluctant."

"Petrified?"

"A creature of habit."

"Frozen in time. You and the dinosaurs."

"Resistant maybe," Kelsey admitted. "I'm a methodical person. There is nothing wrong with that."

"Maybe not, but it's boring."

"You don't cut me any slack."

"And that's why you keep me around." Tasha patted her hair like a preening princess. "Plus, I love you to pieces."

"I feel stuck." Okay, now she was being a Gloomy Gus, and that just wasn't like her. She might never be Little Miss Sunshine—she was too much of a realist for that—but she worked hard to keep a good outlook.

"I know." Tasha wriggled her eyebrows. "And boy howdy, have I got a big surprise lined up. We're gonna blast you right out of that rut."

"And if I say no?"

"Aww, c'mon. You never say yes to anything."

"That's not true. I was about to say yes to Clive."

"But you did-*dent*." Tasha emphasized the last syllable with an exaggerated vocal fry and waggled an index finger.

"Not my doing. I was prepared to say 'I do.'"

"Okay, one instance. I'll give you that. But overall, you don't welcome new experiences with open arms."

"I welcomed you into my life."

"That you did, and look, your life is so much better because of me." Tasha laughed her robust laugh.

"Can't argue with that."

"So, trust me?"

Kelsey heaved another long-suffering sigh. "Okay, what do you have in mind?"

"It's a surprise, remember?"

"No hints?"

"I'll give you a clue."

"Your secrecy is not making me want to say yes."

"Give me a chance," Tasha wheedled. "It'll be fun. I promise."

"*What* precisely will be fun?"

Tasha clasped her hands and a Cheshire cat grin crossed her face. "Why, a Christmas of 'Yes.'"

"What does that mean?" Kelsey narrowed her eyes and her voice.

"My twist on Shonda Rhimes's *Year of Yes*. See? I brought a book into the mix. I know you've read it."

Kelsey had read the book. It was very inspiring, but

she was nervous about applying the concept to herself. "What do you have up your sleeve?"

"You have to say yes to five challenges that scare you from now until New Year's. Shonda did it for a whole year. I'm only asking *you* for two weeks and five measly challenges."

"Yeah, well, she's Shonda Rhimes."

"But she wasn't always. That's the point."

"She was born with another name?"

"Smart-ass," Tasha said. "That's the spirit. Fist bump."

Smiling, Kelsey bumped Tasha's extended fist.

"So, who issues these challenges?" Kelsey asked.

"Me."

"Where do you come up with them?"

"Make 'em up as we go along, based on what we encounter on our adventures."

"I'm not sure I like the sound of that." Kelsey folded her arms over her chest. "I'm not doing anything illegal."

"Of course not. I wouldn't ask that. You in?" Tasha put out her fist again.

Reluctantly, Kelsey bumped. "But I'm scared."

"Ooh, perfect. Say good-bye to Comfort Kitty." Tasha's phone dinged, and she pulled it out of her purse and peered down at the screen. "The Uber is here. You ready?"

"No—"

Tasha gave her a chiding look. "A Christmas of 'Yes.' It's the central theme of this trip. So, let's try this again. Are you ready?"

"Ye*sss*." Kelsey got up and located her purse. "Let's get this over with."

Tasha clucked her tongue. "Don't be such a Debbie Downer."

"Okay." Kelsey circled her wrists as if she were holding lit Fourth of July sparklers. "Yay."

"False enthusiasm. I'll take it." Tasha pulled a blue silk scarf from her purse that was supposed to have been Kelsey's something blue. "But first," she said, "a blindfold."

"A blindfold?" Kelsey balked.

"It won't be a surprise if you know where we're going."

"Tasha."

"Kelsey."

"This is over-the-top."

"Does that make you uncomfortable?"

"You know it does."

"Bye-bye, Comfort Kitty."

"Are the next two weeks going to be like this?"

"Yup." Tasha fluttered the scarf. "Turn around."

"We don't need the scarf. I'll keep my eyes closed."

"The blindfold is part of the deal. Are you in or out?"

"I—"

"In or out?"

Kelsey opened her mouth, shut it again. The muscle in her eye ticked wildly.

"Yes or no?" Tasha asked.

Kelsey nodded. Barely. "I only agree to this because the alternative of spending Christmas alone with Filomena on a sulk sucks."

"I know. Blindfold?"

"Meow." Kelsey purred.

"That's the spirit." Tasha sidled closer, the scarf stretched between both hands. "Here goes nothing. Commit to a Christmas of 'Yes,'" she whispered dramatically.

"I—"

"No more stalling. The Uber is gonna leave without us. Kelsey James, make a promise, make a vow. Gather your courage and do it now. I *dare* you."

Kelsey and Tasha spent the night in the honeymoon suite at the Ritz-Carlton, which Kelsey was supposed to have shared with Clive. They'd no more than walked in when Filomena texted Where R U?

Belatedly, it dawned on Kelsey that she hadn't told her mother where she was going. She'd gotten too caught up in Tasha's scheme.

"Don't answer her," Tasha said.

Kelsey shot her friend a look. "As if I could get away with that."

"Then don't answer her right away. You reinforce her behavior when you jump to do her bidding."

"She signs my paychecks."

"Part of the problem," Tasha mumbled from one side of her mouth.

Kelsey chose to ignore that and texted back: Since I won't be having a honeymoon, Tasha and I R going on vacation for 2 wks.

FILOMENA: Now? How dare you run out on me.

Kelsey winced. I was going 2 B gone anyway.

FILOMENA: But it's Xmas.

Kelsey bit her bottom lip. Being snide with Filomena always boomeranged but she couldn't help texting: Dec wedding was UR idea.

FILOMENA: Well!!! What am I supposed to do while you're traipsing around with Tosha?

Kelsey grunted.

"Did she misspell my name again?" Tasha asked.

"You know she did."

"She does it on purpose."

"I've told her a million times it's Tasha, not Tosha."

"To minimalize me."

"I know." Kelsey sighed. *This* was why she didn't want to go on a trip. Her mother made such a big deal out of everything. Much easier to stay home than buck her. Kelsey met Tasha's gaze. "Maybe I should just—"

"No." Tasha held up the blindfold that Kelsey had taken off when they arrived at the Ritz. "You accepted my dare." Tasha pointed at Kelsey's phone. "Make it clear you are not giving in."

FILOMENA: Kelsey? R U there?

KELSEY: Mom, just do what U were going to do while I was on my honeymoon.

FILOMENA: But U R not on your honeymoon.

KELSEY: Pretend I am.

FILOMENA: Will you be home for Xmas?

KELSEY: We'll C.

FILOMENA: We'll C!!! We'll C!!! What's that supposed to mean?

KELSEY: I need alone time.

FILOMENA: But U R not alone. U R with *her*.

Kelsey groaned.

FILOMENA: Where R U going? Where will U be?
KELSEY: I don't know. Tasha is surprising me.
FILOMENA: I don't trust her.

Kelsey resisted texting back *You don't trust anyone.*
Instead, she wrote: But I do.

Filomena sent a scowling emoji: Text me the minute
U get to the destination and let me know where U R
staying.

KELSEY: Will.do. Bye. Love U.

She waited a minute for a reply, but nothing came.
What did she expect? Filomena was really good at with-
holding affection when she was angry. Sighing, Kelsey
tossed the phone onto the nightstand and fell backward
onto the bed.

Tasha patted her shoulder. "It's going to be okay."

"Easy for you to say. Your mother isn't bat-shit crazy."

"On a lighter note, they have crème brûlée on room
service." Tasha held up the menu book. "Just FYI."

Kelsey groaned and covered her head with a pillow.
Instinct pushed her to go home. Much easier to smooth
things over with her mother and stay in Dallas. But the
part of her that had gone into hibernation when Chelsea
died whispered in her ear, *You'll never break away if
you stay.*

Guilt chewed on her. As difficult as her mother was,
Kelsey knew that Filomena was hurting. She just didn't
know how to show her vulnerability. Filomena viewed
letting down her guard as a weakness and weakness
was the last thing she would ever let anyone see. It made
Kelsey sad.

"Aww, c'mon, cheer up. Don't get morose," Tasha wheedled. She grabbed Kelsey's hand and tugged her off the bed. "Let's go do something. Just because your mother is unhappy doesn't mean you have to be."

She appreciated Tasha, she really did, but the irony wasn't missed on Kelsey. Tasha wanted Kelsey to stop trying to please Filomena by pleasing her instead.

"Just let me decompress, okay?"

"Sure, sure." Tasha bobbed her head. "Fact is, I need to go home and pack anyway before we take off on this jaunt."

"Do that then."

"Only if you swear, swear, swear you will *not* go home."

"I swear."

"Pinkie swear?" Tasha held out her little finger.

"Pinkie swear." Kelsey locked fingers with her friend.

"Okay, but when I get back, we're going to dinner at the swankiest place I can find that'll take us without advance reservations. On me."

"You don't have—"

"On *me*," Tasha insisted. "I'm getting a two-week trip on your dime, remember?"

"Okay." Kelsey nodded, smiled.

"And we'll discuss your first dare."

"Have you thought about something?" Kelsey asked.

Tasha shivered as if she'd thought up the best dare in the world. "How's this? You have to kiss the first random guy that you find attractive."

"Provided he's willing and single."

"Absolutely. I'm all about consent. Just ask Tony, the butt grabber."

Kelsey laughed. "Okay, I'll do it."

"Really?" Tasha looked surprised.

"A dare's a dare."

"That was easier than I thought. Unless . . ." Tasha
narrowed her eyes and tapped her chin. "You're planning
on running out on me."

"I won't leave."

"Just in case, I'm taking your purse." Tasha grabbed
Kelsey's purse and bounced for the door. "Back in a flash."

Even though she'd pinkie sworn, the guilt pushed
her to go home and Kelsey might just have given in to
her emotions, called her mom, and asked her to send
over her personal chauffeur, Lewis Hunter. But she
decided to think this through.

Twenty-seven years of growing up with a controlling
mom with lofty political ambitions had schooled her to
stay calm, quiet, and observe her environment to head
off trouble. Hypervigilance was her watchword. *Be prepared*, her credo.

Kelsey had not ever been able to trust the world
around her, never knowing when Filomena might snap
from love bombing to angry harangues. Or whether she
could count on her father to rescue her from her mother's
quixotic moods. Sometimes Theo would go toe-to-toe
with Filomena. Other times, he'd take off for the golf
course or disappear into his den with beer and pretzels
and watch sports for hours.

After Chelsea died, that one defining moment of pure
tragic horror had cemented Kelsey's worldview. Life
was indeed dangerous. It wasn't safe to trust anyone too
much.

She stuck her hands into her pockets, found Mayor
Berg's card. Studied it. Could it be her ticket to freedom? Or were there too many strings attached? Part
of her thrilled at the idea of managing a gubernatorial

campaign, but did she really want to start a war with her mother? Because that's how she would take Kelsey's defection. A declaration of war.

Her cell phone dinged. *Not again, Mom.*

Leery, she peered at the screen and breathed a sigh of relief when the text was from her runaway groom.

CLIVE: U OK?
KELSEY: Good.
CLIVE: Really?
KELSEY: R U OK?
CLIVE: I've never been more OK. My only regret is U.
KELSEY: Don't worry about me. B true to yourself.
CLIVE: I do love U.
KELSEY: Just not in the right way.
CLIVE: Is there a wrong way to love?

Kelsey chuckled. Suppose not.

CLIVE: Can U 4give me?
KELSEY: Nothing to 4give.
CLIVE: What about Filomena?
KELSEY: Oh, she'll carry a grudge to the grave.
CLIVE: My poor dad. He's getting an earful.
KELSEY: I'm sure.
CLIVE: Kels?
KELSEY: Yes?
CLIVE: Freedom is beautiful.
KELSEY: ???
CLIVE: Search your heart. U know the answer.
KELSEY: ???
CLIVE: Dare to reach for the stars. They R closer than you think.

KELSEY: U sound like a fortune cookie.
CLIVE: I wish for U the very best life has to offer.
KELSEY: U 2 Fortune Cookie.
CLIVE: Gotta go. Our plane is boarding.

Kelsey didn't even ask Clive where he was going. It was none of her business. She stared at the phone in her hand. Looked at his texts—*freedom is beautiful, search your heart, reach for the stars.*

Dare.

Apparently, it was her trigger word today.

Dare.

Dare to take off for two weeks. Dare to step outside her comfort zone. Dare to kiss a random willing guy.

Dare, dare, dare.

She'd agreed to Tasha's Christmas of Yes challenge. But first she had to stick to one big fat *N-O.*

No, she would not go home. No, she would not give in to her mother's wishes. No, she would not second-guess herself.

She was doing this.

It felt good to make a solid decision.

And the next morning, when they got up and headed out, Tasha didn't even have to remind her about the blindfold. Kelsey tied it on herself in the Uber.

CHAPTER 5

Noah MacGregor loved, loved, loved Christmas.

December was his absolute favorite time of year. Cooking brunch at the First Presbyterian Church Hall for The First Love Cookie Club that Sunday morning had left him with a warm glow and a happy smile as he parked his pickup truck in the marina parking garage.

Christmas Island wasn't drivable by car. The island was too small for roads. Guests parked at the marina and were met by a staff member, who greeted them at the bridge archway and ferried them to the *Rockabye* in a golf cart.

He unloaded his truck briskly. As he was leaving the church hall he'd gotten a text from Raylene reminding him that two guests were arriving soon and to get his ass over to greet them.

Anxious to get to the marina before his guests, he'd hustled right over from the brunch, still wearing his white apron, embroidered with cheeky red lettering: *I'm the Reason Santa Has a Naughty List*.

Noah puttered down Marina Drive and arrived at the bridge, which was decorated in garlands, bows, Christmas lights, and mistletoe. He and Sean had put the ornaments up the day after Thanksgiving.

The air was cool, but not too cold. The sky overcast. He parked the golf cart on the middle of the bridge, cocked back in the driver's seat, and stretched his long legs out over the steering wheel and across the top of the golf cart.

Within minutes a black SUV stopped at the end of the ramp, and two women got out, along with the driver who went around the back of the vehicle to unload their luggage. One of the women was dark haired and brown skinned, the other blond and pale as cream. The blonde wore a blue scarf as a blindfold.

Hmm? What was this?

The shorter woman reached up and whisked the scarf off the blonde as if arriving at the marina was a big surprise.

Blinking, the blonde looked around. Squinting against the afternoon sun, she pulled sunglasses from her purse and put them on. She leaned over to say something to the dark-haired woman.

The two were a study in contrasts. The shorter woman was built like a gymnast, petite, compact, and muscular while the sexy blonde looked like a yogini—tall, willowy, lithe. She had her hair pulled into a single long braid that dangled halfway down the middle of her back.

The dark-haired woman wore denim jeans, a red Stetson, black cowgirl boots, and she looked as if she was headed to a hoedown. The blonde was draped in soft floral fabrics that shifted and fluttered with her movements.

In his opinion, the material was way too thin for December weather near the water, even in North Central

Texas. She wore ridiculous high-heeled sandals and a lightweight white knitted sweater as if she'd been planning a vacation someplace more temperate but changed her destination at the last minute.

The way the blonde walked stirred something inside him. Something wild and rebellious. Did he know her?

An unexpected name popped into his head.

Kelsey.

Holy Christmas stockings! Noah plowed a hand through his hair. Why was he still thinking about that long-ago, teenage love?

Forget it.

Forget Kelsey.

Water under the damn bridge.

But the blonde swayed with the same delicate grace as his first crush. From this distance, he couldn't be sure, but it seemed she had the same full mouth, the same heart-shaped face, the same high cheekbones.

The center of his chest, and other parts of his body, far south of his heart, tightened and squeezed.

It couldn't be her. Could it?

Nah. What would she be doing here?

Noah unfolded himself from the golf cart and started toward them, raising a hand in greeting. He realized belatedly that he was still wearing the goofy apron, but he couldn't remove it without taking off his jacket first, and they'd already spotted him.

"Hello," he greeted and sauntered closer, his pulse quickening until he was standing directly underneath the bridge archway. "I'm from the *Rockabye* here to give you a lift."

"Hi!" The bubbly petite woman rushed over. "I'm Tasha Williams."

The blonde was still at the SUV. She tipped the driver, who grinned like he'd won the lottery. The man got back into his vehicle and drove away.

"I keep telling her to use the app to tip the driver, but she insists on paying cash," the shorter woman mumbled.

Slowly, the blonde made her way toward them, head down as she watched where she placed those impractical shoes on the wooden walkway.

Noah extended a hand to her. "Hi, I'm—"

The blonde raised her head and inhaled sharply. She pushed her sunglasses up on her forehead and studied him openmouthed.

Noah's heart bounced up into his throat. His stomach contracted and sweat trickled down his sides as he peered into a pair of startling blue eyes that he hadn't seen in ten long years.

It is *her,* he thought.

Kelsey James.

A boat passed by the island, rocking waves into the marina. Metal rigging clanged against cement posts. The suspension bridge swayed mildly beneath their feet. Kelsey's mouth popped wide in a huge smile, and she said in a breathless gasp, "Noah MacGregor, is that really *you*?"

Kiss the first random, willing, hot guy that you find attractive.

The second Kelsey recognized the hot guy in the kitschy Christmas apron, she knew she'd been hoodwinked.

She'd already been thrown for a loop when Tasha pulled off the blindfold and Kelsey realized she was back in Twilight. But to find herself looking into Noah

MacGregor's brown eyes—and he just happened to be standing under a bridge archway laden with mistletoe—was just too much.

Her heart jumped into overdrive and zoomed off. She grabbed hold of her friend's arm and reeled her backward. "Dammit, Tasha," Kelsey growled under her breath. "You set me up."

"Ta-da." Tasha chuckled, bending to hoist their two suitcases waiting on the wooden walkway where the Uber driver had left them. "I conjured up your fantasy man. Imagine my surprise when I researched Noah further and discovered he opened up a boat motel right in the town where you first met."

"This can't be happening." Kelsey shot a sidelong glance over at Noah, who was lounging insouciantly against the archway post.

"Are you uncomfortable yet?" Tasha giggled like a maniacal villain in a cheesy soap opera.

"Very."

"Oh goodie. This is indeed a Christmas of Yes. You have to stay, and the first dare is to kiss a random hot guy."

"A *willing* random hot guy."

"That man is standing underneath a mess of mistletoe. How willing can you get?"

The stupid dare. Why had she ever agreed to it? Before Kelsey could say anything, Noah reached for their suitcases and took them from Tasha's hands.

"Leave that to me," he said.

Kelsey didn't want to stare at him, but she couldn't seem to stop. Forget that he was wearing a goofy Christmas apron and a light jacket, she could still make out well-developed muscles beneath his clothing.

Actually, the apron was kind of adorbs. And she could easily imagine him cooking up a special holiday dinner. At camp he'd made the best s'mores.

Twinkle lights were strung from the dock and the marina building in the distance. In the grayness of the foggy afternoon, the Christmas lights offered a welcoming invitation.

Come, they invited. Cozy up by a warm fire with a lap blanket, a good book, and a cup of hot tea. Forget about the wedding that wasn't. Forget about the fiancé that picked the exact wrong time to come out of the closet. Forget about the mother who was fuming because Kelsey had taken off with Tasha for the holidays.

All she had to do was say *yes.* Yes, to Twilight. Yes, to stepping outside her comfort zone. Yes, to kissing the hot guy under the mistletoe who also just happened to be Noah MacGregor.

No, no, no.

One thing and one thing only was on her mind—rest, relax, recover. Never mind about Tasha and her ridiculous dare.

But one look into Noah's dark brown eyes changed all that.

She felt something twist low in her abdomen like a savage beast had awakened and wanted out.

Noah was all grown up and filled out in pure masculine glory. The breeze gusted, sending his sexy scent rushing over her.

His aroma was both familiar and foreign. He smelled like the boy she'd once known, but with more layers now. Leather and peppermint. Sandalwood soap and Spanish marjoram and . . . and . . . Kelsey's nose twitched—eggs, Canadian bacon, hollandaise sauce?

Eggs Benedict.

He smelled like eggs Benedict as he stood directly below the mistletoe, with their suitcases hoisted underneath his arms, his gaze pinning her to the spot.

Intentional positioning?

Was he in on the scheme with Tasha? She darted a glance at her friend.

Tasha puckered up, jerked her head at Noah, mouthed, *Kiss him, I dare you.*

Oh, this was beyond nutty.

Kelsey knotted her hands into fists and struggled to catch her breath. A dozen competing emotions surged through her—nervousness, misgiving, fascination, wariness, hope. But at the bottom of them all, the feeling with the strongest wallop?

Delight.

She was *delighted* to see him.

But who wouldn't be? He was cover-model gorgeous, and he had matured into one heck of a man. His shoulders were broader, his thighs thicker, his face fuller. But he still owned that bad boy grin, and the devilish twinkle in his eyes and the saucy apron told her that he had not lost his playful sense of humor.

Her breath flew from her body, leaving her feeling airless and high. She quelled the urge to close her eyes.

Or better yet, dive right off the bridge and swim away.

Jumping into the cold waters of Lake Twilight would be less shocking than seeing her old flame and discovering that the embers still burned.

Especially since she had an equally compelling urge to fling herself into his arms and kiss him until both of them were addled with lust and tearing each other's clothes off to finish what they'd started ten years ago.

"I thought you were getting married this weekend," Noah murmured.

Kelsey fingered her bottom lip. "You heard about that?"

"It was on the news when your mother won the mayoral election. Tell Filomena congrats by the way."

Kelsey would *not* be doing that. Her mother despised Noah with a passion.

"Things didn't work out with Clive," Tasha said. "Kels is free as a bird."

Kelsey shot her friend a hard stare. *Stop talking.*

But irrepressible, Tasha kept right on rolling. "He left her at the altar yesterday. Ran off with the best man."

Noah's eyes landed on Kelsey again. They were full of kindness and sincerity. "Aww, that sucks. I'm so sorry that happened to you."

"Don't be," Tasha said. "She's not."

"Firefly?" Noah dipped his head, lowered his eyebrows. "Is your friend correct? *Are* you okay?"

Firefly.

His old nickname for her tripped right off his tongue as if it hadn't been a decade since he'd last spoken to her. She'd almost forgotten that nickname. He'd dubbed her "Firefly" the first time they'd met as eleven-year-olds at Camp Hope.

While returning from a hike in the forest, they'd gotten separated from the rest of the group and ended up in a meadow filled with fireflies. Thrilled by the sight, she'd spun around in circles, laughing.

He'd told her he'd never seen anyone get so excited over lightning bugs. But he was a country kid raised on the Brazos River, and she was from the city. The sweet flickering lights of the insects had given her hope in that dark time after Chelsea's death.

Later that evening, he'd sneaked over to her cabin with a mason jar filled with fireflies and waited on the porch until she'd come out yawning at midnight, headed for the privies. He'd poked holes in the metal lid so that the bugs could get air.

"For you," he said, shyly toeing the porch boards with his sneaker.

She cupped that mason jar in her hands, feeling awed and special by his thoughtful gift and that he'd been brave enough to risk getting caught for her.

"You could get in big trouble for hanging around the girls' cabins. Why did you do this?"

"Because you liked the fireflies so much."

"It's the nicest present anyone ever gave me." She clutched the jar to her chest. "Thank you."

"You're welcome," he said. "You can use them for a nightlight but let them go in the morning, so they don't die."

That's when she'd kissed him. A quick press of her lips to his.

Her first kiss.

Their first kiss.

His eyes had flown wide, and his mouth dropped open, and he scurried off to his cabin.

Smiling, Kelsey had climbed back into bed, settled underneath the covers with the mason jar, and fallen asleep as the fireflies blinked their magic lullaby.

Now, Noah was staring into her eyes again.

She stared back.

An odd sensation swept over her. A feeling that if she just stretched out her hand, time would fall away, and she could touch the past and the girl she used to be. And Noah would be the innocent boy that he once was.

Silly, whispered her matter-of-fact voice. *The past is the past. It's over and done.*

Seize the day, prompted the wild part of her she never let loose. The secret part that had agreed to Tasha's Christmas dare. *Make a fresh start. Become a new you.*

In a nutshell, that was the push/pull that had defined her life since Chelsea had died. Safety and security on the one hand, versus taking a big, passionate bite out of life on the other. The internal battle had trapped her, arrested her development.

Noah raked a long, measuring gaze over her body and she grew hot despite the cold wind blowing off the lake. The hungry expression in his dark eyes stripped her naked. It felt as if he could read her every thought and knew her inside and out.

She shivered in her vulnerability, feared losing control. Feared what this man could do to her equilibrium.

The muscle at the corner of her eye twitched. That annoying, involuntary tic that her doctor called blepharospasm. It cropped up whenever she felt overwhelmed.

Or scared.

Right now, she was both.

If she'd known she was going to run into Noah, she would have taken a Xanax. While she didn't like taking the stress-relieving medication, her doctor had prescribed it for whenever the twitching got severe.

She'd hesitated to even get the prescription filled, but then her doctor pointed, "It's either an occasional Xanax or you stop working for your mother."

Yes, well, that was easier said than done.

"It's good to see you after all these years." Noah's eyes crinkled in a friendly, welcoming smile, and it seemed he meant it.

"She's happy to see you too." Tasha shifted from foot to foot, thrust Kelsey toward Noah, and whispered low under her breath, "Kiss the first random willing guy you find attractive." Louder she said, "She still has hot sexy fantasies about you—"

Kelsey bumped Tasha with her hip, a light tap, a warning, *shut up*. But she smacked her harder than she intended, and the momentum knocked Tasha off-balance.

Her friend wavered on the edge of the bridge, arms windmilling wildly.

Mortified, Kelsey gasped and grabbed for her. "Oh, oh, I'm so sorry!"

But Noah sprang into action. He dropped the suitcases and caught Tasha by the arm just before she tumbled into the water.

Tasha righted herself. "Hey thanks, hero."

"You okay?" Noah asked, keeping his hand on Tasha's shoulder until she was steady.

"As you can see, Kelsey is still so crazy for you that she'd rather send me into the drink than let you know it." Tasha winked.

Kelsey groaned and pulled a palm down her face. Her eye twitched furiously.

"Is that right?" Noah drawled, tipping his head back and assessing Kelsey from half-lowered lashes.

"This whole setup was my friend's doing," Kelsey said, terrified that he thought she'd come here to Twilight to make a move on him. "I had no idea where she was taking me, or that you owned the boatel we're staying at." Realizing that she was starting to sound frantic, Kelsey caught her breath.

"I believe you," he said. "I saw your friend take the blindfold off."

"This was dirty pool." She pointed at Tasha, who was practicing her innocent *who me* expression. "Blindsiding me with Twilight."

And *Noah*.

"Still the same old Firefly." Noah's chuckle was tender, his eyes lively. "Terrified of your emotions."

"I'm not—"

"It's okay. I get it," he said. "Emotions are hard things to process. Didn't we hear enough about that at Camp Hope?"

Without another word, he gathered her in his arms as if they were friends for life, wrapped her in a brunch-scented hug, picked her up off her feet, and spun her around.

All the air seeped from Kelsey's body and over his shoulder, she saw Tash mouthing again, *Kiss him!*

CHAPTER 6

Did she dare?

His firm masculine chest smashed against her soft feminine breasts. Kelsey flew into a lather. Instantly, she was hot and sweaty and . . . God, but it felt so damn good in his arms.

But scary at the same time.

Incredibly scary.

Anything she was feeling right now, she could not trust. It was adrenaline and hormones and the fact that her fiancé had stood her up at the altar. This was a crazy, surreal Twilight Zone—*pun intended*—and anything that happened here could not be real. A mind-bending paradigm shift.

His muscles contracted as he tightened the hug. His chin brushed against her skin, his beard stubble sexy-scratchy. The contact roused every sleeping erogenous zone in her body.

Kelsey's head swam.

In Noah's embrace, that long-ago night came flooding back to her. And she was hit with the real reason she hadn't resisted when her mother had dragged her off that dock at Camp Hope. Why she hadn't tried to contact Noah afterward. Why she'd burned his picture and cried herself to sleep the night before she went off to Vassar College. Why she'd ended up with Clive.

She was a coward.

Noah was too much man for her—big and strong and powerful. Life-force oozed from every pore. He was everything she'd ever dreamed of and everything that scared her to death, all rolled into one.

And she was emotionally stunted. All she wanted to do was squirm away, run away, just get out of here fast.

"You can put me down now."

Noah laughed, a throaty sound that tugged something deep inside her solar plexus. He released her, but one arm still lingered at her waist as if it belonged there. His chocolate eyes sparkled with mirth. He'd always been so open and fun loving and passionate. It was good to see that he had not changed.

Immobilized, she peered into his eyes, her mind bouncing around. Her body tingling from where he'd touched her, blood pumping hard through her veins.

Energy pulsed from his palm into her waist. Supercharged and electric. If sensation were a color, his aura would be flame blue—burning bright and beautiful.

His touch, his stare.

In a blink, she was transported back in time, and she was that girl again. Seventeen years old and so hot for him, but so very afraid that her feelings would take her down. He was right. She was terrified of her emotions, and he could break into them, and everything she'd been tamping down for years—all the feelings and fears—would come rolling out.

What a mess!

And if that happened, she felt like she would just dissolve. Disappear. Lose herself entirely. That was the attraction and the repulsion.

"You look astonishing," he said, eyeing her up and down.

Her cheeks heated and unable to hold his appreciative gaze, she glanced away. *Not so bad yourself,* she longed to say but didn't. Instead, she murmured, "That's kind of you to say."

"How is your dad?" he asked. "I'm assuming your mom is on cloud nine since she just got elected mayor of Dallas."

"Dad's fine. Filomena's having a cow over the whole runaway groom thing," Tasha piped up. "But she'll get over it. Nothing keeps her down for long."

"Your friend is a pistol," Noah said to Kelsey.

Tasha was Tasha. Her friend didn't care what anyone thought. Tasha's devil-may-care attitude was one of the things that Kelsey admired most about her.

"And you're a hotshot." Tasha used her fingers as pretend guns, pointed them at him, mimed shooting and then blowing invisible smoke from her fingers.

Noah laughed and smiled at Kelsey. "I like her. She's good for you."

"Day-*am*, Noah MacGregor. I dig you too." Tasha winked.

Tasha was a flirt, Kelsey knew that. Her best friend meant nothing by it, and yet a strange heat of jealousy spread up her lower back, into her spine and the nape of her neck.

Noah directed a smile at Tasha, but he was still looking at Kelsey, waiting for her reply.

"Dad has a girlfriend and I suspect they'll marry soon. Mom . . . she's too busy with her career for a love life."

"I can't say I'm surprised. Your mother . . ." He paused as if trying to think of a diplomatic way to express himself. "Is a little high-maintenance."

"A little?" Tasha snorted. "That's like saying that the Pope is a little bit Catholic."

"How are your sisters and Joel?" Kelsey asked him.

His face lit. The MacGregors were a close-knit bunch. Kelsey was a teeny bit jealous of how well they got along. Okay, maybe not so teeny.

"Flynn and Jesse got married," he said. "They have two little ones now. Grace is six and Ian is three and a half. Those kids are adorable. I love being an uncle."

"Aww!" Kelsey pressed her palms together in front of her heart. "What about Carrie?"

"Six years ago, Carrie married her high school sweetheart, Mark, and they moved to California. They don't have any kids yet, but they have a house full of dogs."

"So Carrie succumbed to the town legend too?" Kelsey smiled. "I never thought she'd fall for it."

Local lore said the town of Twilight was founded on the spot where two teenage lovers—separated during the Civil War by competing loyalties—were reunited fifteen years later on the banks of the Brazos River. The town was known for bringing couples together, and capitalized on the story to stir tourism, with a Sweetheart Park, Sweetheart Tree, Sweetheart Fountain, and other romantic landmarks.

"You know how it is," Noah said, still eyeing her. "Anyway, it's also a family tradition to find The One when you're young. How could she resist? Mom and Dad were teenage sweethearts, Jesse and Flynn . . ."

Noah and me.

The thought popped into Kelsey's head, but she squashed it. Thoughts like that were useless. The past was over. He hadn't come for her as he said he would. Hadn't fought for her. Although she couldn't really blame him for that. Filomena was a formidable foe, and he'd been a seventeen-year-old kid.

"That's good to hear that your sisters are doing well. And Joel?"

"Joel and I are in business together. He runs tours on the *Brazos Queen*, while I manage the *Rockabye* Boatel and Christmas Island."

"That's great news. I can totally see you doing that. What about your dad?" she asked.

"He remarried and moved to Stephenville last year. He's still sober, going on twelve years now. We're so proud of him."

"I am happy for you, Noah. It sounds like the Mac-Gregors are thriving."

"We are." He leaned in, his body language saying he wanted more contact with her. Or was it wishful thinking on her part? "Where are you living these days?"

"With her moth-*er*." Tasha arched her eyebrows and emphasized the last syllable.

"It's just temporary," Kelsey rushed to add. "My lease was up, and I was already at Mom's house night and day anyway as we worked on her mayoral campaign so—"

"She's Filomena's campaign manager," Tasha interrupted.

Noah didn't say anything else, just kept eyeing Kelsey like he couldn't believe she was there.

She looked at his sexy mouth, and something just came over her. Something impulsive and rash.

If she had to keep her promise to Tasha and kiss a willing hot guy, why not Noah?

Better than the alternative, right? Some random stranger.

Then again, Tasha had pulled strings. This whole thing was a setup. Was she really going to walk right into her friend's trap?

Noah's smile beguiled.

Kelsey's heart thumped. She was all mixed up inside.

This was supposed to have been her honeymoon. Right now, she should have been on her way to Spain. Instead, she found herself in this surreal *Sliding Doors* reality where it seemed she was living an alternate life in a different dimension.

How had she gotten here?

Why didn't she just leave?

Was she trapped in some bizarre lucid dream?

Oh, what the hell, who cares? Just kiss him and get the dare over with.

She went up on tiptoes, cupped the sides of his face between her palms, and planted a quick kiss on his startled lips.

There.

Done.

The first dare completed.

Check it off the list. On to the next one.

Except the kiss was *not* over.

Not by a long shot.

Kelsey dropped her heels to the wooden bridge planks and peered up.

Noah looked down.

Their eyes met.

The moment was straight out of some romantic holiday movie. Mistletoe dangled in from the archway above them. Woodsmoke from someone's fireplace scenting the dewy air. Holiday music drifting from the marina building. "Santa Claus Is Coming to Town."

Christmas, Christmas everywhere and not a Grinch in sight.

Unless you counted Kelsey.

Noah's dark eyes offered something inevitable.

Of what, she was not sure, but Kelsey couldn't catch her breath. Her stomach knotted, and her body ached, literally *ached*, for another taste of him.

The fairy-tale moment sucked her in—the water, the holiday, that infernal Twilight Sweethearts legend—yanking her down deep into a past she wasn't certain she wanted to revisit.

It felt as if she'd been asleep for a decade, locked away in her mother's ivory tower. Unable to truly feel any emotions. Unable to live her own life. Unable to find out who she was if she was not merely Filomena James's daughter.

But now, here was Noah, and his tender smile untwisting the lid to her jar as if she were a bright trapped firefly he was releasing back into the wild.

Get out, yelled the part of her that prized safety and security. *He's going to dismantle you, and then you'll be in pieces all over again.*

"What," he said, looking shocked, "was that all about?"

She pointed overhead at the handy excuse. "You shouldn't stand under mistletoe if you don't want to be kissed."

"Oh." His eyes crinkled in a happy smile.

Kelsey cleared her throat. "Noah."

"Firefly."

He caressed her cheek.

She went up on tiptoes again.

He dipped his head lower.

She latched onto his gaze.

His thumb stroked her bottom lip.

She touched the tip of her tongue to his thumb.

He pursed his lips.

Her heart zoomed into her throat. Her comfort zone shoved into another dimension. Her eye twitched. Too bad the Xanax was in the bottom of her makeup bag inside her suitcase. She'd dry swallow one if she had it.

Noah's thumb moved from her mouth to her temple. He massaged her skin with soft, rhythmic strokes until the tic subsided. "How's that?"

"Huh?" She stared at him dazed.

"No reason to be nervous with me."

"No?" Her knees knocked wildly.

"I'm going to kiss you again," Noah said. "If that's okay with you. But this time, it'll be a proper kiss."

Noah had no idea what he was doing. He was a guy who operated on instinct. Did what was fun, as long as it was fun, and right now, kissing Kelsey was *fun, fun, fun.*

He knew well enough this wasn't a smart move. She'd just gotten stood up at the altar, for crying out loud, and the last thing he wanted was to rekindle a relationship with the daughter of the woman who had almost ruined his life.

But here he was, happy-go-lucky Noah, pushing his luck.

In answer to his request, Kelsey threaded her arms around his neck and tugged his head down lower. She wasn't short at five-foot-six, but he was still almost a foot taller. A gap to bridge.

Noah captured her mouth and found himself capsized on the wave of Kelsey's lips. He tasted her. He absorbed her. Her flavor. Her warmth. Her Kelsey-ness.

Engulfed.

He was engulfed in the intimate experience of her soft, delicious lips. It had been too long since he'd kissed this pretty woman and he devoured her.

Or maybe she devoured him.

It was hard to tell with so much moisture and heat.

Mouths open and searching, they shared one quivering breath under a network of hot wet kisses. Whew-eee. They still had it!

He hauled her up flush against his body on the gently swaying suspension bridge, in the mist.

She made a soft mewling noise, like an uncomfortable kitten. But feisty too. She nipped his bottom lip between her teeth. Growled. Laughed.

Man, this was fun.

Kelsey slipped her arm underneath his jacket, fisted the back of his shirt in her hand, tugged as if she wanted to rip it off his body.

I'm game.

Noah tilted her head back, dove deep. Held her steady while he poured every ounce of his focus into kissing her.

God! She tasted sweet and rich. He did not remember her tasting this good. But ten years was a long time.

Nibbling, licking, tasting. His hands roving over her body, appreciating her delicate bone structure, her lithe, lean muscles, the rise and fall of her chest.

He felt her knees buckle, her body sway. He held her steady, kissed her again. He thrilled to the zap of wildness rising up through the water, through the boards of the bridge, through the soles of his feet, up his spine. Grounding him in the element. Delivering energy from him to her.

Their mouths fused.

It felt to Noah as if they were caught up in a riptide of past and future all swirling into this one passionate kiss. Incredible, this rush of hope filling up his chest, heady and strange. He shimmered from his toes to the center of his forehead.

Vibrated. Tingled. Burned.

Unbelievable.

Overstating much, Bronco? It's just a damn kiss.

She stilled beneath him, her body stiffening.

He stopped kissing her. Looked into her eyes. Into her bewildered expression as she struggled to process what was going on.

Clueless.

Hey, he was clueless too.

She let go of his shirt. "I've never . . . that was . . . wow," she whispered. "Just wow."

He smiled. "I'd forgotten how much fun it was to kiss you."

"Me too." She fingered her lips.

Lips he wanted to plow through like pudding.

She gave him a foxy smile.

"Mistletoe magic," he said.

"Mistletoe," she echoed, her eye muscle twitching wildly again, but this time he did not try to soothe it. He was unsettled himself.

"Well." Noah dusted his palms together and pretended that she hadn't just rocked his entire world. "How about I give you ladies a tour of Christmas Island on our way to the boatel?"

CHAPTER 7

Breathlessly, Kelsey moved from underneath the archway, crossing the threshold between the marina deck and the suspension bridge, and headed for the golf cart. The bridge swayed gently beneath her weight. Noah bent to pick up the luggage he'd dropped when he'd grabbed for Tasha to keep her from falling.

Grinning, Tasha gave her a thumbs-up. Mouthed, *Go get him, girl*.

But she was not going to "go get him." She kissed him because she'd agreed to the silly Christmas of Yes. Dare One was over and done with. Only four more to go.

Yes, it was a great kiss, but so what? It wasn't as if anything would come of it. She didn't want anything to come of it. She was just getting out of a relationship, and trying to find herself, which was the only reason she was here. Jumping into something with Noah at this juncture would be dumb, dumb, dumb.

Tasha shoved her toward the passenger side of the golf cart, jumped into the backseat and sprawled out, so there was no place for Kelsey.

Kelsey glared at her. "Trade places with me," she hissed while Noah stowed their luggage on the back of the golf cart and got behind the wheel.

Tasha shook her head. "Nothing doing."

Kelsey narrowed her eyes and her mouth. *You are so dead.*

Her best friend giggled, not the least bit threatened, and whispered, "A Christmas of Yes."

"Have a seat," Noah invited, patting the spot next to him.

Kelsey edged down, strapped on her seat belt.

The sleeve of his jacket rode up on his arm, revealing a small tattoo on the inside of his wrist. One word in beautiful black calligraphy script.

Dare.

Really, seriously? Was "dare" becoming her personal theme? She didn't like that. She'd spent her life avoiding rash decisions.

Noah had not had that tattoo when he was seventeen. When had he gotten it? And why?

Dare.

That summed up his personality to a T. Everything he did he tackled with passion and gusto. Even if he didn't have the best staying power in the world because his quicksilver mind tended to jump from one thing to the next.

Dare.

Did he approach sex with that same degree of passion? She recalled how his hot tongue had done strange and wonderful things to her teenage body.

How he'd run his fevered hand up her bare belly as they lay on that long-ago dock, and how his fingers had loosened the strap of her bikini top. How he'd pressed his erect shaft against her soft thigh and how her heart pounded blood into her ears with the tympani of tribal drums.

But mostly, she remembered the longing. Desperate and overwhelming. Yearning and burning.

Obsessed.

With him.

Oh crap.

But that was a long time ago. They had both changed. They weren't reckless kids anymore, acting on instinct and the headiness of puppy love.

So what if his kiss knocked her socks off? She was a controlled person. She wasn't impulsive. Didn't make rash decisions or dive into risky water. After kissing Noah, she felt like she'd walked off a gangplank backward and plunged into the deep end of the ocean.

Her right eye twitched. A hard spasm that lowered her lid. She put a hand to her temple, ducked her head, and took a deep breath. Held it for as long as she could before slowly letting it out through clenched teeth.

Calm down.

"We're going the long way around." Noah started the golf cart.

The marina disappeared from view as he drove around the far side of the island. Gusty wind loosened hair from Kelsey's braid, and whipped the strands into her face. The air smelled of mist and fried catfish from Froggie's diner along the opposite shoreline.

"Does your family still own Froggie's?" she asked.

"Dad sold it when he remarried," Noah said. "The end of an era."

She studied his profile as he guided the golf cart down the dirt path along the water. What contrast. The tall, muscular man in a frivolous Christmas apron sticking out from underneath his jacket.

There was gentleness in the softness of his smile, and the kindness in his eyes—an erotic combo, those hard muscles, and tender ways. And she couldn't help wondering what he looked like naked. Oh, she'd seen him shirtless before, but that had been ten years ago when he was lean and seventeen.

He raised his head, caught her watching him.

Winked.

Sexual energy rolled off him, blasting body heat from him into her. And she had a deep, sudden yearning for him that churned through her blood, heavy and potent.

And it scared Kelsey to her roots.

He was everything she'd spent the last decade avoiding. A man who moved her. A man who stirred her physical desires. A man who had the power to dismantle her with his smile, that wink, and those chocolate brown eyes.

Dismantle, unravel, and shove her so far out of her comfort zone she could never find her way back.

Holy smokes.

Was that why she wanted him? Because he could tear apart her prim safe little life if she dared let it happen?

Dare.

That damn word again.

Craziness. She had to stop thinking like this. Kelsey swiveled her head to see what Tasha was doing.

Tasha had her short legs stretched in front of her, ankles crossed. She sat near enough for Kelsey to reach over and tweak the toe of her boot if she wanted. Her friend's face was tilted up to the cloudy gray sky, her fingers interlaced, palms cradling the back of her head, elbows out, and she was grinning like she was the most cunning matchmaker ever.

Tasha hummed "Reunited" by Peaches and Herb.

Aww, c'mon. Kelsey's eye jumped like mad, and she prayed that Noah couldn't hear what Tasha was humming.

Kelsey bugged her eyes, glared at her friend. *Stop it.*

Irrepressible, Tasha kept right on humming.

The fog grew heavier the farther they went and a fine mist settled over their clothes. She felt her hair frizz. The mist became a gray blanket, wrapping them in a weighted whirl. It felt like some kind of fairy-tale fantasy, as surreal as a dream.

Could Noah be a wild fling? Did she dare? It was a Christmas of Yes, after all.

Why not?

The fog was mysterious and layered. Just like Noah. What went on behind his intelligent eyes? What was he thinking? Did he feel this chemistry as strongly as she? Her gaze trailed to his hands. Big, strong, masculine hands. Then she dropped her gaze to his wrist.

Dare.

It was a motto. A credo. An anthem. A flipping call to action. But at the same time, it felt like a warning. Dare too much, and you could end up damaged.

Her mind said, *Keep away, don't take a chance.* Her soul cried, *Who cares? Look at that body, will ya?*

Her body heated up all over again. And her heart, oh the stupid thing, went all squishy and soft and romantic. Thinking about sex with Noah had Kelsey drawing in a deep breath and sent her irritating eye tic into overdrive.

"There's Camp Hope." Noah pointed out across the length of the lake.

Kelsey didn't need the reminder. That dock, that night, was forever etched in her memory.

"That's where you two met, huh?"

Kelsey looked back at her friend again. Tasha fished a clementine orange from the pocket of her jacket and started peeling, then offered a second orange to her. Kelsey held up a palm. Shook her head. Her stomach was tied up in knots. She couldn't eat if she tried.

"We met there every summer for six years." Noah was studying Kelsey with heavily lidded eyes.

"So you guys were childhood sweethearts?" Tasha popped a slice of orange into her mouth, chewed. The fragrance of citrus spritzed the air. "That's so cute. What's this deal about a sweetheart legend I saw online when I booked the B&B?"

"Marketing silliness," Kelsey said at the same time Noah said, "Soul mates."

Kelsey blinked at him. "Soul mates? You've gotta be kidding me."

"You think the legend is silly?" He gawked at her as if she were a complete stranger and she'd just espoused an opinion that was a deal breaker.

"Ooh." Tasha stuffed the orange peelings in her pocket and rubbed her palms together. "Conflict. I love it."

Kelsey rolled her eyes at Noah. "Tasha loves drama. She was a theater major in college."

"That was before I found my calling in food." Tasha pointed at Noah. "You, go. Tell me why this sweetheart legend is so hot."

He cast Kelsey a sidelong glance and sent her a wolf-ish smile and her pulse, which had finally started to settle down, kicked back up again. He told Tasha the legend of Rebekka Nash and Jon Grant, how they'd reunited on the banks of the Brazos River at twilight. Jon on one side of the river, Rebekka on the other as they'd both come down to water their horses. Noah's voice took on a romantic quality as he described how the two lovers had swum across the river and met in the middle for their legendary reunion kiss.

"It was the power of Christmas," he said, "that brought them together."

"Christmas?" Kelsey shook her head. "Are you telling me Jon and Rebekka met at Christmas?"

"Yep."

"That's the first time I'm hearing *that* version."

"It's true," he said. "You can look it up in *The Fascinating History of Twilight, Texas*, volume one. It's in the library."

"No, no, I'm pretty sure it was summer when they met. They told us the story at camp, remember?"

"It was *summer* camp, so they might have altered the details to suit the audience, but it's not the official version."

"You're telling me Jon and Rebekka swam across the river in December?" She tapped her chin with an index finger.

"Their love was that powerful." He sounded as if he truly believed that cockamamie story.

Kelsey folded her arms. "I can't think of anybody I'd jump into icy waters to kiss."

"I can," Noah said, his gaze hot on hers.

Oh my, was he talking about *her*?

Tasha leaned over to poke Kelsey. "He's talking about you."

Kelsey ignored both Tasha's poke and Noah's look and said logically, "They would have gotten hypothermia if they'd swum across the water in winter."

"Maybe they did." Noah's brows lowered with his voice. "And the power of their love saved them."

Kelsey rolled her eyes hard. "They would have frozen to death. Especially back then."

"But they didn't."

"Which is why I question the veracity of a Christmas swim."

"True love trumps all." The wind ruffled Noah's hair, reddened his cheeks. His teasing smile deepened. "Soul mate magic."

"That's so romantic." Tasha sighed and tucked both palms underneath her chin. "They were willing to die for love."

"It's just a fable," Kelsey said to blunt the sudden sharpness pushing through her chest. "There's no actual proof that any aspect of the story is true."

"When did you get so crusty?" Noah clicked his tongue like she was a lost cause.

Kelsey studied him. "When did you get so sentimental?"

"You gotta remember," Tasha interrupted. "Kels just got dumped at the altar yesterday. She's not normally so down on love."

Kelsey wished her friend would stop talking. From somewhere on the water, the sound of "White Christmas" drifted out to them over a loudspeaker.

People were gathered on a boat dock, lining up to board a paddle wheel boat. Both the dock and the boat were lavishly decorated with lights, wreaths, garlands, the works. But of course: this was Twilight.

"What's going on over there?" Tasha asked.

"That's the *Brazos Queen* taking folks out for an afternoon tour. My twin brother and I own it," Noah said.

"Wait, you have a twin?" Tasha fanned herself. "You mean there are two guys who look like you, walking around in the world? Move over, Property Brothers."

"Up ahead," Noah said, "is the *Rockabye*."

The boatel was a paddle wheel twin to the *Brazos Queen*. The *Rockabye* was also decorated to the hilt with Christmas pageantry.

Kelsey found herself watching Noah as he guided the golf cart closer to the floating B&B. His fingers were long and broad and so darn sexy. Once upon a time, those very same fingers had tickled the underside of her chin while his hot wet tongue explored her mouth.

Deep inside, Kelsey felt a frighteningly strong tug of sexual arousal.

"Who generally stays at your boatel?" Tasha asked. "What's your demographic?"

"During the holidays, tourists throng the town. Twilight is a Christmas mecca. People usually choose the *Rockabye* because it's quiet and off the beaten path, but still near enough to walk to town. Plus, we have a grand view of the New Year's Eve fireworks display. You can sit in the roof dome lounge, have a drink and relax."

Kelsey cocked her head and spied a small glass dome structure on the bridge of the *Rockabye* that had been added as an extension to the pilot house. She imagined herself in the lounge with Noah watching fireworks.

Felt corresponding fireworks shoot through her.

"How many guests can you accommodate?" Tasha asked.

"We have seven bedrooms with their own private baths, plus the suite you reserved," Noah said.

"Nice."

Noah pulled to a stop inside a covered portico that housed two other golf carts along with outdoor supplies.

Tasha jumped from the backseat, grabbed her luggage, and started up the wooden decking toward the boatel, calling over her shoulder, "I'll check us in."

Kelsey heard, rather than saw, her friend bounce up the dock toward the *Rockabye*. Her eyes were full of Noah. He got out and came around to her side of the golf cart, reached out his hand.

"Watch out, the ground is boggy from the recent rains and in those shoes . . ." He shook his head at her high-heeled sandals.

She took his hand. The mist swirled. The air was alive with the electricity of their contact. Her skin prickled and her nerve endings danced.

They hung together for a whispered heartbeat with their hands joined.

Touching.

She didn't know if the magic came from Christmas Island or the evocative weather or from the very real feel of Noah's skin on hers, but there was definitely something going on here.

Something crazy and mysterious and far outside her comfort zone.

Noah was breathing hard, just as hard as she was, in a ragged, rough-edged rhythm.

A nexus of complicated feelings rippled through her. He guided her toward the deck.

The toe of her shoe caught on a loose board. She stumbled and lost her balance. "Oh, oh!"

He was there.

His body, a solid wall, blocking her, keeping her from falling. Noah reached out to caress her jumping eye muscle again. Soothingly, rhythmically.

Why was she suddenly so clumsy? What was it about him that snatched her equilibrium right out from underneath her?

And just what in the hell was she going to do about it?

CHAPTER 8

You're begging for trouble, MacGregor.

He'd known better than to touch Kelsey. Noah had caressed her temple to ease her twitching eye, and to connect with the vulnerability that she couldn't hide. Even as a teenager she'd always cared too much, felt too much. It showed up on her face, even then, and here he was taking full advantage of her weakness.

Because he wanted her.

Wanted her so badly he could taste it.

From the moment it dawned on him that the cool blonde getting out of the Uber was Kelsey James—his first crush, first kiss, first love, first everything—he'd been gobsmacked. She was the last person he expected to show up on Christmas Island.

And when Tasha spilled the beans about Kelsey getting stood up at the altar, his initial impulse had been vengeful smugness—*Karma's a bitch, babe.* After her mother had dragged her back to Dallas, she'd never answered his letters. Never texted. Never called. Even when he'd gone after her . . .

But that was just hurt feelings and unfair to Kelsey. She'd been seventeen with an aggressive, controlling mother. In total honesty, his youthful expectations that love conquers all had been totally unreasonable.

Love did not conquer all.

He felt ashamed for thinking that karma thing.

Forgive and forget.

That was ten years ago. He'd gotten past it. He no longer nursed a grudge over Filomena's threats or Kelsey's ghosting. She'd just been protecting herself.

He got it.

And until he'd come back to Twilight, bought Christmas Island, and saw Camp Hope every time he stepped out onto the deck of the *Rockabye*, he rarely thought about Kelsey.

But deep down inside, a tiny bit of his heart was still scarred from what had happened between them. In some small way, he was still that boy from the wrong side of the tracks that had dared to love Filomena James's daughter.

He wasn't proud of that scar, but it was part of him. Noah was who he was. Good *and* bad. That didn't mean he didn't try his best to be a better person. It just meant that some days, he didn't succeed. And some days he felt like that vulnerable, motherless teenage boy who didn't quite understand why he wasn't good enough for Kelsey.

The old inferiority complex reared its ugly head. In every other corner of his life, it didn't bother him one bit that he came from a lower-middle-class family. But when it came to Kelsey . . . well, it seemed he was seventeen all over again. Self-conscious that her family had money and his did not.

You got money now, Budweiser. He heard his twin brother Joel's voice in his head. Yeah, but *nouveau riche* didn't count to the likes of Filomena James. She'd called him poor white trash and told him to stay away from her daughter.

The memory was a grass burr in his gut, poking him hard.

All the more reason to steer clear of Kelsey. From what Tasha had said, Kelsey was still tightly tied to her mother's apron strings. Noah did not need that kind of hassle, thank you very much.

No matter how hot Kelsey might be.

Keep your hands to yourself, MacGregor.

It was a solid plan, but then a final thought popped into his mind as he stood on the dock staring down into Kelsey's sapphire eyes—a thought which was strictly from his animal brain.

How do I get her between the sheets?

As he looked deep inside her, sudden realization hammered through him. *You still don't know who you are, do you, Firefly?*

Neither in bed nor out of it.

He could see how lost she was in the twitching of the muscles around her eye. She hadn't changed. She was still allowing her mother to call the shots. Telling her who to marry, running her life.

Kelsey was still hiding from herself. Terrified, for some reason, of grabbing life with both hands.

Noah could see it in the way she held herself, rigid and uncertain. How she slanted her eyes downward and glanced away. How she caught her breath whenever things got emotionally intense the way they were right now.

"Breathe," he whispered.

"What?" She blinked.

"You're holding your breath."

"No, I'm not." She exhaled.

He recalled the first time they'd met at summer camp. Two eleven-year-olds processing a lot of damn grief. He'd lost his mom to ALS that Christmas and Kelsey's twin sister had drowned the previous summer. As a twin himself, he understood the bond. He couldn't imagine life without Joel, leading him to wonder if pity was part of the reason he'd been drawn to her.

Joel had been at camp too, but Kelsey, unlike most everyone, never got them mixed up, not even when they'd tried pranking her by getting Joel to pretend he was Noah.

She'd been swinging in a hammock reading a book when Joel had approached her and said, "Hey, you wanna go fishing with Joel and me?"

She hadn't even put her book down, simply yawned, turned the page and said, "Joel, you're not fooling anyone. Tell Noah if he wants me to go fishing with him he's got to come ask me himself."

"How did you know?" Joel asked.

"I was a twin," Kelsey said. "I understand the trading places game."

"Noah," Joel had called over his shoulder where Noah had been hiding behind a tree. "C'mon out. We're busted."

He'd come forward, scuffing the toes of his shoes in the dirt, crushing on her even then. She'd smiled, and his heart tripped, and she'd closed her book and said, "I'll come fishing if you bait my hook."

And that was that.

Their first date.

She had no idea how strong she was. How she was the glue that held her mother's world together. He'd seen the depth of her strength from the moment he'd met her at camp, even if she couldn't see it in herself.

He saw a glimmer of it now. How she straightened her spine and lifted her chin and ironed her features into a cool expression of indifference. But at the same time, her hands were trembling, and he saw the quick throb of the pulse at the hollow of her throat. She was unnerved by him but determined not to show it.

Hell, Firefly, I'm plenty unnerved too.

He recalled the summer where everything changed. When they'd returned to Camp Hope as junior counselors, and she'd stepped out of her mother's Cadillac wearing a crisp short-sleeved white blouse, a knee-length denim skirt, and leather sandals. Her sleek long blond hair was pulled back into a tidy low ponytail at the nape of her neck. Modest gold jewelry. A tennis bracelet, stud earrings, a teardrop necklace. Simple, understated, elegant.

Just like Kelsey herself.

She looked so different from the other girls in their brightly colored T-shirts, short shorts, and flip-flops. It really hit him then that she came from money.

And he did not.

But the gap was gone now, and he had money of his own. He was her equal.

The beautiful woman, who'd once seemed so off-limits, was standing in front of him, just as ripe and sexy as she'd been at seventeen, if not more so. All sensuous curves and provocative lips. She walked with a sexy roll of her hips that could drive a sane man crazy. She might look dignified and restrained on the surface, but underneath she was hungering to be set free.

His eyes met hers.

She inhaled softly but audibly.

He could smell the female pheromones radiating off her soft skin. Could see her need in the slow, alluring way she flicked out the tip of her pink tongue to moisten her lips when his gaze strayed to her mouth. And there was that telltale twitch of her eye.

His nearness stressed her, but she was excited about it.

Damn, so was he.

He wanted to take her in his arms and kiss her until neither one of them could breathe. He yearned to run his tongue over every inch of her body and discover exactly what made her sigh and wriggle. He longed to scoop her into his arms, carry her to his bedroom, and show her precisely what they'd both been missing out on for the last ten years.

Great sexual chemistry.

His pulse hammered, and his belly tightened, and below his belt he got hard in a way he hadn't been hard since he was a teenager. It was *scary* how much he wanted her body.

"Is the stress getting to you?" he said.

"What?" she whispered.

"Your eye." He touched her temple with the flat of his thumb. "It hasn't stopped twitching since you climbed into my golf cart."

"I . . . I . . ." She seemed to have lost her voice.

He dipped his head lower. "Yes?"

"Tasha talked me into coming, against my better judgment. I don't want to be here. I don't like Christmas and Twilight is a Christmassy place, and I don't like the water and we're staying on a damned boat, and . . . and . . ."

"And what?"

"And then . . ." She licked her lips again. "There's you."

Amused, he canted his head. "What about me?"

"Coming here was *not* my idea. I want you to understand that."

"So why don't you just call the Uber to come back?"

She hesitated, bit down on her bottom lip. "You really want to know why?"

"I want to know everything there is to know about you."

"Because I got a job offer to go work for my mother's competition."

"Oh ho." Hmm, this was intriguing. "And you're considering it?"

Kelsey chuffed out a big sigh. "It would be like declaring war on Filomena, so no. But it does have me thinking . . ."

"Aww, that's what's got your eye going wonky."

She touched the corner of her eye. "Stop noticing."

"You're still gorgeous. The wonky eye is not a deal breaker."

"Noah . . . stop it." Kelsey spun on her heels.

Noah grabbed her wrist and stopped her in her tracks. Felt her pulse kick up.

She stilled beneath his touch.

"Hey," he said.

Her gaze met his, and she arched one perfectly plucked eyebrow. How well he remembered that lady-of-the-manor expression she trotted out whenever she was displeased with him.

"I was *teasing*. It was a joke. When did you lose your sense of humor?"

"I didn't—" She snapped her jaw closed.

He meant to tell her she needed to learn how to relax and find the real Kelsey lurking behind the good girl who kowtowed to her mother. To let down her hair and just *be*. But she needed something stronger than mere words to jolt her from her cocoon. "Why did you kiss me?"

"Oh, that." Kelsey shrugged. "That was nothing. Tasha—" She waved a hand. "Never mind. You were standing under the mistletoe. I was happy to see you, and I kissed you. That's all it was."

Noah rubbed his jaw. Ah, either the kiss hadn't rattled her world the way it had rattled his or she was lying up a storm. "That's it?"

"That's it."

"So, you wouldn't be interested in—"

"God no!"

"Okay, just checking." He raised both palms. Apparently, he'd misread the signals. "Sometimes sex can clear the cobwebs. I was just throwing it out there."

"I'm out of my head, okay? Can you overlook my outrageous behavior?"

"If you can overlook mine." Noah leaned down and kissed her again. This time, unlike before, she did not respond.

Feeling like a dope, he let her go, stepped back. "Really? Nothing?" Then he finished with the one word that had always made her smile. *"Firefly."*

Hamburger.

Beneath Noah's enigmatic stare and his whispered, *Firefly*, Kelsey's heart shredded to hamburger. He was a steamroller, and she was . . .

Squashed hamburger.

Cover it up! Quick!

She schooled her features, making herself impervious. She was a master at hiding her real emotions. You couldn't live with, and work for, Filomena James, and not perfect that skill. If she let him see how much he had affected her, he could crush her safe little world to dust.

Um . . . maybe he already has, murmured a voice in her head. *And maybe that's a damn good thing.*

She'd kissed him on a dare, and that's all there was to it. They were not going to date or have sex.

"I should go inside," she said, dropping her gaze to her luggage that was still in the golf cart. "I'm sure Tasha's wondering where I've gotten off to." Kelsey started for her suitcase.

But Noah put out a hand to stop her. His fingers slid around her elbow. "Wait."

She straightened and met his gaze even though she really didn't want to. "What is it?"

"I'll bring in the suitcase in a minute, but first I think we should talk."

"About what?"

"About what's going on between you and me."

She tossed her head, and her braid bounced off her spine. "I don't know what you mean. Nothing is going on."

He laughed heartily. A booming sound that echoed out over the water.

"What's so funny?"

"You. Set yourself free, Firefly."

"Please don't call me that."

"Why? Because it reminds you of who you used to be?"

Exactly. "I'm not that girl anymore."

"No." His dark eyes lost their luster. Nuts. She felt as if she'd kicked a puppy. "You're not. *You* got lost along the way."

"We were young," she said, ignoring the last part of what he'd said.

"We hurt each other."

"I . . . I . . ." She cleared her throat to swallow back the jitters.

"Things were left unfinished," Noah said, giving voice to her thoughts. "Your kisses . . ." He rubbed his mouth. "Wow, they brought it all back."

She kept her spine rigid and did her best to ignore the longing blazing inside her.

"We *could* finish those things," he said. "Get our closure so we can move on."

"Wh-what do you mean?"

"I mean . . ." He hooked his thumb under her chin and lifted her face up, so she had to look him squarely in the eyes.

His hand was dry and warm despite the cold, damp afternoon. How easy it would be to melt into his arms and stay forever.

"What I'm trying to say is that if you want to set yourself free, Firefly, I'd love to be the one to take the lid off the jar."

She heard a gasp, the sound coming from somewhere dark inside her. She could see the tattoo on his wrist.

Dare.

Just jump in. Just do it. Just take a risk. She took a deep breath to say *no* or laugh it off. Anything to stave off the fear.

Her cell phone vibrated in her pocket. A welcome relief from the starkness of Noah's stare. Kelsey took out her phone. Glanced at the screen. Groaned.

"Filomena?" Noah guessed.

"Shh, shh." She put a finger to her lips as if her mother could hear him before Kelsey even accepted the call.

He grimaced, shook his head, and walked away to the golf cart.

Wincing, Kelsey answered. "Hello."

"Where are you?" her mother demanded.

"On vacation. We had this discussion, remember?"

"I know that," her mother snapped. "*Where* are you on vacation? Have you arrived at your destination?"

Kelsey turned her back to Noah and walked several paces up the deck away from where he was taking her suitcase from the golf cart and lowered her voice. She didn't want him to hear this. Especially since her mother sounded as if she were gearing up for a fight.

"We're still in transit." It wasn't a complete lie. She hadn't stepped onto the *Rockabye* yet. Still, it wasn't completely honest either, and a ping of guilt plucked her ribs, but she wasn't about to let her mother know she was in Twilight.

With Noah.

If Filomena knew that, her head would spin around like the little girl in *The Exorcist* and she'd spew angry word vomit all over Kelsey.

"Forget your plans, turn around, come back, come home now, I insist," Filomena said all on one long breath.

Kelsey got an immediate ache in her stomach and a sour taste in her mouth. "Why? What's wrong?"

"Lionel Berg is running for governor."

"So?" Kelsey held her breath. Did her mother also know that Berg had offered her a job?

"I can beat him."

No, Filomena must not know about Berg's offer. She would have let Kelsey have it with both barrels if she did. Unless . . . she was plotting something. "Mom, you just got elected mayor. It's not your time to be governor."

"We need to start planning *now*."

"Your time for the governor's race is at least four years away."

"We need to talk strategy, get a solid plan in motion—"

"It'll keep until after the holidays. I need some time to myself, Mom."

Filomena huffed like a fire-breathing dragon. Kelsey knew that sound. She was gathering her emotional armor, preparing to fight and fight hard. "Darling, let's not quibble. Come home. All is forgiven."

Kelsey fisted her hand. Her eye twitched so hard it hurt. "Excuse me? I've done nothing to be forgiven for."

"I'm your *mother*. You ran off and left me all alone when I needed you most. Reporters have been hounding me about that disaster of a wedding."

"You're blaming Clive's leaving on me?" Kelsey's jaw dropped. Gaped. Yes, her mother was self-centered. She always had been, but this was beyond the pale.

"You could have kept him from running off with the best man. If only you'd—"

"Wait, wait." Kelsey's head was spinning, and her eye was jerking so hard she couldn't keep her eyelid open.

But her mother did not wait. "Come back and give your story to the media. You can say you knew all along that he was gay, and you were just trying to help him find himself."

"Mother! Listen to yourself. Just stop it!"

"Do *not* speak to me like that, Kelsey Anne James!"

"I am not coming home. I am on vacation for the next two weeks. I will see you then."

There was a long, cold, hard silence.

Kelsey didn't dare breathe as she waited for the other shoe to drop.

Then it came.

The fury.

The roar.

The rage.

Kelsey had been avoiding her mother's foul moods for twenty-seven years, and now she was in the midst of the hurricane.

Filomena let loose, howled. "You *will* get back here. Right now. You have to put on a good face for the media. Running makes you look like a coward. And if *you* look like a coward, *I* look like a coward."

Kelsey bit down on her bottom lip. Outrage trembled through her. How many years had she catered and kow-towed to her mother? Why had she put up with her mother's abuse for so long? How come she hadn't been able to see the abuse for what it was?

Her mother had been psychologically abusing Kelsey her entire life. And she had allowed it to happen. In the wake of Chelsea's death, she'd clung to the shore, both literally and figuratively.

Afraid to step outside the bubble. Afraid to take a risk. Afraid of her mother.

Desperate to keep Filomena happy. Desperate to make up for Chelsea being gone. Desperate to deny what she knew deep down in her heart of hearts.

Filomena loved herself far more than she loved her

daughter. She always had. She always would. Kelsey was just a pawn to move around the chessboard of her political ambitions.

Tasha had been trying to tell her this for several years, but she hadn't wanted to hear the truth.

Enough was enough. It was way past time she drew a line in the sand. She'd let love and guilt blind her to the fact that her mother did not have her best interest at heart.

"I'm hanging up now, Mother."

"Don't you dare hang up on me!" Filomena's voice grew shrill.

Typically, when her mother sounded like that, Kelsey would immediately back down, backtrack, apologize to stave off her growing wrath. But no more. Time to set boundaries for this relationship.

Severe boundaries.

"Mother, I am hanging up now. I do not want you to contact me for the next two weeks. If you contact me, I *will not* respond. And every time that you do contact me, I will add another day onto the clock before I get back in touch with you."

"You can't cut me off. We have things to discuss. You're going to be my office manager. I need you." Filomena quickly pivoted from rage to victimhood trying to elicit Kelsey's guilt. "You are essential."

"Mother, this is it. I'm not kidding. These are my terms. If you violate them, there will be consequences." Kelsey was shaking all over, terrified but proud of herself.

"Consequences?" Filomena snarled.

Kelsey could practically see her mother's lip curling back over her teeth. She'd spent her whole life skating around that snarl.

"You're giving *me* consequences, little girl." Her mother crackled. "You have no idea what consequences are. You don't get to cut me off. I'm cutting *you* off. You're a horrible child. What kind of monstrous woman does this to her own mother? You—"

Then, for the first time in her life, Kelsey hung up on her mother.

Every cell in her body quivered with raw emotion. Her throat seized up, and she couldn't swallow. Could barely breathe.

She felt Noah's big calming body standing behind her. Tears pushed against her eyes, but she could not let them flow. If she did, she didn't know if she'd be able to stop crying.

His gentle hand touched her shoulder.

She was so glad he was here when this thing with her mother blew up. Ten years might have passed, but Noah had always been in her corner.

She had finally taken a stand, and it felt magnificent. But her knees were also weak, and she was sick at her stomach, and she knew she had to do something to chase away the fear before she gave in to old patterns, caved, called her mother back and apologized.

Although she knew what an ordeal of groveling that would entail. It was the pattern ingrained in her from early childhood. A pattern that required something monumental to break it. Her mother had stolen so much from her. Her childhood. Her choice of careers.

Even her twin.

Yes, she finally dared to place the origin of Chelsea's death where it belonged. At her mother's feet.

It was the ugly truth she'd never allowed herself to admit. Her twin had gotten in that canoe because her

mother had screamed at her for tracking mud in on the
pristine white lake house rug. As punishment, she'd not
only taken away Chelsea's flute—music had been everything to her sister—Filomena had thrown it into Possum
Kingdom Lake.

Kelsey drew in as much air as she could to settle herself. Her blood pumped through her veins as hard and
fast as if she'd just sprinted a four-minute mile. The fog
was everywhere. She could barely see, and she needed
something to latch onto.

Something to ground her.

Her gaze searched the area.

There on the deck, she found it. Just a few steps away
sat a large plastic locker. The kind people stored lawn
furniture cushions in for the winter. The container was
labeled in the same black script as the tattoo on Noah's
wrist.

Dare.

A strong message for her. Instructions to follow. A
code of conduct to embrace. If she was going to do this
thing, face her mother, set boundaries, stop the lifelong
emotional and verbal abuse, she might as well start with
Tasha's Christmas of Yes and those five dares.

Bring them on! She couldn't wait to take control of
her future.

CHAPTER 9

"Filomena?" Noah nodded at the phone Kelsey shoved back into her pocket. His heart ached for her.

She was trembling hard and her face had lost all its color. The red blinking lights from the Christmas decorations on the *Rockabye* twinkled behind her, creating a misty crimson halo above her head.

She closed her eyes, swayed.

"Kels?" Noah caught her just as her knees gave way and she almost tumbled over the deck railing and into the water.

"I seem to keep falling into your arms today," she whispered and gave him a ghostly smile.

"I'm not complaining." He held her in the crook of his arms, surprised by the tender feelings sweeping through him. *Careful.* A blast from the past was not always a good thing. "But you're shaking like a leaf. Let's get you inside and warmed up."

He wrapped an arm around her waist and walked her up the dock to the gangplank leading to the *Rockabye*. Held on to her as she stepped up onto the paddle wheel boat, guided her up the steps, through the front door, and into the reception area.

The front desk was empty, but Noah could hear voices from the dining area. Raylene was serving afternoon tea to the guests.

"Here." He parked Kelsey on a chesterfield in front of the gas fireplace. To one side of the fireplace stood a Christmas tree so tall that the tip of the star topper grazed the ceiling.

"Still big into Christmas, huh?" she said.

"Yep. You still a grinch?"

"Yep," she echoed. "Christmas is just more trouble than it's worth."

"You've never spent Christmas in Twilight," he said. "I aim to change your mind."

"Good luck with that." She was shivering harder. Her clothes were damp from the mist. Strands of her beautiful blond hair, breaking free from her braid, had started to frizz around her face in a totally adorable way.

He picked up the lap blanket draped across the back of the couch and wrapped it around her.

She groaned.

"What is it?"

"Even the throw blanket is Christmas themed." Kelsey traced Santa's cherubic face in the fabric.

"It *is* December, and this *is* Twilight. I'm not apologizing for that." Noah tucked the blanket around her. "Sit tight. I'll be back with something to warm you."

Noah left Kelsey huddled in front of the fire and scooted into the kitchen where Raylene had come back from the cookie club brunch to put out eggnog, hot chocolate, coffee, cookies, and pastries for the guests.

Raylene was regaling the six people seated around the

farm-style table with stories of her glory days as a Dallas
Cowboys cheerleader, and they were eating it up.

Quickly, he greeted his guests, grabbed a mug of hot
chocolate and a stack of frosted sugar cookies, and took
them back to the reception area.

"Here." He thrust the mug of hot chocolate into
Kelsey's hands and settled the plate of cookies on the
end table beside her. "Drink this."

Kelsey accepted the warm mug, curled her hands
around it. Her face dissolved into a smile. "Aww, little
marshmallows."

"I remember how you loved marshmallows when we
were at camp. Figured a few in your hot chocolate might
cheer you up."

"That was nice of you."

He crouched in front of her and slipped off her sandals.

Looking alarmed, she pulled her feet away. "What are
you doing?"

"Your toes are turning blue." He took one icy foot into
his hand and rubbed it.

She tensed at his touch, and her reaction triggered his
own brand of tension. A decade ago, he had put her in a
box, marked it "unpleasant memories," and jammed it as
far back in his brain as he could get her. It had worked
well. He'd forgotten how much he'd once yearned for her.

Until today.

"Why are you wearing high-heeled sandals in December?" he asked.

"I was packed for a honeymoon in Spain. And Tasha
did not give me a heads-up where she was taking me
when she kidnapped me."

Honeymoon.

Yeah, she'd been about to marry someone else.

A surprising knife of jealousy sliced through him. Why? What did he have to be jealous of? Kelsey's ex was gay. Besides, Noah had no claim to Kelsey whatsoever.

"Why do you think your friend ambushed you? Sounds kind of disrespectful."

"No, it's not. We had an agreement."

"An agreement?"

"She dared me to a Christmas of Yes. I have to say yes to a series of dares."

"Why?"

"She's says I'll never change as long as I stay inside my comfort zone."

"And you want to change?"

"I need to change."

Yeah, he could see that. "Hey, did one of those dares happen to include kissing me under the mistletoe?"

Kelsey nodded, looking embarrassed.

Ahh. So she had not been overwhelmed by a desire to reconnect with him. *Chump.* Noah rocked back on his heels.

"You know," he said. "Kissing me should invalidate the dare."

"Why?"

"I'm familiar. Safe. Still in your comfort zone."

She shook her head. "I'm not the least bit comfortable."

"Good," he said, surprised by how spiteful that sounded. Maybe he was still carrying a small grudge.

Once her foot pinked, he moved to the other one.

She sipped her hot chocolate and peered at him from behind the rim of her mug. The muscle at her eye had stopped twitching, and she looked so damned cute.

Noah sucked in air.

Stared into those blue eyes he'd once known so well. Once upon a time, he could stare into them for hours. First when they were kids sharing their grief, then later as horny teens with their hands all over each other.

She wriggled her toes in his palm. "It's warm now. You can stop rubbing."

Her skin was still cold, but he was happy to let go because touching her petite feet was undoing him in a dozen different ways.

A bit of chocolate foam formed a mustache on her upper lip. He wanted to lick away that bit of foam and kiss her again.

She flicked out her tongue, dispensed with the chocolate mustache. Depriving him of the thrill of doing it for her.

Damn.

Unreal. Even after a decade, Kelsey still possessed the power to turn him upside down.

She set the mug of hot chocolate on a coaster next to the cookies, pulled her knees up to her chest, and wrapped the ends of the blanket around her feet. She didn't meet his gaze.

Her innocent vulnerability stirred him. To see her so out of her element and thrown off-balance pinched him.

"That locker on your dock," she murmured, "and the tattoo on your wrist. Dare? Does that stand for something?"

"Yes," he said, rocking back on his heels but staying crouched in front of her, reluctant to move. "Joel and I became scuba diving instructors to help put ourselves through college. Now we offer diving lessons with our summer vacation packages. 'Dare' is the name of that part of the business and we also have a retail section in Jesse's motorcycle shop. I got the tattoo to remind me that when the going gets rough, dare to do something to shake things up."

"A lesson you hadn't yet learned when we were together."

"What's that supposed to mean?"

"When things got rough between us, you didn't dare to come after me."

"Yes, I did."

"What?" She looked startled.

"You didn't know?" Did she really not know about what her mother had done to keep them apart? He'd assumed she had known but had knuckled under to her mother's wishes.

"Know what?"

Noah narrowed his eyes against the softening in his chest. Yep, he was still clinging to some resentment. Surprise!

"Noah?"

"Ask your mother," he said curtly.

Eyes hollowed, she rested her chin on her knees and whispered, "Oh God, what did she do?"

Noah fidgeted, plowed a hand through his hair. He'd been able to compartmentalize his feelings because he told himself she'd been too afraid to fight for him. To learn that wasn't true—well, it changed things.

"I thought you'd written me off," she whispered.

"How could you think that? I texted and called dozens of times. Tried contacting you through social media."

"Mom," she whispered. "She must have blocked you. I should have known."

"You didn't try to contact me," he said, trying hard not to let the hurt creep into his tone.

"I was trying to protect you from her." The pain in Kelsey's eyes was genuine.

"The next morning after she dragged you off, I drove to your house in Highland Park. She met me at the door and told me that if I didn't leave you be, she would have my basketball scholarship to UT revoked. And when I didn't immediately go, she threatened Joel's scholarship as well."

"Noah!" She gasped and pressed a palm to her chest. "No!"

"The scholarship was my one big chance to make something of myself. I took your mother at her word. I couldn't risk losing that scholarship or putting Joel's in jeopardy. I didn't push it."

In his seventeen-year-old mind, he'd formed a plan. Go to college, make it in the NBA, and then come back to claim Kelsey. But four years was a long time. Especially for a wet-behind-the-ears kid. Life got in the way, and eventually, he forgot about her. But he couldn't tell her this. For one thing, from all evidence, she was still Filomena's puppet, so he couldn't completely trust her. He had too much to lose to get involved with Kelsey again. Way too much.

"I can't believe her." A furious expression crossed her face. "No, I can. That's the problem. I've seen her do things like that to people dozens of times. I believe you."

"I should have fought harder," he said. "I gave up too easily."

"I don't blame you." She dropped her feet to the floor and threw off the lap blanket, her eyes taking on a feverish sheen. "My mother doesn't make idle threats. She would have found a way to take your scholarship. Count on it."

"How have you survived with her?"

"As long as I toed the line and did what my mother wanted, life was good. But the minute I dared step out of line, to have my own wants and needs and desires . . ." Kelsey stopped, gulped.

"It can't be easy having Filomena for a mother. No one is blaming you either."

"*I'm* blaming me. I've wasted so much time. I want . . . I need . . ." Anguish twisted her features.

He reached for her hand, squeezed it. "It's not too late for you to find yourself. Step outside that cocoon she's got wrapped around you."

"That's what I'm doing here. I want to be different. I want to change." She leaned forward and cupped her palms around his face. "Noah, can you help me do that?"

Had she honestly just asked him that question? "Never mind. That was stupid."

"Not stupid." He growled. "In fact, it's brilliant, and my answer is *yes*. Whatever you need to get free, I'm on board."

Kelsey stared at the handsome man on his knees in front of her. He was still wearing that goofball *I'm the Reason Santa Has a Naughty List* apron and he looked utterly captivating.

Noah was about to say something when Tasha bopped into the room alongside a good-looking man. Trust Tasha to find herself a guy right off the bat. Who could blame her, the guy was hot. Not as hot as Noah in her estimation, but right up Tasha's alley.

The man's cheekbones were high and prominent, his features perfectly symmetrical. His skin was light brown. His black curly hair clipped short. He wore faded

Levi's, hiking boots, and a green plaid flannel shirt that brought out the color of his green eyes.

"This is Sean," Tasha introduced him. "He is Noah's handyman, but he used to be a navy SEAL."

"How do you do, ma'am?" Sean nodded at Kelsey.

"We met in the parlor," Tasha explained. "Did you know Sean baked and iced those cookies?"

"Tasha is quite charming," Sean said.

"She's a live wire." Kelsey smiled, happy that her friend had found someone to entertain her. Maybe now Tasha wouldn't pester Kelsey if she wanted to stay in the room and read.

Noah looked straight at Sean. "Should we invite them?"

Sean splayed a palm to his nape. "I dunno, man, it might not be their jam."

"Invite us to what?" Tasha asked, bouncing on the balls of her feet. "This vacay is for Kels, but I wouldn't mind having some fun along the way."

"We've got this thing tonight . . ." Slyly, Noah grinned, as if sitting on a secret.

"What kind of thing?" Tasha looked from Noah to Sean. "Is it a sporting event? Basketball? I'm on board for that. I love seeing hot men run around and get sweaty. Or is it a musical gig? I love music." Turning to Kelsey, Tasha said, "Sean plays the guitar."

"Not basketball," Noah said. "Or guitar playing."

Intrigued, Kelsey studied his face. "What is it?"

"We belong to this little club. . . ." Sean's smile grew. He and Noah kept trading looks like high school boys up to some kind of prank.

"What kind of club?" Kelsey asked.

"Just a little program we put on for charity at Christmas," Noah said.

"You guys are killing me here with the suspense. Just tell us." Tasha pressed her palms together.

"We're the Christmas Bards," Sean said.

Tasha blinked. "The what?"

"The Christmas Bards," Noah repeated, looking mischievous. These two were up to something.

"Do you mean barbs?" Tasha's forehead puckered. "Like barbed wire? Is it a stand-up comedy act? That might be okay. I like comedy clubs. Especially the uncensored ones."

"No." Sean chuckled. "It's *bards*, with a *d*."

"What are bards?" Tasha narrowed her eyes.

"Poets," Kelsey said. "Like Shakespeare."

"Oh, that kind of bard." The disappointment on Tasha's face said she thought this event sounded *bor*-ing, cute former navy SEAL or not. "Let me get this straight. You two hotties are members of a Christmas club that recites poetry?"

"Something like that." Sean grinned as if reciting poetry was the most awesome thing ever invented. "We attract huge crowds."

"We write our own rhymes," Noah added.

"So," Sean said. "Do you two want to go?"

"Umm, you know," Tasha hedged. "I promised my mom I'd do a little Christmas shopping for her while I was in Twilight. I saw some cool artisan gift shops when we drove in."

"You can shop tomorrow," Kelsey said, not the least bit inclined to help Tasha wriggle off the hook. "We'll be here two weeks."

"Yeah, I don't want all the good stuff to be gone." Tasha ran a palm over her mouth.

"Your loss," Sean said. "We always sell out."

"Tasha," Kelsey said. "Are you afraid you'll be bored?"

"No." Tasha snorted and sent Kelsey a help-me-out-here stare.

"She's got a touch of ADHD," Kelsey explained. "It's hard for her to sit still if her attention wanders."

Tasha threw darts at Kelsey with her eyes, and said through clenched teeth, "That's not it at all."

Kelsey measured off an inch with her forefinger and thumb. "You're not the least little bit uncomfortable at the thought of poetry?" Two could play this comfort zone game. If Kelsey had to do a Christmas of Yes, Tasha should too.

"Okay." Tasha held up both palms, surrendering. "All right. You've got me. No offense guys, but poetry just isn't my cuppa."

"No offense taken," Noah said. "We've got plenty of fans. Don't feel bad for skipping out on us."

"I'm sure you're really good . . ." Tasha said.

"It'll be our pleasure to accept." Kelsey placed a hand on her friend's shoulder, squeezed lightly. "Right?"

"Yes," Tasha mumbled. "All right, I'll go."

"You won't regret it." Sean winked.

"Hmph." Tasha folded her arms.

"We have to get into costume," Noah said. "And hook up with the other Bards, to go over our routine . . ."

Kelsey stood up and retrieved her sandals from where Noah had left them on the floor. "And we'll go unpack and get settled."

"Show up at The Horny Toad Tavern just before eight," Sean said. "We'll arrange VIP seating for you."

"That's so kind," Kelsey said.

Tasha linked her arms through hers and dragged her down the hall toward their room. "Oh Lord, just what I wanted. Front row seats to a poetry reading. Thankfully, it's in a tavern. If we have to go to a god-awful poetry reading, at least there will be beer."

"Look at it this way," Kelsey said. "We're in this together. Just try to enjoy yourself tonight. I dare *you*."

"Speaking of dares," Tasha said. "You did really well with the first one. I'm proud of you. Planting a big wet one on Noah like you did." She paused outside their room and searched her purse for the key card. "By the way, I've thought of your second dare."

"Hmm," Kelsey said. "What's that?"

Tasha opened the door, and they stepped inside the quirky nautically themed room. "You have to do something that totally embarrasses you."

"Like what?" Kelsey asked.

"Your choice. Sing karaoke, wear your clothes inside out in public, dance naked in the rain—"

"I'm *not* dancing naked in the rain!"

"Get up onstage and read a poem . . ."

"Ah-ha. You're just trying to get back at me for getting you involved in this poetry reading."

"Ding, ding, ding, my BFF." Tasha tapped the end of Kelsey's nose. "If I have to suffer, so do you. I have the perfect poem in mind for you to recite, a limerick really. There once was a lass from Nantucket . . ."

"You know, you're really lucky I can't bear to be on the outs with two people at once," Kelsey said.

"I know." Tasha grinned. "I was totally counting on that."

CHAPTER 10

In the breezy evening, Tasha and Kelsey walked the mile from Christmas Island to the marina. As they passed underneath the mistletoe-strewn bridge arch, Kelsey thought about her first dare.

The kiss had been bold. It had been sassy and look where it had landed her.

Having unwanted feelings about her teenage crush.

All right, maybe not so unwanted. Noah was one hunky tall drink of water, and she was dying to slurp him up.

Chill out. She had just gotten out of one relationship. She was not jumping into another.

A sexless relationship.

Yes, okay, she might be a bit sex starved.

What about a casual fling? Hot sex and nothing more?

Gak! To drown out the voice in her head, Kelsey hummed along with the sounds of "Rudolph, the Red-Nosed Reindeer" wafting from the marina.

One dare down, four to go.

She pondered Tasha's new challenge. What could she do that was embarrassing, but not completely humiliating?

At least her friend had left the manner of the humiliation up to her.

"Are you doing your second dare tonight?" Tasha read her mind as they climbed into one of the pedicabs lined up at the marina and told the driver, "Horny Toad Tavern."

"Imposing a time limit?"

"Take it at your own pace, but reciting poetry would be quick, and relatively painless."

"You just want a bawdy limerick to break up the boredom."

"God yes." Tasha pressed her palms together. "Please do the limerick."

"Forget the poems, just enjoy the eye candy."

"Sean *is* yummy." Tasha sighed dreamily.

"Do I sense a spark between you two?"

"Baby, there's a forest fire in my pants over that man."

"Eloquence, your best quality."

Tasha guffawed.

The pedicab cycled through the lively town square, packed with people in period costumes turning out for Twilight's annual Dickens festival. Literary characters strolled the sidewalks—Scrooge, Tiny Tim, Miss Havisham, the Ghost of Christmas Past, Marley . . . The smell of hot wassail, roasting chestnuts, and funnel cakes filled the air.

On the courthouse lawn, booths were set up for games of chance—a snowball throw, elf bowling, Whack-a-Santa. There were amusement park rides for children—a small Ferris wheel, a reindeer carousel, bumper cars.

In the middle of it all was a North Pole tent, complete with Santa on a sleigh taking gift requests from boys and girls.

"Would you like to lap the entire square?" the pedicab driver asked. "No extra charge."

"Absolutely," Tasha sang out.

"You're stalling," Kelsey accused.

"Yep. If we take our time, maybe the place will sell out before we get there. Darn the luck."

On each corner of the square was an elaborately decorated tree. On the west side, a flocked tree with white and gold decorations and angel ornaments, and a plaque saying it was hosted by the Presbyterian church. The north tree was filled with book ornaments put up by Ye Olde Book Nook. The east tree, decorated by Twilight General Hospital, featured hospital-themed ornaments: Santa on crutches, Rudolph in a wheelchair, an elf with a bandaged head. The fourth tree to the south was sponsored by a pet store and covered with whimsical animal curios.

Music bled from everywhere. Piped into the square from outdoor speakers on the courthouse. Oozed from the open doors of the stores. A delightful cacophony of competing Christmas tunes.

Kelsey would have thoroughly enjoyed the sights, sounds, and smells if Tasha hadn't whined all the way to The Horny Toad Tavern.

"This is going to be so *boring*," Tasha chuffed.

"Probably."

"I wish we could just hang out in the town square."

"Maybe the stores will still be open once the poetry reading is over and we can enjoy the festival a bit," Kelsey soothed.

"I cannot believe you roped me into a poetry reading."

"Hey," Kelsey said. "You're the one who came up with a Christmas of Yes."

"I blame Shonda Rhimes," Tasha muttered and jammed her hands into her jacket pockets. "I should never have read that book."

"C'mon," Kelsey said. "It'll be fun."

"Famous last words."

"Cheer up, you're supposed to be the optimistic one."

"Horny Toad Tavern," the pedicab driver announced.

Kelsey paid, and they turned to go inside. A line of women queued up outside the door for half a block.

"Whoa." Tasha stopped short. "What's going on?"

"Do you think there's another event going on here as well?" Kelsey said.

"Gotta be cheap drinks. No way are women lining up to hear Christmas poetry."

"Noah did mention the event is for charity."

"That has to be it. Generous-hearted folks getting lit."

Heading to the back of the line, Kelsey spoke to the woman in front of them. "Are you all here for the Christmas Bards?"

"Oh absolutely." The woman was in her early twenties, wore hip designer clothes and a shiny alcohol-tinged smile. "Those guys are *scrumptious*."

"Yeah," Tasha said, "but they're reading *poetry*."

The young woman tossed Tasha a you-dumb-bunny look and gave a knowing smile. "You've never seen the Christmas Bards, have you?"

"Guilty as charged, and proud of it." Tasha tossed her head and with an exaggerated drawl, said, "Poetry's not my *thang*."

"You'll change your mind after tonight," the young woman said. "I guarantee."

Tasha blew out her breath and threw Kelsey a this-chick-be-psycho-if-she-thinks-I'll-ever-dig-poetry grimace.

The line moved quickly, but when they got to the threshold, the muscle-bound bouncer pulled up a velvet rope to block the doorway. "Sorry. We're at max capacity. Fire code."

"For a poetry reading?"

"Yep. The Bards be unreechy," the bouncer said.

"What does that mean?" Kelsey mumbled to Tasha, who was far hipper than she.

"Unreechy means they are so good they've achieved lofty heights." Tasha sidled closer to the bouncer. "I don't believe that for a minute. What *poets* are unreechy?"

The bouncer chortled. "You be in the woods."

Kelsey leaned down to whisper in Tasha's ear. "What does—"

"Innocent, uneducated, babe-in-the-woods. Kind of like you."

"Oh."

The bouncer folded his arms. "Sorry. No more tickets. Maxed."

"You said that already," Tasha pointed out.

Kelsey interlaced her fingers, surprised by her nervousness. "What are we going to do, Tasha? We promised Noah and Sean. I had no idea it would be this crowded."

"Oh well, we tried." Joyously, Tasha turned and headed back toward the square.

"Wait." The bouncer raised a palm. "You're Kelsey and Tasha?"

"Yes." Kelsey lifted her chin.

"You've got reserved seats," the bouncer said. "Right up front."

That's right, Kelsey had forgotten Sean said the guys would reserve them VIP seating.

"Yay," Tasha said in a "nay" voice.

"This way." The bouncer unlatched the velvet rope and led them inside.

Women packed the club. Kelsey didn't see a single man in the audience. Odd. Yes, Noah and Sean were good-looking guys, but come on. There should have been a few literary-inclined fellows in the bar.

The crowd was noisy, excited. On the stage, which normally hosted a live band on Friday and Saturday nights according to the posters at the entrance, a lone spotlight was centered on a single microphone. The rest of the stage was dark, the house lights still high. Behind the microphone was a single straight-backed kitchen chair.

The bouncer led them to a table for two at the stage apron. Kelsey noticed several women shooting them jealous glances as they walked past.

"Enjoy," the bouncer announced and departed.

Right after he left, a waitress appeared. "What'll you have? On the house. Courtesy of the Christmas Bards."

"Two shots of Fireball whiskey." Tasha held up two fingers. "And I'll have whatever draft beer you've got on tap."

"And for you?" The waitress set cocktail napkins and a bowl of mixed nuts in front of them.

"Pinot grigio," Kelsey ordered. She preferred red wine, but her mother had indoctrinated her that when she was in social situations she should always order white wine. No stains if you spilled, and white wine didn't discolor your teeth. "No, wait . . ."

The server paused. "Yes?"

"Make it pinot noir." Take that, Mom.

When the drinks arrived, Tasha pushed one of the shots of cinnamon whiskey toward Kelsey. "A toast."

"To what?"

"Obliterating Comfort Kitty for good." Tasha grinned and clinked her shot glass against Kelsey's. "Bottoms up."

Happy that her friend had cheered up, Kelsey downed the shot.

The house lights lowered. The crowd quieted. A few coughs, the tinkling of ice in glasses, the rustling of clothes, but no one spoke as the music started.

An instrumental version of "You Can Leave Your Hat On" started to play. Then seven trim, fit men in Santa Claus costumes pranced onto the stage.

Immediately, the women went wild—clapping, cat-calling, whistling as if they were in a strip club. Some, in the back of the room, stood in the seats of their chairs for a better view of the stage.

What was going on?

Kelsey's pulse quickened, and her palms got sweaty.

Noah was impossible to miss. He was the tallest of them all and positioned in the middle of the bunch. He took center stage, smiling down at Kelsey.

She swooned. He was one seriously sexy Santa.

Sean was the first in the lineup. He sauntered to the microphone.

The music quieted.

With his eyes on Tasha, Sean began to recite a Christmas poem, rife with sexual innuendo and double entendres. As he went along, his voice shifted into a rap-style beat and hard-driving music began pulsing from the surround sound speakers.

Behind him, the other Santas broke into a choreo-graphed dance and . . . took off their fake beards to reveal their handsome faces.

The women applauded, cheered.

Tasha pressed both hands to the left side of her chest. "Be still my heart!"

Have mercy! This wasn't a poetry reading. This was a striptease! No wonder there was a sellout crowd.

Each Santa took a turn, rapping out his poetry to the tune of instrumental Christmas music. While one Santa recited, the others danced to choreographed steps, taking off an article of clothing one number at a time.

Kelsey's jaw hit the floor. The closer it got to Noah's turn at the mike, the faster her pulse ticked.

Then he was in front of her. Bare chested by this point, swaying in time to the beat.

"Yes, yes, yes," the crowd cheered and clapped in unison.

Even though her cheeks were burning hot, Kelsey could not look away even if she wanted. She did not want to look away.

Noah was mesmerizing. Each muscle in his chest and abdomen was honed and delineated. Tight and righteous. She had an overwhelming urge to scoot onstage and lick him like an ice cream cone.

The women in the room screamed as if it was 1965 and the act was The Beatles.

Noah zeroed in on Kelsey and clutched her gaze as he recited his poem set to a Christmas-themed rap beat.

She didn't hear a word of it.

Her body was on fire. Burning. Every nerve ending tingling. She wanted him. More than she had ever wanted any man in her entire life. She had crazy images of running her fingers along those washboard abs and playing him like a musical instrument.

Inscrutable. He knew how hot he looked, and he was proud to show off for her.

Tasha leaned over to pinch her lightly.

"Ow," Kelsey said, rubbing her arm. "What was that for?"

"To let you know that you are *not* dreaming. This is really happening. Your guy is a firecracker!"

"He's not my guy."

"The drool on your chin says otherwise."

"What!" Kelsey touched her chin.

"Gotcha."

"What about *your* man?" Kelsey nodded to Sean who was dancing like there was no tomorrow.

Strobe lights flashed across the stage as Noah finished his rap and stepped back into the chorus line of sexy stripping Santa poets. The group behind the microphone pivoted, putting their backsides to the audience and wriggling their butts.

The next rhyme-spouting Bard stepped up to the microphone.

Kelsey paid the new guy no mind. Her eyes were transfixed on Noah's butt as he did the bump and grind in time to the music.

Oh God, she was ogling him. If Filomena could see her now, she'd drag her out of the nightclub by her braid.

The music turned slow and sensual. All bump and grind. No longer a Christmas tune. The men took off their shiny black belts, danced close to the edge of the stage, tossed the belts out into the audience.

Women dove for them.

Tasha caught Sean's.

Kelsey snagged Noah's.

Noah winked at her.

Her heart took an express elevator to her throat and her impulse was to run as fast as she could. But another part of her, a brazen part she didn't even know was there, said, *C'mon, don't you want to see what he's packing underneath those pants?*

Comfort zone? What comfort zone? There was nothing the least bit comfortable about this striptease, but damn was it exciting. Comfort Kitty was gone and in her place was Feral Cat.

Meow.

Tasha draped Sean's belt around her neck, danced in her seat.

Feral Cat took things one step further. She lifted Noah's belt to her nose. It smelled of leather and pure male testosterone, primal and real.

Her stomach quivered, and her breath flew from her lungs, thin and thready. She put the belt between her teeth, bit down.

And when Noah's hand went to his zipper, she stopped breathing altogether.

Only his pants, boots, and Santa hat remained on his sizzling body. He crooked his finger at her.

Kelsey buried her face in her hands and laughed a little hysterically.

Tasha poked her in the ribs with her elbow.

She parted her fingers, peeked out.

Noah was gyrating straight for her, coming down the steps of the stage, one at a time.

The crowd loved it. Hollered, "Pick me! Pick me!"

But Noah was coming for *her.*

Kelsey thought her pulse was going to jump right out of her chest and take off down the street.

Noah swaggered up to their table. Held out his hand.

She shied away, sinking back in her chair, shaking her head.

"Pick me, pick me, pick me!" the women chanted.

Noah stood patiently waiting. The other men were still dancing onstage, but Kelsey wasn't watching them.

"Pick me, pick me, pick me!"

Tasha nudged her. "If you don't take his hand, one of these other chicks is gonna knock you out of the way and do it for you."

"It's embarrassing," Kelsey whispered.

"Precisely."

Dare number two was staring her right in the face. Oh crap!

"Come," Noah whispered in a midnight deep voice.

That did it.

Kelsey came, embarrassment be damned.

Blocking all sensible thoughts, she slapped her palm into his and followed him. Noah led her up onstage to that chair.

The same chair all the Bards had been dancing around.

Noah's big calloused fingers curled around her soft ones, and he walked backward, twitching his hips to the beat. Damn, if her body didn't take over and match his moves.

The spotlight shifted to focus directly on the chair.

Sweat ran between her breasts. Her heart galloped. She'd never been a fan of public speaking, but she could do it when necessary. This however, was something else entirely.

Smiling tenderly, Noah met her gaze and eased her down into the chair.

The audience members were on their feet clapping and singing to the song that started. Apparently, they were all familiar with this part. A jazzy, upbeat tune called "Back Door Santa."

Kelsey's cheeks flamed.

Noah began to dance for her and her alone. The other dancers faded into the background, letting him have center stage.

Shaking her head, Kelsey sank her face into her palms again.

Gently, Noah guided her hands away from her eyes, forcing her to watch him.

She was beyond embarrassed, but at the same time she was thrilled. For once, it was all about her. Uncommon in Kelsey's world.

Velcro straps broke away as Noah yanked off his pants. The material made a hot, tearing sound.

He flung the pants to the side of the stage and swayed in front of her. Bumped and grinded and shimmied in nothing but a Speedo, boots, and Santa cap.

Provoked, the crowd let loose with more squeals and applause.

Kelsey covered her eyes with her long braid.

Noah took her hands in his. Her hair dropped. He shook his head, mouthed, *No more hiding.*

She put a palm to her mouth to camouflage her smile. "You Sexy Thing" by Hot Chocolate was playing.

Noah was directly in front of her, almost naked.

She had no idea he was that well-endowed. She didn't want to look, but she couldn't help herself. How fast could your pulse race before you had a heart attack?

Why was she so scared? This was Noah.

Ah, but he was the man her body craved. Apparently, a man that hundreds of women craved as well. Not in a million years would she have guessed she'd find herself here.

Onstage.

Her dream man doing a public striptease for her. Maybe this wasn't really happening. Maybe it was a dream.

Yes, that was it. A sweet, sexy dream.

But Tasha had pinched her. It wasn't a dream.

Oh dear. This *was* happening.

People had their cell phones out. Snapping pictures. What if someone uploaded it to social media? What if her mother saw? The thought of Filomena's rabid indignation had every muscle in her body clenching. She did not even want to think about that tailspin.

Relax.

Even if a picture did end up on social media, no one knew who she was. That was the nice thing about being a background player. No one would think to tag her. They only wanted Noah's picture.

Kelsey glanced off in the distance, unable to bear the pressure.

That's when she spied him.

Middle-aged, ruddy face, black suit, looking completely out of place in the sea of estrogen. So familiar. The man looked like Lewis Hunter. The latest driver in a long line of her mother's revolving door of employees.

CHAPTER 11

Noah had lost her.

He was nearly naked, and he still couldn't hold Kelsey's attention? What did a guy have to do to get her to notice him?

She's embarrassed.

Yeah, well, so was he. This Santa striptease shindig was not his thing. He was not a fan of being ogled. Not thrilled with taking off his clothes to get a reaction. But the Christmas Bards performed strictly for charity. Each Bard donated their part of the take to the charity of their choice.

His star power and physical fitness was why the group had invited Noah to join them. What motivated him to perform was to get as much money as he could to defeat the terrible disease that had claimed his mother's life. That's what got him to put his embarrassment aside and do the Magic Mike thing.

His mind was on Kelsey, but he had an audience to please. They'd come for a show and he wasn't going to let them down. In time to the music and wild catcalls,

Noah took off his Santa hat and settled it onto Kelsey's head.

She turned her gaze back to him, reached up to touch the hat. It was too big for her and the brim dropped to the level of her eyebrows.

God, he'd missed her. Noah's gaze gobbled her up.

Kelsey wore a blue angora sweater that molded to her lovely breasts. Through the material and the layer of her bra, Noah could see the pert poke of her nipples. She was turned on.

His stomach pitched.

If they were back at the *Rockabye*, he would not stare at her so overtly. But here? Amid the sexually charged striptease, he didn't hide a thing.

With a fast, adept twirling move, he spun on his heels. A full three-sixty, winking at the crowd as he whirled past before spinning back to Kelsey.

He bent down, grasped both arms of the chair and leaned in until his face was inches from hers. He touched her bottom lip with the pad of his thumb.

She parted her lips, showed him her teeth. Touched his thumb with her tongue. She might be hesitant, but she wanted this.

That realization pushed *him* to push her. She deserved to be the center of attention. To recognize and indulge her inner playful self.

The music throbbed.

The crowd stomped, and cheered, clapped, and hollered, "Kiss her, kiss her, kiss her!" He knew the audience was putting themselves in Kelsey's shoes. Letting her be their proxy. Chanting what *they* wanted from him.

She shuddered and closed her eyes.

Overwhelmed?

Well, she wasn't alone. So was he.

An inferno of savage need blasted straight to his groin. It was all he could do not to scoop her into his arms, carry her offstage, and whisk her back to the *Rock-abye* as fast as he could.

She peeked open one eye.

He held out his hand to her, pulled her up off the chair.

The music boomed "Sassy Sexy Wiggle."

Noah gyrated to the slow-paced, but hard-driving beat. Kelsey's cheeks blazed red. She grinned shyly. He did a deft little two-step shuffle, took her in his arms and spun her in a circle.

She gasped.

The crowd went nuts. "Kiss her, kiss her, kiss her!"

He righted her, let her go, danced away. Crooked his finger for her to come toward him.

She stood staring at him.

Deer in headlights.

Sweat dripping off her forehead, but a coy smile creeping across her lips. She liked it. She just needed some encouragement to let go and enjoy the moment.

Wiggle, he mouthed silently and bopped his shoulders.

She dropped her gaze to Tasha, who was standing in the seat of her chair whistling, clapping, and shouting her approval.

From where Noah was standing, he saw rather than heard Tasha mouth *dare you.*

Kelsey's gaze darted back to him.

He smiled, encouragingly. It was hard performing under these circumstances, but he knew after she'd done it, she would feel exhilarated.

Noah held up his wrist so Kelsey could see his ink.

Dare.

Crooked his finger again. *Come to me.*

"Do it, do it, do it!" chanted the crowd.

Hesitantly, Kelsey started to dance toward him. She was naturally graceful, even if she wasn't a practiced dancer. Her body moving in sensuous, serpentine undulations. There was an earthy carnality to her that she worked hard to keep boxed up.

That's it. Let yourself go, babe.

She wore a hot black leather skirt over black leggings and black kitten heels. Her curvy little butt bounced in time to the beat.

Yeah, give me that sassy sexy wiggle.

Swinging her hips, she sauntered closer. She had pinup queen legs, showcased by that tight leather pencil skirt. Shapely thighs and foxy knees. Slim but muscular calves that tapered to narrow ankles.

Divine.

She reached him. Placed one palm on his shoulder and then the other. He put both hands on her waist and they moved together.

Dancing.

Closer.

Bodies rubbing.

Just the two of them now. The audience forgotten.

Noah cradled her in his arms. She smelled like summer. Honeysuckle and lemonade. He dipped her so low that her long blond braid grazed the ground.

The crowd gasped, "Oooh."

He righted her.

She stood in front of him, cheeks the color of scarlet roses in full bloom. Panting. Her breasts heaving with rapid breath.

He dipped his head, anxious to taste her again.

The crowd started in again with "Kiss her, kiss her, kiss her!"

Her crystal blue eyes were twin full moons in her face, glittering like diamonds in the spotlight.

He rested his forehead against hers. Stared into her until they were both cross-eyed. "Firefly," he murmured huskily. "I've missed this so much."

"What?" She chugged in air. "Performing a striptease?"

"No." He laughed. "You. Me. *Us*."

"Well," she said. "What are you waiting for? We can't disappoint the audience. Kiss me."

As the last notes of the song ended and the spotlight faded, Noah pulled her close and kissed her.

The minute Kelsey got back to her seat, Tasha grabbed her hand. "Let's go backstage before the rest of these hungry wenches get their claws into our men."

"Huh?" Kelsey felt dazed, her eyes glazed.

In the heat of dancing onstage with Noah, she'd forgotten about Lewis Hunter being in the club. She glanced around but didn't see her mother's driver. Anxiety nibbled at the back of her brain.

Trouble.

She was in trouble.

"C'mon." Tasha urged. "They're lining up at the back door to accost *our* men."

"Our?" Kelsey giggled.

"Now is not the time to play coy. I'm jonesing for Sean and you are burning up for Noah. Even a blind person could see that. I swear that dance you two did was the sexiest thing I've ever seen outside of an X-rated movie."

"I . . . we . . ."

"Come *on*." Tasha thrust Kelsey's coat at her. "I need me some Sean."

"You just met him."

"So what? You know me. When I want something, I go after it." Before Kelsey could slip on her coat, Tasha yanked her by the hand. "Let's move it."

"We haven't paid for our drinks—"

"They were on the house, remember. Move it."

"Tip?"

"Already left one." Tasha shot a frantic glance out the window.

Kelsey followed her gaze. Women were lining up in the alley at the back door of the bar to get the Christmas Bards' autographs.

The house lights had come up. The nightclub was a mess of crumpled napkins, bent straws, overturned chairs, empty glasses, and spilled popcorn. Tasha latched onto Kelsey's elbow and dragged her around the side of the stage.

"Where are we going?" Kelsey asked, struggling to get her arm into her coat.

"Backstage."

"The guys are getting dressed. Shouldn't we wait outside with the others?" Kelsey worried.

"Don't be a putz."

"We can't just barge into their dressing room."

"Why not?"

"That would be rude."

"Does barging into their dressing room embarrass you?"

"I see your point," Kelsey said. "Let's go."

Tasha tugged her behind the stage and down the hallway, Kelsey's pulse ticking at a fast clip.

"What was it like up there with Mr. Hot Body?"

"Intimidating."

"But exciting?"

"Well . . ."

"Admit it. You're scorched. Why do you have such a hard time having fun?"

"I saw Lewis Hunter in the audience."

"Huh?" Tasha wrinkled her forehead. "Who?"

"Mom's latest driver."

"She has a new one every few weeks. How do you remember their names?"

"I try to get to know them. They vote, you know."

"You might be hallucinating. I didn't see anyone in the audience that looked like a chauffeur. You were freaked, and your mind conjured up one of your mother's henchmen."

"Maybe so." Kelsey worried her bottom lip. "But I wouldn't put it past her to send him after me."

"Me either, but I would tell you if I'd seen him." Tasha was opening each door as they went past. Bathrooms and a janitor closet and an office. One door left at the very end of the corridor.

Tasha paused outside the final door in the narrow hallway, where the sound of laughing masculine voices greeted them.

Kelsey's pulse buzzed like a chainsaw.

"Here we are," Tasha announced.

"We are here," Kelsey said. "Maybe we should—"

But Tasha wasn't given to self-reflection. She was a go-getter, not a thinker. Considering the wisdom of barging into a room full of half-naked men didn't enter her mind. Her friend twisted the knob, barreled her way inside, hauling Kelsey along with her.

A riot of male voices came to an instant halt as seven guys in various stages of dress stopped and stared at them.

For a split second there was nothing but silence.

"Hi!" Tasha chirped. She propelled Kelsey toward Noah, who was wrestling into a long-sleeved black T-shirt. "There you go."

Noah's eyes lit up at the sight of Kelsey and she felt a corresponding light flood her senses. Overstimulated, she glanced at the floor.

Across the room, Sean was leaning his shoulders insouciantly against the wall watching Tasha. His gaze was inscrutable.

Tasha marched up to him.

He smiled. "Yes?"

"What are you doing after this?"

"What do you have in mind?" Sean folded his arms over his chest, pushed off from the wall. His biceps bulged. On one shoulder he had a navy SEAL tattoo, on the other, lettering that said *Get Comfortable with Uncomfortable.*

"Kels and I were going to cruise the square and get in on the Dickens thingy. You and Noah want to come along?"

Kelsey wasn't sure how she felt about Tasha's open invitation.

Sean shrugged, looked amused. "I'm in."

"Me too," Noah said.

Whew. Kelsey let out her breath. Sometimes Tasha's bold approach worked. Sometimes it didn't. This time she'd scored. They officially had dates for the evening.

What about Lewis Hunter?

He was bound to tattle to her mother. If it *had* been Hunter. She could have been mistaken.

Guilt played up and down Kelsey's spine. Maybe she should just go back to the *Rockabye* and lie low. She tried to catch Tasha's eye, but her friend was busy ogling the former navy SEAL's buff body.

Sean snapped his fingers next to his temple. "My eyes are up here, darlin'."

"If you don't want people to stare, maybe you shouldn't look so hot," Tasha sassed.

"I could say the same to you," Sean drawled.

The air fairly crackled with their chemistry, but Kelsey had plenty of stewing chemistry of her own.

Boy, Noah was something else. His hair damp from a quick shower, and his masculine cologne teasing her nose. "You guys ready?" he asked.

Sean pulled on a white T-shirt and topped it with a black leather jacket. He held out his hand to Tasha. "Are we?"

"Oh yes!" Tasha sank her hand into Sean's.

Not to be outdone, Noah slipped his arm around Kelsey's waist. Possessive gesture, but she liked it. Giddy with desire, Kelsey stepped closer, absorbing his warmth.

"Later, fellas." Noah lifted his hand at the other guys in the room. "Great show tonight."

"Let's sneak out the side exit," Sean said. "Avoid the Bard Babes."

Tasha cocked her head. "Your groupies have a name?"

"We didn't name them," Noah supplied. "That's what they call themselves."

"You must get a lot of . . ." Tasha paused.

Kelsey was terrified her sassy friend was going to say *tail*, but she didn't finish her sentence. Tasha could be outrageous, and Kelsey worried she might scare Sean off. But face it, the guy had to like Tasha for who she was, or it wasn't going to work.

Still holding hands with Tasha, Sean led their small group through The Horny Toad Tavern. The bartender and waitresses were cleaning up after the stage show. Sean escorted them past the kitchen. Waved at the cooks as they slipped out the side door into the cool night. It wasn't freezing, but there was definitely a bite to the air.

Kelsey shivered, not from the cold, but from the delight of being here with her friends. She felt seventeen again and ready for adventure.

"You guys hungry?" Noah asked.

Not for food was on the tip of her tongue, but Kelsey quelled the impulse. "I love street food if any of the vendors are still open."

"Really?" Noah looked surprised.

"Me too," Tasha chattered. "I'm a sucker for junk food. Cotton candy. Funnel cakes. Soda. I'm bad."

"Uh-hmm." Sean eyed her.

"From the looks of you," Tasha told him, "I'm guessing you're Mr. Paleo or Keto or something anti-carby-o."

"Actually," Sean said, "I'm vegetarian and I like a slice of hot cheese pizza as much as the next guy." He patted his taut, hard belly. "I just don't get to indulge often."

"How about you?" Kelsey asked Noah.

"I'm game for pizza." Noah dropped his arm from her waist and took her hand. "Be careful on the cobblestones. They've been here since the 1880s and are pretty unlevel."

The four of them walked toward the town square. It was nine thirty and the foot traffic had lightened considerably, but the midway was still open, as were the food kiosks.

Sean stopped at the pizza vendor. Held up two fingers. "Veggie slice for me and . . ." He turned Tasha.

"Pepperoni, no, wait," she said. "Make mine a veggie pizza too."

"You don't have to eat veggie just because I do," Sean said.

"Oh yeah, right. Like I can nosh on meat now. If you kiss me, you'll taste it on me."

"*If* I kiss you?" Sean's mouth twitched.

"Am I getting ahead of myself?" Tasha splayed a palm to her chest. "Am I being too forward?"

"I've got a solution," Sean said.

"What's that?"

"How about I kiss you *before* we eat pizza?" Sean murmured.

"This is our clue to give them some privacy," Noah said to Kelsey and led her away as Sean enveloped Tasha in a hot embrace.

CHAPTER 12

While Tasha and Sean were getting frisky under the awning of a closed law office, Noah and Kelsey purchased their pizza—they both got the Margherita—and walked the square, taking in the sights.

Noah didn't say anything. Kelsey got weirded out by the silence and cast around for a topic of conversation. "So how long have you known Sean?"

"Sean was my roommate in college and when he got out of the Navy, he didn't know what he was going to do with his life. Joel and I offered him a job working as a scuba instructor and tour guide. So that's what he does in the summer. In the winter, he's our handyman."

"How long has he been out of the SEALs?"

"Why all the interest in Sean?"

"Noah MacGregor, are you jealous?" she teased.

"Sean *is* a hot guy."

"Not half as hot as you."

"You're biased." He finished off his pizza, wiped off his fingers with a napkin, and offered one to her.

"You have a point." She dabbed her mouth with the napkin and tossed the remaining pizza crust into a nearby receptacle. "The truth is, Tasha really likes him, and I don't want her to get hurt."

"Do you always run interference in your friend's love life?"

"Her last boyfriend was a jerk. She's been through a lot."

"And you haven't?"

She ignored his question. "Who knows? Maybe she's grilling Sean about you on my behalf."

Noah glanced over his shoulder, and Kelsey followed his gaze to where Sean and Tasha were still deep in the throes of a grappling kiss. "I don't think she is."

"She's rather spontaneous."

"I gathered." Noah took her hand again and they meandered toward Sweetheart Park, adorned in a wealth of Christmas lights.

They paused at the Sweetheart Fountain, a stony depiction of Jon Grant and Rebekka Nash locked in a lovers' embrace.

"Should we throw a coin in the fountain and make a wish?" he asked.

Kelsey caught her breath. The old legend. Throw a coin in the fountain, wish to be united with your childhood sweetheart and you would be. It was mythic, of course, but what was he suggesting? Did he want to rekindle the old flame? Did she?

"I mean . . . I was just joking," he amended quickly. "No expectations."

"No?"

"Do you *want* me to have expectations?"

Kelsey studied his face, trying to get a read on him. "Do you want me to want you to have expectations?"

He laughed, a rueful sound that landed hard on her ears. "Firefly, you're doing it again."

"Doing what?"

"Trying to figure out what I want so you can please me."

"Am I doing that?" she asked mildly.

"You know you are."

"What do you want from me, Noah?"

"To speak your truth. I can handle it. If you're regretting the hell out of the kisses we shared today, just tell me and I'll back off. I have no intention of pressuring you."

"I see."

"But you were the one who kissed me first, so I thought maybe . . ."

"On a dare."

"But you chose me."

"You were under mistletoe. It was an opportunity I couldn't pass up."

"That's it?"

"I just got stood up at the altar, Noah." A waspish note crept into her voice.

"I understand that. It's why I want you to tell me what's going on here."

What was going on here?

"I feel . . ." Kelsey paused, searching her body for areas of tightness in the places where her emotions got trapped. Anxiety lived in the muscles around her eyes. Fear turned her stomach into a rock tumbler. Guilt strummed the strings of a headache.

"Yes?" He waited on her, patient and kind.

"Confused."

"By me?"

"By everything."

"Is there anything I can do to help?"

"Just be my friend."

"I can do that." He paused, cleared his throat. "To be clear, are we friends who kiss?"

She wanted to laugh at the earnest expression on his face. "I'm *not* looking for love."

"Oh me either." He shook his head vigorously. "I'm happy as a clam."

"So you weren't hoping . . ."

"Not to be rude or anything, but while you *are* smoking hot and I would love to have all kinds of fun with you, we haven't seen each other in ten years. Lots of water under that bridge."

"Yes." She nodded. "You are absolutely right. I agree."

"You didn't have any lurking dreams of coming here to reconnect with me after your wedding fiasco?"

"No. As I told you, Tasha sprang this whole thing on me."

"So, what *are* you looking for?"

"Me."

"A noble goal."

"I'm a little late to the party in finding myself. But if I'm going to find me, I can't get distracted by—"

"Me."

"Yes."

"Whew." He blew out his breath, put his palm to his nape. "I'm glad we had this talk."

"Me too."

"So . . . is it okay to hold hands?"

"If it's okay with—" Kelsey cut herself off, realized she was doing it again. Feeling him out before she gave an opinion. "No, you know what? I'd love to hold hands with you, Noah. And I enjoy kissing you. And if other things unfolded, I wouldn't be opposed."

"But no strings attached?"

"No strings attached. Believe me, the *last* thing I want are strings."

"Me either."

"For the next two weeks, I don't want to think about *anything* but having a good time," she said.

"Why, Firefly, I can guarantee you a good time." He held out his hand and she slipped hers into his, feeling more solid and grounded than she had since . . . well, since Camp Hope.

As they continued on through the festively decorated park she felt the bah-humbug roll off her shoulders.

"It's a beautiful night," she murmured.

He squeezed her hand, his eyes on her. "Yes, it is."

She cast him a sidelong glance, studied him in the winking and blinking of twinkle lights. He was such a handsome man.

Her heart fluttered, and her breathing slowed.

He dipped his head.

Was he going to kiss her?

Her eyes widened.

So did his grin.

"Do you remember where we carved our names?" He pointed behind her.

Kelsey turned to see the two-hundred-year-old pecan tree thick with branches. Hundreds of names had been carved into the trunk. The oldest was *Jon loves Rebekka 1874* engraved into the center of the tree. The carving was weathered and faded but still visible. After that famous local couple declared their love on the tree, many others followed their lead. Writing their names in Twilight history with pocketknives.

Sometime in the 1960s, a botanist threatened that if the desecration continued, it would eventually kill the pecan and the town had built a white picket fence around the tree. Along with a stern sign declaring "Do Not Deface the Sweetheart Tree."

"Do you remember where we carved our names?" Noah repeated.

Kelsey stepped over the low fence and squatted at the base of the tree. "We were stretched out here on a blanket."

She squinted in the dark, trying to find their names among all the others.

"We were lying on our stomachs, trying to make ours the lowest of them all."

"But really you'd just gotten too comfortable after our picnic and you were too lazy to stand up," she reminded him.

"Oh yeah." His grin was as lazy as his name-carving ambitions had been. "It was warm, I was full, and you were soft. I hated to move."

"Here we are." She reached to trace her fingers over the names. *Noah & Kelsey 4 Ever.* "You didn't even spell out 'forever.'"

"But I carved an actual heart," he said, coming over to crouch beside her. "That suggests I wasn't as lazy as you're making me out to be."

"Cutting too close to the bone, am I?" She laughed.

Their faces were so near, the rich smell of winter soil permeated the air. She could feel his warm breath on her cheek.

"I'm not too lazy to do this." He leaned in and touched her mouth with his. Light, teasing. Just the right amount of casual pressure.

But were they trying too hard to recapture the past?

Kelsey pulled back, offering him a soft smile to let him know he hadn't crossed any lines, that retreating was all on her.

He looked puzzled but easily let her go. It was not the first time he'd let her go without a fight.

That's unfair.

Noah *had* tried to see her again after that night on the dock, even though she hadn't known it. But Filomena was too formidable; especially for a seventeen-year-old kid with a basketball scholarship to the University of Texas.

Kelsey grappled with insecurity. Part of her was still the girl who felt abandoned by her twin, her father, and her first love. Yes, as an adult she understood how complicated and complex life was, but deep inside, there was a scrap of that wounded child who'd never quite healed.

That was really the root of why she was here in the first place. To heal. Tasha had known what she was doing when she cooked this whole adventure up. She needed to thank her.

Noah stood, straightened. His imposing height towering over her. He reached down a hand to help her up.

She accepted his hand, studied his kind face, felt her heart trip over itself. She was reconsidering that kiss when Noah's phone dinged, signaling that he'd gotten a text.

"Sean and Tasha are heading on back to the *Rockabye*," he said, checking the phone screen.

"It's getting late."

"Almost midnight." The cell phone cast shadows across his face in the darkness, giving him a spooky, but sexy look.

The park lay empty, no one else around.

Noah guided her toward the rear exit of the park, sheltered by thicker trees, and the road leading back to the town square.

On the street, a few people lingered. Couples holding hands. Laughing and joking, a group of twentysomethings drifted out of the wine bar, Fruit of the Vine. The town felt safe, comfortable, happy.

Noah didn't speak. Neither did Kelsey. It was a companionable silence. Enjoyable. A nice night.

She inhaled deeply, and a soft sense of peace settled over her.

They walked along the cobblestones, their footsteps echoing. At the loudness of their footfalls, Kelsey realized the Christmas music had stopped playing.

On the courthouse lawn, kiosk vendors were packing up and closing down their stands. She could smell the lake even from here. The wind drifted the loamy scent over them.

The familiar aroma stirred images, both bad and good. In her mind's eye she saw Chelsea in that canoe on Possum Kingdom Lake, her sister's determined chin set. She saw Camp Hope and Noah and how he looked at eleven years old on the first day they ever met. Then that last day she'd been with him, as Filomena dragged her off the dock by her hair.

As they headed toward the marina, the few people in the area dispersed to cars, until they were the only ones left on the sidewalk. Noah wrapped his arm around her shoulder. Contented, Kelsey snuggled against his side.

Behind them, a car moved slowly down the street, but Kelsey didn't pay it much attention. She was wrapped in her reverie and the feelings of happiness combined with sadness churning through her. The urgency to change mixed with fear. Regret mingled with guilt. Possibility collided with redemption. All of which was the result of this midnight walk with a man she hadn't seen in ten years. A man who'd once meant so much to her and might mean a lot to her once again.

Abruptly, car tires squealed.

The vehicle behind them revved and sped up. Simultaneously, Noah and Kelsey jerked their heads around.

A black Lincoln Town Car jammed on the brakes in the middle of the road right beside where they stood on the sidewalk.

Oh Lord, she knew that car.

A big bulky man, dressed all in black, leaped from the passenger side and pounced onto the sidewalk in front of them.

Kelsey recognized him right away, despite the ski mask he wore.

Clifford Steel, her mother's personal bodyguard.

Before she could react, Steel roughly shoved Noah into the side of the building, grabbed Kelsey's wrist in a vise grip and forced her into the backseat of the Town Car.

Steel tumbled in beside her, and as he grappled to slam the door closed he yelled at Lewis Hunter sitting behind the wheel, "Go, go, go!"

Stunned, after hitting his temple on the side of the stone building when the assailant shoved him, Noah shook his head.

Kelsey was being kidnapped!

His noggin throbbed, but he shrugged it off and jumped for the door of the Town Car before the assailant could close the back door.

Chaos ensued.

"Gun it!" the kidnapper screamed at the driver.

"He's half in the car!" the driver shouted back.

Noah punched the guy who'd taken Kelsey, slamming him in the nose. Blood spurted. It had been a long time since Noah had been in a brawl and Kelsey's assailant was much faster than he.

The man dodged Noah's next punch and delivered one of his own, smacking his fist into Noah's left eye.

Noah groaned.

The assailant kicked at Noah's hand clinging to the inside door handle.

No way, asshole.

Noah was not going to let them get away with Kelsey. He clung to the door as hard as he could, his upper body angled across the other man's lap.

"Let go," the assailant growled.

"Kelsey, get out the other door!" Noah said.

"I can't," she cried. "The child locks are on."

The assailant grabbed hold of Kelsey's braid with one hand and yanked her back. She yelped in pain, fueling Noah's anger. With his other hand, the assailant pressed his palm into Noah's face and kicked him in the shoulder.

Noah grunted but hung on.

"Noah, Noah," Kelsey said. "Let go. I don't want them to hurt you. It's okay. My mother sent them."

"You know these bozos?" Noah asked.

"Yes."

He couldn't see her. Too much hammy palm in his face. "Do you want to go with them?"

"No!"

"Well, then." Noah punched the assailant again. *Bam, bam, bam.*

"Stop it," the man howled. "This will not end well for you!"

"Let me go. Let me out of here." Now, Kelsey was kicking the assailant from the other side.

Hot blood seemed to be everywhere. Noah didn't know if it was from the assailant's nosebleed, or the cut stinging his cheek, or if Kelsey had also been hurt. Alarmed, the hairs on his nape lifted.

The man couldn't handle both of them. Not two at once. "Drive, Hunter, dammit!"

Noah needed to strike before the chauffeur decided to take off, with Noah's legs still dangling outside the car, and drag him. Leveraging his body weight, he leaned back and jammed his elbow hard up against the guy's Adam's apple.

The man made a strangling noise, and immediately let go of Kelsey so he could snatch hold of Noah's arm with both hands.

Noah added pressure to the guy's throat, holding him still. "Driver, if you want your buddy to keep breathing, undo those locks. Now!"

The driver swiveled his head around to see what was going on, eyes widening at the situation. "Steel?" His voice quivered.

Steel made gurgling noises, and Noah could feel the fight going out of him. Fear streaked through him. He didn't want to kill the guy. He just wanted them to let Kelsey go.

"Do it," Noah said.

The driver looked unsure.

Noah stared right into Steel's eyes. "I'll let up off your throat if you tell him to do it."

Steel shot bullets at him with his glare, but he blinked and nodded as best he could.

Noah eased off the pressure, but kept his elbow positioned on Steel's Adam's apple just in case there was still fight left in him.

Gasping, Steel sucked in a big gulp of air. Grunted. "Do it."

The door locks clicked, disengaging.

"I'm sorry, I'm sorry," Kelsey said, apologizing for something that wasn't her fault, and flew from the backseat, slamming the door behind her.

"Shit," the driver said. "I didn't sign on for *this*."

"Me either," Steel said, but his voice was garbled, and it came out sounding like "Mefever."

With his enemy neutralized, Noah eased up, and extracted himself from the car. "Tell Filomena James she can kiss my—"

"Tell her *this* is not the way to bring me home." Kelsey came around the Town Car to stand beside him.

Noah wrapped his arm around her waist, tucked her against his side. Her entire body was shaking. Fury at her mother wound around his spine like a cobra. All four of them were breathing hard.

"Don't wuwwy," Steel slurred, raising a hand to his throat, his face covered in his own blood. "I quit."

"Me too," the driver added. "Kidnapping is way outside my comfort zone."

CHAPTER 13

"You're bleeding," Kelsey exclaimed after the Town Car had driven off, leaving them standing underneath the streetlight. "And your poor eye! It's swelling shut."

Sure enough, Noah squinted, reaching up to touch his cheek, and felt blood. His body was still numb from adrenaline. "Forget about me, are you okay? Did they hurt you?"

"I fell getting out of the car and skinned my palms." She held up her hands for him to see her wounds. Bits of dirt and gravel were embedded in her skin.

Noah winced. "Assholes."

"And my head hurts where he pulled my hair, but I'm okay. You're in much worse shape."

"Your friend Steel is in the worst shape."

"I can't believe how well you handled yourself."

"What?" He grinned even though it hurt. "You believed I'm too laid-back to put up a fight?"

"Well, kinda."

That sobered him. "Kelsey, are you telling me that you seriously thought I would let those hoodlums just whisk you away?"

"They were my mother's henchmen. I didn't expect you to fight them."

"I admit it. I'm an easygoing dude, and not much gets under my skin. I'm not a fan of conflict and I would rather patch things up than hold a grudge, but I would *never*"—he cupped her chin in his palm and tilted it up so that she had to meet his stare—"allow anything to happen to you, woman. Got that?"

"Got it." Through long lashes, Kelsey peered at Noah as if he'd been the one to decorate the sky with the moon and stars.

In her eyes, he was some kind of hero.

Uncertain how he felt about that, Noah dropped her chin and glanced away. They'd just had a big discussion about keeping things casual, but if she kept looking at him like that, all bets were off.

A bicycle bell chimed, and a man's voice called out, "Noah."

The pedicab driver, who was named Alonzo, pulled up at the curb. He lived just down the road from the marina and had once worked at Froggie's as a dishwasher. "You guys need a ride? I was just heading home . . . whoa, what happened to you?"

"Wild night out," Noah said, drawing his arm around Kelsey's waist again.

Alonzo eyed him up and down. "I'll say."

"We'd love a ride, thanks."

"Hop in."

They climbed inside and covered themselves with the wool blanket Alonzo kept on hand in cold weather.

On the way back to the *Rockabye*, Kelsey sighed and rested her head against his shoulder and Noah couldn't help smiling. He felt like a gladiator returning victorious from a heated battle to the loving arms of the woman who'd waited for him.

Uh-oh.

He was feeling too much too fast. He needed to slow things down and figure out why he was so willing to jump in headfirst.

In the ten years they'd been apart, Noah had gained and lost an entire career, blown out his knee, been married and divorced, and started his own business. He had dealt with his life changing course one hundred percent.

Did his attraction to her have something to do with those rapid and complicated life changes? Did she represent security and continuity and that's what he was really longing for, not Kelsey specifically?

Were his hopes childish and impossible?

Could they really start anew and this time around develop a steady, reliable, mature love?

It was a good question.

But Noah did not have an answer.

Surreptitiously, Kelsey checked her cell phone in the pedicab. Bracing herself for a barrage of angry texts from her mother.

Nothing.

Uh-oh.

Silence from Filomena was often worse than her rage. Silence meant she was gathering her resources and plotting her strategy for the next attack. Kelsey knew because she was normally by her mother's side as she manipulated and maneuvered.

Now she was on the receiving end, it wasn't pretty.

You did tell her not to contact you for two weeks.

Yes, but that was before Filomena had sent her toad-ies to attempt a kidnapping. Nibbling her bottom lip, and careful of her skinned palm, Kelsey slipped her phone back into her pocket, refocused her attention, and tried to enjoy the ride. If she wanted to ruin her mother, she could. Kidnapping was against the law. She could have her arrested, or sue her, or at the very least, go to the press.

But she knew her mother. Filomena would find some way to turn the blame back on Kelsey. If she had to lie, cheat, or gaslight to do it. Of that, Kelsey was certain.

The clouds had blown away, exposing a nearly full moon shining down as they headed toward the marina. Kelsey rested her head on Noah's chest, listened to the steady thumping of his heart, and wished she could freeze time and hang suspended in this moment where she felt like a damsel who'd been rescued by a storybook knight.

Silly of course. She didn't believe in fairy tales, but it was fun to pretend for a few minutes. He had slain two dragons for her.

But they were lesser dragons. The main dragon was far more powerful, and only Kelsey could slay *her.*

Oh heavens, what kind of daughter was she? Thinking of her mother as a dragon in need of slaying.

Guilt and shame burned her ears. Closing her eyes, she gulped and struggled to push back the feelings.

Failed.

She should go home. Smooth things over before this standoff got too ugly. She checked her phone again. No texts or missed calls.

"It's going to be okay," Noah said.

Easy for him to say. He didn't have to eventually go home to Filomena. And yet, she took hope from him.

Maybe things *would* be okay. She was feeling emotionally stronger after completing two of Tasha's dares. Perhaps there *was* something magical about a Christmas of Yes.

"You were so brave," he murmured.

"Me? You were the one who risked being dragged by a car."

"I just reacted," he said. "Instinct. But you could have just told me to step away from the car and gone passively home with them . . ."

He didn't finish the sentence, but she knew what he was thinking. The way she had their seventeenth summer when he tried to pull her out of her mother's car, and she'd told him to leave. It had been for his own protection, not because she hadn't wanted him to fight for her.

"You took a chance on me," he said. "On us. You got out of the car. You stayed."

Kelsey wasn't brave. Not at all. If it hadn't been for Tasha hijacking her to Twilight, she wouldn't be here.

From the pedicab, they transferred to Noah's golf cart and a few minutes later were at the *Rockabye*. The Christmas lights were off, but the porch light was on, guiding their way into the boatel.

Tiptoeing so as not to disturb the other guests, they slipped inside the front door and Noah locked up behind them.

In the light from the lobby lamp, Kelsey could see how badly his left eye was swelling shut. Dried blood had settled in the cut on his cheek. Thankfully, it didn't look deep enough for stitches. Adhesive butterfly strips should close it up if he had a first aid kit.

"We need to doctor that eye of yours," she whispered.

"And your palms," he whispered back.

"Do you have a first aid kit?"

"Fully stocked. It's in my bathroom. C'mon."

"First," she said. "Frozen peas for your eye."

"Okay." He nodded. "This way."

Noah led the way into the kitchen and flicked on the light. Kelsey pulled out a kitchen chair. "Have a seat."

"Taking charge, are you?"

"Does that bother you?"

"Not at all," he said, his good eye crinkling in amusement as he watched her. He turned the chair around backward and sat with his chest against the high back.

She tilted her head and studied his smashed face in the brighter light, sucked in her breath.

"Well, doc, what do you think? Am I gonna make it?"

"I could throttle Steel for doing this to you," she seethed.

"The guy was just following your mother's orders."

Too true. Exhaling, Kelsey went to the stainless steel commercial freezer in the corner. Being careful with her abraded palms, she used her fingers to dig out a bag of frozen peas, and gingerly wrapped them in the kitchen towel she found dangling from the oven door handle. Then she brought the makeshift ice pack to him.

"Actually, the guy didn't put up much of a fight. I don't think his heart was really in it. Kidnapping his boss's daughter is probably not the high point of his résumé."

"Looks to me like he did plenty of damage." Tenderly, she fingered his forehead just above where he held the ice pack to his swollen left eye.

Her hand trembled. She was furious with her mother. Kelsey's stomach grumbled loudly, upset by her fuming emotions.

"Are you hungry?" Noah asked. "You only had one slice of pizza."

"No, no." Kelsey shook her head. "I have a nervous tummy that rumbles when I'm upset."

"Anxiety," he said. "Like your eye tic."

She nodded. "When I was a kid, and my stomach would growl in public, Filomena would pinch me. Of course, that only upset me more and my tummy growled even louder."

"What?" He scowled.

"Right under here." She fingered the flesh on the underside of her upper arm. "So that people couldn't see the bruises."

"As if you can control how loud your stomach growls." Noah shook his head. "The more I hear about Filomena, the more I dislike her."

Kelsey's defenses shot up. He was talking about her mother after all. "You have to understand. My mother grew up with parents who neglected her and her older brother. Yes, they had money, but my grandparents were never there for her. She grew up with servants and when she was just eight years old they sent her off to boarding school. She vowed never to do that with her children."

"Boo-hoo, poor little rich girl. I'm beginning to think you would have been better off at boarding school."

"I'm making her sound terrible. There were good times."

"Yeah? When?"

"When she was pleased with Chelsea and me. She could be a lot of fun. Took us for mani-pedis or a concert or afternoon tea at the Ritz. That's why we

worked so hard to stay on her good side. For those rare
nice times."

"I guess I get that . . ." Noah paused. "To some degree.
After my mom died, my dad turned to alcohol. Although
he never abused us, we four kids were careful to keep
things light to head off the depression that could send
him on drinking binges."

"Maybe that's why you're so mellow."

"Maybe . . ."

"I wish—" She stopped, bit down on her bottom lip.

"What?"

No point wishing for something she couldn't have.
"Time to get that blood cleaned off your face and that
cut closed up."

"All right," he said, thankfully not pressing her on
her thoughts, which were jumbled and nonsensical in the
first place. "This way."

Still holding the ice pack pressed against his eye, he
stood up and guided her to his bedroom.

The hallway was narrow and there was no one else
about as they took the stairs down to the lower deck
of the paddle wheel boat where guests were not allowed. Briefly, she closed her eyes, but that only made
things worse as she felt Noah's hand at the small of her
back. Imagined him pressing hot kisses down her spine.
Dreamed of his erect shaft throbbing against her backside.

*Holy freaking cow, what was wrong with her! She
was losing it.*

Her eyes flew open.

Moving in what felt like slow motion, Noah stopped
outside a closed door, took keys from his pocket, and
unlocked it. Time stretched, elongated.

Dangled.

"After you." Noah swept his arm over the threshold. His tattoo visible. *Dare.*

She would be entering his bedroom suite. Just the two of them. All alone.

Not smart, not smart.

Taking a bolstering breath, Kelsey stepped past him. The room was tidy. Simple. A queen-sized bed made up with a sage green comforter. A bookcase. A dresser. Braided rug on hardwood floors.

Pictures on the wall. Noah on the basketball court and in scuba diving gear. More pictures of him with Joel and the rest of his family. A small Christmas tree sat in the corner. Even here, she could not escape the relentless holiday cheer.

The place smelled of him. Pine and sandalwood and Noah. It felt way too intimate.

She wanted to run. She should run.

"First aid kit is in the bathroom," he said.

The bathroom was larger than she expected, but still a small space to be sharing with this big man.

"Who should go first?" she asked.

"I'll bandage your hands, then you can bandage my face."

"Good plan," she murmured.

He lowered the toilet lid. "Have a seat."

She sat. The lid was cool against the back of her legs. If she'd known she would be involved in a thwarted kidnapping, she would have worn pants instead of a short skirt and leggings.

He towered over her. Reached in the medicine cabinet above her head. His shirt rode up and she got a glimpse of his taut flat belly, and immediately she was transported back to The Horny Toad Tavern where Noah stripped in time to the music as she sat in the chair on-stage, transfixed.

Kelsey's face flushed hot.

Noah kneeled in front of her, the first aid kit in his hand. This was a heavy-duty first aid kit, not the cheap kind from the big-box stores. Professional grade. He un-peeled the Velcro closures on the kit and it reminded her of the sound his pants made when he ripped them off onstage. He rolled the heavy canvas kit open on the bathroom sink counter.

"Let's see your hands."

She held out her palms.

He clucked his tongue and shook his head. "It's going to sting when I clean out the abrasions."

"Got a bullet for me to bite on?" she joked.

"How about a candy cane." He reached into a jar on the shelf and pulled out a candy cane wrapped in cello-phane.

"You keep candy canes in your bathroom?"

"It's a long story."

"I'm not going anywhere."

He unwrapped the candy cane.

She opened her mouth and he settled the candy across her teeth. She bit down lightly. Ran her tongue over the candy cane crook. "Hey, it's cinnamon not peppermint."

"Cinnamon is Grace's favorite flavor."

"Grace is your niece, right?" Remembering what he'd told her when they met on the bridge that morning. So much had happened this evening, it seemed eons ago. "Flynn's daughter."

"Yep. Grace is how the candy came to be in the bath-room. I was babysitting her and Ian a couple of days ago and they were running around the boat, bothering the guests with their high-octane kid energy. To keep them quiet, we made candy cane reindeer. You might have seen some of them hanging from the tree in the lobby."

She had noticed the candy canes with glued on googly eyes and antlers made of brown pipe cleaners. It touched her that he did craft projects with his young niece and nephew.

"Ian kept eating the candy canes. Grace got frustrated and hid the jar from him in here."

"They sound like fun kids."

"They are." He beamed, the proud uncle, and took an antiseptic swab from the packaging. "Time to bite down on that candy cane."

He rolled the medicated swab over her right palm.

"Shhhittt," Kelsey hissed around the candy cane.

"Warned you."

She chomped on the candy. The taste of cinnamon burst into her mouth and she bit the cane right in half, closed her eyes and busied herself chewing as he ran a fresh swab over the left palm.

"Wave your hands to dry them, and I'll get out the burn cream."

She flapped her hands while he loaded the burn cream on a cotton ball. When the antiseptic had dried, he coated her abrasions with the thick white cream. Kelsey stared down at her greasy palms. "What now?"

"I'm going to bandage them." He had his head lowered over her lap as he wrapped her hands. First with nonstick sterile pads, then with a white gauze roll. His poor left eye almost totally closed, dried blood still streaked across his face.

Her heart wrenched. "Can you see out of it at all?"

"Well enough to get you patched up."

"We're a sight," she mumbled, her senses overwhelming her. The close proximity to Noah, the overheated warmth of the tight quarters, the taste of cinnamon in her mouth, the rich aroma of this outdoorsy man. Kelsey was drunk on his scent and the teasing glint in his good eye.

The moment shouldn't have been particularly erotic, but damn if it wasn't.

When was the last time someone had taken care of her needs?

Well, Tasha had whisked her off to Twilight. So there was one time. But other than that, she was generally the caretaker in her major relationships—Filomena, Theo, Clive . . . and before she'd died, Chelsea.

Kelsey had been the responsible twin. The one who pulled back when Chelsea plunged them recklessly into adventure . . . and usually trouble.

"All done." Noah adhered the gauze with medical tape and lifted his head.

Their gazes met.

She placed her bandaged hands to her heart and stared at him wide-eyed and awestruck by his handsomeness. "Your turn."

CHAPTER 14

They swapped places. Noah sitting on the toilet lid, and Kelsey doing the doctoring. Since he was so tall, she didn't have to kneel.

Jittery, Kelsey soaked a washcloth in warm water, wrung it out, and carefully washed the dried blood from his face.

He flinched.

"I'm sorry," she whispered. "Bet you're regretting hanging out with me now."

"Never do I regret hanging out with you, Kelsey Anne James." His one good eye drilled a hole through her.

"You remembered my middle name."

"You were my first love, Firefly." His voice lowered, turned Sam Elliott deep. "I remember a lot of things about you."

"Oh yeah?" she said, gently rubbing the blood from his face with the warm wet washcloth. "Like what?"

"That little starburst birthmark, right here . . ." He reached around her leg to touch the spot high on her back thigh where she had a pigmented dark spot in the shape of a starburst.

His touch fired her up inside.

"You bought me a sack full of Starburst candy to tease me about it. No one else caught the joke."

"I loved seeing you in a swimsuit so that I could get a good look at the birthmark." He gave her an adorable lopsided grin.

"Yeah, that was why."

That look in his eye tickled her far more than it should have. Her feelings for Noah were complicated. His lazy smile and tender tone only muddled her more. Was he trying to start something? Attach those strings. Did she want him to?

Half of her was screaming, *yes, yes, yes*, while the other half said, *cool your jets*. They hadn't worked the first time around, why would they now?

Because you're grown-ass adults this time around, she heard Tasha's voice say in her head.

"Thanks again for doing the whole Sir Galahad thing." She dabbed the last of the blood away, got a good look at the cut on his cheek underneath the black eye. Not deep at all. Clifford Steel must have cut Noah's face with that gaudy pinkie ring he wore. "It was nice of you."

"Nice?" His tone turned caustic. "You think I jumped in and started kicking ass because I'm nice?"

"You *are* nice."

"Do nice guys look like this?" He touched his cheek.

"Okay, okay." She laughed. "You're a nice badass."

"Now you're just trying to make me feel better." He pretended to look wounded by her words.

"Noah, you *are* a badass. Basketball star. Boatel owner. Striptease artist. But you're still a nice guy. You're happy-go-lucky and laid-back. It takes a lot to ruffle your feathers."

"You make me sound like a dufus."

"Oh no, no, no, Noah. I love the way you are. I wish I could be like that. I'm a bundle of nerves. I have no idea how to relax. Hell, I can't even enjoy Christmas."

"That's because you've never hung out with me during the holidays." He tried to wink, but it didn't work. "Ouch, ouch. FYI don't try to wink with a black eye."

"I'll keep that in mind." She dropped the washcloth in the sink, his face cleaned of blood, and went for the antiseptic swabs. "This is gonna sting."

"Turnabout is fair play." He slouched against the toilet's tank, legs outstretched.

"You want a candy cane to bite down on?"

"Absolutely."

She gave him a candy cane. He looked adorable pretending he was a tough gunslinger biting down on a bullet. Chuckling, she cleaned the cut. His breath was warm against the back of her hand. "May I ask you a personal question?"

"You can ask," he said. "Doesn't mean I'll answer."

"What really happened between you and your ex-wife? Tasha read that she dumped you after you got injured, but I know the media doesn't often get things right."

"You friend is trying hard to play matchmaker," he said mildly.

"She just wants me to be happy. She thought this trip might . . ." Kelsey fell silent.

"Might what?" Noah nudged.

"She thought seeing you again might bring closure. Hit a reset button and help me to figure out what it is I need out of life."

He studied her for a long moment and then said, "Melissa and I wanted different things."

"What did Melissa want?"

"Status, money, trips, keeping up with the Joneses, penthouse apartment, and all the trappings of success." He shrugged. "I had all that for a short time, but it really didn't do anything for me. I was much happier here in Twilight, being plain old Noah. She said I lacked ambition. Maybe I do. But I know myself. I don't need the latest gadgets or priciest car or to be seen at the poshest parties. I'm perfectly satisfied drinking lemonade and swinging in a hammock on a Saturday afternoon. Face facts, I'm a simple guy."

That sounded like heaven to Kelsey.

"Melissa didn't leave me because of my injury. Sure, the timing sucked, and she took a lot of flak for pulling up stakes when she did, but to be honest, we were never a good match. We had chemistry, but that's not enough to sustain a long-term marriage. Plus, she had a thing for one of my teammates."

"I'm sorry things didn't work out."

"I'm not," he said. "When I think about my marriage, 'Unanswered Prayers' pops into my head."

"The Garth Brooks song?"

"Yes. At first, I was hurt of course, and I prayed Melissa would come back, but now . . ." His heated gaze met Kelsey's. "I'm so glad she didn't."

Kelsey gulped. She was very glad too, but she wasn't going to say that. Unsure what was happening here, she sealed the cut on his cheek with a butterfly closure and stepped away from him.

"Well . . ." she said, dropping her gaze and her bandaged hands. "It's super late and I should be going."

"Thanks for this," he said and touched his cheek.

"Ditto." She raised her bandaged palms and met his gaze again.

"Some night, huh?"

"Some night," she echoed. Her feet pointed toward the door, anxious to get the heck out of that tiny, intimate room. But her heart, that crazy organ, surged forward, leaving her in a weird, twisted position.

Noah stood. "I'll walk you to your room."

"No, no, I can find my way," Kelsey said and zoomed right out the door.

Once in the narrow corridor, pulse zipping, she turned in the wrong direction, corrected and headed back toward the stairs.

The lobby was silent. The Christmas tree was turned off, but floor lighting led the way to the guest rooms.

As if she were sucking through a straw, her breath slipped from her lungs, thin and swift. Before she ever reached the door of the room she shared with Tasha, Kelsey saw the blue scarf, which her friend had used on her as a blindfold, wrapped around the doorknob.

Uh-oh.

A telltale sign that Tasha had company and Kelsey should find somewhere else to spend the night.

Sean and Tasha must have hit it off big-time.

Good for her!

Except now, Kelsey had nowhere to go.

She stood in the hallway a moment, considering her options. She could sleep on the chesterfield in the lobby, but then people would come trooping through. The thought of being that exposed bugged her.

Or . . . she could go back to Noah and see if he had a spare bedroom she could use for the night.

Back in front of Noah's door, she took a deep breath and blew it out slowly. What if he thought she'd returned because she wanted to spend the night with him?

Indecision grabbed hold of her. Maybe she should just camp out on the chesterfield after all.

"Dammit, Tasha," she muttered. "Thanks a lot for putting me in this position."

She was about to rap her fingers against his door, but making a fist hurt, and the door suddenly opened. Noah sailed over the threshold, frozen peas in his hand, and almost ran into her.

"Whoa." He halted. Backed up. "Hey."

"Headed to the kitchen?" She nodded at the peas.

"Yeah. They were thawing. Did you get lost?"

Yes, she wanted to say. *About ten years ago when I told you not to fight for me.* Instead she said, "There was a scarf on the doorknob of our room."

"No kidding? Tasha and Sean?"

"Tasha moves fast. I worry about her."

"Sean's a good guy."

"I'm sure he is, but she's been through a lot of heartache—"

"I hope she doesn't hurt him."

"I hope *he* doesn't hurt her."

"They're both consenting adults. We should probably stay out of it."

"Agreed." She paused. "Listen, do you have a spare bed I could sleep in tonight?"

"We're booked up," he said.

"Could I stay in Sean's room?"

"He doesn't live on the *Rockabye*. Or even in Twilight for that matter. He rents a house out in the country, which is probably why they came back here instead of going to his place."

"Oh, I see."

"You could bunk with me." The alarm sprinting through her bloodstream must have shown on her face because he quickly added, "Just to sleep. I'm not suggesting anything hinky."

Why not, she wondered. *Did he not want her?* He must not yearn for her as much as she yearned for him.

Crazy woman.

What the heck was with her? One minute she was freaked out about the thought of sharing his bed, and the next second she had her nose out of joint because he didn't want to jump her bones?

"I didn't think you were."

"It's not that I wouldn't want to do more than sleep . . ." He wriggled his eyebrows and tried for a smile, but he looked exhausted.

Gosh, how selfish was she? Thinking about her sexual desires when he'd taken a beating for her.

"Of course, we'll just sleep. Who thought we'd do anything else? I didn't think we'd do anything else. Why would we do anything else?" she babbled. "We've only been back together for a day. Not even a full twenty-four hours. Not that we're back together. We're not back together. I—"

Good grief, Kelsey, just shut the hell up.

He stepped aside, the bag of thawing frozen peas still clutched in his hand. Held the door wide open.

She could see his bed from here. That comfy looking queen-sized bed. Too bad it wasn't a king. They could both sleep on opposite sides and never touch, but a queen-sized bed . . .

"C'mon in," Noah invited, then shut the door behind her.

The notion of sleeping beside Kelsey and yet keeping his hands to himself was more than Noah could process.

"I promise I'll stay on my side of the bed," she quipped as they both stood in the middle of the room, staring at his bed. "You could even rig up a sheet between us, like in the old black-and-white Clark Gable movie, *It Happened One Night*."

She grossly overestimated the stopping power of a sheet and underestimated her sex appeal. Thank heavens he was feeling like hammered meat and didn't have the energy to follow his impulses.

Still, he needed to set up some ground rules to keep them both in check. "Nothing will happen," he assured her. "You are safe with me."

She looked slightly disappointed by that, or was it his imagination? "Thank you."

"No kissing. No caressing. No snuggling." No matter how much he might want to do all three, and more, so much more. Taking things to the next level so early in their reconnection would be a huge mistake. Noah knew it. He could see that Kelsey knew it too.

If they had sex she'd just be using him to salve her emotional wounds.

Yeah, what's wrong with that? whispered the blackguard in him.

"Got it." She bobbed her head.

"Swear that you will stay on your side of the bed?" he asked, sounding desperate even to his own ears.

"I pinky swear." She stuck out her hand.

Noah looped his pinky around hers, stared into her gorgeous blue eyes, and thought . . . *it is going to be a very long night.*

Three A.M. and Kelsey was wide awake.

How could she fall asleep when she was lying beside the man who heated her blood and sent her heart dancing sideways in a lopsided reel?

She rested on her back, arms ironed to her sides. Eyes fixed on the ceiling, listening to the soft sounds of his breathing. Not snoring. Just a rough but steady and reliable rhythm.

It comforted her. His sound. Curled her toes. Caused her to feel all warm and cozy inside.

To be so close to him . . . and yet so far away.

She'd promised to keep her hands to herself, but Kelsey was seriously regretting that promise. When she pinky swore to his terms, she'd no idea just how difficult this was going to be.

She ached to snuggle up to him. To wrap her arm around his waist with one hand, to let her other hand trail under the covers to touch his—

Stop it.

Right. She needed to stop thinking about sex. Stop visualizing him pouncing on her and pouring his hot self into her and—

Geeze, do you not know the meaning of the word stop?

Okay, okay. She closed her eyes, tried to think of something else. Hmm, what was a surefire desire killer?

Oh yeah, Filomena.

Umm, no. She certainly did not want to stir that pot, which would keep her awake for a totally different reason.

Her bandaged palms throbbed, reminding her of what had happened on Twilight's deserted main street just a few hours ago. Her mother sending her henchmen to whisk Kelsey back to Dallas. Noah, bravely standing up for her. Filomena was going to be so furious at him. At her. At them both.

Emotion flooded her. Anger at her mother. Pride and admiration for Noah. Frustration with herself that she couldn't easily turn off her preoccupation with pleasing her mother.

It wasn't the first time her mother had tracked her, spied on her, yanked her away from her leading her own life. Kelsey didn't know why she was so surprised about what Filomena had done.

When she'd gone off to Vassar, away from her mother's direct control, Filomena had sent someone to follow her around campus, to spy on her and report back. Of course, "spying" wasn't the way Filomena put it. In her side of the story, she'd employed a bodyguard to watch out for Kelsey's safety.

Yeah, without telling her about the "bodyguard." So yes, Mom, it *was* spying.

Filomena had also hired PIs to gather dirt on Theo to use as ammunition in their custody battle. To the point where Theo had threatened to sue her for harassment. Filomena had backed off the private detectives after that, but she did have a long history of using others to do her dirty work.

Forget about her. Forget about Noah. Think about sleep. Count sheep. Breathe in. Breathe out. Focus on your breath.

After several rounds of that, her body finally relaxed, and her mind grew fuzzy as she drifted between consciousness and a dream state. The problem with the dream state, however, was the dreams.

Floaty images dotted her brain. Images of arms and legs and tongues and mouths as she and Noah did sweet, wicked things to each other. Kelsey sighed, melting into the dream, letting her imagination take her to places she wasn't brave enough to go in waking life.

A solid arm went around her waist.

Her eyes flew open. She didn't know how much time had passed, but she was suddenly wide awake, and Noah's hard, strong arm was resting along her ribs, just below her breasts.

Apparently, he'd flopped onto his stomach, and his arm had landed across her without him being aware.

Or maybe it was a sly test to see what he could get away with.

"Noah," she whispered.

No answer.

She tried to move his arm, but that caused him to curl his fingers around her side and pull her down closer against him.

"Noah, are you awake?"

Nothing.

But she heard a low, soft snore. Not awake. His snuggling was an accident. He was not trying to push boundaries. Not trying to sex her up.

Disappointment nibbled at her. Gosh, he was a sound sleeper.

She recalled one time at Camp Hope, the year they were fourteen. She'd sneaked over to the boys' dorms and threw pebbles against the window above his bed trying to get him to wake up and hang out with her.

She'd had a nightmare about Chelsea, couldn't go back to sleep and needed to talk.

But instead of Noah, she'd gotten the attention of the seven other boys in his dorm, who'd all come to the window to see what was going on.

She'd hidden in the shadows, terror sending her pulse into overdrive, and then she ran back to the girls' dorms, tripping on a tree root in the dark and busting her lip when she fell.

Kelsey blushed at that memory, recalling how she'd been teased for the rest of summer camp for "sleepwalking"—because that was the excuse she'd given. At fourteen she wasn't about to admit she'd had a crush on him.

That had come three years later, when they'd returned to Camp Hope as junior counselors.

All these years they could have been together if not for her mother. Then again, maybe not. What had happened, had happened. Wishing and hoping couldn't change the past.

Kelsey let out a wistful breath, and forced herself to stop thinking about what might have been.

Right now, she was in bed next to Noah, wearing one of his T-shirts that was so big on her that it fell to her knees. A San Antonio Spurs T-shirt that smelled of his scent. She pulled the neck of the T-shirt up over her nose and breathed in the smell of him. Flared her toes. Savored the weight of his arm resting on her chest.

And at last, drifted off to sleep with a happy smile on her face.

CHAPTER 15

At eight o'clock on Monday morning, less than twenty-four hours since Kelsey had popped back into his life, Noah tiptoed into his bedroom with a cup of hot coffee and one of the French pastries that he'd gotten up to bake at six A.M.

He waved the pastry under her nose, hoping to rouse her with the yeasty scent.

When she didn't move, he bent at the waist and whispered in her ear. "Wakey, wakey, Firefly. Time to let your light shine."

Slowly, her eyes fluttered open. Kelsey stretched and offered him a shy, sleepy smile. "Hey."

His heart torqued. Damn, but the sight of her in his bed did strange things to him. "Hey, yourself. How are you feeling?"

She held up her palms as if she'd forgotten about the abrasions. "Sore, but I'll live. How about you?"

"The ice pack helped. I can see out of my left eye this morning. Thank you."

"What are you telling your guests about your face?"

"That they should see the other guy." He chuckled.

"It *would* be pretty interesting to see how Clifford Steel looks this morning."

"I suspect he's cursing our names," Noah said.

"Or Filomena's. If he's not too hoarse. You did have your elbow jammed right up against his voice box."

"Hey, I wasn't about to let *anyone* hurt you."

Kelsey cheeks pinkened and she smiled softly. Noah felt a corresponding softness slide through him. Uh-oh, he was leaving himself wide open to pain by liking her too much.

Noah picked up a bottle of over-the-counter anti-inflammatory pills sitting on the bedside table. "Take some of these. I did, and it made a world of difference."

"Have you seen Sean and Tasha this morning?" she asked, holding out her bandaged palm for him to hand her the pills.

"I've seen Sean. He looks like Sylvester the Cat with Tweety Bird stuffed into his mouth. Guilty, but not the least bit ashamed about it. When I asked him how he slept last night, he grinned but didn't say a word."

"Hmm. I need to go check on Tasha and see how she's doing." Kelsey tossed the pills in her mouth and took a sip of coffee. "Oh yummy. Cappuccino. You remembered."

"Firefly, you're unforgettable."

She dropped her gaze. "You used to tease me about cappuccino and you said I was only a play-like coffee drinker."

"See, you remember a lot about me too."

She sobered, set the coffee aside. "Noah," she said. "What are we doing?"

"What do you mean?" He held his breath, not knowing how he wanted her to answer.

"You . . ." She waved a hand at him. "Bringing me breakfast in bed."

"I just wanted to spoil you."

"To what end?"

"Can't a guy do something nice?" he asked. "I'm not your mother. I don't have a hidden agenda."

"Sorry." Her eye twitched slightly. "I didn't mean to sound so antagonistic."

"You didn't. It was a legitimate question." Noah sat down on the end of the bed. Studied her. How could he give her an answer when he was just as confused as she?

Underneath the covers, Kelsey drew her knees to her chest, and wrapped her arms around her knees.

"I don't know what we're doing, Kelsey. I care about you, and I'm damn pissed that your mother still treats you like you're seventeen."

"I care about you too," she murmured.

"I don't know where that leaves us. I don't know if it's smart for us to be anything more than friends, especially after last night."

Her mouth dipped in disappointment, but she nodded vigorously.

Good. They agreed. It disappointed him to say they should just be friends, but he had a good life going here. It wasn't smart to mess things up by getting involved with Filomena James's daughter again. He'd been down this road before. Had the scars to prove it.

"I'm sure she's been blowing up my phone with angry calls and texts." Kelsey cast a glance at her purse, which sat near the bedroom door where she'd dropped it the night before.

"Do you want me to get your phone?"

"Not yet. Let me just enjoy this yummy coffee and pastry first. Then I'll figure out a way to smooth things over with my mother."

"Why do you have to smooth things over? You've done nothing wrong. She's the one who sent people to kidnap you. That's not normal behavior. You should be able to go wherever you want, do whatever you want, without getting her approval first. You're not seventeen anymore."

Kelsey sighed and slumped back against the headboard. Surrender was her default position when it came to her mother. "It's just easier to calm the waters and keep the peace than to argue with her."

"So, Filomena always gets her way? At your expense? That doesn't seem fair . . ." He paused. "Or emotionally healthy."

She winced, her mouth pressing into a thin you-don't-get-it line. But he *did* get it. He'd been at the receiving end of Filomena's barbs.

Kelsey folded her arms over her chest, tucked her bandaged hands into her armpits.

Empathy rolled through him. Being raised by a woman like Filomena had to be brutal. Even more so because society put motherhood on a pedestal, as if some mothers weren't downright toxic to their children.

He might be hot for Kelsey, and having some gang-buster sexual fantasies about her, but until she started living her life for herself, there was no hope for them. Bummer. The biggest obstacle keeping them apart as teens was as big as it had ever been.

If not bigger.

Kelsey was older now. More entrenched in the pattern. Less likely to fight back. Was it too late for her to change?

Bigger question, why should he rock his own safe little boat? Life was good. Simple. Easy. Just the way he liked it.

Your life could be better, whispered a voice at the back of his mind. *With Kelsey in it.*

"What if Filomena demands you come home?" he asked.

"I won't go."

That lifted his hopes, but he was afraid to let them get off the ground. He was happy. Why muck that up by lusting after the wrong woman? In all honesty, they'd never been a good match. She came from an elite, hoity-toity world. He was a water rat from the wrong side of the river. He'd had the rich and famous lifestyle for a short time and he'd never felt comfortable in that privileged world.

"You sure?" he asked, testing her.

"I'll tell her I'm staying because Tasha put together this great trip to help me get over the whole botched wedding thing."

"That'll put Tasha in the hot seat."

"Ahh, Tasha won't mind. She loves ruffling Filomena's feathers."

"I really like Tasha," he said.

"I do too." Kelsey forced a ghost smile, pale and gone quickly. "She's the only one who's not afraid of my mother."

"I'm not afraid of her."

"Excuse me? You let her bully you into backing down ten years ago."

"Hey, we were just kids. And she threatened to take away my scholarship. I—" Noah shoved his hands through his hair, pivoted on his heel, did a complete three-sixty. "No, I'm not doing this. I'm not justifying myself. You might feel like you have to constantly justify yourself to her, but I don't."

Kelsey's bottom lip trembled, and that damn eye muscle of hers was twitching so hard she could hardly hold her eyelid open. "Why are you yelling at me?"

He had raised his voice in frustration. It must feel like yelling to her. The rapid twitching of her eye seemed to suggest that was the case.

He was no shrink, but he knew a few soldiers with PTSD. Military personnel and victims of crimes weren't the only ones who could suffer from it. A lifetime of chronic emotional and verbal abuse could trigger PTSD too.

His heart cracked. His mind filled with images of all the ways Filomena must have made Kelsey suffer. Cruel, sinister, underhanded ways that left deep scars that no one could see. Scars far more damaging than the ones he'd suffered when he'd lost his mother to ALS. After his mother had died, he would get angry when kids complained about their moms. His thought had been that at least they *had* a mom.

But listening to Kelsey's story, seeing the damage done, he realized there *were* worse things than having your mother die when you were young. His mother might have left the earth early, but while she'd been here, she'd been nothing but a radiant light of unconditional love. Giving him the strength he needed to keep his heart open and his mind clear. He couldn't imagine growing up with a parent who manipulated and emotionally abused their child every step of the way.

Noah ached to bring Kelsey into his world. To change her direction and have her find safety in his arms. He wanted her to see that every single day could be like Christmas when you had the courage to claim happiness. To see the world with fresh eyes.

To see *him* with fresh eyes.

He was no longer that seventeen-year-old kid, terrified of her domineering mother. And he was no longer willing to simply be the blast from her past.

Right or wrong, Noah wanted more.

So much more.

He gave Kelsey the most loving look he could muster, peered deeply into her eyes, and whispered, "Let me know when you've figured out what it is you really want out of life, Firefly. Your freedom or your shackles."

Noah's parting words shook Kelsey up and pissed her off a little. He acted as if he knew her, and what was in her heart. The man hadn't seen her in ten years. He didn't know. He didn't understand.

Dreading what she would find, Kelsey picked up her purse and rummaged around for her phone. Held her breath. Turned it on.

There was nothing from her mother. No texts. No missed calls. No emails. No private messages.

Total silence.

The hairs on her arms lifted. Her right eye jumped, and her stomach grumbled. This was not good. Not good at all. Filomena did not stay silent unless she was plotting revenge or on a giant sulk.

Both were equally dangerous.

If last night's encounter was a squall, currently Kelsey was standing in the eye of the hurricane. Huddled in the deceptive moment when all went quiet, while outside the small zone of calm, a chaotic, ferocious storm raged.

Freaked out, Kelsey got dressed, left Noah's room, and went in search of the one person who understood.

She found Tasha in the lobby having a gabfest with Raylene.

Tasha took one look at Kelsey's bandaged hands and gasped. "What happened to you?"

"Filomena." It was the only word Kelsey could get out. She gave Tasha a look that said *I need to talk, now.*

"Um," Tasha said to Raylene. "I gotta go. Looks like my friend is at Defcon 5." Tasha linked her arm through Kelsey's. "Let's go outside. Housekeeping is cleaning our room."

They stepped out onto the deck of the paddle wheel boat. Sean was on the island, standing on a ladder in front of the gazebo stringing Christmas lights.

"Hi!" Tasha waved madly.

Sean dropped the strand of lights to wave back just as madly.

"Whatcha doin'?" Tasha called to him.

"Finishing up the gazebo before the decorating committee gets here this afternoon for the first round of judging," Sean said. "Wanna help?"

"Maybe later," Tasha called to him across the gap between the paddle wheel boat and the island. "Me and my BFF got things to discuss."

"Am I one of those things?" Sean asked.

"Curiosity killed the cat," Tasha said. "But if you feel your ears burning . . ."

Sean covered his ears with his palms and laughed out loud.

"C'mon," Kelsey mumbled, grabbing Tasha's wrist, dragging her down the gangplank and off the boat.

"Where are we going?" Tasha asked.

"Somewhere we can talk in private." Tension twisted up every part of Kelsey's body and her right eye jerked hard.

"You're acting really weird. I'm scared."

"Me too." Kelsey walked over to the shed where the golf carts were stored and commandeered one. "Get in."

"Mmm." Tasha sent a lingering look at Sean. "Okay."

Not even knowing where she was going, Kelsey maneuvered the golf cart over the dirt path, putting the *Rockabye* behind them. But it was a small island. How lost could they get? "Did you have fun last night with Sean?"

"Yes, we had a fab time, and Sean tastes as delicious as he looks. But forget about me. You're ready to spew like Mount St. Helens. What *happened*?"

"It *was* Lewis Hunter I saw at The Horny Toad last night." Kelsey told her about her mother's foiled attempt at kidnapping her.

"That explains Noah's face. Omigosh." Tasha rested her hand on Kelsey's forearm. "Your mother is a flat-out witch. I bet she's been blowing up your phone."

"No. That's the truly scary part. Not a word. Not a peep." Kelsey drove to the edge of the island overlooking the water. She could see the outlines of the buildings of Camp Hope in the distance. "Not a whisper."

"Uh-oh."

"I know." Kelsey stopped the golf cart and sat trembling.

"I'm so sorry." Tasha gathered her up in a tight hug.

Kelsey didn't mean to cry, she didn't want to cry, but a fat tear rolled down her cheek. Tasha pulled a packet of tissues from her coat pocket and passed them to Kelsey.

"Got any more of that Fireball?"

"We finished it off at the Ritz, remember?"

"Rats." Kelsey straightened in her seat, dabbed at her eyes. She'd left the *Rockabye* with only a sweater and this close to the water she regretted not wearing a coat as a cold shaft of wind cut through her.

"I should go home. I need to go home and make this right before it gets worse."

"Make what right? The fact that she can cause you to knuckle under just by giving you the silent treatment?"

Yes.

"You know this is actually a good thing, right?" Tasha got out of the golf cart, picked up a handful of pebbles and started skipping them across the lake.

Kelsey got out and joined her. Maybe moving around would generate some body heat and stave off the cold. "What is a good thing?"

"Radio silence from Filomena."

"It just means she's busy gathering her forces."

"Like the Wicked Witch in *The Wizard of Oz* calling up her flying monkeys." Tasha's stone skipped four long hops across the lake. "Yep, I get that. But you can turn it into your advantage."

Kelsey poked her tongue against the side of her cheek, pondered that theory. "How?"

"You gather *your* resources while she's gathering hers."

"What are my resources?"

"Me for one."

Kelsey picked up a flat stone, curled her finger around it and flung it out across the lake in the direction of Camp Hope. The stone skipped a full six hops before sinking into the water.

"Good omen." Tasha applauded.

"For what?"

"Your third dare."

Kelsey stopped throwing rocks, turned to look at her friend, her long braid whacking against her shoulders. Tasha's first two dares had paid off. She'd reconnected with Noah and while her mind was in a tizzy, she *was* feeling stronger, braver.

"Let's hear it."

"Turn off your phone for the rest of our vacation."

"I can't do that."

"Why not?"

"What if I have an emergency?"

"You can use my phone."

"What if my mother has an emergency?"

"If it's a real emergency she can call the hotel. She's been tracking you. She knows where you are."

"What about my dad?"

"You can tell Theo to call me if he needs to get hold of you."

Kelsey felt a sharp sense of loss as it struck her that limiting contact with her mother also meant limiting contact with her father in order to keep him from the heat of battle.

Did she dare accept Tasha's challenge?

"Filomena's silent treatment is driving you crazy. Did you know that the silent treatment is actually a form of emotional abuse? I say fight fire with fire. Turn off your phone. Besides, you can't really relax and do what you came here to do if you're constantly checking your phone."

"But if I turn off my phone, isn't that giving her the silent treatment in reverse?"

"No, it's setting boundaries. The woman tried to have you kidnapped, for crying out loud." Tasha went on tip-toes to tap Kelsey's forehead. "Let that fully sink in."

"How about I just turn it off for a few hours?"

Tasha gave her a pointed stare.

"What if by ghosting my mother, she turns up here?"

Tasha shuddered. "Yeah, neither one of us wants that, but what's the alternative? You have to break away sometime."

Kelsey cocked her head. "Maybe I could turn it off for a day, since she's ignoring me anyway."

"Dammit Kelsey, you didn't do anything wrong."

Slowly blowing out a long breath, Kelsey nodded. "Two days?"

"Five."

"I'm just worried."

"About what?"

"She'll fly into a rage."

"She's going to do that anyway. And you won't be there when it happens."

"No, but then, the *worst* will happen."

"What's the worst, Kelsey?" Tasha asked, stepping closer to her. "What is the bottom line that you're so terrified of? Do you think Filomena will get physical with you? Even if she had dragged you back home, do you think she's going to lock you up?"

Kelsey paused, and said nothing for a very long time, and when she spoke her voice was the tone of a small child. "She'll *ignore* me. Until she thinks I've been adequately punished. Not for an hour, not for a day, not for a week, but for *months*."

"All right," Tasha relented. "Seventy-two hours. I dare you to turn your phone off for seventy-two hours and spend the next three days just enjoying yourself. Not only that but give me your phone and I'll hide it, so you can't find it in a moment of weakness. Do you accept?"

Kelsey massaged her temple, getting an instant headache at the thought of confronting Filomena. Her eye twitched. Every instinct inside her urged her to give up the futile goal of a relaxing holiday, go home, and beg her mother's forgiveness as she'd done for the last twenty-seven years whenever Filomena's nose got out of joint. Anything to avoid a showdown.

Because if she didn't, the showdown *was* coming.

But she didn't have to think about that now. If she accepted Tasha's challenge she'd have seventy-two hours of peace at any rate. Every word her friend spoke was true. Kelsey knew it deep down. Had known for a very long time.

But she'd been a coward. Unable to face the loneliness and isolation that came from being frozen out by Filomena. When she had thoughts of leaving her mother's employment, and making her own place in the world, her eye started the miserable twitching. And eventually, the twitching, unchecked, would settle into a mind-numbing migraine.

In the past, to stave off the guilt, stress, and pain, she would list Filomena's good qualities, because *come on*, even the worst person had good traits.

And Kelsey kept telling herself that her mother wasn't the *worst* person. Kelsey could see past Filomena's bluster to the hurt child inside her who had never gotten the attention she craved. Filomena had grown up in a household full of money, competition, and contempt without an ounce of tenderness or compassion.

Filomena's childhood had made her quite cunning. She was smart, charismatic, and could be very witty. The trick was not to spend too much time in her company. To get out before the criticisms, blaming, gaslighting, and hate-fueled gossip began. Unfortunately, Kelsey spent the majority of her workday hours with her mother.

She fished around in her purse for Lionel Berg's card. Stared at it. Thought about how enraged her mother would be if she accepted Berg's offer. Did she really want to be his campaign manager? Or was something inside her attracted to the idea of hurting her mother?

Working for her mother was unhealthy. She could see that now. Tasha had been trying to get her to see it for a long time. But Kelsey had worn blinders for twenty-seven years and it was only seeing the pity in Tasha's eyes that reality fully hit her.

If she stayed within her mother's sphere of influence, and kept allowing her to violate her personal boundaries, she would never be happy. Never be free. Never be fulfilled. The truth was hard to look at.

It was as if she'd been sporting mud-smeared glasses and Tasha had taken them off, cleaned them up, and put them back on and she could see the world with startlingly clear eyes. And for the first time since she could remember, Kelsey felt real hope that things could indeed be different.

"Ticktock. This is your life calling," Tasha said. "For real."

She looked at Tasha, at the card from Berg, and the phone she'd fished from her purse. This was it. Her defining moment. Now or never. Let the damn chips fall where they may.

Resolute, Kelsey turned off her phone and gave it to Tasha. "Put the thing somewhere I can't find it. My future is in your hands."

CHAPTER 16

"What's eating you, boss?" Sean asked from his place on the ladder, a string of lights in his hands. "I mean beyond trying to see from behind that shiner?"

Noah stood on the ground, hands on his hips, head cocked back, squinting up at the gazebo. They were behind schedule. The decorating committee was coming by at four thirty and it was almost noon. They weren't going to finish in time.

"Don't call me boss. It makes me feel old."

"Why not? You sign my paychecks."

"I'm also younger than you."

"Doesn't matter. You're the man in charge."

Hmm, Noah supposed he was, but he wasn't even really sure how that had happened. "The design scheme we were working on is taking too long. Let's shortcut and skip putting lights on the cupola. That's good enough."

"Good enough? That's not something you say to a navy SEAL." Sean shook his head. "No such thing as good enough. Don't you want to win? Think of that money for ALS research."

Noah shrugged. "If we do, we do. If we don't, we don't."

"Joel could take the competition. Have you seen the *Brazos Queen*? It's epic."

"If he wins he'll give the money to ALS research, so no biggie." Noah shrugged.

"Where's your spirit of competition? Or are you just too lazy to put up a fight?"

To tell the truth, he was dragging after the beating he'd taken last night, but Noah would rather lay his lackadaisical attitude off to laziness than admit he was feeling raw and vulnerable.

"If you'd get a ladder and get your butt up here, it would go much faster," Sean said.

Noah didn't want to look like a wimp, but his head was throbbing like a bastard and he'd gotten up at the crack of dawn after not sleeping much with sumptuous Kelsey curled next to him and a "no touching" policy between them.

"It's cold," he grumbled. "The wind's kicking up, and it's dangerous on a ladder. You shouldn't be up there either."

"Excuses." Sean scoffed. "I'm not half-assing this. I take pride in *my* work."

Noah jammed his hands in the pockets of his leather jacket. "Fine. I'll go get another ladder and assist. We'll blow away together."

He retrieved a second ladder from the shed, erected it on the opposite side of the gazebo. His cut cheek tingled, and his eye burned, but he wasn't going to whine about it.

"Here," Sean said, feeding a strand of Christmas lights toward Noah. "This goes up the right side of the cupola."

"I know. I designed it."

"You're in a mood."

Was he? He didn't know what to make of Kelsey or these feelings he kept having. Noah was seldom out of sorts, and whenever he was the least bit grouchy, people noticed.

"What's up between you and Blondie?" Sean asked as Noah scaled higher on the ladder, the strand of lights clutched in his hand.

"Don't call her Blondie—it's demeaning. Her name is Kelsey."

"My bad. What's up with Kelsey?"

"Why do you care?"

"I saw her coming out of your bedroom this morning. Not that I'm judging, but if reconnecting with your childhood sweetheart is going to make you so prickly, I advise not to throw a coin in the Sweetheart Fountain."

"Don't worry about me."

"I can't help but worry when I see a friend on the fast train to a broken heart," Sean said.

"What makes you think I'm going to get my heart broken?" Noah challenged.

"For one thing, Blondie . . ."

"Kelsey."

"Kelsey is a go-getter and you . . ." Sean met Noah's gaze over the metal cupola roof. "Are not."

"So? Opposites attract."

"And she just got stood up at the altar, on what, Saturday?"

"Yes."

"That's *Saturday*, as in two days ago." Sean inched up to the very top of his ladder and stretched long to anchor his strand of lights. "You're looking a whole lot like the rebound guy from here."

"There is nothing for her to rebound from. Her fiancé chose his wedding day to come out of the closet."

"You think that makes things easier? The woman's mind has got to be as disheveled as hell after something like that. Have fun together, but don't start picking out wedding rings."

"Good Lord, why would you even think that? All we've done is a little kissing—"

"And you slept in the same bed."

"Nothing happened!"

"But you're a hopeless romantic. Now your brother, Joel . . . there is a sensible guy. But you? When it comes to love, you leap before you look. Melissa, case in point. You knew that from the beginning you two had nothing in common. You ignored it."

"Melissa was different. I was young and riding the high of a big basketball contract . . ."

"And Melissa was there drooling over you. No effort on your part. You had a hot chick, and money in the bank, and you thought why not get married . . ."

"I'm not paying you to psychoanalyze me."

"Then there's the fact that you earned yourself a shiner over Kelsey."

"How do you know Kelsey has anything to do with this?" Noah touched his eye, but the ladder wobbled in the wind and he grabbed hold with both hands.

Sean snorted. "You're the most easygoing guy in Twilight. It would take something mighty serious for you to get into a fight. Two plus two equals four, my friend."

"Meaning?"

"Beautiful mystery woman from your past shows up in town, next thing you know, you're sporting a black eye. Doesn't take a rocket scientist to decipher that chemical equation."

"Fine, you're right." Noah grunted, and told him what had happened with Filomena's Town Car thugs.

"Shit, that's even worse than I suspected." Sean ran a palm over his head. "I figured some guy grabbed her ass or something and you stepped in."

"It's not as serious as my face makes it look."

"And you're rafting down a river with Cleopatra."

"Huh?"

"De Nile."

"Ha-ha. Hand me your staple gun and the lights."

"I'm serious, Noah." Sean paused to pick up the staple gun from where he'd rested it in the roof gutter and passed it across the roof to Noah. "I'm worried about you."

"I know what I'm doing."

"Do you?"

"You're one to talk. You took Little Miss Thing to bed on the first date."

"Don't call her Little Miss Thing. It's demeaning. Her name is Tasha." Sean got moony-eyed. "And you got that wrong. Tasha is the one who took *me* to bed."

"And you're giving me dating advice?"

"I tried to resist."

"I'm sure you tried so hard."

"What can I say?" Sean shrugged, grinned. "Tasha is a firecracker. But we're not talking about me. I'm not the one who falls willy-nilly into relationships at the drop of a hat."

"Me either."

"Excuse me? In college alone there was . . ." Sean ticked off names on his fingers. "Neve, Tiffany, Ginger, and—"

"Remind me again why I hired you?"

"I keep you on the straight and narrow."

"Is that really what you're going with? Putting you in charge of the straight and narrow is like throwing gasoline on a campfire to put it out."

"Just keeping it real, man."

"I'm trying to help Kelsey, you know? She's been through a lot and her mother is a doozy . . ."

"And?"

Out of habit, Noah started to pull a palm down his face, but the minute his hand touched his sore cheek, he stopped. The wind gusted, cutting through him like a blade and rocking his tenuous perch on the ladder.

"And?" Both Sean's acid tone and hard-edged gaze held his feet to the fire.

Noah *liked* being happy. His friend's prodding stirred up emotions he'd rather not feel. He should have fought harder for Kelsey ten years ago. If he had, maybe she would have already broken free from Filomena's claws. She'd needed him, and he'd let her down. But he couldn't say all that to Sean.

"At least I'm housebroken," Noah quipped, reciting a line from his favorite movie.

"Don't quote *The Big Lebowski* to me," Sean said. "I see right through your Dude act. You skim through life on your looks and charm, never digging too deep."

"Wanna go knock down some pins when we get done here?" Noah asked, trying to ease his way out of the conversation with another *Big Lebowski* reference. "Elf bowling started on the first. And we could check out the new fondue restaurant on the square."

Sean clicked his tongue and shook his head. "How is it that you own a boatel and I'm *your* handyman."

"You went into the Navy, while I on the other hand opted for the NBA."

"Oh yeah, my bad for not being born with six-foot-five genes."

Before Noah could think of a comeback, he heard the sound of a golf cart motoring up the trail, and spied Kelsey and Tasha pulling up to the *Rockabye*.

Kelsey swung out of the golf cart all long legs and golden braided hair.

One look at her and his chest swelled, and his pulse skipped, and his breath caught . . . and Noah knew what Sean had said was true. If he wasn't careful, Kelsey James *was* going to break his heart into a hundred little pieces.

Again.

But this wasn't about him, was it?

She deserved to be happy and free.

While he might not figure into her long-term equation, he *did* know how to relax and have a good time. He could flip things for her. Give to Kelsey what she gave to others—attention, kindness, caring. She hadn't had enough of those things in her life. He could be good to her. Treat her like the goddess she didn't realize she was.

His good deed for the holidays. And if he ended up with a wounded heart, well, those were the breaks. He expected nothing in return.

As she and Tasha walked toward the gazebo, Noah felt a surge of joy so great he almost fell off the ladder. And when she came to stand beneath him, shading her eyes with a bandaged hand, a genuine smile crossed her face. Kelsey was as glad to see him as he was to see her.

"Hey," he called down to her.

"Hey, yourself." Kelsey's blue eyes twinkled in the sunlight.

Her beauty took his breath and he almost backtracked. If he fell now, he'd hit the ground hard, and he wasn't talking about falling off the ladder. "Got a question for you."

"What's that?"

"Ever eat fondue?"

An official date.

She and Noah were going on their first official date in a decade. Should she feel this giddy? Kelsey didn't think so. It seemed too dangerous.

After she and Tasha returned to the *Rockabye*, Kelsey was desperate to distract herself from her cell phone. She suggested they roll up their sleeves and help Noah and Sean finish decorating the gazebo.

They'd had a blast, the four of them laughing, joking, and bantering as they worked.

Noah looked fantastic.

He stripped off his red plaid mackinaw to reveal a black wool turtleneck pullover that clung to his hunky broad shoulders. His dark hair ruffled in the breeze and his black eye and steri-stripped cheek cut lent him a rakish, bad boy air. He wore rugged Rockport boots and she liked the way he looked in the ensemble—a suave lumberjack.

At dusk, just minutes before they finished, the preliminary round contest judges showed up. The island, boatel, gazebo, and suspension bridge archway were aglow with lights, and Christmas music from the speakers on the *Rockabye* accompanied the light show.

Joel, who'd just made the finals for the *Brazos Queen*, came to join his twin for his judging. Raylene too had joined them.

Noah said he didn't care if he won or not, but to Kelsey his body language said that he wasn't being honest with himself. His usual laid-back slouch vanished. As the judges, two men and a woman who looked vaguely familiar, oohed and aahed and took notes, he pulled up his spine as if his height could influence their decision.

He fiddled with the zipper on his coat and shifted his weight from foot to foot. Ran his palm over his head repeatedly. Made too many jokes about his facial bruises.

He desperately wanted that prize money for ALS research. He and his mother had been close and losing her at a young age impacted him more than he liked to admit. Kelsey's heartstrings tugged. She crossed her fingers and said a little prayer that he would win.

But wishing and hoping didn't seem like enough. What more could she do to help?

"I love how Noah synched the music to the light display," Kelsey pointed out, in case the judges hadn't noticed that when "Winter Wonderland" played all the lights turned frosty blue. Or when "All I Want for Christmas Is You" came on, the lights chased each other at a quickening pace, mimicking a racing pulse.

Noah cut his eyes at her. "They get it, Kelsey."

Goodness, had she stepped on his toes? Quelled, she pressed her palm against her mouth.

"Wait a minute," said the female judge. "I know you. You're Kelsey James. We met at the Fourth of July gala for the Dallas Symphony Orchestra. We donated to your mother's mayoral campaign because of how impassioned you were about the good she could do for Dallas." The woman stuck out her hand. "Judy Paulson."

"Mrs. Paulson, yes, yes. What a delight to see you again." Kelsey clasped her hand and went into full political diplomat mode. "Thank you so much for supporting my mother's campaign."

"I know Filomena will do a world of good for the city."

Kelsey struggled to keep her smile genuine. She could only pray that her mother's desire to look good in public translated into her doing the right things for the city. "Do you still live in Dallas?"

"No, we just moved here to Twilight. We bought the historical Spencer House on the river bluff overlooking the town." Judy Paulson pointed in the direction of the biggest house in Twilight, a looming Greek Revival three-story mansion. The roofline was visible through the bareness of winter. "What are you doing in town?"

"I'm visiting for the holiday."

"Is your mother here too?" Judy Paulson craned her neck.

"No, she's in Dallas readying to take office."

"And you're not by her side?" A disapproving look crossed the woman's face.

"Shh . . . it's not for public knowledge, but Kelsey came to reunite with her childhood sweetheart." Tasha nodded at Noah. "They went to Camp Hope as kids." She went on to create a dramatic story of two heart-broken kids who'd forged a bond, then had found a second chance at romance.

"I—" Kelsey started to set Mrs. Paulson straight, but Tasha bumped her in the back of her knee.

"Oh my." The sunshine smile was back on Mrs. Paulson's face. "That is so romantic! Just like the Twilight Sweetheart legend."

Noah cleared his throat as if he intended to say something. The judges looked his way, but Tasha rushed in again.

"Exactly," Tasha said. "Why do you think Noah cued up 'All I Want for Christmas Is You'? It's all for Kelsey."

"What a darling story! Another tale for the Twilight legend." Judy Paulson motioned for the two male judges to follow her over to one side. They held a whispered conversation.

Kelsey looked at Noah to see how he was taking this. His expression was blank. Unnerved, she dropped her gaze to Tasha.

Her friend raised her eyebrows and her shoulders, held out her palms.

Judy left the huddle and came back to where Kelsey, Noah, Tasha, Sean, Joel, and Raylene were standing beside the gazebo. "I have great news. The design is terrific, and the scale of your display is impressive, but what really puts you over the top, Mr. MacGregor, is Kelsey herself and your heartwarming love story. We're pleased to announce that your entry advances to the final round in the small business category."

The judges shook Noah's hand, and congratulated him on both the display and his renewed association with Kelsey. Mrs. Paulson invited them both to tour the Spencer House.

As the judges departed, Raylene turned to Tasha. "You laid it on pretty thick about the reunited sweethearts thing."

"Hey, it's all about the marketing, am I right? You heard Mrs. Paulson. Kelsey is the reason Noah is a finalist."

Noah put his mackinaw back on, jammed his hands into his pockets. Kelsey still couldn't read his reaction, but she feared he didn't approve of the turn of events.

"You're a shoo-in as a finalist." Raylene put a hand on Noah's shoulder. "No one in town has as much Christmas spirit as you and now you've got this whole Sweetheart Legend schtick going on with Kelsey . . ."

"Hey, hey!" Joel snapped his fingers at Raylene. "I resent that remark. I have Christmas spirit too."

"I couldn't have done it without you all." Noah's smile was humble, but he did not meet Kelsey's eyes. "You guys rock my world."

"And don't you forget it." Raylene elbowed him in the ribs.

"I'm glad you finalled, little brother." Joel was two minutes older. "It's no competition if you're not in it."

"Just wait until I take you *down*." Noah dropped his knees to the ground to demonstrate how low Joel would sink.

Joel laughed. "Gonna whup your ass, bro. Better put on your crying pants."

Seeing Noah and Joel together in their good-natured teasing and brotherly playfulness plucked strings of longing deep inside Kelsey. It had been seventeen years since Chelsea's death, but she still missed her twin something fierce.

Tasha rubbed her palms together, cast a sideways look at Sean. "So, about that fondue . . ."

"Mind if we tag along?" Sean asked Noah.

Noah quirked an eyebrow at Kelsey. Waiting for her approval?

"The more the merrier," Kelsey said, even though she longed to be alone with Noah. She'd not yet shared the news that she'd relinquished her phone to Tasha for seventy-two hours, but feared looking selfish if she said no. "Please come along."

Noah shrugged. "Sure. Come along. My treat, y'all, for helping finish the gazebo." He turned to his twin. "Joel, you coming?"

"Can't. Gotta prep for Christmas Casino," Joel said.

"Christmas Casino?" Tasha cocked her head. "What's that?"

"A Christmas-themed gambling party." Joel grinned. "Just like it sounds."

"Ooh." Tasha rubbed her palms. "I'm in."

Kelsey noticed her friend studying Sean from the corner of her eye while the former SEAL moved to adjust a piece of garland that was drooping a bit on the lip of the gazebo gutter.

"Christmas Casino is our second annual black-tie charity event," Noah explained. "Last year it was our biggest fundraiser of the season. We're hoping to top it this year. All the profits raised go to support ALS research."

"You guys do a lot of charity events," Kelsey said. "The Christmas Bards, cookie club brunch, Christmas Casino . . ."

"That's not half of it." Sean caught Tasha eyeing him and smiled. "Together these two are the biggest fund-raisers in Twilight. I mean look at 'em." He waved his hands at the brothers. "Tall, good-looking. The way they

smile at you makes you want to crack your wallet wide
open . . ."

"You ladies are invited too," Joel said. "We'd love to
see you there."

Tasha crinkled her nose. "Neither one of us brought
anything black-tie-y to wear."

"That's easily solved." Noah nodded in the direction
of the Twilight town square. "There's a formal wear
rental shop in town."

"Are you going to the event?" Tasha asked Sean.

Sean shook his head. "Someone has to hold down the
fort at the *Rockabye*."

"Sooo . . ." Tasha eyed Sean. "You'll be here all alone
on Friday night?"

"I will."

They locked gazes.

Kelsey shifted her attention back to Noah and Joel.
"Congrats again to both of you on making the final
round."

"Thanks again for your help. You made it possible,"
Noah said, his voice even and his eyes inscrutable.
"Without your connection to Mrs. Paulson and Tasha's
creative embellishment of our relationship, the *Rockabye*
wouldn't have made the cut."

"You don't know that," Kelsey said. Noah might look
easygoing on the surface, but she sensed the Mrs. Paulson thing had gotten under his skin.

Why? Shouldn't he be happy that she'd helped him
cement his advancement to the final round?

Doubt pulled at her. Maybe it was the way Tasha had
played on their story. She had made it sound like they
were lovers.

"Believe me," Noah said, a bite of icy steel in his voice. "I know all too well how the rich manipulate people to get what they want."

"Oh right," she shot back, surprising herself by speaking her mind. "Like the poor don't manipulate."

"I'm not saying they don't. I'm just pointing out that money gives clout and clout gives the power to make or break people's lives." He touched his cheek.

Kelsey's eye twitched. "Maybe we should call this dinner off."

He looked surprised at that. "Why?"

"You seem upset with me."

"Not with you, Firefly. With myself."

CHAPTER 17

The fondue restaurant, The Swiss Melt, was Bavarian themed, with high-backed booths covered with sheep-skin, thick ceiling beams, and wood-paneled everything.

The curtains were designed to look like Swiss flags, and cuckoo clocks hung on the wall. In the center of the room was a wood-burning two-sided fireplace, alive with crackling logs. Christmas trees flanked either side of the dining room, fondue pots bubbled on nearby tables, and a hurdy-gurdy version of "We Wish You a Merry Christmas" filtered through the speakers.

But Noah barely noticed. In his head, he kept turning over what had happened with the contest judges. How he hadn't been a shoo-in until Judy Paulson recognized Kelsey.

Political clout wins again.

He was disappointed in himself. That he let it get to him. Why should he care? He was in the finals. One step closer to winning the money for ALS.

And yet the kid he'd once been, that kid from the wrong side of the river, the kid who'd lost his mother, the kid whose father started drinking heavily to deal with his grief, still lived inside of him. The inferiority complex of not being good enough for the likes of Kelsey James reared its ugly head. The self-doubt he hid behind a lazy smile and easygoing attitude still lived within him.

Noah helped Kelsey off with her coat and Sean did the same for Tasha. They hung their outerwear on the moose antler coatrack beside their table.

Kelsey and Noah sat together on one side of the booth. Tasha and Sean on the other. A double date.

It felt awkward at first. Uncomfortable.

No one said anything.

Noah cast around for something witty to say, but he was so overwhelmed by Kelsey's intoxicating fragrance he came up empty. "You smell good."

"Thank you." She folded her hands in her lap.

"How are your hands?"

"Good. The burn cream you put on them is helping them heal."

More silence.

Yikes. Okay, this was not going according to plan.

Stop thinking about how awkward you feel. Operation Kelsey, remember? This is about making her feel special.

A perky server named Samantha, dressed in a uniform that looked like it came straight off a box of Swiss Miss cocoa, appeared with menus. Noah recognized her right away—she'd dated Joel for a couple of months the previous summer.

Samantha took one look at Noah's face and her eyes widened. "What happened to you?"

"Long boring story." Noah waved a hand.

"Of course, it is. Nothing exciting ever happens in Twilight," Samantha said, passing out the menus.

Noah didn't agree. He sent a sidelong glance toward Kelsey and met her gaze. She grinned, and he couldn't help grinning back. He might not deserve her, but he enjoyed being with her.

"Bite your tongue, woman," Noah told Samantha. "Twilight is a hotbed of excitement."

"If you believe that, then I really don't want to see what you consider boring." Samantha crossed her arms.

"She's right," Sean said. "I moved to Twilight because it is boring."

"But you do like some excitement, right?" Tasha sidled closer to Sean.

Kelsey leaned across the table and whispered, "Be prepared. She's a swashbuckler."

"Not that I don't love you," Tasha said to Kelsey, "but keep to your lane, sister."

"Burn." Sean chuckled. "She got you."

"See what I mean?" Kelsey said. "Tasha is really good at swordplay."

Tasha stuck out her tongue. "For the record, Sean *enjoys* the way I play with swords."

"Joel was really good at swordplay." Samantha sighed.

"TMI." Kelsey put her hands over her ears.

"You're no fun," Tasha teased. "Noah, lighten her up. She's in desperate need of some swordplay herself."

"Tasha!"

Tasha grinned, shrugged. "Just speaking my truth."

Noah looked over at Kelsey.

She sat so contained, so proper. Spine straight. Shoulders back. Her blond hair braided in that long, restrained braid. She wore a high-necked white blouse with all the buttons done up underneath a simple gray cardigan, black designer-label slacks.

He ached to ruffle her up, turn her back into the adventuresome young woman who'd once sneaked away to meet him on the dock.

Firefly, he thought. *You light up my world.*

She was the first woman he'd been interested in since his divorce. Kelsey supercharged him, but the timing was all wrong. She was stinging from getting stood up at the altar and the last thing he wanted was to be her rebound man.

She tilted her head and met his gaze, a slight smile tugging at her lips and it felt like Christmas morning when he ripped open the packages and found absolutely everything he'd wished for.

"What should we order?" Kelsey studied the menu.

"Here's the thing," said Samantha. "It's basically all the same. You pick the items from the list on this side"—she leaned over to run a finger down Kelsey's menu—"that you want to dunk in cheese, and on the opposite side, you pick the kind of cheeses you want to melt. My fave is the nutmeg-infused Gruyère paired with lamb."

"That's quite helpful," Kelsey said. "Thank you."

"I'll get you guys started with some drinks," Samantha said. "What'll you have?"

"Beer," Sean and Tasha said simultaneously, then looked at each other and laughed.

"What kind?" Samantha asked.

In unison, Tasha and Sean said, "Whatever is on tap."

"I'll have iced tea, unsweet," Kelsey said.

"You don't want an adult beverage?" Noah asked.

She shook her head. "I want to keep my wits about me."

Hmm, what did that mean? "I'll have the same," Noah told Samantha, "but make mine sweet tea."

"Well, I see who's going to be the life of this party." Samantha nodded at Tasha and Sean, who were busy peering into each other's eyes. "I'll get your drinks and be right back to take your food order."

The conversation lagged, and Noah had a feeling that Tasha and Sean were playing footsie underneath the table.

Those two were in their own little world, and the awkward silence was back between him and Kelsey.

"How long has this place been here?" Kelsey asked, grasping at conversational straws. "Looks like it's the happening place in town."

"A couple of months," Noah said.

It was six P.M. on a Monday, and the place was filling up with families. Dads in jeans and Stetsons, coming in off the local ranches. Or the chinos and collared shirts of office workers or small business owners. Moms in skirts or slacks and yoga pants. Kids with backpacks and electronic devices. People greeted one another. Raised hands and hearty voices. Shoulder claps and handshakes. Folks in Twilight talked slow and moved slower. People congregated near the door, visiting, catching up, touching base.

How's your mom after her surgery?

Did you get the text I sent about the toy drive?

Congratulations to little Billy for winning the spelling bee.

Hey, I heard your car is in the shop. Do you need a ride to work tomorrow?

Twilight. Communal. Gossipy. Bighearted. Noah loved his hometown.

He knew without having to ask that this was a far cry from Kelsey's monied world of political glad-handing and campaign fund galas. What did she really think of Twilight? Did she find it quaint and amusing? Or hopelessly backwater and old-fashioned? Would she ever consider living in a place like this?

Whoa there. Slow down. Gotta cut thoughts like that off at the knees.

"Ooh." Kelsey nudged him with an elbow and nodded to a fir tree in the corner. "I just now noticed that Christmas tree is decorated with Swiss Army ornaments."

"The restaurant is donating real Swiss Army knives as prizes for our Christmas Casino event." His side felt tingly where her elbow had prodded him, and he caught a whiff of her hair, which smelled like strawberries.

"Fun! What are some of the other prizes?"

"The mattress store is donating memory foam pillows."

"Comfy." She hugged herself. "I adore memory foam. Who knows, maybe I'll win one. Although I've never really gambled before."

"You are *such* a comfort kitty." Tasha gave Kelsey a meaningful look.

"What's that?" Noah asked.

"She loves her creature comforts. Give her books, a bubble bath, and a cup of hot tea and she's in heaven."

"Really?" Noah said, trying hard not to imagine Kelsey lounging naked in a sudsy tub, her long hair pinned to the top of her head, reading glasses on the end of her nose, book in hand. The song "Hot for Teacher" ran through his head. He slid a glance at Kelsey. "What's your favorite tea?"

Kelsey's cheeks turned pink. "I like a lot of different varieties."

"Tell the truth," Tasha popped off. "Her favorite is passion tea. That's because tea is the only place she gets any—*ow!* Why did you kick me?"

Kelsey smirked. "Oh, did I kick you? I'm so sorry. I was just moving my foot."

Noah hid his grin behind his hand. Kelsey might come off as straightlaced on the surface, but underneath, fire lurked. She'd just been suppressing it for so long, she'd forgotten it was there.

"So." Noah propped his elbow on the table and his chin in his upturned palm and gave his full attention to Kelsey. "What do you like about passion tea?"

"I like mint tea too. And chamomile."

"But they aren't your favorite. What is it about passion?"

She shot him a stare that said she wished he'd stop saying *passion*. "The tea is healthy and caffeine free."

Tasha exaggerated putting her palm over a big fake yawn.

"The brand I like comes in the prettiest pink packaging." Her face brightened. "It's made from hibiscus flower—"

"FYI," Tasha interrupted. "Kels has always wanted to go to Hawaii, but Filomena says it's too full of tourists."

Kelsey crossed her eyes at Tasha.

"Oops, sorry. I have a big mouth." Tasha pantomimed locking her lips with a key and tossing the key over her shoulder.

"You were saying about the tea . . ." Noah nudged. He didn't give two shakes about tea, but what he did care about was what made Kelsey happy. If that was tea, then he wanted to know all about it.

"No one wants to hear of my love for tea." Kelsey waved a hand. "Oh look, here is Samantha with our drinks."

She reached over to take the tea glass Samantha offered, and Kelsey's thigh brushed against Noah's. He could feel her body heat radiating through the layers of their clothes and seeping into his skin.

He enjoyed the contact, and his body responded, instantly stirring in a masculine way and making him glad that he was sitting down with a napkin over his lap.

"Put frozen peas on that," Samantha said and for a wild second he thought she was talking about what was going on inside his jeans.

Your eye, goober. She means your eye. "Um, already did. Thanks for the tip."

Samantha took their food orders and disappeared again.

"Hey, little brother."

Noah looked up to see his sister Flynn standing beside the table. "What are you doing here?"

Flynn held up a to-go bag. "I was checking out and saw you guys over here."

"To-go fondue? Dining in *is* the experience," Noah said.

"I have a microwave." Flynn seemed like she was up to something.

"You remember Kelsey." Noah put his arm around Kelsey's shoulder.

Flynn's smile tightened. "Yes, hi, good to see you again," she said on one long breath.

"This is her friend, Tasha," Noah said.

Tasha wriggled her fingers. "Hi. Love your hair."

Flynn had long naturally curly hair that fell in corkscrews about her shoulders. "Thanks." She gave Tasha the same cool smile she'd directed at Kelsey, then turned her attention back to Noah. "Could I speak to you a minute?"

"Sure. Shoot."

"In private."

"Okay." Noah measured out his tone, put his napkin on the table, and followed his sister, who led him out the side door and into the alley.

The harsh wind whipped between the buildings, coming off the lake with chilling force, but his sister seemed oblivious. He recognized the crusading look on her face. She was on a mission.

"What is it?" he asked, not even trying to cloak his irritation.

She clutched the fondue take-out bag to her chest. "What are you doing?"

"Excuse me?" He hunched his shoulders against the cold.

"Messing around with Kelsey James."

"I'm not messing around."

"Don't tell me you're seriously going down that road again."

"What bee crawled in your bonnet, sister?"

"She's going to hurt you just like before." Flynn leaned in, glowered at his face. "It looks like she already has. Noah, you know her mother could destroy you."

"Kelsey didn't do this."

"No, but her mother's thugs did."

"Where did you hear that?" He hadn't told anyone but Sean what had really happened to his face, and the SEAL was not a gossip. But this was Twilight. Things had a way of getting out, and Raylene had big ears and an even bigger mouth. Raylene could have eavesdropped on his conversation with Sean.

"I dropped off some donations at the *Rockabye* for your toy drive—"

"So, the take-out is a charade?"

Flynn tightened her grip on the bag. "I've been meaning to try this place and I didn't feel like cooking tonight—"

"And Raylene told you we'd be here . . ."

Hardening her chin, Flynn shrugged. "You can't blame me for worrying about you, Noah. You were crushed when Kelsey disappeared on you the last time."

"I was seventeen. I don't need you to clean up my messes anymore."

"So, you admit this is a mess?"

Noah huddled, shivered, wished he had his coat. "While I appreciate your concern, dear sister, who I date is none of your damn business."

"Then you *are* dating her."

"She's a guest at my boatel and I'm taking her out to dinner."

"That's it?"

"For now."

"Noah—"

"Flynn, I mean this in the nicest way, butt out."

Her eyes widened as he continued.

"Go home to your family. Microwave your fondue and have a nice night." Surprised by the anger spurting through him, he pivoted on his heel and started back into the restaurant. Noah rarely got mad, especially with Flynn. She'd pretty much raised him and Joel.

"I won't be there to pick up the pieces for you like last time," she called after him.

"That's fine. I'm not seventeen anymore, *sister*. And I'm no longer your worry."

"Noah, I'm sorry, okay." She shifted gears, wheedled. "I worry."

"Sounds like a personal problem to me," he said and closed the door behind him.

He had to stand in the hallway a moment to compose himself. It took several deep breaths to calm down before he returned to the table with a smile.

The food had arrived, the black fondue pot simmering with cheese. Meats, cubed bread, and veggies were arrayed on a tray in front of his friends. He didn't dare meet Kelsey's gaze in case she read the upset in his eyes.

All the fun was sucked out of the evening.

Thanks a lot, Flynn.

This was what he did not like about his hometown. How family and friends felt free to meddle in his business.

He slid into the booth beside Kelsey.

"Are you okay?" Kelsey rested a hand on his thigh. Her touch jolted him like an electrical shock.

His nerves were shot. His muscles wiredrawn. "Yes, fine." His voice squeaked out an octave higher than normal.

Holy guacamole, he was in trouble.

It wasn't just Kelsey's hot body or her gorgeous blond hair that got to him. It wasn't the orgasmic look on her face when she talked about passion tea. It wasn't the amazing way she smelled or the way her eye jumped when she got anxious—like now. It wasn't because she was a creature of comfort who liked memory foam pillows and warm bubble baths and good books.

All right, it *was* all those things, but it was so much more. It was their past and the cherished memories he had of her. It was the sound of her voice and the look in her eyes whenever she smiled at him. It was the taste of her kisses and the flavor of his hopes.

One thing was clear. If he kept up hanging out with her, things were going to get serious.

And he just didn't know if he was ready for that. Maybe it was time to call the whole thing quits.

CHAPTER 18

Kelsey was no dummy. Flynn's curt greeting and Noah's anger when he returned to the table made her realize she was a bone of contention between brother and sister.

Kudos to Tasha, who picked up on the vibe and tried to save the evening with a lively game of Never Have I Ever, but it backfired miserably.

While they noshed on fondue, Tasha cajoled Noah and Kelsey into playing the drinking game, ordered a pitcher of beer and two extra mugs.

"Here's the rules," Tasha said. "Whoever goes first gives a simple statement about something they've never done, by starting with 'never have I ever.' Anyone who has at some point in their lives done that thing must take a drink. I'll go first. Never have I ever injured myself trying to impress someone I was interested in."

Noah looked at Kelsey. "Would you call last night trying to impress you or rescue you?"

"The eye is pretty impressive," Kelsey ventured, unable to gauge his mood. He still seemed disgruntled. Was he mad at her or was it residual fallout from his argument with his sister? She'd seen them outside the window and he'd looked pretty pissed. "And I didn't need rescuing. I could have handled the situation in a less violent way."

Noah grimaced, nodded, and took a long drink of his beer.

Definitely still pissed.

Sean took a drink as well.

"Ah," Tasha said to Sean. "What did you do to injure yourself while trying to impress a girl?"

Sean flashed Tasha a sultry look. "Pulled a groin muscle last night."

"Poor baby." She touched his shoulder. "Why didn't you tell me?"

"I am a SEAL. I learned a long time ago to get comfortable with uncomfortable." Sean rolled up his sleeve to show off his tattoo.

Tasha squeezed his biceps and sighed longingly. Sean grinned and ruffled her hair. "We're going counterclockwise. Your turn, Kels."

Kelsey locked eyes with her friend. "Never have I ever pushed someone out of their comfort zone."

Noah cleared his throat. Loudly.

Kelsey shifted her gaze to him. "Yes?"

"Not true."

"Are you saying I've pushed you out of your comfort zone?"

"Every time I'm around you." His eyes drilled into her and she couldn't tell if he considered that a good thing or not.

"In what way?" Kelsey's stupid eye muscle started its jerky dance.

"In every way."

"Are you saying you don't want me at *Rockabye*?" Her stomach knotted. Noah didn't want her.

"I've pushed people out of their comfort zone. I do it all the time. I should take two drinks for that." Tasha hoisted her glass.

"Me too. Comfort zone pushing is my thing." Sean raised his mug, clinked beers with Tasha and they each took a big gulp.

"You're pushing me right now," Noah murmured, his gaze drilling Kelsey to the spot.

"By asking you a question?"

"By suggesting that I want you to leave the *Rockabye*."

"Do you?"

His gaze was a steel trap, holding her hostage. "Do you want to leave?"

"You know what? I don't think I pushed you out of your comfort zone. I think your sister did and you're taking it out on me."

"Noah," Tasha said. "It's your turn. Never have you ever—"

"Never have I ever spent so much of my life pleasing people that don't even know who I am, or what I want out of life." Noah's tone was barbed.

Kelsey gasped, indignation bouncing through her like a bullet. "I don't believe you just said that to me."

"Just playing a game." Noah's tone was neutral, but she heard the spikes beneath it.

"You gotta take a drink on that one, Kels," Tasha said.

She whipped her head around to gape at her best friend. *"Et tu?"*

Tasha pulled one side of her mouth down in a the-truth-hurts expression. "He's got a point . . ."

Sean drummed his fingers on the table. "Maybe this game wasn't such a hot idea."

"Hey." Tasha squeezed Sean's biceps again. "I thought you were comfortable with uncomfortable."

Kelsey wagged a finger at Noah. "You're still holding a grudge because I didn't contact you after my mother dragged me away."

Noah raised his palms. "Maybe I am."

Stunned, Kelsey sank her top teeth into her bottom lip, put a hand to her throat. He'd gone for her most vulnerable spot, which wasn't like him, or at least not like the Noah she'd known ten years ago. What in the world had Flynn said to him?

Noah's eyes softened, and he held up both palms, a gesture of surrender. "I was out of line. I shouldn't have said that."

"I think I've had enough fun for one evening," Kelsey said, still stinging from Noah's comment. It hurt because it was true. "I'm going to walk back."

"I'll drive you," Noah said. "You're not walking the streets alone. Not after last night."

"I'll take a pedicab."

"You two go on," Sean said, resting a hand across Tasha's shoulder. "We'll finish the fondue and pick up the check."

Kelsey telegraphed Tasha a look that said *leave with me now.*

Tasha pretended to be deeply engrossed in spearing a piece of steak and rolling it in melted cheese.

Noah stood up, extended his hand. "Kelsey?"

What else could she do? Falling back on her people-pleasing ways because she was uncomfortable with fighting in public, damn her. She accepted his hand and let him help her on with her coat.

Five minutes later, they were sitting in his truck, staring at each other.

"You know the best thing about having a fight?" Noah asked her.

"Clearing the air?"

"No." He gave her his most charming grin. "Kissing and making up."

"I'm a butthead," Noah said contritely. "You were right. I was ticked at Flynn and I took it out on you."

"And I was hypersensitive. I know I take things too much to heart. It's a flaw of mine."

"Is it a flaw? Or is it a reaction to the criticism your mother dishes out?"

"Does it matter? I need to work on toughening my skin, especially in intimate relationships."

"Are we in an intimate relationship?" Noah asked.

Kelsey licked her lips. Noah's gaze tracked her tongue. "I'd like to be intimate with you."

"There's nothing I'd like better, Firefly."

Noah studied her profile. She was class all the way and that was the part that made him stumble. He was from humble beginnings. His NBA success was far behind him. Now, he'd never be more than a regular guy from Twilight. He could offer her his undying love, this quirky community, and a comfortable but modest lifestyle by her standards.

She was part of the world's elite one percent. A wealthy family pedigree that stretched back generations. She could travel when and wherever she wanted. He'd made a little dough, sure. But it was all invested in his business. A business that tied him down. He had no flexibility. Hadn't really wanted any. Now, all he could think about was all the things he could not give her.

"But right now," she said, "I'm kind of a mess emotionally."

"That's okay. I'm not asking for any big lifetime commitment or anything."

"Oh wow, whew." She dragged the back of her hand across her forehead. "You don't know how relieved that makes me."

"So we're talking . . . what?"

"A no-strings fling?" She set her teeth, eyes widening. "Would you be okay with that?"

He wanted more, but he would take what he could get.

"I'd kind of like to finish what we started that night on the dock ten years ago."

"Me too," he said, unsure of what he was feeling, but his body knew what the hell it wanted—*Kelsey*.

In the parking garage at the marina, Noah pulled Kelsey into his lap and she ran her palm up under his shirt and things got really steamy really quickly.

"Oh, God. I can't wait to get you in bed."

"I've been thinking," he said, removing his hot lips from her neck. "Maybe we should slow things down."

"What do you mean?" Panic flared inside her. Was he bailing out already?

"I want to enjoy every minute of our time together. Why don't we focus on that tonight instead of going straight for the kill?"

"What are you saying, Noah? You don't want to make love to me after all?"

"I'm just saying wait a few days . . . build the anticipation."

"All right," she agreed. "But you owe me something really fun to make up for the slow burn."

"Done," he said. "How about I make this a Christmas to remember? We'll do all the kitschy Christmas things there are to do in Twilight."

"You know I'm not a fan of Christmas."

"Exactly."

"You plan on turning me into a holiday lover?"

"I want to show you Christmas through my eyes."

It wasn't that she truly *hated* Christmas. It was just all so overwhelming. The crush of parties she never wanted to attend in the first place, but Mom's career always came first. Glad-handing and forced smiling a must. So much rushing around. And for what? Buying expensive gifts for a mother who'd turn her nose up at them and ask why it wasn't more, wasn't better.

And on one hand, Filomena would buy Kelsey the gifts that she wanted for herself—designer clothing in bold colors, ostentatious jewelry, heavy baroque furniture. Or on the other hand, she'd buy Kelsey things she didn't need: a KitchenAid mixer, a sewing machine, snow skis.

When Kelsey was twenty-one, she set herself the task of finding that perfect gift that would at last please Filomena. She scrimped and saved. Skipped lunches and nights out with her friends. Pooled her tax return money and cashed in her vacation savings fund and dipped into her inheritance from her paternal grandmother.

She'd bought her mother one of those extravagant fantasy gifts from the Neiman Marcus catalogue. It was pricy, it was prestigious, it was precious. One of a kind.

Meeting all of Filomena's criteria for the appropriate gifts for her.

A perfume created by a master French perfumer, exclusively for Filomena. And it cost twenty-five thousand dollars. It was the loveliest perfume that Kelsey had ever smelled.

Theo had proclaimed the perfume a perfect hole in one. "If this perfume were golf clubs it would be Callaway."

"That's good?"

"The best."

"But do you think she'll like it?" Kelsey had asked her father.

"I don't know, you know how she is. Don't get your hopes up too high, Kels."

But Kelsey had been so excited for Christmas Eve when they traditionally opened gifts in the James household. She'd plopped the gorgeously wrapped package in her mother's lap, danced around on happy toes, clasped her hands to her chest and cried, "Open it, open it."

Filomena had made a big show of unwrapping the ribbon, saying, "Oh my, what could it be that's got you so fired up?"

Kelsey held her breath as her mother took the perfume from the box.

"*Filomena*." She read the name etched into the crystal bottle, and then the caption underneath. "A perfume of unbearable loveliness."

"I had it made just for you," Kelsey squealed. "From the Neiman Marcus fantasy catalogue. It's by famed French perfumer Luca Alméras. It's unique. No one else in the entire world will ever have this perfume."

Filomena had spritzed a bit on her wrist, sniffed. Turned up her nose. "It has clary sage in it."

"I don't think so," Kelsey said.

"I have a very sensitive sense of smell." Her mother gave a haughty toss of her head. "There's clary sage in this and I'm allergic to clary sage."

"It's not on the ingredients list. I was given the formula so that it could be replicated in the future. It's there in the bottom of the box on a rolled parchment scroll."

Filomena had pulled up her spine and leveled Kelsey a hard glare. "Are you calling me a liar?"

"Not at all, Mom. I'm saying it's not on the ingredients list. I just wanted to give you a nice gift for Christmas."

"Well, if you bought it from the Neiman's catalogue, I know you spent too much," Filomena had said, putting the perfume bottle aside. "What else did you get me?"

The unused bottle of *Filomena* perfume still set on her mother's dresser, as a mockery of Kelsey's stupid hopefulness.

Later, her father had pulled her aside and urged her to stop trying so hard. "No matter what you do, Filomena will always find fault with it. That's the one thing you can count on with your mother." Each year, he bought Filomena a bottle of her favorite expensive scotch for Christmas because that way, at least he knew it would get used.

After that, Kelsey followed his lead and each year got Mom a bottle of Pappy Van Winkle bourbon. Which Filomena promptly gave to some top-tier campaign contributor, but it was the thought that counted, right?

With a start, Kelsey realized that the perfume fiasco was when her ambivalence toward Christmas had turned into downright dislike. If she could have skipped from Thanksgiving to New Year's each year, she would gladly give up those weeks of her life.

But now here, with Noah, whole new vistas were opening up. What if she was actually able to enjoy Christmas for once? It was a giddy thought.

Don't get your hopes up.

But it was so hard not to as they rode up to the *Rockabye* in the golf cart, the festive lights twinkling and changing in time to the music.

They went inside to find Raylene putting on her coat. "I'm out of here," she said. "All the guests are still out. I just put another log on the fire and I put out the dessert tray and loaded up the coffeemaker if anyone wants a cup when they get back."

"Thanks," Noah said.

Once Raylene was gone, Kelsey turned toward him. "Are we still kissing and making up?"

"Oh yeah," he said, and gathered her close for a long kiss.

He scooped her up in his big strong arms and carried her to his room. He didn't even set her down to open the door. Just cradled her against him while he expertly twisted the knob with his hand and carried her over the threshold into the bedroom illuminated only with the glow of Christmas lights dangling above the headboard.

Those lights, his bed, made her fall in love with Christmas just a little. His holiday whimsy was touching.

Noah settled her down onto the mattress.

Overwhelmed, she reached out to trace his face with her fingertips. Was she really here with him? The man she'd loved with all her heart and soul when she was seventeen? That was a dangerous thought.

She was different. He was different. The past was a link to those old emotions that could wreck them both in their current lives.

Wildly, impulsively, Kelsey didn't care because his mouth merged with hers once more.

Noah stayed standing on the floor, leaning over her. He tasted so good. She laughed, and he deepened the kiss. His hot lips kinetic and pliable.

A fever fired through her. Turbocharging her lust.

She drank him in like eggnog on Christmas Eve, in quick, eager gulps. Tangled her arms around his neck, pulled him down on top of her.

Kelsey hadn't had a lot of sex in her life. There had been the eighteen-month "no sex" interlude with Clive. His kisses had been warm and mild, nothing like this relentless, rampant heat.

She'd had a boyfriend in college. It lasted a year and ended when he'd gotten a job in London. No hard feelings. No real heartbreak. They'd just been on separate paths. She'd had a couple of casual things between college and Clive. Nothing serious. No one had turned her upside down and inside out like Noah.

Noah's arms slipped to her pelvis, his weight sank into the mattress as he rolled onto his side, and he moved her so that he could fold her close to his body.

In that precious moment, his warmth leaking into her, she felt safer than she'd ever felt in her life.

For a moment, he simply held her like that and all was wonderful.

Okay, yeah, her body was throbbing with need. How could it not when he was pressed so close against her and she could feel his erection poking her through his jeans?

But it was a special moment as he stared into her eyes and smiled at her like he'd just opened the best Christmas present he'd ever gotten in his life, and gently brushed a strand of hair from her face.

"I need you to do something for me," he said.

What's that? she wondered. Was he about to ask her to do something kinky? That thought both intrigued her and scared her a bit. "Yes?"

"I want you to lie back, relax, and let me take care of everything."

"Um . . ." Now she really *was* nervous. "What do you mean?"

He rearranged her, so that she was on her back again, her head cradled by the pillow while he slid down the length of her body and ended up kneeling on the floor at the end of the mattress.

She propped herself up on her elbows, studied him. "What are you up to?"

He gave her a wicked smile.

Kelsey caught her breath, felt her toes curl involuntarily inside her ankle boots. Felt her eye muscle twitch. Oh no, not that stupid tic.

"Relax," he said. "Let go and let Noah."

"Are you about to do what I think you're about to do?"

"Blow your mind? Oh yes, Firefly."

Kelsey gulped. "Um . . . I don't know if I'm comfortable with that."

Surprise lifted his eyebrows. "You don't like oral sex?"

"I've never . . ." This was embarrassing to admit. "I've never been lucky enough to have anyone do that for me."

"Well, darlin'." His eyes lowered, and that devious smile lit up his entire face. "I'd say your luck just took a turn for the better. Now shh, shh . . . *relax*."

Yeah, that wasn't so easy.

He took off her boots and let them drop to the floor. Then he took hold of her hips with both hands and dragged her to the edge of the mattress, positioning her right in front of where he was kneeling. Noah slipped his hands up her skirt, took hold of the waistband of her leggings and eased them down her legs.

Her body tensed.

"Let go," he crooned as he whisked off her panties along with the leggings and the next thing she knew his hot mouth was on her.

Kelsey squirmed. She was embarrassed.

He was tender. Stroking slow and easy.

She gasped and finally sank down into the mattress and she gave up all control. Noah was in charge and holy freaking Fireball whiskey, did that man know how to use his tongue. She allowed herself to get lost in his mouth and what he was doing to her.

He increased the pressure.

She wriggled her hips to let him know she liked it just like that. Wave after wave of pleasure rolled over her, rippling, growing. His touch made her tremble and she was completely unprepared for her body's hot-blooded response. He was dismantling her cool exterior. Exposing her to all kinds of wild, frantic thoughts and feelings.

As things escalated, she lifted her hips, pressing herself forward, anxious for more of his wonderful mouth. More licks from that powerful tongue.

He manipulated her with such ease. Showed her pleasure centers she'd never known existed inside of her.

She moaned and writhed. Twitched and quivered. She was close, so very close, to the orgasm she'd never had with a partner. To date, she'd only been able to come when flying solo. She wadded the sheets in her fists. Bucked against him.

Then the audacious man slipped his finger inside her and he went at her with both digits and thumbs. He caressed the blazing core of her and she mewled like a helpless kitten.

The sensations rocketed her to a dizzying height. He was more than she could take. Where had he learned these tricks?

And then . . . *detonation.*

Pleasure blew up inside Kelsey in hard, shattering jolts.

Gone. She was out of her mind and fully, completely inside her body. Everything was raw and achy and filled with the most exquisite pleasure.

Oh! She could get so addicted to this. To Noah. And his magical tongue.

He climbed up on the bed beside her. Took her in his arms and squeezed her tight. That's when a buzzer sounded.

"What's that?" she whispered, curling tighter against him.

Noah sighed. "There's a guest at the front desk. Sorry, Firefly. I had other plans for this moment, but an innkeeper's work is never done."

"I had plans for you too."

"Oh yeah?" His eyes glistened in the twinking lights. "Like what?"

"You'll just have to wait until next time to find out . . . now, go tend to your guests." With that, she stood on shaky legs and got dressed.

CHAPTER 19

An hour later, the key slipped into the lock and Tasha stumbled into their suite at the *Rockabye*. She was tipsy and flipped the overhead light on without thinking.

Blinking, Kelsey sat up in bed and peered blearily at the clock. A few minutes after midnight. "You're back already? I didn't expect you until the wee hours . . . if at all."

"I blew it." Tasha groaned and fell backward onto the bedroom sofa.

"Um . . . do I dare ask what it was you blew?"

"My chances with Sean," she announced gloomily.

"What happened?"

"He told me that he wanted to slow things down." She slapped her palm over her eyes. "That last night we'd jumped the gun by having sex too soon. I tried to convince him otherwise, but he said no."

"He turned you down for sex?"

"Yep. Get this. He wants a *meaningful* relationship."

"And you don't?"

"Dude, I'm just off a three-year, tilt-a-whirl with Tag. I don't want to climb back on another amusement park ride. Well, I *do*, but I want a weekend pass, not season tickets."

"Hey, at least Sean let you know up front where he's coming from. You have to appreciate his integrity."

"Integrity-schmegrity," she grumbled. "I was primed for hot sex and I got squat."

"I'm sorry," Kelsey said, trying to sound properly sympathetic. "Maybe it was just the pulled groin muscle talking. Maybe he's not as comfortable with uncomfortable as he likes to pretend."

"No, you're not sorry. You think it's funny."

"Well, it *is* a little amusing. Big, sexy former navy SEAL just wants to snuggle-wuggle."

Tasha blew a raspberry. "That's the most action my tongue is seeing tonight. I know I sound dramatic, but this is dire." Tasha sat up and clutched a couch pillow to her chest. "It's been a really long time since I've been *this* hot for a guy."

Kelsey knew what she meant. She was feeling the same way about Noah. "The feeling will blow over," she said, more to herself than to Tasha.

"Will it, Kels? Will it really?"

"Look, we don't have to stay here. We can call an Uber right now and go home."

Tasha narrowed her eyes. "Is that what you want to do?"

Did she? Kelsey thought about her mother. No. She was not ready to face Filomena just yet. She wasn't done finding out who she was or what she really wanted out of life. But let's be honest, was she really going to find that here in Twilight between now and Christmas?

"If we stay . . ." Tasha picked a thread on the sleeve of her sweater. "Maybe I could wear Sean down. Get him to understand that a fast pass is better than no pass."

"On the other hand, you might end up unraveling yourself the way you're unraveling that sweater." Kelsey nodded as the thread Tasha was tugging on kept growing longer and longer.

Tasha stopped pulling the thread and lifted her sleeve to her face to bite it off with her teeth.

"I brought scissors."

"Of course, you did, Girl Scout."

"What do you mean by that?"

"Always prepared for anything. Always following the rules."

"I don't *always* follow the rules."

"Name one time you broke them?"

Kelsey poked her tongue against the inside of her cheek, pondered that. "I parked in a loading zone once. I was late picking Filomena up at the airport, so I just parked right in that loading zone."

Tasha rolled her eyes, rubbed her teeth over the thread. "That was self-preservation, not a serious intent to flaunt the rules."

"Here," Kelsey said, unable to watch Tasha try to gnaw the thread in two. "I'll be right back with the scissors."

"Stay put. I'd rather chew it off. I'm in that kind of a mood."

"Sean doesn't know what he's missing." Kelsey laughed.

"You got that right. Stupid, gorgeous man." The thread snapped. "Ha! Got it."

"The cuff of your sleeve is half-gone."

"Eeh." Tasha shrugged. "I don't like this sweater anymore, anyway. It'll forever remind me of the night Sean turned me down for sex."

"You're taking this kind of hard."

"No harder than you. Why are you here in bed alone instead of with *your* hottie? Did you two not make up?"

"A guest interrupted—"

"And you didn't wait?"

"It wasn't like that."

"Oh no?" Tasha lifted an eyebrow. "Face it. You play it safe the way you always do."

"There's a flaw in your theory," Kelsey pointed out.

"What's that?"

"You didn't play it safe and you're here with me and not in Sean's bed."

Tasha waved a dismissive hand. "That's different."

"Why?"

"Sean said he'd love to be with me, but only if I wanted to go steady."

"Did he actually say, 'go steady'?"

Tasha blew another raspberry. "Not in so many words, but that was the upshot. You, on the other hand, *want* something meaningful."

"Says who?"

"Oh please, you were willing to wed Clive so you wouldn't be alone. You *want* a relationship."

"I didn't know Clive was gay."

"Honey, you need glasses. Big thick ones. That ceiling fan up there could tell Clive was gay."

"Why didn't *you* tell me he was gay?"

"How was I supposed to break that news without ruining our friendship?"

For sure. Kelsey was pretty talented at believing the best in everyone and seeing only what she wanted to see. How else could she work as her mother's campaign manager?

"So." Tasha rubbed her palms together. "Did you two kiss and make up?"

Kelsey ducked her head to hide her smile. "Yes. We did do some serious making up tonight."

"How serious?"

"We're going to do Christmassy things around town this week."

"Deets. Since I'm not getting any myself, I need to live through you vicariously."

She intended on playing it cool, but the memory of the kisses they'd shared had imprinted on her tongue, and what had happened in his bedroom, whew! She giggled like a teenager. "It was amazing."

"As good as ten years ago?"

"Better."

"C'mon. I'm dying here. Spill it."

"Well . . ." Kelsey clasped her fingers. "When we were kids we were fumbling and frantic, spilling over with hormones. Now, Noah is so controlled, and he knows exactly what he's doing." Kelsey lowered her voice.

Tasha gave an exaggerated shiver. "I've got goose bumps. I'm so happy for you."

"I'm just having fun. Don't blow it up to be something big. I'm on the rebound and very aware of it."

"From a guy you were never in love with."

"I loved Clive."

"But not in the right way."

"What is the right way to love someone?" Kelsey asked.

"With all your heart and soul."

"The way you loved Tag?"

Tasha glowered. "You can hush now."

"I'm just saying it cuts both ways."

"And I'm saying I'm happy you've decided to give Christmas—and Noah—a chance."

"It's Noah more than Christmas. You know me, Tash. I've never been a magical thinking kind of gal."

"That's a bit sad when you think about it. Where's the whimsy? Where's the fun? Look what being all practical and stuffed-shirted got you. Working for your mother. Gak. Engaged to a gay man. Your whole life filled with routine and precision. Nothing ever breaking the monotony, not even in your daydreams."

"I've got you to add spice to my life," Kelsey said. "Besides, you make it sound awful and it's not. I'm good at what I do. Yes, my mother is a challenge, but that also keeps things interesting. I don't need sparkle and razzmatazz to feel alive. I like a cup of hot tea and a good book before I go to sleep every night. It's not glitzy or fancy, but it's me."

"Is it really? Or are you just comfortable with settling and terrified to let your passions off the leash? Deep down, are you secretly afraid that if you fully embrace the wild and messy side of life that you won't ever be able to go back to the way things were?"

Ha! Little did Tasha know . . .

Kelsey paused, and a shiver of fear ran through her. "What I'm worried about is getting sucked into a fantasy world and then real life will pale by comparison. That's why I dislike Christmas. It sets up unrealistic expectations. Some kindly old guy flying a sleigh at night to brings toys to good little boys and girls in the world." She snorted. "Manipulative hogwash."

"I wonder if Noah has any idea what he's getting himself into with you, Grincharina. You're a hard-core case, my friend."

"Not hard. Just realistic. Down-to-earth."

"Hmm," Tasha said. "Maybe you should hook up with Sean and leave Noah to me. That man is looking for a ball and chain."

"Maybe Sean just wants his own happily-ever-after."

"Now *that's* magical thinking."

"You don't believe people can be happy together for life?"

"And you think Santa is a hard sell?" Tasha shook her head. "That happily-ever-after stuff is for saps."

"Now who's being Grincharina?"

"What are your plans with Noah? Rekindle old flames. Fall madly in love. Who is living in a fantasy now?"

Kelsey sighed. She hated to admit it, but Tasha was right. Filomena would throw a hissy fit if she hooked up with Noah.

All the more reason to do it, whispered a subversive voice in the back of her mind.

"You know what you ought to do?"

Kelsey was almost afraid to ask. "What's that?"

"Something that symbolizes you're taking charge of your life, like getting inked. What about a firefly tattoo, since Noah keeps calling you that, right here on your shoulder." Tasha touched her own shoulder to demonstrate where Kelsey should get a tattoo.

"I'm *not* getting inked."

"That was just an example," Tasha said. "But if you did something that represents throwing off your old life, it might loosen those manacles Filomena's got you wrapped up in."

"For example?"

Tasha lifted a shoulder. "I dunno. Maybe cut off that Rapunzel hair."

Kelsey fingered her long braid and twisted it around her hand. "Beyond trims, I haven't cut my hair since Chelsea died."

Tasha's eyes met hers. "Exactly. You're still holding on to your sister. And holding on to her is binding you to your mom. Cutting your hair is symbolically clipping the ties that bind."

"That seems pretty drastic." Kelsey twisted her braid around her finger.

"It's just hair. You could always grow it back if you hated it."

She felt the resistance rise up in her hard and solid as concrete. Her hair was her security blanket. Her attachment to her twin.

All the more reason to cut it. Set yourself free.

She undid the band at the end of her braid, felt her hair tumble around her like a curtain as it fell below her waist.

"You know," Tasha mused. "You haven't once asked me for your phone back. I expected you to pester me all day."

"Honestly, I got so caught up in helping decorate the gazebo, the contest judging, and hanging out with our guys, I forgot about it."

"I think this means you're ready for another dare." Tasha steepled her fingers.

"The fourth one? So soon?"

"The time seems right."

"Let's hear it."

"I dare you to get a total makeover, starting with a new haircut. We can cut it now, symbolically, then you can go to a salon tomorrow and get it done right. We'll get you a sexy new outfit to wear to that casino thingy and we'll hit the makeup counter for some up-to-date tips and techniques. I saw a Sephora when we came into town."

Kelsey still wasn't sure about cutting her hair, but a makeover might be fun.

"Do it, do it," Tasha challenged. "Go get your scissors, Girl Scout, and I'll lop off those locks and set you free."

CHAPTER 20

The hair salon came first.

The chatty stylist turned Tasha's amateur cutting job into long sleek layers that framed Kelsey's face, and added honey-colored highlights for depth. Kelsey couldn't believe the difference. She looked—and felt—like a brand-new version of herself.

Then they hit the makeup counter at Sephora and the makeup artist showed her how to deftly create a smoky eye. Kelsey bought all the products needed for her transformation.

Next came the boutiques where Tasha gave two thumbs-up to a red velvet ankle-length gown for the black-tie Christmas Casino event on Friday night. The dress had a stylish low-cut bodice and a long slit up the front of one leg that revealed her upper thigh when she walked. Very sexy. Filomena would have disapproved.

Kelsey, however, loved the dress and bought it along with a pair of black four-inch stilettoes with bright red soles.

She bought other clothes as well to complete her metamorphosis. Clothing she would normally never wear. Low-cut blouses, short flirty skirts, leather pants, thigh-high black boots. She felt sexy and wild. The kind of woman who had romantic sexual liaisons, enjoyed herself, and never experienced a drop of guilt over it.

The stores buzzed with activity and she caught snatches of down-home conversations she would never hear in Dallas. Crappie were biting something fierce in Sanchez Creek. Some rowdy kids had smuggled a longhorn into the high school and left a mighty mess for Principal Bullock. The most popular B&B in town, the Merry Cherub, was completely booked up throughout the entire holiday season, except for the presidential suite of course, because who could afford that?

Kelsey took it all in, remembering how much she'd enjoyed visiting this quaint small town each summer, and felt a stab of nostalgia. She had treasured those two months every year, and until now hadn't fully realized how much she'd missed Twilight.

They grabbed lunch at a sandwich shop and while they were eating, Tasha's phone dinged with a text notification. She frowned at the screen. "It's from Theo." And she slid her phone across the table for Kelsey to read her father's text.

Tash, please tell Kels that Lionel Berg upped his offer by 50k a year.

"Fifty thousand a year extra?" Tasha gasped. "That's some serious moolah. Fifty K is what I'm making as La Fonda's executive chef. See if Berg needs a personal chef, Kels. No, don't really. I'm kidding. Sort of."

Oh wow. Out of proportion distress seized Kelsey by the throat. If Berg was offering that kind of money, he was serious about hiring her as his campaign manager. The scary part was she wanted to take the job, but couldn't imagine doing it because of her mother.

"I shouldn't have showed you that," Tasha said, palming the phone and sticking it back into her pocket. "You're supposed to be relaxing and enjoying yourself. Not dealing with the real world right now. I'll text your dad back and have him tell Berg to cool his jets until you're off vacation."

Kelsey bobbed her head but couldn't finish her lunch.

When they got back to the *Rockabye*, Noah was behind the desk waiting on a guest. He glanced up, caught her eyes, and smiled.

The smile melted her.

There was another reason she couldn't glibly accept Lionel Berg's job offer and he was standing right in front of her. No matter how much she told herself that she could keep things casual with Noah, her feelings for him ran deep.

She inhaled sharply. She needed time alone to collect her thoughts.

"Young man," said the woman at the desk in a snooty voice. She was greyhound thin and wearing a mink coat. "I told you those pillows in our room were way too uncomfortable."

"I replaced them myself, Ms. Grant." Noah gave her his world-class grin.

"Hmph." The woman tilted her head in a haughty gesture that reminded Kelsey of Filomena. "So you claim, but I have a trick when I stay places to test if my special requests are taken seriously. This morning, before I left my room, I placed a small piece of pink string over my pillow and when I got back the string was *still there*." Her voice dripped acid with those last two words.

"I saw your string and I put it back when I replaced the pillows," Noah countered.

The woman's jaw snapped shut. "Those pillows are simply unacceptable and unless you do something to make this right, I'm not paying my bill and I will leave you a scathing review on Yelp."

Laid-back Noah upped the wattage in his grin and pulled out his good old boy charm. "Now, Lila," he wheedled in a good-natured but slightly chiding tone, calling the woman by her first name. "I know you're a good person and you wouldn't try to slip out on your bill over something as trivial as pillows."

The blowtorch glare in Lila Grant's eyes said that if she were a fire-breathing dragon she'd burn this boat to ashes. "Don't you dare call me Lila, you—"

"Ms. Grant," Kelsey interrupted, unable to bear the conflict. "Everything will be made right. I will personally make sure you have the finest European feather pillows brought to your room immediately."

"Where are you—" Noah started to say, but Kelsey threw him a look that quelled him in his tracks.

"Triple layer? I am very sensitive." Lila Grant sniffed.

"Triple layer." Kelsey nodded. "And for your inconvenience, you may stay an extra night free. Plus, a complimentary bottle of Dom Pérignon will be sent to your room. How does that sound?"

"And chocolate-covered strawberries?"

"Yes."

"Made with Godiva chocolate?"

"Yes, ma'am."

"Don't try to pawn off any old chocolate on me." She shook a bony finger. "I have an acute sense of taste."

"Of course, you do." Kelsey kowtowed the way she'd learned to fawn over Filomena when she was in a mood. "You're a woman of elegance and substance, and you deserve the very best."

"I do, don't I?"

"In fact—" Kelsey turned her back to the desk, leaned in close and lowered her voice as if sharing a secret. "A woman of your caliber should be staying at the Merry Cherub, not a damp and dank boatel. If you like, I'll call the Merry Cherub for you and let them know you want the presidential suite."

"Hey!" Noah said.

Kelsey waved a hand at him behind her back where Ms. Grant couldn't see, and he shut up.

"Yes, do that." Lila Grant tossed her head and drew herself up tall. "You are exactly right. I don't belong *here*." To Noah, she said, "Please give me my bill and I will be on my way."

Once he'd sent Lila Grant off, Noah turned to Kelsey. "Love your hair."

"Thanks."

"That was pretty slick how you handled Lila Grant. How did you know the presidential suite at the Merry Cherub was available?"

"Overheard town gossip."

"Damn, Kelsey. You are phenomenal." He came around the desk and wrapped his arm around her waist. "One question."

"Yes?"

"What would you have done if she'd stayed here? Where would you have gotten European goose down pillows, Dom Pérignon, and Godiva chocolate-covered strawberries?"

"I have the Dom Pérignon in my suitcase that was supposed to be for my wedding night, I could have gotten random feather pillows at Walmart, cut off the labels and embroidered them with a fancy name, and as for the chocolate, I would have used whatever chocolate I could find and dunked the strawberries myself."

"You would have gambled that the 'sensitive' Ms. Grant couldn't tell the difference in the pillows and the chocolate?"

"Trust me. I know the Ms. Grants of the world. As long as they think they are getting the best, as long as you make them feel special, you'll have them eating right out of your hand."

"She does know." Tasha bobbed her head. "If you ever need someone to handle difficult guests, Kelsey is your woman."

"Yeah, my usual go-to smile wasn't working." Noah scratched his head.

"Your charm works on regular people. But with someone who believes they are better than others, the only way to keep things easy is to let them have their delusions."

"And that is how you've managed to deal with your mother for the last twenty-seven years."

She stepped from his arms, looked up into his face. Sadness shimmered in his eyes.

It plucked something inside her, his pity.

"You don't have to feel sorry for me. My life might not have been a bed of roses, but I've learned how to navigate it well."

"That you have." He nodded slowly. "And I admire you for it more than words can say."

Noah took Kelsey to Pasta Pappa's for the Tuesday night dinner special.

She wore a black turtleneck sweater and a short, red plaid wool skirt over black leggings, and cute matching ankle boots. The leggings couldn't hide her shapely legs, and the sweater showcased her pillowy breasts.

Ahh, to rest his head there and dream.

But what really grabbed him by the throat and stunned him into silence was her hair. Gone was the long, tidy braid. Her hair, which had once fallen below her waist, now floated about her shoulders in big soft curls.

The new hairdo was engrossing, alluring. The style suggested whimsy, delight, and fun. It accentuated her perky blue eyes and her high rosy cheekbones. She looked as if she'd stepped right off the cover of a Norman Rockwell Christmas painting.

Wholesome, yet sexy and totally irresistible.

Testosterone shot through his body like a bullet, tore through his brain with a wild salvo of completely un-wholesome visuals.

They sat on the same side of a corner booth and kissed between feeding each other bites of pasta and reminiscing about the time they'd had pizza in the very same booth on their day off from Camp Hope ten years earlier. The restaurant was an adorable cliché with red-and-white-checked oilcloth tablecloths, Chianti bottles with candles in the middle of the tables, and Dean Martin crooning Christmas music over the sound system.

After dinner, he took her ice skating. She wasn't a very good ice skater and he spent the next hour with an arm around her waist as they circled the rink, which was absolutely fine with Kelsey. Then afterward, they stopped by the Fruit of the Vine winery storefront on the square for a Christmas trivia game.

Tasha and Raylene were already there, sipping cranberry wine. Kelsey and Noah sat next to them and after the round ended, joined their team. When the server came over, Noah ordered a beer and Kelsey opted for cranberry wine.

Before the next round began, Flynn and her husband, Jesse, came in, followed shortly by Sean. Flynn eyed Kelsey and gave her a begrudging smile. Kelsey pretended all was well and smiled right back.

"Who's manning the front desk at the *Rockabye*?" Noah asked Sean as he sauntered over.

"Joel." Sean sucked the foam from the top of his beer and Tasha seemed enthralled with the process, her gaze locking on the handyman's lips. "He offered to give me the night off, so that I could come play Christmas trivia." Sean slanted Tasha a sideways glance. Tasha practically melted off her stool. "He knows it's my favorite night at Fruit of the Vine."

"Uh-oh," Noah said.

"What's wrong?" Kelsey leaned against his shoulder, drawing comfort from his warmth.

"Joel is up to something. He doesn't just drop by and offer to give Sean the night off without an ulterior motive."

"Like what?"

"A practical joke most likely."

"Those two are always trying to get one up on each other," Raylene said. "Don't be surprised if when you climb into bed, you find yourself short-sheeted."

"Oh yeah," Kelsey said. "Joel did that at camp once and someone saw him coming out of the girls' cabins and thought it was Noah and he got into big trouble. You should have seen us all trying to jump into bed that night. It was hilarious."

"My twin is sneaky," Noah mumbled. "And he's not above pretending to be me if it gets him out of trouble."

"He says the same thing about you," Raylene pointed out.

"I wonder what he's up to . . ." Noah mused.

"How are we going to divide up the teams?" Flynn asked. "There are . . ." She did a quick head count. "Seven of us. We need an even number." She glanced around the room at the crowd. "Who can we draft to join us?"

"I'll sit this one out," Kelsey said. "I'm pretty rotten at Christmas trivia."

"All the more reason you should play." Noah threw his arm around her shoulder. "Kelsey and I are a team."

Sweet words to her ears.

"I'm heading out," Raylene said. "Noah's got me scared at what Joel is doing over at the *Rockabye*. I'm gonna go check up on him."

"Thank you," Noah told her. "We'll be back at the *Rockabye* in an hour."

"Take your time." Raylene waved a hand. "Earl's out on a hunting trip with his drinking buddies. I've got nothing else to do." She pointed at Sean. "You. Take my seat."

Raylene got up and Sean took her spot next to Tasha.

Tasha grinned and wriggled her chair closer to Sean.

"So, all six of us on a team," Flynn said. "That'll work."

"Are you sure you want to be on a team with me?" Kelsey asked. "I'm worried about bringing you down."

"It's all in good fun." Jesse picked up a controller.

"I'm going to the bathroom before we get started." Flynn pushed back her chair. "Kelsey?"

"Uh-huh?"

"Would you like to join me?"

No, no she would not, but clearly Flynn wanted to talk to her. Kelsey picked up her purse and followed.

Tasha immediately jumped to her feet. "I'm coming too."

"It's okay, Tasha. I've got this." She smiled at her loyal friend.

"You sure?" Tasha's hands were clenched.

Kelsey nodded and followed Flynn into the ladies' room.

"Listen," they both said at once.

Flynn laughed, and that eased Kelsey's fret a little. "I'll go first. I love my baby brother. Ten years ago, after what happened between you two, he was a complete wreck. He'll never let you know that, but when Noah loves something, he puts his heart and soul into it." She paused, cocked her head. "Noah is chill and laid-back, but—"

"You don't have to worry," Kelsey said, keeping her tone as calm and steady as she could with her pulse jumping like crazy. "Your brother and I are just—"

"Friends?"

After what happened last night in his bedroom, how could she say that with a straight face?

"Please, anyone with two eyes can see that you two still have feelings for each other. I just don't want to see him get hurt again."

"The last thing I'd ever want is to hurt Noah."

"You know he feels like he's not good enough for you."

"Why would he feel that way?"

"Oh, I don't know. Your family is rich. Your mother is the mayor-elect of Dallas. You went to Vassar."

"And Noah played in the NBA."

"He never felt worthy of that either. I think it's part of the reason why he didn't fight harder to rehabilitate after his knee injury. Plus, his ex-wife made him feel like crap because he didn't want any part of the glamorous, jet-setting lifestyle she craved. You know he was offered a job as a sports commentator for ESPN."

"I did not."

"That's the reason Melissa left him. She told him he was river riffraff and he had blown his one chance at making something out of himself."

Fury pushed up Kelsey's spine at the woman who'd treated Noah so shabbily. "He didn't tell me that. He made it sound like he and Melissa had just drifted apart."

"Well, he's not going to admit that, is he? Noah's a good guy, but he has simple taste. Home, family, and his community mean the world to him. Don't expect him to suddenly become the kind of man who enjoys political galas and jetting off to Paris at a moment's notice."

"None of that matters to me."

"They matter to your mother and from what I can tell, you still answer to her."

"Not that it's any of your business," Kelsey said as gently as she could. She didn't want to offend Noah's sister, but she wasn't going to let herself be pushed around either. "But I'm no longer at my mother's beck and call."

Flynn folded her arms, studied Kelsey a long moment. "I really like you, and Noah lights up like a Christmas tree whenever he's around you, so I'm trusting you on this. Don't hurt him."

"I won't," Kelsey promised.

"All right, then. Now that we've gotten that out of the way, let's get back out there and kick some holiday trivia ass."

CHAPTER 21

"Who's up first?" Jesse asked upon their return.

"I'll start, and we'll just go around the table." Flynn sat down next to her husband again.

"Everything okay?" Noah leaned over to whisper in her ear.

"It is."

Noah reached under the table to take her hand. "My sister is a Christmas trivia wizard. Flynn is hard to beat."

"Good thing. Someone has to pull my weight for the team."

"Don't worry," Sean said. "We've all got you covered."

"Here we go." Noah pulled Kelsey close and they directed their attention to the computer screen where the questions would pop up.

What is Mrs. Claus's first name?

Underneath the question scrolled a list of possible answers.

A. Martha
B. Josephine
C. Meredith
D. Jennifer

"Martha," Flynn said and hit the button for A. Their computer screen lit up green. She'd answered before anyone else in the winery. She crowed to the players at the next table, "Suck it, losers."

"I should warn you. Flynn is very competitive," Noah said.

"How in the world did she know such an obscure thing?" Kelsey asked.

"Darlin'," Jesse drawled. "Twilightites know everything there is to know about Christmas."

"Pay attention." Flynn elbowed her husband in the ribs. "You're going to miss the next question."

In the 1964 classic *Rudolph the Red-Nosed Reindeer,* what is the name of Rudolph's faithful elf companion?

"I got little kids," Jesse said. "I'd have to turn in my father-of-the-year award if I didn't know it was Hermey." He punched the appropriate button on the controller and the green light lit up again. "Your turn." Jesse tossed the controller to Tasha, who was sitting to his left.

"Oh boy, don't get mad if I blow this." Tasha shook out her hands.

The question flashed on the screen.

In what modern-day country was Saint Nicholas born?

"Oh, oh, I know this." Tasha bounced up and down in her seat and when the possible answers popped up on the screen, she pounced on *Turkey*.

Another green light. Three right answers in a row. Their team was smoking the rest of the players in the bar.

"How did *you* know that?" Kelsey asked her friend.

Tasha beamed. "I lived in Turkey for a year when I was in college, remember?"

"You"—Flynn pointed at Tasha—"are my new favorite person."

Kelsey pulled a palm down her face, dreading her turn. She was going to blow it and competitive Flynn would blame her for the loss.

Sean took his turn. What was Frosty the Snowman's nose made out of? "Button."

"No, it's not," Kelsey said, remembering when she and Chelsea had built a snowman on the front lawn. They'd used a carrot for his nose and Chelsea had said, "Just like Frosty." That was before Filomena saw the snowman and knocked it down because it looked tacky. "Can you change your answer?"

"No, no," Flynn said. "Button is right." She proceeded to sing the "Frosty the Snowman" song. Corncob pipe. Button nose.

But Sean had already changed it and the screen lit up red.

Kelsey plastered a hand over her mouth, shame lighting her up from inside out. "I am so sorry."

"It's okay, it's okay." Flynn bobbed her head and clapped her hands like they were contestants on *Family Feud*. "We're still in the lead."

Kelsey's palms were sweating. She hated letting the team down. Why had she said anything? She didn't know a thing about Christmas.

Noah patted her forearm. "You did fine."

"I didn't."

"Your turn, little brother." Flynn nodded at Noah.

Noah's question flashed on the screen. Where is Christmas Island located? "Slam dunk!" Noah gloated and hit the button that corresponded with the answer *Indian Ocean.*

"No fair," a man at the adjacent table complained. "You bought your own Christmas Island. You were bound to know that."

"Luck of the draw," Noah said and settled the controller in Kelsey's palm.

"My hand's skinned up," she said. "Let Flynn take my turn."

"No can do," Flynn said. "We'll be disqualified. You have to answer."

Ugh. She was *not* in a Christmas-loving mood.

"What's the worst that could happen?" Tasha said. "You suck like an Electrolux. We lose. That team"—she jerked her thumb at the next table—"does a really big happy dance because Flynn was so gloaty, and we move right on to a drinking game."

"No, no more drinking games after last night," Kelsey said.

"Go, go." Flynn snapped her fingers. "Your question is on the screen."

Paralyzed, Kelsey stared at the question.

Mistletoe is poisonous.

There were two choices. True or False. A fifty-fifty chance.

Kelsey backed into it through logic. Mistletoe was a parasite. So wasn't the stuff at least poisonous to the host plant that it fed off? Kelsey selected *True*.

The screen lit green.

She blinked. It took a second for it to register that she'd answered correctly.

Flynn whooped and reached across the table to hug the stuffing out of her. "We win! We win! Go, Kelsey! Way to get your Christmas on!"

Kelsey flushed, grateful that she hadn't blown it. She glanced over at Noah, who was grinning like she held the key to his world.

The server brought over their winning prize—another bottle of cranberry wine. There was much toasting and merriment, and Kelsey realized that despite her performance anxiety over Christmas trivia, she was having a blast.

Noah leaned over and whispered in her ear, "It's good to see you looking so happy."

"It's good to *be* happy." Kelsey laughed, grateful for the joy swelling inside her. She didn't know how long this wonderful feeling would last and she was determined to enjoy every second of it.

"You ready to get out of here?" he asked as their friends prepped for another round of trivia. "Or do you want to play again?"

"Let's quit while I'm ahead." She grabbed her coat from the back of her chair.

"You were a good sport." He helped her on with the coat.

"I had fun."

"I'm glad." His smile dusted her with happiness.

They told the others good-bye and headed out the door. She pulled on mittens to protect her sore hands that were touchy after manning the controller. Healing, but not yet healed. Closing wounds took time.

But she felt better than she'd felt in years.

The joy was fresh and exciting. She wanted to wrap her arms around it and squeeze, but she was terrified if she embraced the joy too hard it would pop like soap bubbles.

They meandered back through town. At ten P. M. on a weeknight, things had wound down. The stores and restaurants were closed. Fruit of the Vine remained the lone lively spot on the square at this hour.

The outdoor music had been switched off and the silence brought a calmness that settled her soul. The air was cool but not too nippy.

Noah settled his arm over her shoulder, tugged her close. They walked side by side, shoes crunching leaves that the wind had blown over the sidewalk.

It was a special moment. A precious moment. Kelsey breathed it in, riding the high of the trivia contest win and the sheer joy of traveling the quiet, empty streets with Noah.

Kelsey glanced over her shoulder.

"Thinking about the night your mother's goons tried to kidnap you?"

She nodded.

He pulled her closer to him. "I've got you, Firefly."

It took almost an hour to walk back to the *Rockabye*. They didn't speak. Just enjoyed each other's company. They paused on the bridge to admire the decorated arch and the glow of the marina beyond. Then hand in hand, they traversed the cobblestone path to the boatel.

When they reached the paddle wheel boat, Raylene was coming down the steps, headed home, as they went in. She was shaking her head.

"What's up?" Noah asked.

"Your brother." Raylene chuckled.

"What did he do?"

"See for yourself." Raylene waved a hand. "I'm outta here. I'll be in late tomorrow. Night, Kelsey."

"Good night." Kelsey smiled at the elderly woman.

"Wait," Noah said, "and I'll walk you across the bridge to your car."

"No need." Raylene nodded toward the walkway where an older man stood with his hands in the pockets of his jacket. "My white knight is here."

"Hey, Earl." Noah nodded at the man.

"Hey, Noah." The man sized up Kelsey. "Hey, Noah's girl."

"Hey, Earl," she said, feeling like one of them.

It was a dizzy, blissful feeling and she wished she could capture it in a jar when she was back at home. Back to her real life.

What if this could be your real life, whispered a voice in the back of her head. Calm, quiet. Filled with love and laughter and community.

Kelsey held her breath. It was a heady thought. One that was too exciting to seriously entertain. Her life was way too complicated to unknot it so easily.

Earl and Raylene went off into the darkness.

Noah led Kelsey inside the B&B.

Raylene had left the light on in the lobby and as soon as Noah closed the door behind them, he started laughing.

"What is it?" Kelsey asked.

"Look up." Noah pointed.

Kelsey tilted back her head. Every square inch of the ceiling was covered with mistletoe, and dangling from each sprig was a white tag that read "Kiss Here."

"Joel?" she asked.

"Who else? I knew he was up to something."

"Your twin is a cutup." She chuckled.

Noah's eyes glistened. "You know what this means, don't you?"

"What?"

"We're going to have to kiss all the way across the room."

After twenty-seven kisses—yes, Kelsey counted each one—they made it across the room, and Noah walked her to her door. He kissed her one last time bringing the tally up to twenty-eight.

Kelsey placed a palm against his chest, fingered the collar of his shirt. "You sure you won't change your mind and come in?"

"There's Tasha," he said.

"She's still at Fruit of the Vine with Sean."

"We're going for the slow burn, remember?" His eyes smiled at her.

"They're our rules, we can always change them."

"I want it to be right, Kelsey."

"It feels right to me."

"Don't tempt me, woman. I'm hanging by a thread."

"Good." She went up on tiptoes and planted her lips against the underside of his jaw. Nibbled.

"Sweet baby Jesus, you gotta stop that."

"When?" she said. "If not tonight?"

"Give it time."

"I'm only here for eleven more days and we're wasting them."

"Not wasting, indulging."

"You're driving me crazy, MacGregor."

"Ditto." He kissed the top of her head. "Now go to bed. I'll see you tomorrow."

"Are we going out again tomorrow night?"

"Maybe. Who knows? We might stay in."

"What are we doing?"

"You'll just have to wait and see."

"You're a tease, you know that?"

"Yep, and you love that about me."

It was true. She did.

He sent her off to bed with one more sizzling kiss and Kelsey fell into a deep sleep filled with hot sexy dreams about her tall, handsome man.

On Wednesday after Noah finished work, they drove around town looking at Christmas lights and ended up at a lover's lane spot. They necked like teenagers until Sheriff Hondo Crouch drove by and knocked on their car window.

Again, Noah left her at her bedroom door with a passionate kiss. Kelsey went to bed revved up and frustrated.

On Thursday, Noah was busy getting ready for the Christmas Casino event. Kelsey offered to help, but he insisted she should be relaxing and enjoying herself, so she and Tasha went on the Tour of Homes.

On Friday, Kelsey slept in, dreaming of Noah, and waiting for it to be late enough to start getting ready for the party. At ten A.M. a knock sounded on her door. Tasha had already left to go for a run with Sean.

Kelsey drew on a plush *Rockabye* bathrobe, ran a hand through her hair, and went to peek through the peephole. A fit young woman she didn't know stood in the hallway holding a collapsible massage table.

"I didn't order a massage."

"I'm Po Morgan from Hot Legs Spa. Are you Kelsey James?"

Kelsey opened up the door. "I am?"

"Mr. MacGregor arranged for you to have a hot stone massage in your room. Is now not a good time?"

That Noah. Kelsey couldn't help grinning. He was spoiling her. "Now's a great time. Come on in."

Ninety minutes later, feeling limp as a noodle, Kelsey sighed happily and pressed a generous tip into Po's hand.

"Mr. MacGregor included the tip in your bill." Po tried to give the money back.

"Keep it. Have a merry Christmas."

Po grinned. "Merry Christmas to you . . ." She paused a moment. "You do carry a lot of tension in your temples. So much, that it's beyond massage. But acupuncture might help."

"Thank you for the advice. I'll look into it." She closed the door after the masseuse and considered taking a hot bath in the jetted spa tub. She started toward the bathroom, when a second knock sounded on the door.

It was another employee from Hot Legs Spa. A manicurist named Shirley. "Noah sent me," she said, and Kelsey waved her inside.

Shirley was sixty if she was a day, and dressed in outrageous colors—purple, orange, chartreuse—and she was a nonstop talker, but Kelsey didn't mind. She liked hearing about Shirley's dating exploits after she found herself newly single when her husband left her for a—in Shirley's words—"a 'twinky' half his age."

Kelsey picked a sedate pink for her mani-pedi, but Shirley shook her head. "No, no. For your age and coloring you need something daring."

Daring. Dare. There was that word again.

"I recommend Fire Engine for the background color, but how about I paint a cute little design on for you as well."

"I normally prefer something more polished."

"Aww, c'mon. You're young. You only live once. How about we do something Christmas themed?" Shirley snapped her gum and the smell of watermelon wafted around her. "Red background, and the designs in white. A snowflake on one finger, a gingerbread person on another, a star, a Santa suit on another. Whadya think?"

"Go for it," Kelsey said.

"That's the spirit." Shirley laughed and got to work.

When it was done, the artistic mani-pedi was better than many Kelsey had gotten at her high-end salon in Dallas. Shirley wished Kelsey happy holidays and left smiling with an extra big tip.

Kelsey sat admiring her manicure, feet propped on the couch, when the third knock sounded on the door.

Grinning, Kelsey raced to open it.

This time it was a delivery boy carrying a white box labeled "Twilight Bakery," a pink tin of passion tea, and a candy cane–colored Christmas amaryllis.

She grabbed her purse, gave the delivery guy a tip, and kicked the door closed behind him with her heel.

There was a card with the flower. She opened it up.

The spirit of Christmas is all around you, Firefly.

She set the flower on the counter along with the tea tin. Stepped back to admire the arrangement. She couldn't deny it. Being pampered like this was pretty darn sweet. As her mother's assistant she was usually the one sending other people flowers—campaign donors, people Filomena was sucking up to, folks she was trying to charm.

It was nice being on the receiving end.

Her eye twitched.

Why?

She felt happy. Not stressed at all. Was it because she was unaccustomed to having attention focused on her?

What you resist, persists. Embrace the feelings. Happy, sad, weird, all of them. Don't run from them. Let your eye twitch.

She didn't know where the advice came from. Somewhere deep inside of her maybe? But it sounded a lot like something Noah would say. That wise, laid-back man.

Turning her attention to the white bakery box, she opened it to find a gigantic cookie. On the inside lid, written in red script, was the legend of the kismet cookie. Followed by:

Bake kismet cookies on Christmas Eve, put them under your pillow before you go to sleep and you will dream of your one true love. PS—don't forget, the dream thing only works on Christmas Eve.

What cute, whimsical fun! Par for the course in Twilight.

Below the legend was the recipe, which included rolled oats, white chocolate chips, cranberries, and macadamia nuts. Yum!

Kelsey turned her attention to the cookie.

Inside the box, she found another card.

She was so excited, she didn't even try to open the card delicately. Just ripped the envelope to get at the message.

Eat me.

She laughed. That Noah. What a scamp!

Kelsey didn't need any more encouragement than that. She sat down at the counter barstool and broke off a piece of cookie. Closed her eyes to savor it. Chewed. How sweet this whole thing had been.

But of course, Noah had always been a romantic. She'd been the sensible one. Which was why she'd never tried to contact him after that night on the pier at Camp Hope when her mother ruined their night and took her away.

Suddenly the moist cookie turned dry in her mouth at the memory. She tried to swallow the mouthful, along with the past as her eye twitched again.

Don't hide from it.

Feel it.

All of it.

The blazing shame. The abject grief. The trembling fear of her mother. The heartbreaking loss of never seeing Noah again.

Kelsey let the feelings wash over her.

All these years, she'd resisted examining that moment that had defined her life for the last ten years. Tamping it all down. Denying her feelings. Hiding behind a cool exterior and an unruffled smile. While deep down inside, there lived a throbbing ache, like a tooth gone bad.

She began to sob.

A frame-shaking, gut-wrenching silent sob that took hold of her and wouldn't let go. Her insides twisted. Her heart clenched. Salty sorrow rose up past the taste of cookie.

Finally sound emerged.

A first a helpless mewling. A tiny cry against the past that she'd turned a blind eye to all these years. Her mother's culpability in her sister's death when Chelsea had decided to run away because Filomena threw her flute into the lake as punishment. Her mother's cruelty that night on the dock at Camp Hope. Her mother's hardness that chased away her father. Her mother's meanness toward Noah. The recent kidnapping attempt.

And then the wail grew, keening and forlorn. Denial. For years she'd been in denial about her mother's mental health. Filomena was so good at deflecting blame onto others, at gaslighting and making Kelsey feel like everything was her fault. Even as the realization hit her that her mother was not a well woman, the kindness in Kelsey would not let her hate Filomena. Her mother was a victim too. Something had twisted her. Whether genetics or environment or both, Kelsey could not say.

But how could she judge Filomena? She had flaws herself. And she loved her mother, no matter how broken the woman might be. She couldn't hate her.

Instead, her heart was utterly broken with the sadness of it all.

The keening turned into one long, wretched howl. The sound seemed yanked from her throat by unseen forces.

She cried for her lost sister, for her damaged father, for her irrevocably broken mother. Grieved the normal mother-daughter relationship that she would never have.

The emotional storm she'd been running from her entire life coalesced there over the giant kismet cookie sent to her by a kind, fun-loving man. An emotional hurricane created by his tenderness. It was a riptide that threw her this way and that. She cried until there wasn't a drop of moisture left inside her.

She grappled for tissues. Blew her nose. Wiped her eyes. Sighed. Straightened. Sighed again.

Felt empty.

And cleansed.

Oh so cleansed.

Her eye stopped twitching.

She took stock of herself. She smelled of massage oil. Her fingernails decorated with Christmas. Cookie crumbs scattered over the counter.

Did Noah MacGregor have any earthly idea exactly what he'd done to her?

CHAPTER 22

The day of the Christmas Casino, Kelsey had spent most of the time holed up in her room, taking stock of her life.

Everything had changed.

Not just her hairstyle and clothing, makeup and nails, but her entire outlook. Finally, she understood the gnawing self-doubt that had ridden with her for the past twenty-seven years. Understood where the anxiety came from and how to alleviate it.

Kelsey claimed her power.

Call her a late bloomer. Say she'd taken a damn long time to clip the apron strings. It didn't matter. She'd gotten here. She was finally free. She no longer needed anything or anyone to validate her. She was done seeking her mother's approval. Done seeking *anyone's* approval. She was staking her claim to live her own life as she saw fit.

And to her own sexuality.

After the crying jag, she'd taken a trip into town, where she'd visited a tiny little boutique store off the town square that specialized in slinky lingerie. The store, which she and Tasha had stumbled into the day they'd gone shopping, was called—quirkily enough—She Sparkles.

The name fit her mood. She *felt* sparkly and bright. A brand-new person. From now on, she was putting her healing first.

And she intended to celebrate her emergence tonight. Beneath the sexy dress, Kelsey wore a G-string and a black lace bustier. She couldn't wait for Noah to see her present to him.

His gifts had ripped her control to shreds. Now it was her turn to do the same to him.

Just as Kelsey finished getting ready, Tasha came bopping into the suite. She'd been gone all day, with only a single cryptic text telling Kelsey that she wouldn't be able to meet her for lunch. Which in light of the crying spree, had turned out to be fortuitous.

"Get a load of you!" Tasha's eyes widened as she took in Kelsey in her red velvet dress, upswept hairdo, and the stilettoes. "What the hell happened?"

"What?" Kelsey asked, tucking a final hairpin into her French twist. "You've seen me decked out before."

"Nooo." Tasha swiveled her head back and forth. "Not like this. Something is different."

"What do you mean?"

"You look . . . different. Lighter . . . happier." Tasha assessed Kelsey with a chin tilt. "Free. What happened? Did Filomena kick the bucket?"

It was a scandalous thing to say. Pure Tasha.

Kelsey offered a modest smile. "This has nothing to do with Filomena."

Tasha's grin widened. "You don't say? I like the sound of that."

"Enough about me," Kelsey said. "You better hurry and get ready. The party starts in thirty minutes."

"Oh." Tasha made a humming noise and plunked down on the bed with so much enthusiasm the mattress jumped. "I'm not going."

"What? You love casinos and it's for charity."

"Yeah, I think I'm just going to hang around the *Rockabye*."

"You? What will you do? You don't like to curl up by the fire and read. Especially when there's a party going on."

"Hey, wherever I go, that's where the party is."

A sound philosophy, but still, Tasha was not one to pass up a good time. "Wait a minute, does this have anything to do with Sean manning the front desk this evening?"

A coy expression crossed Tasha's face and she was anything but coy.

"Wait, is Sean the reason you canceled lunch with me?" Kelsey asked.

Tasha's expression turned butter-wouldn't-melt-in-her-mouth. "Maybe."

"What's changed? Did you win Sean over to the promise of casual sex?"

Tasha ducked her head. "We're going to pop popcorn, make hot chocolate, and watch Christmas movies in the lobby. What do you think?"

"Ah!" Kelsey slapped a palm over her mouth. "He won *you* over?"

Tasha shrugged. "You've seen the guy shirtless. A girl's gotta do what a girl's gotta do to get next to *that* chest."

"Well, okay then. Here's to you and Sean."

"Wish me luck in wearing him down altogether. He

says we're only going to hold hands. But I've got kissing planned."

Kelsey gave her a thumbs-up. "You go girl."

"If you want to make your party on time—" Tasha tapped the bedside clock. It was seven forty-five. "Better get a move on."

"How do I look?" Kelsey twirled for her.

"Noah ain't gonna know what hit him."

"There's a giant cookie in the kitchenette. Grab it for your movie-watching party if you want."

"Thanks. Now scoot!"

"I'm in your way, huh?"

"You better believe it."

"Thrown out of my own room." Laughing, Kelsey shook her head.

"You'll thank me for it later."

Kelsey picked up her clutch purse and headed for the door.

"Wait."

She paused.

Tasha fished around in the pocket of her jeans, tossed something to Kelsey.

She caught it with one hand.

A condom.

"Stay safe."

Blushing, Kelsey put the condom in her clutch. It never hurt to be prepared.

Her entire body blazed with sexual energy as she left the *Rockabye* and caught one of the water taxis waiting to ferry guests from Christmas Island over to the *Brazos Queen*. This trip was much shorter over the water than it would have been going via the bridge and catching an Uber to the other side of the lake.

Excited to see Noah again, she took a seat at the front of the ferry. She wanted to be the first one off. The other guests on the boat were staring at her. She shifted, pulling the slit of the dress closed to cover her exposed leg.

Lifted her chin. Grinned.

It took less than five minutes to reach the *Brazos Queen*. Men in tuxedoes and women in formal wear similar to hers were lining up on the gangplank to get in.

Head held high, Kelsey joined the queue. Music pulsed out over the water. A techno version of "Santa Baby" with the singer putting added emphasis on the words *hurry down the chimney*. Weird, but oddly sexy.

Setting the tone for the night?

Kelsey shifted her weight from foot to foot anxious to get in. To get to Noah. Her blood flowed hot as lava. Her heart thumped to the pulsing beat.

But her eye did not twitch. No telltale sign of her heightened emotional state.

Yay!

And there at the door, greeting the guests, were two tall, sexy twin brothers in tuxedoes. Her eyes met Noah's and her heart swooned.

What a romantic figure he cut. Dashing, darling, daring, and dangerously hot. Oh, so many delightful *d* words.

It was her turn. She was at the door.

"Welcome," Noah said as if she were just any other guest, but his dark eyes raked over her body and the smile he gave her was wickedly wonderful.

Her heart tumbled over itself.

He took her hand.

She forgot to breathe.

"The bar is open," he said. The same line he'd given everyone else. But then he leaned down, pressed his mouth next to her ear and whispered, "I'll come find you."

She smirked. Nodded. He was going to come find her! A little game of hide-and-seek for when his hosting duties ebbed?

Feeling the heat of his gaze follow her as she headed to the bar. Kelsey did not look back. Let him feel the same level of anticipation churning inside of her.

"Hello," the bartender greeted her and pushed the drink menu toward her. "Here's what we're serving and the prices, or you could have our complimentary cocktail."

"What is it?' she asked, intrigued.

"A white Christmas martini." Just as he said that, the music shifted to "White Christmas."

"I guess that's a sign," she laughed. "Give me the white Christmas."

"Your wish is my command," he said and rimmed a martini glass with honey and sanding sugar, then in a shaker mixed vanilla vodka, white chocolate liqueur, white crème de cacao and half-and-half. Shook it. Poured it into the glass and passed the martini to her.

"It's too beautiful to drink," she exclaimed, putting a tip into his jar.

"Take a sip. One taste and you won't care about how beautiful it is."

She sipped. It *was* freaking delicious and the liquor sent a nice warm tingling through her body. She smiled, nodded, and gave him a thumbs-up. She was too busy taking another drink to say anything.

He winked and turned to the next guest.

Kelsey stepped away from the bar and moved to one side so that she could study the room. Noah and Joel were still at the front door as a throng of guests moved inside.

In the center of the room was a buffet table loaded with hors d'oeuvres and a dessert table piled high with scrumptious cookies and pastries. Guests lined up at both sides to fill small plates. There were tables scattered about the room where people could sit and eat, but many just held their plates while they mingled around the room.

"Hi there." A man in an attention-grabbing white tuxedo glided up to her. The style told her that he'd probably worn it to his high school prom ten years ago. And he had a wedding-band tan line on his left hand as if he had recently stopped wearing it.

She gave him a cool, not-interested smile. "I'm waiting for someone."

"Too bad." He raked his gaze up the length of her to the top of the slit in her dress. "You look good enough to eat."

"Shoo," she said, without malice. "Go find someone else to pester."

"I like you." He laughed.

"It's not going to work."

"You sure?"

"Positive."

He shrugged good-naturedly, giving up easily. "Your loss."

"I'm sure I'll pine about it for years to come."

"I really *do* like you."

"Bye." She gave a beauty-pageant wave.

"Whoever he is, he's a lucky man."

"I'll let him know you said so." Kelsey turned and smiled at Noah, who was making his way through the crowd toward her.

"Wow, you're with MacGregor?" the guy said. "No wonder I'm dirt beneath your feet."

"You're not dirt," she said. "You just come on a little too strong. Go find someone else to sweep off their feet."

The guy grinned and sauntered off.

Leaving Kelsey free to turn her full attention to the long-legged man coming toward her. His hair was just the right length. Neat and tidy, but with enough thick waves to run her fingers through. She couldn't wait to muss him up. The tuxedo fit him like he'd been born to wear it, hugging his broad shoulders. He looked like he'd stepped right off the cover of *GQ*'s Man of the Year issue.

Tingles quivered up Kelsey's spine one vertebra at a time.

Their gazes jammed into each other. Slam. Bam. Knocking the breath right out of her.

He pierced her with his eyes. A right solid puncture. She felt it to her core. He *knew* her. And it was as if the past ten years dissolved into nothing and they were right back where they'd been. Shiny and new at seventeen.

Kelsey felt it like a punch.

It was that visceral. That primal.

They still belonged together.

Her pupils widened of their own volition, expanding to take in more of him. Her hands trembled, and her body flooded with warmth.

He came toward her like a heat-seeking missile. He glanced neither right nor left. Nothing was going to divert this man from her.

He stopped just short of Kelsey, held out his hand.

She accepted it.

He pulled her to him.

She gasped. Thrilled.

"Come with me," he said.

Setting down her glass, she followed. There was nothing else she would rather do. He led her from the main room, where the food was being served, to a room with a big dance floor. Four decorated Christmas trees flanked every corner and couples waltzed to a live band playing George Strait's "Christmas Cookies."

Kelsey recognized the lead singer as country star Cash Colton and wondered how Noah and his brother managed to get such a big-name artist to play at their charity event. Colton might be a celebrity, but Kelsey's eyes were on Noah.

Swinging and swaying his hips, Noah waltzed her out onto the dance floor. He moved with an Elvis-style swivel that set her pulse pounding. With his height, he cut a commanding figure and she saw many surreptitious glances following his moves.

Cash Colton sang about how much he liked Christmas cookies.

"How in the world did you get Cash Colton to sing at your event?" Kelsey asked as Noah pulled her close and waltzed her around the dance floor.

"Cash is my cousin-in-law. That's his wife, my cousin Paige, over there." He waved to a petite pregnant woman sitting in a chair to the left of the stage. Paige waved back with an enthusiastic smile.

"Lucky you, having a famous cousin-in-law."

He peered deeply into her eyes, grinned. "I am a lucky, lucky man."

Feeling powerless against his charms, Kelsey swallowed that grin hook, line, and sinker. He held her tightly against his body. She could feel his heat and the jut of his arousal. She lowered her lashes. Rested her head against his chest, let him guide her to the beat of the peppy tune.

"Kelsey," he whispered.

She turned her face up to him.

He ducked his head, brushed her lips with his. Soft and gentle. But when the kiss ended and she met his gaze, the look in his eyes was anything but soft or gentle. His expression was lusty and wicked.

"You look red hot in that dress, woman." His tone was husky as a cornfield.

Delighted, she shivered. Her toes curled inside her stilettoes as she quelled a runaway urge to pull his head down and French kiss the hell out of him right there in front of God and everybody.

Decorum. Filomena's voice clanged in her head.

Flipping screw that.

Kelsey followed her impulse for once. Wrapped her arms around Noah's neck, pulled his head down, parted her lips, and kissed him. She flicked out her tongue and boy, was he on board! The next thing she knew, he was kissing her with wolfish primal hunger.

People were staring. She could feel their gazes. And for some kinky reason, that only made her hotter.

This was so not her. These wild displays of public affection. But her body ate it up. Clenching and tightening and yearning for more.

So very much more.

Maybe it was her. The new and improved her. The sexually adventuresome Kelsey.

His buttery lips tasted sweet. His scent filled her nose. She drank him in. Finally, he broke the kiss, so they could dance.

Cash Colton and his band struck up a slow, romantic song. The lights dimmed. Couples embraced. Danced closer.

She and Noah couldn't get any closer with their clothes on. Moving as one unit. Step for step. Kelsey could feel the ripples of his muscles beneath his tux. Perspiration dotted his forehead and she realized she was perspiring too. Not so much from exertion, but from the sheer heat of desire.

With each step, each breath, their passion for each other ramped higher, rocking them on a river of need. His arms tightened around her and she could feel his heart drumming inside his chest as crazy as her own.

When the song ended, Noah took her hand and led her off the dance floor. She hadn't noticed a spiral staircase at the back of the room before. He guided her there and he went up the staircase first, but kept firm hold of her left hand with his right. Interlaced their fingers.

"Where are we going? she whispered.

"To the casino."

She teetered a bit as she tucked her clutch purse underneath her arm, while lifting her dress hem with her free hand to keep from tripping on the stairs.

He looked down with an indulgent smile on his face. She felt like Cinderella at the ball. Full of joy but aware of that ticking clock at the back of her mind. Eventually, she was going to have to leave this fantasy Christmas world and head back home to Dallas and her real life.

Not now. Don't think about that now.

On the upper deck, they found the casino packed.

Guests in formal attire gathered around the roulette wheel. There were blackjack and craps tables. Three other tables housed poker players. All were vying to win various prizes that local merchants had donated, arrayed on a long table.

Which game were she and Noah going to play?

Kelsey didn't gamble, so she had no clue how to play any of them. But it was for charity, so she didn't mind looking foolish. But to her surprise, he did not stop at any of the tables. Instead they bypassed them all and went down a narrow hallway similar to the corridor on the *Rockabye* that led from the lobby to the dining room.

"What games are back here?" she asked.

"*Our* game."

That thrilled and intrigued her. She wanted to ask questions, but she trusted Noah, and she didn't ask, eager for the surprise. After the massage and the mani-pedi and the giant kismet cookie and amaryllis, who knew what else he had up his mysterious sleeve?

Whee!

"What do you want me to do?" she asked.

"Take down your hair."

"What?"

"Let it loose. You cut it for a reason. Don't keep it pinned up."

Boldly, she plucked the pins from her hair. Tucked them into her purse and let her hair cascade around her shoulders.

His grin was reward enough, but then he took her hand again and off they went. As they walked past the long wide window that looked out over the lake, Kelsey caught a glimpse of her reflection and almost did not recognize herself.

Who was that woman with the wide blue eyes enlarged by the artful application of mascara, the bouncy blond hair floating about her shoulders, her body wrapped in scarlet velvet, lips puffy from the pressure of Noah's red-hot kisses?

She was a fox.

A hottie.

A bodacious babe.

No longer the buttoned-down conservative woman desperate to manage her image for the sake of her mother's career. Tonight, with Noah, she could let her sexuality out of the bag. Tonight, she was no longer straightlaced Kelsey James worrying about what the constituents would think. Tonight, she was a woman who fully embraced her sexuality.

Her pulse spiked.

She was loving this. She felt free. Was this what Clive had felt like when he ran off with Kevin? Her discovery of her true self was just as profound as Clive's had been.

"Here we go." Noah grinned at her, winked, pushed in on a wooden bifold door and took her into the provocative cubbyhole. Closed the door, sealing them into the small space together. It looked like the space might have once been a wet bar converted into a storage closet, except the closet was empty.

"What—"

But that was as far as she got.

He scooped her into his arms, picked her up, and settled her bottom on a narrow counter. Then he wrapped his arms around her and proceeded to kiss her senseless.

CHAPTER 23

Only a thin paneled wall separated the storage area from the casino main room. She could hear bets being taken and wheels turning and excited voices rising above the strains of "Santa Claus Is Coming to Town," the Bruce Springsteen version.

She thought about Noah and how he'd looked in his Christmas Bard costume, and thought, *Oh yeah, Santa, come*.

Slowly, he drew back, pressed an index finger to his lips. "Shh."

Sitting on the counter in front of him, they were eye to eye. Giggling, she leaned in and dropped her forehead on his shoulder. His cologne, an exotic blend of yeasty French pastry and Thailand spice market, startled her. Kelsey's first thought, *What is this scent?* The second: *he smells handsome*.

What a rush!

"Shh." He purred the sound. "They can hear us."

Those four words shot her arousal skyward. Her body instantly softened, moistened. Got ready for him.

The slit of her dress had fallen open to reveal her bare leg. A wicked gleam came into his eye as he ran a hand up her thigh.

Kelsey shivered. Closed her eyes. His touch felt so good.

"How does that feel?" he whispered, his calloused fingertips belying his sophisticated attire.

"Mmm," she purred.

He bumped against her knees with his pelvis, urging her legs to part. He settled himself between her legs. The material of his trousers rubbed against her thighs.

His hand crept higher, tickling her skin. Her eyes flew open. His chocolate brown eyes were wide, filled with awe.

When his fingers found her G-string panties, his grin overtook his face. He pushed the skimpy piece of lace to one side.

Her heart tripped over itself.

His hips were still wedged between her knees. She squeezed him tighter. He made a guttural sound and his eyes turned murky with need.

The room was hot, but Kelsey was hotter. Her blood practically boiled. Her head spun with the heat and for one moment she thought she might pass right out from the scalding temperature of their escalating lust.

Noah leaned in closer, dipped his head, pressed his lips to the pulse throbbing at her collarbone. Kelsey threw back her head, barely managed to contain her groan. They were not tentative kids anymore. They were full-grown adults, ready, willing, and able to explore every inch of each other's bodies and revel in the process.

He slipped off his tie and wrapped the silky black material around his fingers.

"What are you going to do with that?" she whispered, excitement raising the hair on her arms.

"Trust me?" he murmured.

She nodded mutely.

"Close your eyes."

She obeyed.

He wrapped the tie around her like a blindfold, and it felt like a scandalous dare. He tied it at the back of her head. The man was whimsical even in his sex games. But of course, that was Noah.

She sucked in her breath. Nerves jangling. She wanted this so much, and yet she felt so vulnerable, not being able to see him while he got to watch—and control—her every move.

He gets to control you only if you allow it, whispered the bold voice in her head. *You can stop this anytime you want.*

Yes, she was nervous, but her eye did not twitch.

Victory!

Maybe *good* stress did not trigger the tic. Maybe when she was in control of the stress it was okay.

His mouth was on hers again, halting her wayward thoughts and pulling her back into the sweet, hot moment. His hands cupped her breasts. He hissed in air.

"What is it?" she whispered.

"Shh."

Stay quiet. Yes. People were in the other room. Milling. Talking. Gambling. She was taking her own kind of gamble right here, right now. If anyone opened that bifold door . . .

"Santa Clause Is Coming to Town" had turned into "O Christmas Tree." She heard someone say "All in."

Yes, that was her. Smart or not, she was all in.

He stopped kissing her, his hands still at her breasts. "Noah?"

When he spoke, his voice was thick and clotted. "You're wearing a bustier?"

She nodded.

"Damn, Firefly," he said. "That's so freaking sexy."

It pleased her that she'd turned him on even more. She could hear the escalating tension in his voice. Feel the steel of his shaft pressing against her thigh through the thin material of his trousers.

She was just as hard. Her nipples beaded like pebbles beneath her lingerie.

Noah slipped his palm up her nape, fingers splaying through her hair, cupping the back of her head in his hand. Held her in place while his hot, wet mouth nibbled at her throat.

She'd never done anything remotely like this. Make out with the risk of such public discovery. The closest she'd come had been with him on the dock that summer night so long ago. And despite what had happened then, this felt more dangerous than that.

And far more erotic.

Adulthood added a whole new spin on things.

If she didn't trust him so much, Kelsey wouldn't have been able to do this. But she knew Noah had only her best interest at heart.

Grinning, she wrapped her legs around his waist, pulled him even closer to her, flexed her thigh muscles to show him just how much she wanted him.

He made a helpless gurgling noise.

She squeezed tighter.

His breath was raspy and warm against her skin as he stroked her collarbone with his tongue. *Mind blown!*

She heard voices in the corridor, people passing by. Her stomach contracted and her breath stilled. Just a thin bifold door stood between them and public humiliation. At any moment, someone could push in on them.

His hand moved from the back of her head to cup her chin in his palm and spread his fingers out along her jawline. His skin was hot, his hand firm and powerful. He ran his thumb over her lips and she bit down, not too hard, but not lightly either. He tasted slightly salty and delicious.

Noah groaned softly and arched his back so that he was fully pressed against her. His pelvis lodged right between the V of her legs. If it wasn't for clothing, he would have been inside of her.

Her desire rocketed. She was cocked and ready to go off.

Voices again. Right outside the door. Someone mentioned Noah's name. Asked if anyone had seen him.

Momentarily, Kelsey's heart stopped. She couldn't see a thing. The cubbyhole was already dark, and the blindfold blocked out any remaining light.

The voices faded. Footsteps walking away.

Whew. Safe.

Except, without warning, Noah lifted her up, set her down on the floor.

She was disoriented, barely balancing on those thin high heels, but Noah's hands were still on her, guiding her. He turned her away from him, gently bent her over the shelving she'd just been sitting on, slipped the hem of her dress up over her bottom.

She gasped. Thrilled to her core. Mystery and excitement filled her. What was he going to do to her?

He leaned over her, whispered in her ear. "Is this what you want, Firefly?"

She nodded, unable to speak, aroused beyond measure.

"Say yes," he said. "Say yes to adventure."

"Yes," she whispered, terrified and thrilled all at the same time. What was he up to?

He kneed her legs farther apart.

Kelsey balanced precariously on her stilettoes.

Noah wrapped one hand around her waist to hold her steady, furled the hem of her long dress until it lay across her midback, revealing her naked buttocks. With a flick of his finger, he pulled the G-string to her knees.

Her pulse was a wild thing, beating like a rabbit running from a fox.

He stroked her bare cheek with a knuckle, sending ripples of desire pooling through her in waves. His other hand, the sinful thing, slipped between her legs touching her in all the right places.

With her eyes covered, blocking out her sense of sight, all her other senses blasted into hyperdrive.

Then his mouth was on her bare butt. Hot and wet.

She hissed in air through clenched teeth.

He chuckled. "More?"

"Please."

He nibbled, his teeth taking small erotic bites.

Holy sex machine. She whimpered, squirmed. Arched her spine and pressed her bottom up to him. She wanted more of that mouth!

His tongue danced over her skin, playfully drawing a figure eight. Or was that an infinity sign?

To infinity and beyond!

Yes.

He kept the one hand at her waist, the other doing mind-blowing things between her legs, and his mouth trailed down her backside.

The pressure inside her built.

She whimpered, aching for release.

"You are so gorgeous," he whispered, his breath hot against her skin. There was such admiration in his tone. Such reverence.

Her heart reeled, drunk with anticipation of what was to come.

Where is this going? the part of herself that Tasha called Comfort Kitty cried. *You're playing with fire. You're going to get burned. Back off. Back away. Go home before it's too late.*

But it was already too late.

Had been too late from the moment she'd seen him standing there on the dock in his adorable Christmas apron.

You're falling in love with him and what if he doesn't feel the same way? What if he breaks your heart? What if you break his? What if, what if, what if . . . her cautious side repeated like a computer glitch.

Heavens, the last thing she ever wanted was to hurt him again. She couldn't begin to imagine how hurt he'd been when she hadn't responded to his texts and phone calls ten years ago. Why had she allowed Filomena to control her life and keep her away from Noah?

You were seventeen and scared. You didn't know how to handle your feelings.

That was rational, yes, but was it also a rationalization?

Get out of your head, interrupted her body. *Be here now.*

Yes, stop missing out. She should concentrate on the wondrous things that Noah was doing to her. Forget thinking. Come what may, she would handle it. She was good at managing outcomes and consequences.

Resolutely, she brought her awareness back to his mouth.

That wicked, skilled mouth.

Immediately, goose bumps carpeted her skin.

Carefully, he eased one tender finger inside of her. "Firefly, you are so wet."

The goose bumps turned into an all over body shudder.

His pinky finger gently stroked the hooded head of her throbbing clitoris while a second finger joined the first one inside of her. His pinky flicked that tender spot with just enough pressure to send her straight into orbit.

She was so sensitized she felt everything. The gentle rocking of the paddle wheel boat in the water, the heat of his breath on her bottom, the slightly musty smell in the cubbyhole, the steady movement of his hand sending her higher and higher.

The smooth friction, the climbing pressure, the exquisite surge of sensation as he strummed her like guitar strings.

Her head spun, a crazed carousel of commotion.

It was too much. He was too much. Like eating an entire chocolate lava cake in one sitting. She wasn't prepared for this.

For him.

Faster and faster his hand caressed her.

She grasped the counter with both hands. Held on.

Her knees were so wobbly, she feared they would give out and send her tumbling noisily to the ground.

He tightened his grip around her waist as if sensing she was about to fall, but he never stopped what he was doing with his other hand. His ability to multitask astounded her. And that's what worried her.

How easy it was for him to mold her.

Each hot kiss, each calculated stroke, pushed her nearer and nearer to the brink of her sanity. His masterful fingers manipulated and controlled her. While his pinky kept up the steady rhythm, his two middle fingers sank deeper inside of her.

She sighed. If she died now, she'd die utterly happy.

He picked up his pace, and her muscles went rigid. He was magic. Electric. A right sexy Santa gifting her with pleasure beyond measure.

How special she felt. Pampered and cared for. For too long, she'd been the one doing the caretaking and nurturing. How good it felt to let go and let Noah take the reins.

And that alarmed her almost as much as it soothed her.

She floated in a sweet limbo land. Joyously hung out on the narrow strand of time. Dangling here and now. For this moment, she accepted everything, just as she feared that as soon as the moment was over, she'd snap back into her old, worrying ways.

They were down to the nitty-gritty. She was close, so very close to losing her mind.

The knowledge that at any second someone could shove open that bifold door and discover them in flagrante delicto—sent her around the bend.

Shocked, she embraced it. She couldn't get enough of him.

He was pressed against her back, his chin touching the top of her head as she clung helplessly to the counter, the scent of his cologne combined with his musky masculine aroma surrounding her. God, he smelled so good!

Kelsey wanted to eat him right up.

His erection poked hard at his zipper, straining to get out. To get to her.

Inside the blissful daze, inside the heat of her own skin, Kelsey simmered. In the darkness, she listened to the *bump-thump* of her drumming heartbeat. Her blood rolled hot through her veins and pooled deep inside the most feminine part of her.

The part of her where she ached for Noah to be.

If he could do this to her with his fingers, oh my heavens, what would he do to her with the hardest part of his body?

Lust fired her nerve endings. Endorphins flooded the pleasure centers of her brain. Cravings for him swallowed her whole.

Gone. She was absolutely gone. Wandering lost on a sea of sensation.

No. Not lost. Noah was there guiding the way. Offering her sweet sexual magic. Giving her his whimsy, his sense of adventure. Leading her where she'd been so afraid to tread.

"Come," he whispered softly in her ear. "Come, Firefly."

Firefly. Even his nickname for her was whimsical and spoken in a tone of wonder.

She felt so safe with him. So unafraid. He would never steer her wrong. Never knowingly hurt her.

The pulsating bass of the music throbbed up through the floorboards. A hard rock version of "I Saw Mommy Kissing Santa Claus."

Sensory overload.

Too much input. Her velvet dress. His silky pants. The cool air against her bare butt. She bit her bottom lip, writhed against his hand, accepted that he was driving her mad with lust. Embraced it.

"That's it, sweetheart," he cooed, his voice raspy with desire of his own. "Yes, yes. Let go. I *dare* you."

A dare. A challenge. A Christmas of Yes. She had to accept.

He touched her one last time, pressing in as if it were a secret button.

Kelsey burst. Flew right over the edge.

Her body felt both weighted and featherlight. She felt as if she'd been jettisoned into a warm black pit of squishy pudding. Time stretched, elongated, while at the same time, it seemed to shrink to the size of a BB and then pop wide open, until she was free floating through the cosmos.

She couldn't think. Couldn't form a coherent thought. Only fragments of words that floated through her head like Christmas snowflakes. A slow peaceful drift. Which was nice.

Noah. Her. Music. Fingers. Warmth. Tenderness.

Aah. Touch. Lips. Tongue. *Yesss.* Sweet. Hot. Precious. *Mmm.*

And finally, as her world exploded into a shattering of stars . . . *Noah, Noah, Noah.*

Her body lit up with the most incredible orgasm she'd ever had. The music and voices behind the thin walls of their cubbyhole were loud enough to drown out her mewling cries of release.

But it could not drown out the swelling of her over-flowing heart, and the realization that this was the life she *should* have been living all along.

CHAPTER 24

Edgy and fuzzy headed with lust, Noah tugged Kelsey's little G-string panty back into place, lowered the tail of her sexy velvet dress, untied her blindfold, stuffed the tie in his front pocket, and reached for her.

Noah cradled her in the crook of his arm.

She trembled against him.

He grinned. He'd wrecked her to rubble. Which had been his plan all along.

She rested her head against his chest. Slipped her arms around his neck. Sighed like she'd just run a marathon. He had defiled Mayor James's daughter. If she knew, Filomena would be livid.

Noah's grin widened. Gloating was not an honorable trait, but damn if he wasn't proud of himself for helping Kelsey cut off the leg iron of her mother's control. Yes, he was using sex as a weapon, but it was for Firefly's own good.

Sometimes the end *did* justify the means.

Still, he suddenly felt as if he was pulling the wool over Kelsey's eyes with sexual tricks. Was he being underhanded? Using her vulnerability to bond her to him?

He'd already started this, he had to finish it. No bailing
out now. Whether she knew it or not, she needed him.
And here was the important part: he needed her just as
much.

Although he'd done his best to hide it from himself,
he'd felt adrift after his divorce and his retirement from
the NBA. Yes, he'd rebounded. He had the support of
family. He'd bought the *Rockabye* and was making a go
of it. He was happy and doing well.

But still there had been this part of him, the seventeen-
year-old inside him, that had unfinished business with
Kelsey.

Time to be honest with himself. He wanted to be with
her. Was he rushing things? Was he being unrealistic?
He did have a habit of building sandcastle fantasies in his
mind before the groundwork was solidified. He should
slow his roll.

Kelsey's breathing came fast and shallow. She stepped
back as far as she could in the cubbyhole and tossed a
satisfied grin his way. Her eyelids lowered seductively.

Then he had to ask himself the biggest question of all.
Was he more invested in her than she was in him? That
was a startling thought. Sandcastles. Be careful. A fat
wave could knock them over and wash them out to sea.

Looking into Kelsey's eyes, his defenses dissolved
like soap bubbles. What a woman! How could he not
spin fantasies about her?

How had this happened? How had he lost himself to
her so completely again and in such a short time. Yes, they
had history, but they hadn't seen each other in ten years.

Yet from the moment he'd seen her again it was as if
no time had passed instead of a decade. And now, here
was this need to move heaven and earth to make her his.

They stared at each other. Gazes locked. He wondered if her thoughts were as complicated and jumbled as his. They belonged together now as much as they did the night he'd carved their names into the Sweetheart Tree in Sweetheart Park.

Kelsey looked baffled, ducked her head and glanced away, color rising to her cheeks. She put a hand to her temple, to her twitching eye.

He knew what that tic meant. She was anxious, stressed.

Without a word, he pulled her to him again. Gently massaged her temple. Felt the muscle jump faster beneath his fingertips. Was *he* the cause of her stress? Or was the tic due to him pushing her outside her comfort zone?

Much as he wanted to make things better for her, he wasn't going to stop pushing. Seeing the world in a new way was what she needed to break her mother's hold over her. It was what they both needed to bring closure to the past and pave the way for the future.

There's those sandcastles again, MacGregor.

Noah had an uphill battle ahead of him. He knew that, but he wasn't going to stop trying. He'd given up ten years ago because Filomena had pulled out the big guns and threatened his scholarship. But now? The woman had no hold over him.

Except for the way she treated Kelsey.

"Your turn," she said.

"No—"

Her hand locked around his wrist. "Yes."

"I—"

"Turnabout is fair play," she said, her tone brooking no argument.

She pulled out the blindfold.

He gulped, overwhelmed with lust for her.

"Turn around," she commanded. "Now."

"That's kinda bossy."

"I'm a campaign manager. How do you think I keep people in line?"

Wow, this was a whole new side of her. Noah approved. Heartily. Firefly was turning the tables on him and he loved it.

Chuckling, Noah obeyed, and turned his back to her.

"You're going to have to bend down a bit, tall man."

Noah loosened his knees, crouched halfway while she tied the blindfold over his eyes.

His pulse kicked up the way it had on the basketball court whenever he broke away from the pack to make a run for the basket and score a layup to win the game.

She turned him around and kissed him.

It felt as if they were kissing for the very first time. A kiss bursting with heat and adventure, with passion and gung-ho exploration. Something was definitely different about Kelsey tonight. Something had changed. She was no longer hesitant or holding back. She was fully embracing her sexuality.

What caused the shift?

Noah had no idea. He only knew that kissing her was the hottest, most heartfelt thing he'd ever done.

"Who are you?" he joked. "And what have you done with my cautious Kelsey?"

"I booted her," she said. "She was boring."

"Not boring—"

"Boring. She would never dare do something like this . . ."

"Something like what?" His mouth was so dry it felt like he'd swallowed the desert.

"Like this." She positioned him against the wall. "Spread your legs."

He did as she commanded, his belly and pelvic muscles clenching tight. He felt her sink to her knees in front of him.

His heart was a drum—*bam, bam, bam.*

Kelsey reached for the zipper of his trousers.

Noah blew out his breath in a swift, hot rush.

Slowly, she eased the zipper down.

Holy shit, was this really happening? By the time she got his pants and boxer briefs shucked to his knees, he was granite hard and ready for her.

She touched him, and his shaft jerked. "You are so big," she murmured, her voice in awe. "I'm going to love tasting you."

Noah groaned.

"This will teach you to lure me into casino cubbyholes, mister." She blew her breath across his skin.

He sucked in air.

She touched the tip of her tongue to the head of his shaft.

A low feral growl flew from his lips. He wanted to tell her so many things. How beautiful he thought she was. How even after ten years apart she still made him tremble. How he would gratefully give up everything he owned to be with her forever.

But his throat was too dry and tight for any words to emerge. He'd been reduced to guttural animal sounds. His brain had left the building. All he could focus on was the feeling of her lips wrapping around his throbbing shaft.

He was lost, absolutely lost.

But what a way to go!

She turned him inside out and upside down and every which way but loose. He did not know where she'd learned her tricks. He did not care. An orgasm shook through him, an earthquake of a release.

And when she was finished with him, he was left a quivering shell of a man.

"You . . . that . . ." he gasped. He shook his head. What could he say. His mind—and his body—had been completely and utterly blown.

He sank down the length of the wall, joined her on the floor. Stripped off the blindfold, reached with Jell-O arms to cup her cheeks between his palms and hold her still while he stared deeply into her eyes.

"Firefly," he whispered and then he pulled her to him so that she was leaning over his long legs. He kissed her eyelids, her forehead, each cheek, her cute little chin. Then finally he took her mouth and showed her just how much he loved and appreciated her.

But that was the problem, wasn't it? He still didn't know if she loved him back. And wouldn't know until he was brave enough to say the words.

"Thank you," she whispered.

"Shh." He pressed his lips to her twitching temple. "Thank *you*."

"I . . . this . . ."

"You're feeling weird," he said.

She bobbed her head. "You know me too well."

"Don't forget that." He gave her the kindest smile in his arsenal.

They sat for a long moment in each other's arms, listening to the racket outside their safe little cocoon.

"How exactly do we come out of this closet now?" she asked.

"We strut right out. No regrets. We're grown consenting adults. We have nothing to be ashamed of. Hold your head high." He wasn't going to give her time to fret. He pulled her off the floor, clasped her hand in his, pushed open the bifold door and led her back to the casino.

The room was wall-to-wall with people in formal attire gathered at the gambling tables. From the decorated trees in the corners to the mistletoe garlands strung over the doorways to the festive, white, holiday cocktails people clutched in their hands, the place screamed Christmas.

The merry location was why he'd invited her to the event, but now he wished for a more secluded venue than Twilight's biggest shindig of the season. There were too many people, too much noise, just too much of everything after their very private encounter.

"Hey." Kelsey elbowed him lightly in the ribs. "There's Sean and Tasha."

Yep, sure enough, over by the roulette wheel stood his handyman and Kelsey's best friend placing their bets. Tasha's head rested on Sean's shoulder. Sean's eyes were bright and there was a pile of chips and empty martini glasses in front of both him and Tasha. What happened to snuggling up at the *Rockabye* to Netflix and chill?

"Do you want to go say hello?" he asked. "Or slip out the back way?"

"Noah!" Sean caught Noah's eye and raised a hand. "Over here."

"Too late for escape." Kelsey chuckled and headed over to the roulette wheel.

Noah followed.

"Where did you get the formal wear last minute?" Kelsey eyed Tasha's outfit. The dress was sunflower yellow and looked more appropriate for a senior prom than a black-tie Christmas party.

"Raylene Pringle," Tasha said. "She came to the *Rockabye*, insisted we come to the party while she held down the fort. Brought along this dress. Beggars can't be choosers."

"Bets, bets, place your bets," the roulette dealer called.

"Join us," Sean invited, kicking out the empty chair on the other side of him. "We're on a hot streak. Tasha is charmed. Rub her shoulder for good luck and place a bet."

"I credit the yellow," Tasha said. "It's an attention-getting color. Go ahead. Rub."

"I can't," Noah said. The only woman he wanted to rub on was Kelsey. "I'm running this charity, so gambling is a conflict of interest."

"Oh yeah," Sean said.

"How about you, Kels?" Tasha said, extending her arm. "Wanna rub me for good luck and place a bet?"

"I'm not a gambler." Kelsey stepped back to let a server go by.

"Christmas of Yes," Tasha said.

"Place your bets, ladies and gents," said the roulette dealer dressed in old-school Monte Carlo casino attire.

"Do it, do it, do it," Tasha chanted.

"Place your bets."

"I don't know how," Kelsey said.

"High time you learned." Sean leaned over to hand Kelsey a pile of chips.

"Oh wow, okay." Kelsey glanced at Noah.

He nodded, encouraging her. Raised his sleeve so she could see his tattoo. *Dare.* "Rub me." Tasha flapped her arm like a wing.

"I don't believe in good luck charms," Kelsey said. "It's magical thinking—"

"Place your bets," the dealer said. "Last call." The other people at the table were starting to look irritated.

"Okay, okay. I'll play along." Rolling her eyes and smiling sheepishly, Kelsey rubbed Tasha's elbow. "Now what do I do?"

"Give the man your chips," Sean instructed. "And bet exactly the way Tasha does."

"Here goes . . ." Kelsey looked at the chips. "How much is this?"

"Fifteen dollars."

"Here goes fifteen dollars," she said and bet it all on red.

The dealer closed the betting, spun the wheel. The ball landed on red. Everyone at the table had bet on red. A cheer went up. The dealer paid out the chips. People hopped up to rush over and rub on Tasha, who was looking like a puppy in a nursing home. Adored and fawned over.

But Noah had eyes for only Kelsey. She was, he decided, the most mesmerizing woman in the room. All high-society elegance and class. He licked his lips, remembering what they'd just done in the storage room. She was counting her chips, unaware that he was studying her. He had a desperate urge to whisk her back to the *Rockabye* and make love to her good and proper.

Doubt ate at him. Why would a woman like her want anything to do with him long-term? She'd made it clear she didn't want any strings attached. Why did he keep hoping? He was cruising for a bruising.

"Wow, I can see how people get addicted to gambling. Winning is fun!" She beamed.

"Wanna another hit of this?" Tasha held up her elbow again.

"I think I'll quit while I'm ahead." Kelsey cast a surreptitious glance over at Noah. Gauging his reaction? "Here are your chips back." She extended her winnings to Sean.

Sean held up a palm. "Keep it. My gift to you. Go claim your prize."

"Wait, wait," Tasha said. "There's one rule though."

"What kind of rule?" Kelsey asked.

"You have to pick something fun. Nothing practical. No toaster oven. No flat iron. It has to be *fun*."

"I'm afraid to ask what you think constitutes fun," Kelsey said.

"Better yet," Noah added. "Something Christmassy and fun."

"Ooh, good idea." Tasha rubbed her palms together. "Go help her pick something out, Noah."

"Ignore her," Kelsey said to Noah. "She gets off on telling people what to do."

"Is that true?" Sean lowered his voice and leaned in closer to Tasha.

Tasha giggled and pressed her nose against Sean's. "I have this dominatrix costume . . ."

Kelsey placed her hands over her ears. "TMI, TMI."

"Oh, like you have any room to talk," Tasha said. "We saw you two coming out of the closet readjusting your clothing. And hey, wasn't your hair in an upsweep earlier?"

Kelsey's face reddened.

Noah took pity on her, looped his arm through hers. "C'mon, I'll help you select your prize."

Kelsey stuck her winnings into her pocket and Noah guided her over to the prize table so that she could cash in her chips. He enjoyed the feel of her body so close to his. He moved his hand from her arm to the small of her back. God, he loved touching her.

He slid her a sidelong glance as she stepped up to the table and examined the prizes. She picked up a food processor.

"If you like to cook, that might be fun," he said. "But it's not the least bit Christmassy."

"What if I use it to make Christmas treats?"

He made a noise like the buzzer on *Jeopardy* whenever a contestant gave a wrong answer.

"Okay, fine." She put the food processor back down. "How about this Christmas blanket?" She fingered a flannel throw blanket with a picture of Santa's face on it.

"Is it fun?" he asked.

"It would be fun if you snuggled underneath it with me."

"How about this?" he asked, reaching for a strand of battery-powered Christmas lights that changed colors to different patterns and played holiday music to boot. "I could wrap them around you, turn them on, and we could have all kinds of fun."

"Sold," she said, cashing her chips for the musical lights.

The cashier bagged up the lights for her. Winked. "Make sure you pick up extra batteries. I have a feeling you two are going to use them up fast."

CHAPTER 25

"That was embarrassing," Kelsey said as Noah escorted her away from the gift table.

"Small town." He shrugged. "What are you gonna do? Gossip will always be the lifeblood of this place."

"It doesn't bother you that everyone knows we're . . ." She paused. What were they?

"Not at all." His voice was smooth and velvety. "I'm proud to be seen with you."

Suddenly, it felt as if things were moving too fast. She didn't know whether to slam on the brakes or mash the gas pedal and drive right over the cliff.

Her life was so complicated and looking at his bruised face, it occurred to her just how much she could complicate his. She cared for Noah deeply and the last thing she ever wanted was for blowback from her mother to land on him. Filomena had threatened him once. What was to say she wouldn't do it again?

"Listen," Noah said. "The party is winding down, but I have to stick around to help clean up. I'm going to put you in an Uber and send you back to the *Rockabye*."

"I could stick around and help."

He cut his eyes at her. "Dressed like that?"

"You're dressed in a tux."

"I brought a change of clothes. I'm putting on jeans as soon as everyone leaves. Besides, you need your rest. You're not going to get much sleep tomorrow night."

"Oooh," she said. "I like the sound of that. What have you got up your sleeve, Noah MacGregor?"

"You'll have to wait and see." He bent to kiss her. "Grab your coat and I'll walk you out. Do you want me to call you a car, so you can go back via the road, or do you want the ferry so you can go back by water?"

She shivered. "A car. It's gotten colder."

"Your wish is my command." He pulled his phone and ordered a car on the Uber app.

"Listen," she said. "I want to thank you for the gifts you sent me. The masseuse, Shirley for the mani-pedi, the kismet cookie, the amaryllis. I felt pampered and cared for."

"Good. That's how I wanted you to feel."

"It was very nice, but tonight . . ." She smiled. "Well, that was perfect."

"I'm glad you liked it. Not so bad yourself, Firefly."

"But I do want to set something straight."

He looked a little worried but pasted on a gung-ho smile. "Sure, what's that?"

"I get the feeling that you're expecting something more than I can give you right now."

"No, no, no." His smile didn't slip for a minute, but she saw the muscle in his jaw tic. "My only goal is to make you happy."

She blinked at him. "Are you sure, because I was getting the distinct impression from those gifts you showered on me that—"

"Absolutely not. We discussed this. Keep it caz. No strings attached. I get it. We're cool."

"Oh good." She let out a long-held breath. It wasn't that she didn't hope for more from Noah, it's just that she wasn't ready for him.

"Does this mean you don't want to get together tomorrow night?"

"I'm looking very forward to that. Especially after tonight." She licked her lips.

"Glad to hear that because do I have some fun things planned for you." His smile was genuine this time. He winked. "Just you wait and see."

Mind churning about the pleasures Noah had in store for her, Kelsey headed for the coat check area. Her imagination was so revved, she hardly heard Tasha call her name.

"Kelsey!"

She tipped the coat check clerk and turned to find her friend standing behind her. Sean hovered, a few steps away, as if he were Tasha's bodyguard.

"Hey," she said. "What's up?"

"It's time to give you this back." Tasha held out Kelsey's phone to her. "Past time, really. It's been over seventy-two hours and you haven't asked for it back."

Was it possible she'd forgotten about her phone? Her thoughts had been so full of Noah, she hadn't missed it.

"Did you turn it on?"

Tasha shook her head. "It's your phone."

Kelsey took the phone, sudden dread hooking into her.

"You know, you don't have to turn it back on until we leave," Tasha said.

"I should go ahead and face it head-on." Bracing herself for a barrage of angry messages, Kelsey hit the power button and watched the screen as it booted up, her muscles tense. Her eye started to twitch.

"Do you want me to hang around?" Tasha asked. "Or would you rather have some privacy?"

"I'm okay. Go be with Sean. Enjoy the party while it lasts."

Tasha's brow wrinkled. "You sure?"

"Positive." Kelsey whipped up an encouraging smile. She tucked a strand of loose hair behind her ear. She was still getting used to the shorter haircut.

"Okay, if you need me, just text."

"I'll be fine."

She waited until her friend and Sean had gone back to the dance floor before she looked down at her phone.

Nothing from her mother.

No texts. No missed calls. No email.

It had been five days since Filomena had sent her goons to try and kidnap Kelsey and not once had she tried to contact her.

Wow. What did it mean?

Could her mother be acting like a normal human being for once and giving her space to figure things out?

It was a nice thought, but a highly dangerous one. Only fools underestimated Filomena and Kelsey was no fool.

Her mother was plotting revenge. Kelsey knew it in her bones. At this point, the rage-fueled harangues and tirades were preferable to total silence.

By letting her mother control her life, she'd missed out on so much. How had she gone so long without the freedom to decide what she liked and what she didn't? She'd been nothing but an extension of her mother, doing what she had to do to maintain the peace.

But at what cost?

She'd sacrificed her sense of self for calm. She'd run from a fight, knowing she could not win against her mother. It had never occurred to her to just walk away.

"You ready to go?" Noah appeared in front of her wearing a sexy smile, blue jeans, cowboy boots, and his familiar plaid shirt. The man looked just as delicious in work clothes as he did in a tuxedo. "Your Uber is here."

She glanced around and saw that most of the guests had gone or were at the door wishing Joel good-night. "Yes," she said, stuffing her phone in her purse. "I'm ready."

Noah slipped his arm through hers and guided her outside.

The night air was bracing in an it's-good-to-be-alive kind of way. She felt brave, she felt free, she felt as if she were living life large. Never mind what her mother was up to.

It was time for Kelsey to embrace who she was. She wasn't a grinch. Far from it. She was falling in love. With Christmas, with Twilight, with Noah. She didn't know what that meant long-term. She didn't have to figure it out tonight.

Letting go of planning was a revelation for a woman who organized everything to the nth degree. It was okay not to know. Okay to embrace the uncertainty. Okay to just enjoy the beautiful gift of this moment without having to have all the answers or know what the future held.

He walked her down the pier to the vehicle waiting at the boat ramp. All along the shore Christmas lights twinkled. Even though it was close to midnight, the good people of Twilight kept their Christmas spirit shining out into the night. A carpet of stars glittered above them.

The very same stars that had once shined down on them when they were teenagers in the throes of their first romance.

Kelsey burrowed deeper into her coat and snuggled closer to Noah. The smell of cedar rode the air and from a Mexican restaurant on the shore, the smell of fajitas. He held her tight.

When they reached the end of the pier to where the Uber waited with the engine running, Noah turned to kiss her temple at the muscle that tended to get twitchy.

But she wasn't twitchy now.

She felt settled and safe. She wasn't scared of the dark or the water. Which was weird, but at the same time liberating. She had nothing to fear. Noah held her in the circle of his arm. He wouldn't let anything happen to her.

The wind ruffled her hair as his lips shifted from her temple to her lips. "Good night, Firefly. Sleep well."

"Wait!" Tasha came bounding down the pier after them, slipping into her coat on the fly. "I'll ride with you."

Noah held the back door open for them. Kelsey scooted across the seat as Tasha slipped underneath Noah's arm and piled in beside her.

"Get home safely," Noah said. "I'll see you ladies to-morrow." He shut the door and waved good-bye as the Uber drove off.

"Well?" Tasha asked, squirming around in the seat until she was facing Kelsey.

"Put your seat belt on."

"Yes, mother." Tasha had to rearrange herself again to get her seat belt buckled.

"How come you're here with me instead of with Sean?"

"He's staying to help clean up, but said I had to leave since I looked way too hot in this banana cream pie dress. Turns out banana cream pie is his favorite dessert. Who knew?" Tasha giggled.

"Too much temptation, huh?"

"I'm gonna wear him down yet, you wait and see. But enough about me. What was on your phone?"

"Nothing."

"Eww." Tasha pulled her lips away from her teeth and hissed in a breath. "Scary."

"Yeah."

Tasha reached across the seat and squeezed Kelsey's forearm. "I'm here."

"Thank you, Tash. I don't know what I'd do without you."

"Same deal-ee-o from this side of the car, sister. I love you unconditionally, even if *she* can't."

Kelsey felt tears press at the back of her eyelids, but she blinked them away. She'd cried enough for one day.

"But things with Noah are good?"

"So good."

"Awesome sauce! When are you guys seeing each other again?"

"Tomorrow evening."

"Squee! I'm so excited for you." Tasha slapped both thighs with her palms. "I think it's time for your last dare."

"Already? We still have a week left in Twilight."

"You're making such great progress. I'm proud of

you. Blowing through those dares like they were easy and I know they weren't."

Kelsey thought about how much she'd changed in one short week and Tasha's dares had been a big part of her growth. Sure, Clive leaving her at the altar had been the main catalyst, but Tasha bringing her to Twilight and Noah and issuing those dares had kickstarted her goal of finding herself.

"What's the final dare?"

"Please yourself."

"What?"

"I dare you to please yourself."

"Are you talking about—"

"Masturbation? No, but that's not a bad idea either."

"Tasha!" Kelsey inclined her head toward the Uber driver.

"Kelsey!"

"Elaborate . . . on the dare, not the other thing."

"I dare you to do what pleases *you*. Not your mother, not your father, not Noah, not me. *You*. What do *you* like? What do *you* want?"

"In regard to . . . ?"

"Anything, everything."

"That's too broad. Could you narrow it down for me?"

"Okay, let's start with your career. Do you really want to work as the mayor's office manager? Or would you rather run Lionel Berg's gubernatorial campaign? Or is there something else you'd rather do entirely?"

"I don't know."

"Then that is your fifth dare. Figure out what it is you truly want to do with your life and then please yourself. Don't factor anyone else into the equation. This is about you and you alone."

"But that feels so selfish—"

"Ptt, ptt, ptt." Tasha held up a palm. "No excuses. This is your Christmas of Yes. The only thing I want to hear out of you is, 'Yes, Tasha, I accept your dare.'"

"Yes, Tasha." Kelsey grinned like a loon. "I accept your dare."

"Perfect, now tell me all about what happened in that little closet and don't you dare leave a thing out . . ."

"Why are you looking so glum?" Joel asked Noah as he sat counting money. Noah was sweeping up, shoving an industrial push broom over the casino floor. Everyone else had left the *Brazos Queen*. "We had a great night. It looks like we're going to double last year's take. ALS research is going to have a very merry Christmas courtesy of the MacGregor twins."

"I'm not glum," Noah denied, his mind tangled up on what Kelsey had told him earlier. She'd made it abundantly clear she hadn't changed her mind about the no-strings-attached thing. He thought he'd accepted it the first time she'd brought it up, but now he knew he'd been holding out hope that she'd change her mind. That he could change her mind and make her want him the way he wanted her.

"Trouble with Kelsey?"

"Not trouble, no."

Joel stopped counting. "You've fallen in love with her all over again, haven't you?"

"No," he mumbled, outright lying to his twin.

A week ago, if anyone had told him that Kelsey James would come storming back into his life and sweep him off his feet, he'd have laughed his ass off. But now? He felt as muddled and confused as the night he'd watched the taillights of her mother's car disappear into the darkness.

Nothing had really changed.

She might be finally breaking away from her mother and finding herself—and he was damn happy for her about that—but between the two of them, well, she was still that unreachable princess in her ivory tower and he was still plain old Noah MacGregor living on a houseboat on Lake Twilight. He had nothing to offer a woman like her. Never had, never would.

"She's more relaxed when you're around," Joel said.

"Huh?" Noah blinked. He'd zoned out leaning against the push broom.

"Kelsey. Whenever you're around, she smiles more and her eye stops doing that twitchy thing." Joel toggled a finger near his own eye. "You're good for her."

His twin must have been reading his mind. They had an uncanny ability to know what the other was thinking.

"And she's good for you."

"How's that?"

"Your eyes are brighter, your step quickens, you have more get-up-and-go. She fires you up and you calm her down. Looks like a good match from where I'm sitting."

"Yeah, well, I don't fit in her world and she doesn't fit in mine. Never have, never will."

"How can you be so sure?"

"She's made it clear that all she wants is sex."

"And that's bad because . . ."

"I want more."

Joel sighed. "I'm sorry, bro."

"I know she's out of my league. I've always known it, but that doesn't stop me from loving her."

"You underestimate yourself. That's always been your problem."

"I do not."

"You gave up on basketball."

"I got injured."

"You could have recovered from it."

"There's plenty of great basketball players out there. The world didn't need another one."

"See, underestimating yourself. Until you stop doing that, you're never going to attract the love you deserve. Whether it's with Kelsey or someone else."

"Oh yeah?"

"You've got this happy-go-lucky thing going on and that's great. People love to be around you, but you use it as a reason for not showing up in your own life."

"Have you been watching *Dr. Phil* again?"

"No. I've just been watching you breeze through life, keeping everything smooth and on the surface for the last twenty-seven years. Here's the deal, bro. You pursue what you think will bring you satisfaction—"

"Doesn't everybody?"

"Not to the degree that you do. You believe you are only good or okay if you feel good. You got injured on the basketball court. You felt bad. Therapy made you feel worse, because that's what physical therapy does for a while until it starts making you feel better. That's what you did with Melissa and that's what you're doing with Kelsey. Giving up too soon."

"I'm not following you."

"Are you really that dense or are you just hiding out from yourself? Kelsey is as crazy about you as you are about her. Anyone can see that. But you tell yourself this story about not being good enough for her, because relationships are hard. As soon as turbulence hits, you bail."

Did he really? Stunned, Noah stared at his twin.

"Don't let her get away by brushing her off just because it's easier to let her go than fight for her."

"What are you saying? Brass tacks?"

"Tell the woman you love her, dumbass."

"She made it clear she doesn't want me for the long term."

"She's just throwing up a wall to protect her own feelings or maybe, hell, she's trying to protect you."

"I'm not sure about that."

Joel rolled his eyes. "Okay. Have it your way. But don't come crying to me when you lose the love of your life for a second time."

CHAPTER 26

Pulse beating in his veins, Noah knocked on Kelsey's door. He was so keyed up and ready to make love to her that he couldn't stand the tension.

She was dressed in a modest, long-sleeved green wrap dress. He couldn't wait to take it off and get his hands on what was underneath.

"What do you have in store for me tonight?"

"Just you wait and see."

"Where are we going?"

"We're staying right here on the island."

"Hmm," she said going up on tiptoes to nibble his earlobe. "Your room?"

"No. You'll need your coat."

"I can't wait." She slipped into her coat.

He took her by the hand and led her down the corridor. The hallway was empty. Since it was Saturday evening, most of the guests were out on the town.

They climbed the stairs that led to the upper deck. Cold wind blasted them when Noah opened the door and Kelsey huddled deeper into her coat.

"This better not be our destination," she said. "I know

I'm stepping out of my comfort zone but sex on the bridge is not my idea of a good time."

"Not the bridge," he said. "The dome."

He led her around the bridge toward the glass dome he'd built for night sky viewing on the river. Tonight the sky was overcast. No stars to be seen. But that was okay. They wouldn't have much time for stargazing anyway.

"Oh look," she said, stopped at the railing. "You can see the town square from here."

He stopped behind her, put his hands on her shoulders. Her sweet scent tangled up in his nose.

"It's so beautiful all lit up."

"The spirit of Christmas," he murmured.

She took a deep breath of cool, bracing air. Held it. Noah realized he was holding his breath too. At last, she exhaled. "I can feel the Christmas spirit here. In Twilight. With you."

He wrapped his arms around her, cuddled her against him. In this moment, he was the happiest man in the world. She turned into him, went up on tiptoes again, tugged his head down to meet hers.

"Your nose is cold," he whispered.

"So is yours."

"Let's get warm," he said.

"And then we'll get naked?"

He laughed. "Slow your roll, hotshot. We've got all night."

"Are you sure you can last that long?" She winked.

"C'mon," he said. "Let's get inside where it's warm."

He opened the door to the glass-domed room. There was an electric fireplace spreading warmth throughout the room. The dome had been built for maximum comfort, the furnishings designed so guests could lie back and gaze up at the stars. Two big comfy sectional couches with ottomans for lounging were positioned directly under the center of the dome. On the wall above the fireplace hung a seventy-two-inch flat screen TV and it was playing a winter scene of snow falling.

The room had been decorated with Christmas lights. Five thousand in all. He hit the remote in his pocket and the lights came on, glowing their special magic.

"Oh my," Kelsey whispered and touched her chin in awe.

Noah shrugged out of his coat, helped Kelsey off with hers, and then he drew her to him and kissed her beneath the twinkling lights.

With each kiss, things just got better and better. Her mouth was a honeypot, sweet and hot, stoking the fires of his desire. He was nervous about this. Tonight, no more fooling around. They were finally going to go all the way.

There had been enough buildup. The time had come for the real deal. He'd been waiting for this moment for ten long years.

And Noah had every intention of loving her until the sun came up.

They were fated. He knew it to the very center of his bones. After his talk with Joel last night he realized his brother was right. He'd been underestimating himself . . . and Kelsey.

Tonight, he would show her how much she meant to him. Tonight, he would touch and taste every inch of her beautiful body. Tonight, he would prove his love for her.

There was food and drink in the mini-fridge, a deadbolt on the door, and black velvet curtains that would be drawn around the lower portion of the dome, sealing them into their love cocoon.

His lips, his tongue, his eyes, his hands would traverse the sweet territories of her soft form, exploring the boundaries, pushing beyond them to tap into her heart, her mind, her soul.

Slowly, he undressed her in the misty glow of Christmas lights, his humble fingers tugging at the back of her dress.

She slipped the dress off her shoulders and let it pool to her feet, stepped from the circle of the material, looked up at him with shiny tears. She wore a purple bra and matching silk panties, all frill and lace.

He stared at her, enrapt.

It was her turn to undress him. She worked the buttons on his shirt with deliberate slowness, slanting him coy sidelong glances as she took her time. And when he was down to his boxer briefs, she ducked her head and giggled like a schoolgirl.

God, he loved hearing that carefree giggle.

They took off their own underwear at the same time, staring into each other's eyes as they stripped, then left their clothes on the floor in a heap. He reached out and took her hand. Together they walked toward the sectionals that formed a giant square filled in by the big ottomans.

Gleefully, they piled into the middle of the setup. The cushions were soft and bouncy. Earlier, he'd brought a king-sized sheet and blankets and together they made a pallet over the ottomans.

"We're going to be able to see the sky while we make love," she said.

"Yes."

"People could stumble up on the roof and see us through the glass."

He reached for the remote he'd left lying on the back of the sectional, hit the button that brought the heavy black curtains from where they were hidden inside the wall, and slowly the mechanism spooled the curtains out to join at the back of the sectionals.

She applauded. "It's like we're floating on a cloud."

"A Christmas cloud," he corrected, as he hit another remote and soft Christmas music seeped through the speakers.

"I feel like I'm in one of those old 1960s romantic comedies where the playboy guy has all these gadgets of seduction."

He wriggled his eyebrows as Dean Martin started singing "Baby, It's Cold Outside."

She crinkled her nose. "Boy, how times have changed since that song was popular."

"Good thing I'm not a playboy." He drew her closer.

"Nope?"

"Not in the least."

"Not even with all the women chasing you?"

"I'm a one-woman man."

"And I'm that woman?"

"You are." He kissed her forehead. "It's always been you, Firefly."

"Even when you were married?"

"I've always carried a torch for you. Might have been why it didn't hurt so badly when Melissa left me."

She cuddled against him. He inhaled the scent of her hair.

"I could die happy right now." She sighed.

"Let's not do that," he said. "Let's live to the fullest and make up for lost time."

"I'm on board."

"Oh," he said. "I almost forgot your Christmas present."

"But it's not Christmas."

"Trust me. You're going to want to open this package. Be right back." He dashed to the restroom where he'd stashed his props. Wrapped himself in the battery-powered strand of Christmas lights she'd won at the casino, then topped it with his Christmas Bards costume.

He came out and did a personal striptease for his woman, complete with blinking holiday lights that played "All I Want for Christmas Is You."

Kelsey applauded and catcalled. He winked and performed for her with everything he had inside him. She patted her palm against her heart as if it were about to beat out of her chest.

He grinned, gyrated closer.

She giggled, blushed, ducked her head, peeked at him from behind a strand of hair falling over her face.

When he was stripped of all his clothes and was left draped only in the blinking lights, she reached out her hand and wriggled her fingers in a come-hither gesture.

He dove onto the sectional with her, the lights all going red and him blinking like Rudolph on Christmas Eve.

While the fire blazed and the snow fell in the TV scene and music played and Christmas lights twinkled, and the clouds moved to reveal stars twinkling overhead, they plowed underneath the covers together.

She touched him in the right places and his shaft rose hard into the palm of her hand. Noah was overwhelmed by how easily she manipulated him.

And she was loving every minute of it.

Their mouths met, and his fingers traced her jawline. She was hot. Burning with passion and power and feminine strength. Touching her seared his skin with a blistering energy of his own.

Kelsey encircled him in her arms, tugging him down into the covers, her kisses growing more and more demanding.

She was beautiful, and he was so lucky. She was a goddess, rare and splendid. Her cool exterior had completely melted. Her inner firefly, bright and free, had emerged. The vivid woman he'd always known was hidden beneath her hesitation and self-doubts. She shed her reserve for him. Let go of her fears.

For him.

For them.

She touched his body without caution or fear. Not holding back. Giving him her all. She didn't hesitate. She was his past, his present, and he prayed that she was his future too. Never before had a woman possessed him so entirely. Her tongue was sweet torment. Her fingers delicate tools of exquisite torture.

Her courage.

Her confidence.

Her daring.

Yes. She'd dared to leave her comfort zone and join him in his world. He loved her for that and for so many other things. She had surrendered her mask. Allowed him to see the real Kelsey beneath. Engaging with him in the flow of their bodies as they caressed and kissed each other.

They were directly under the vast expanse of sky. It felt as if they were entangled in the Milky Way, mating in the stars. Her feminine energy merged with his masculine essence. Together, they were complete. Whole.

Kelsey pushed Noah onto his back, let out a wicked little laugh, and straddled him. She locked her legs tight around his waist, pressing her pelvic bone against his.

His erection pulsated. He ached to be inside her.

To at long last be joined with her in the sacred dance as old as the stars.

Noah felt as if he'd been given a most cherished gift. A second chance at love. And she was the prize, his golden-haired goddess.

Over the years, he'd tried to forget her. To move on with his life. And he'd managed to cobble out an existence many people envied. But no matter what he did, what he achieved, who he was with, there was always this secret longing at the back of his mind. The sad realization that there was something missing.

His life had been like one of those complicated puzzles that took months to finish, only to find when the puzzle was finished that there was one piece missing. One piece gone.

Now he felt as if he'd finally found that lost piece and snapped it into place. His puzzle complete.

Their lips traveled the landscape of each other's skin, with measured, meticulous movements. Lingering now and again to finger or lick the boundaries of an erogenous zone. To investigate and uncover deeper and deeper layers of sensation.

They whispered sweet nothings to each other as they nibbled earlobes and breathed over clefts and valleys. Lips buzzing vibrations over bellies and breasts, napes and necks.

He groaned.

She moaned.

He whimpered.

She mewled.

The surface beneath them was so soft they sank lower and lower into the cushions.

He kissed her face, her eyelids, her nose, her temples. She stroked his abs, the V-shaped musculature that ran along his pelvis. He licked a trail from her nipples to the triangle between her thighs.

Kelsey threaded her hands through his hair, stopped him from sliding farther. "No." She breathed. "I want more. I want *you*. Inside *me*."

"It's too soon," he whispered.

"No, it's not soon enough."

"If we go now, I won't last five seconds."

"I don't mind. We'll go, then start again."

"I have a better idea," he said.

"What's that?" she asked.

"The deep freeze."

"Deep freeze? That sounds cold."

"'Tis the point." Noah winked wickedly, grabbed her hand, and hauled her to her feet.

"Wh-where . . . Noah . . ."

He didn't give her a chance to back out, just draped a blanket around them both and hustled her to the door.

"Where are we going?"

"Outside," he said and plunged them from the warm cocoon room into the brisk air on the dark bridge. Naked save for the blanket thrown over their shoulders. The air was brisk, and snowflakes began drifting from the sky. The wooden flooring beneath chilled her feet. The moment was surreal, crazy.

It was absolutely epic and nothing she would ever in a million years have imagined herself doing.

"What now?" she asked through chattering teeth.

"Ten deep breaths," he said. "Then we go back in."

"Oh thank God, I thought you were going to suggest we jump into the water."

"There's deep freeze and then there's hypothermia," he said. "We want to avoid the latter."

"Good thinking."

They inhaled together, cold filling their lungs. Noah's skin turned pink and his cheeks flushed red and she supposed hers did the same. His grin hung from his face like a Christmas wreath. He was still wearing those silly lights, though some of them had come unwrapped and were dragging behind him.

"You're amazing," she said, shivering alongside of him as they breathed in tandem.

"Me?" He speared her with his gaze. "For dragging you naked into the cold?"

"By giving me new experiences that crack my world wide open."

"Let's get back inside, Miss Adventuresome. You're starting to turn blue."

"But we've only taken six deep breaths."

"Good enough. I no longer have a hair trigger."

"Our goal achieved."

He swept her back into the dome, shut and locked the door behind them. Wrapped the blanket tightly around her and whisked her to the fireplace. "Warm up," he said. "I'll get us a hot toddy."

After tippling some rum into the eggnog, he heated it in the microwave, brought the mug over to her. They sipped eggnog and stood by the fire until they were warmed inside and out and then he led her back to their makeshift bed.

As she looked into his eyes, Kelsey understood that this was going to be the most erotic moment of her life.

Noah lay down on his back and pulled her on top of him. Her knees straddling either side of his body. The strand of lights still wound around his head like a crown, still blinking their fun Christmas magic. His hands went around her waist, holding her snug against him.

"Firefly," he said. "You're in charge. You set the pace."

He produced a condom and she put it to use, rolling it onto his erection. She felt daring and dangerous, hot and horny. This, at long last, was the real Kelsey.

"Take your time," Noah coached. "No rush."

"I'm so excited," she confessed. "This feels like we're in a safe little Christmas cocoon."

"We are," he said. "That's the point of being here."

"You made tonight so perfect."

"It's not over yet. Not by a long shot."

She touched the tip of her tongue to her upper lip and gently eased herself down over his throbbing shaft.

Noah sucked in a short breath.

It felt so good to have him inside her at long last. So precious. And so damn daring. Slowly, she began to move over him, sliding up and down over his long frame.

Noah threw back his head, exposing his Adam's apple. His dark hair curled against the white sheet.

She moved like water, fluid and light. Up and down. Picking up the pace. Going faster and faster.

Their slick friction welded them together. She swayed, slippery, electrified by the contact of their sultry bodies. They were fully merged, and it was impossible to tell where she started and he ended.

Leaning over his long torso, she kissed him, her knees locked at his hips so that he couldn't slip out of her. She pulled her head back and looked into his face, her hair falling like a curtain around his head.

They stared at one another, both awestruck.

She tightened her inner muscles around his throbbing shaft.

"Kelsey," he gasped, unable to say anything more. His hands clutched at her waist as he pulled her down harder on him.

She rotated her hips.

He groaned. "Faster."

She galloped. Giving him everything she had. Christmas music spun around them. The fireplace flickered. Lights blinked. It was a sensual symphony for the senses.

They were one. The rider and the ridden. Ensnared in the whirl of red-hot sensation and the miracle of long-held dreams coming true. Saying yes to adventure had led Kelsey here. To this man. Her first and only love.

The world belonged to them.

They owned it.

And when their release was upon them, they came together on one shattering crescendo, calling each other's name as they tumbled into the sweetness of their own special Christmas magic.

CHAPTER 27

Afterward, they lay in each other's arms. Every muscle in Kelsey's body ached, but in a glorious way. She breathed in his scent, so grateful to be here. Marveling at the changes in both her body and her mind. Accepting Tasha's crazy Christmas dares had turned out to be the very best thing she'd ever done.

She had not one single regret and would eagerly do it all over again if given half a chance. Thanks to Tasha prodding and Noah egging her on, she had pushed herself beyond the limits of what she'd ever thought possible. She'd set boundaries with Filomena. She had faced her fears. She had made love to Noah in a glass-domed room.

Things were changing.

Good changes.

Long-overdue changes.

She thought about Tasha's fifth dare to her. *Please yourself.* Yes. Long past time to please herself.

And she was starting to believe that she and Noah had a real chance at a future together. He'd shown her he loved her in a dozen different ways. By the lovely gifts he'd given her. By the way he accepted her for who she was, fears and all. By the way he'd helped her safely step out of her comfort zone and embrace a new way of being. By the tender look in his eyes when he called her *Firefly*. How he'd saved her from being kidnapped.

She loved him so much and if he wasn't yet ready to say the words, she was.

"Noah," she whispered and turned in his arms so that they were facing each other.

"Kelsey." His entire face lit up when he smiled at her.

"There's something I want to tell you."

"There's something I want to tell you first."

"Oh?" She sucked in her breath.

He took her hands in his. Rubbed her palms that were healing from where she'd skinned them when she'd fallen getting away from Clifford Steel. He pressed his lips to her wounds, kissed them lightly.

Her heart fluttered.

"I love you, Kelsey James. With all my heart and soul. I love you unconditionally. No matter what."

"Noah." She sucked in a second breath on top of the first one and her chest ached in a beautiful way. "I love you too. I have always, and I always will."

A cell phone played the specialized ringtone she'd given Tasha.

His eyes widened. "Is that your phone or mine?"

"Doesn't matter." She burrowed against him. "We're in our cocoon, remember? That's what voice mail is for."

The phone, wherever it was, rang three more times before it went to voice mail. Kelsey was busy planting kisses on Noah's chest. The phone stopped than started again.

Sighing, Kelsey kicked aside the covers, slid off the sectional, searched around in the heap of her clothes for her phone. Her friend sure had rotten timing.

"Hello," Kelsey answered, sounding none too friendly.

"Are you near a television?" Tasha asked without so much as a hello.

Kelsey eyed the flat screen TV still playing the repeating winter scene. "Yes. What's up?"

"Turn it on."

"Why."

"Just do it. Hurry. They're coming back from commercial now. Switch on the local news to Channel 8."

Apparently, Noah could hear Tasha's frantic voice over the phone, because he picked up the remote, switched off the snow scene and clicked over to the Channel 8 ten o'clock newscast.

There on the seventy-two-inch screen was her mother's face.

"Filomena called a press conference," Tasha said in Kelsey's ear.

"Oh dear God, what about?" But she didn't need to ask, she could read it in the caption scrolling across the screen. *Dallas Mayor-Elect Calls Press Conference. Announces No Campaign Staffers Will Follow Her to the Mayor's Office.*

Stunned, Kelsey waved at Noah to turn up the volume. He complied.

Filomena was at the podium speaking into the microphone. "I will be starting with fresh blood. None of my campaign staffers will be filling a position on my team. Nor will any of the previous mayor's staff remain in their jobs."

But that was ludicrous! Filomena was firing *everyone*?

"You aren't there to talk sense into her," Tasha said, sounding a little gleeful. "She's burning down her own house and doesn't even know it."

"Mayor-Elect James!" hollered a reporter. "What about your daughter, who's been your loyal campaign manager for years? Surely, Kelsey will have a seat at the table."

Filomena's eyes darkened, narrowed, and her mouth turned mean. Kelsey had seen that expression more times than she could possibly count. "My former campaign manager has decided to move on. Next question."

"Oh shit," Tasha whispered.

"Somehow she must have heard about Berg's job offer and this is her way of punishing me."

"I guess you shouldn't have blocked her calls."

Kelsey felt strangely calm. "It's not the end of the world."

"She just fired you in a very public way. She won't backtrack on this. You're out and you'll have to crawl the Sahara naked to get back into her good graces."

"You know what?" Kelsey said, feeling like a canary who suddenly realized that the door to its cage had been open all along. For years she'd been blind to the fact that she could fly through the door to freedom. "I really don't care."

"You say that now, but this is the tip of the iceberg. If she's dead set on punishing you, the misery is just beginning. I'm scared for you. I should never have found Noah, never have given you that dare. Never have brought you to Twilight. It was wrong of me—"

"It's okay. I can handle whatever happens." But could she? A snake of fear whipped through her. Had she grown enough to accept things as they were?

Kelsey had always been the peacemaker. The one to calm her mother's stormy waters. She'd been the golden child and Chelsea the rebel. Who would calm Filomena now that she'd turned Kelsey into a scapegoat?

"I'm so sorry," Tasha said.

"I have to go now, Tash."

"I understand. I love you."

"I love you too."

Trembling, Kelsey switched off the phone. Found Noah standing beside her, a solicitous look on his face.

"C'mere," he said and opened his arms wide. "You look like you need a big hug."

She sidestepped his hug, too knocked down for comfort. "I have to go home. I have to face her."

"Kelsey." Noah dropped his arms, looked worried. "That's exactly what she wants. It's why she held the press conference in the first place. She's counting on your guilt and shame to bring you to heel. It's all a ploy to lure you back."

Was it?

She felt the old pull. The need to make things right. To ensure her mother's happiness at all costs. She'd been doing it for twenty-seven years. How could she stop now? She picked up her clothes, started getting dressed.

Noah did too. He pulled on his jeans, stabbed his fingers through his hair, and looked dazed.

"Isn't that what the spirit of Christmas is about?" Kelsey said to him. "Hope? Isn't that what you've been trying to teach me?"

"There's realistic hope and then there's false hope." His voice was soft with tenderness, his eyes even softer with pity.

Irritated, her eye twitched. "Isn't the whole Santa nonsense a study in false hope?"

"No," Noah said. "Because Santa is only a symbol. He's a fantasy and everyone knows it. But the myth of Santa, just like the myth of kismet cookies and coins thrown into the Sweetheart Fountain to reunite lost first loves, is based on the reality that human beings have the infinite capacity for love and generosity of spirit. You've been resisting the window dressing while ignoring the truth beneath it."

"Which is?"

"Christmas is about faith and *real* hope."

"I'm not seeing the difference between your hope and mine. You hope things will turn out okay, I hope my mother will change."

"Real hope combines a positive outlook with a firm grip on reality. What you've been doing is vacillating from false hope that your mother will change to despair because she is incapable of loving you unconditionally."

"You don't know that she's incapable of loving me unconditionally."

"No," he said. "But you do. Deep in your heart. You've been using false hope to deny the reality of your relationship with your mother."

"How can you say that?"

"For one thing, the tic is back." He touched the muscle twitching at her temple. "For another thing, she just fired you for taking some time away from her and setting boundaries. If she loved you unconditionally, would she do that?"

Kelsey's shoulders fell like anchors. She felt as if she'd been drop-kicked. Of all people, she thought that

Noah would understand and support her in going home to smooth things over with Filomena. She stared at him, feeling blindsided and betrayed. He was supposed to be in her corner no matter what.

And yet here he was, challenging her.

She was rocked to her core, confused and grief stricken. Feeling as if she'd been abandoned by both her mother and her lover in one fell swoop. She'd been relying on his optimism to bolster her hope that things could eventually change with her mother. But now, he was taking that away from her. Forcing her to look at a reality she just couldn't face. Her mother was incapable of loving her the way a normal mother loved.

You've known it all along, whispered a voice in her head that sound eerily like Chelsea's.

"Hope is not a strategy," Noah said. "You can't keep hoping for your mother to change. You're the one who has to change. That's where hope works. That's where you have control. Until you can accept that, you'll never be happy. And I'm sorry as hell, Firefly, but I can't supply that for you. I wish I could, but I can't."

Her bottom lip trembled. Her chest felt hollow as if her heart had been sucked out. "What are you saying, Noah?"

"You're letting Filomena come between us just as you did ten years ago."

"She's my mother."

"And I'm the man who loves you."

"You're saying I can't have both?" Was he really giving her an ultimatum? Him or her mother?

He shook his head. "I think maybe it's best if you *do* go home."

Kelsey gasped and drew back as swiftly as if he'd actually struck her. "Are you breaking up with me?"

"No. I'm setting firm boundaries. Until you're able to make peace with your situation, and break free from your mother's control, it's better that we're apart."

"But . . . but you said you loved me unconditionally. And here you are putting conditions on me."

"I *do* love you unconditionally. I accept you for who you are. I know you are kind and loving and want to help people. But loving someone unconditionally doesn't mean standing by and watching them destroy themselves in order to please someone who can't appreciate their sacrifice."

He was saying one thing but doing another. Telling her he loved her unconditionally but at the same time sending her on her way. Pain stabbed her.

"Because I do love you unconditionally, I'm setting you free, Firefly. I'm not going to tell you what to do. Go. Figure things out for yourself. When you're ready, I'll be here waiting for you."

"You're telling me to leave."

"Would you stay if I asked you to stay?"

She stood there, one hand on the doorknob. Torn right in two. On the one side was the only life she'd ever known—strict obedience to Filomena in order to earn her mother's love. On the other was the hope of a future that beckoned her to accept reality and let go of the past.

Was it false hope?

And how could she break the patterns of a lifetime without trying to see if she could get through to her mother? How could she let go without knowing for sure that there was nothing to hold on to in the first place?

She sent someone to kidnap you.

"Kelsey?" His voice was kind. "What are you going to do?"

"Right now, Noah? To my way of thinking, you're being just as manipulative as my mother. You're no better than she is."

"You don't really believe that."

Then something occurred to her. Something heart-breaking and earth-shattering. She didn't want to believe it, just as she didn't want to believe her mother had hired someone to kidnap her, but the evidence was stacked up like cordwood.

"Noah," she said. "Is this whole thing a ploy?"

"What whole thing?"

"You, me, this." She flapped her hand at the room.

"What ploy, Kelsey? What are you talking about?"

"To get even with my mother. Did Tasha contact you about my coming here? Did you two set me up?"

"I'm not even going to dignify that with a response."

"Tasha's been trying for years to get me to cut my mother out of my life. Maybe she saw you as an instru-ment to get the job done." Even as she was saying it, she could hear how irrational she sounded, but she could not stop the words from spilling out. Her greatest fears spewing from her lips. Terrified that she couldn't trust anyone to love her without strings attached.

"After all we just shared, you can stand there with a straight face and say that to me? Kelsey, you've got a lot of things to sort through. You've allowed your mother to warp your mind. Not everyone is manipulative and calcu-lating and out for their own self-interests. Tasha loves you. I love you. What your mother did to me, to us, is in the past. I'm not holding on to that stuff, but clearly you are."

Heart reeled against her ribs, eye twitching furiously, Kelsey's stomach quivered as adrenaline sped through her. "I don't think this is going to work."

Noah flinched. "If that's the way you feel, maybe you should go."

"Maybe I will."

"Stay, go. It's your choice."

But it felt like no choice at all. Either way she went, she was going to displease someone. Confused, and hurting beyond measure, Kelsey turned her back on him and walked out the door.

It was only then that Kelsey realized she utterly failed at completing her fifth dare.

Because no matter what she did, there was no pleasing herself. The Christmas of Yes had turned into a big fat miserable Christmas of No.

No relationship with her mother.

No job.

No boyfriend.

And most of all, no self-respect.

CHAPTER 28

Not knowing where else to turn, Kelsey packed up and left Twilight. She went to see Theo. She knew her father was headed out on a Christmas cruise with his girlfriend, Leah, in a few days, but maybe he could spare a few minutes for her. She didn't ask him for much.

Standing at the door of her father's condo in the choicest part of Plano, Kelsey took a deep breath. It was late, well after midnight. She'd driven straight here after her fight with Noah, her head all over the place.

This was dumb. She shouldn't have come here. Theo and Leah were probably in bed by now. She should go get a hotel room and sort this out in the morning when she'd had time to calm down.

Just as she was about to leave, the elevator door opened, and Theo stepped out with Leah on his arm. Leah was in a formal gown and her father wore a tuxedo much like the one Noah had worn the night before. Thoughts of Noah tore through her heart like a tornado.

She was so confused. Her life wrecked.

"Kels!" her father exclaimed, letting go of Leah, and moving toward her. "What's wrong?"

"Oh Daddy, do I look that bad?"

"You always were an ugly crier," he said kindly and wrapped his arm around her shoulder.

Leah handed her a tissue she pulled from her purse.

Kelsey dabbed at her eyes and sank against Theo. Inhaled her father's comforting scent.

Unlocking the front door to the condo, Leah stood aside to let them go in ahead of her. "I'll get you both a stiff drink. Looks like you're going to need it."

Theo ushered Kelsey into the living room. Leah kicked off her stilettoes and padded across the room to the wet bar where she poured two tumblers of scotch, neat. Kelsey and her father settled onto the couch.

Leah handed them the glasses, pressed a kiss on Theo's forehead. "I'll leave you two alone. This looks like a private conversation."

"Thank you, sweetheart." Theo touched Leah's arm. He smiled at her the way Noah smiled at Kelsey.

Kelsey's heart thumped. She was happy for her father. Glad he'd gotten free from Filomena, and glad he'd found Leah. She loved Theo. That much was clear.

Leah wriggled her fingers and disappeared down the hallway to their bedroom.

Theo took Kelsey's hand in his. "Did something go wrong with your getaway?"

Kelsey nodded, terrified that if she spoke she'd start crying again. She'd bawled almost the whole way of the seventy-five-mile Uber ride from Twilight. She reached for the tumbler. Took a hit of scotch. Felt brave enough to whisper, "It's more than that."

"Let me guess." Theo sighed. *"Filomena."*

As succinctly as she could, Kelsey told him about the press conference, and her fight with Noah.

Theo shook his head. "I probably made things worse by bringing Lionel into the picture. I was just trying to help you get out from under your mother's thumb, but in retrospect I can see that was a misstep."

"It's not your fault."

"It is. I shouldn't have left you with her. I should have fought for full custody."

"It's not a fight you would have won, we both know that."

"Kels, I'm so sorry for all my mistakes. But I can't regret marrying your mother, because I got you out of the deal."

"Why is she like this?" Kelsey wailed. "What's wrong with me that she can't love me the way a mother is supposed to love her children?"

"No." Theo took hold of Kelsey's chin in his palm, tilted her face up, and forced her to meet his gaze. "You stop that right now. You've done nothing wrong. You're taking the blame for something that is not your fault. She's trained you to think everything is your fault, but it's not. Her behavior is abnormal and it's part of her pathology."

"Pathology?" Kelsey stared in her father's eyes, saw sadness and compassion in equal measures.

"I'm going to tell you something I should have told you a long time ago. I didn't tell you before because you were the one person who seemed to have a good relationship with her and I didn't want to spoil that for either of you."

A chill went up Kelsey's spine. In her heart, she'd always known something was wrong with her mother. As a child, even before Chelsea died, she'd look at her mother at times and feel such bone-deep loneliness and despair without knowing why. The feelings had only worsened after Chelsea's death. She'd buried her feelings in work, but now those feelings were roaring back to life.

"Once you know the truth, it changes everything, and I wasn't sure you were ready for that shift. But I can see you're ready to hear it now," Theo went on.

"Tell me," Kelsey whispered. "What is wrong with her?"

"Your mother most likely has Narcissistic Personality Disorder," Theo said.

"Well of course she has a big ego," Kelsey said. "She has to have a big ego to believe she can make a difference in the world."

"That's a common misconception about NPD. While all people with NPD have big egos, not everyone with a big ego has NPD."

"What's the difference?"

"It's healthy to believe in yourself and have high self-esteem. There's nothing wrong with that. But narcissism is on a spectrum. Most narcissistic people are just a little selfish and when you point out how they are hurting other people, they *can* change their ways."

"Hmm." She let his words sink in.

"But people suffering from full-blown Narcissistic Personality Disorder are incapable of understanding that other people having feelings of their own. People with NPD have an exaggerated sense of self-importance to the detriment of others. They truly believe they are superior to everyone in every way, and they have a grandiose sense of entitlement."

Kelsey's mouth dropped. It was all so true of Filomena and it explained why she would often go against the advice of experts. Filomena believed she always knew what was best and had convinced Kelsey that she was the ultimate authority.

"People with NPD have low empathy," Theo went on. "They see their spouses and children as an extension of themselves, not as separate people with lives of their own."

"How does this happen? How does someone get NPD?"

"It's very sad," Theo said. "The experts don't know for sure. They believe it's a mixture of genetics and environmental influences. When people who suffer from NPD were children, weak and defenseless, something happened that caused them to feel so insignificant and ashamed that they built a false self—this grandiose mask, that they must protect at all costs."

A sick feeling rose inside Kelsey and for a moment it took all she had not to throw up. This explained everything about her mother's behavior. Incidents from the past flashed through her, a kaleidoscope of validation that indeed, her mother suffered from this terrible mental disorder. The times Filomena pinched her when Kelsey's stomach growled in public, the way she'd squashed Kelsey's individuality, how she'd insisted she be the one to walk Kelsey down the aisle.

"People with NPD can be quite charming. That's how they suck you in. It's why your mother is so good at politics. She's great at first impressions. First she charms, then she manipulates and has her victims squirming on a hook. It's a merry-go-round of idealize, devalue, and discard. When people try to break away or fight back she bullies them into backing off through lies, blaming, gaslighting, or smear campaigns. You've seen her do it. She did it to me. She almost ruined me, financially, emotionally, physically. I was wrecked. Too messed up to help you the way I should have."

Yes, Filomena had done this, time and time again. She'd bought into her mother's lies, made excuses for her, championed her to others. Helped her get elected.

Kelsey put a clammy palm to her sweaty forehead. After Chelsea died, her mother had idealized Kelsey, put her on a pedestal, and as long as Kelsey praised and adored her mother things were good. But as soon as she expressed an opinion not in keeping with Filomena's way of doing things, she'd start to devalue her. To stay on her mother's good side, she'd always backtracked.

Until she'd listened to Tasha, gone to Twilight, met Noah.

And then Filomena had discarded her in a very public way.

"People with NPD are unable to love anyone but themselves and if it looks like they're giving you love, it's only to get something from you. They simply do not know how to love without conditions."

"I'm gonna be sick." Kelsey's stomach roiled. She hopped up and fled to the bathroom.

Reality was a sledgehammer smacking into her head. She'd always known that her mother was difficult to deal with and needed to control every aspect of Kelsey's life, but it never occurred to her that Filomena had an actual mental disorder. Kelsey had always assumed *she* was the problem in the relationship. That she wasn't a good enough daughter, didn't try hard enough, that she was the defective one.

Because of course, that's what Filomena had told her often enough.

Her mother's lack of maternal warmth, her inflex-
ibility and refusal to compromise, her touchy hyper-
sensitivity. Seen through the lens of a mental disorder,
her mother's vexing behavior suddenly made terrible
sense.

Including the tragedy of Chelsea's death. Her twin
sister had drowned trying to get away from their mother's mental abuse. Chelsea had been the rebel, the scapegoat, the lost one, while Kelsey had assumed the role of
golden child, trying forever to please Filomena.

The pieces of the puzzle fell neatly into place. Click-
ing like a key in a lock. Solving the mystery that had
plagued Kelsey for years. Answering the question that
she'd long wanted answered.

Why couldn't she ever please her mother?

Her father followed her into the bathroom. Held
Kelsey's hair back while she threw up. Afterward, he
gave her mouthwash to rinse with. Pressed a damp cloth
to Kelsey's forehead. Sat on the floor with her in his
tuxedo. Something Filomena would never have done in
a million years. He rested his back against the wall, put
his arm around Kelsey and pulled her close.

"I'm so, so sorry."

"How did you find out about this?" Kelsey asked.

"I learned it in therapy. I started going after the
divorce. I still go sometimes when things get rocky. I
had to learn why I was attracted to someone like your
mother and address my part in the relationship. Of
course, my therapist says that she can't diagnose Filomena without treating her, but from everything I've
told her, she believes that your mother has full-blown
NPD."

Any remaining guilt Kelsey had been feeling over

establishing boundaries with her mother instantly evaporated.

"I know this is hard to hear," Theo said. "I know you've held out hope that one day she'll love you just for being you, without any strings, or consequences attached to her love, but she simply will not. It's like she's color-blind and you're asking her to appreciate a rainbow."

"I feel sorry for her."

"So do I. But you can't surrender yourself to change her. She'll never go to therapy. Never admit she has issues. Never work on herself. Because denial is at the very core of her illness. She believes she's *always* right. And that's the insidious nature of NPD."

"I wish you'd told me before. I wouldn't have wasted so much time trying to make her love me."

"Kelsey, you are the only one who has ever been able to navigate a successful long-term relationship with her. I didn't want to take that away from either one of you."

"Oh no, Dad, you don't get to do that to me," Kelsey said, standing up for herself. "That's what you tell your-self to make it easier to live with the truth. You left me to her. Even when you were still living at home. You ran off to the golf course every chance you got."

"You're right." He hung his head. "You're so much stronger than I am."

"You abandoned me to her."

Tears misted his eyes. "I abandoned you girls to her. I didn't know how to deal. I was screwed up and selfish myself. And I have to live with that for the rest of my life."

"I don't know if that's enough, Dad."

He looked wretched and remorseful. "What can I do to make amends?"

"You're doing it," she said softening. Knowing that for all his flaws, he did love her unconditionally. "Being here for me now."

"I love you, sweetheart."

"I know, Dad." She did understand that her father had done his best under the circumstances. That he had a boatload of his own problems or he would never have married Filomena in the first place. "I love you too."

Theo hugged her hard. "I hope you can find a way to forgive me."

"If you'll forgive me for feeling angry with you."

"Always, sweetheart. You can be as mad at me as you want, and I'll never stop loving you."

Kelsey moistened her lips. "May I ask you something?"

"Anything. Everything."

"How did your therapist suggest you handle Filomena?"

"Besides leaving her?"

"Yes."

"She said to accept your mother for who and what she is. Filomena does have good qualities."

Maybe, but right now, Kelsey was blind to them.

"And while appreciating those qualities, to stop holding out hope that things will be anything other than what they are."

"Tall order."

"Understand that you are *not* the crazy one, no matter how many times she might tell you that you are. Don't get drawn into a battle with her."

"Another tall order."

"You've managed to keep the peace all these years . . ."

"That's shot to hell now. Once I stood up to her."

"Don't take the blame. Don't say you're sorry for something that is not your fault."

"Tall order times ten."

Her father stroked Kelsey's cheek with his knuckles. "You're strong. You'll get through this."

"Anything else?"

"Besides take care of yourself and figure out what it is *you* want *your* life to look like?"

Kelsey nodded.

"Basically," Theo said, "my therapist's advice is to live life by the serenity prayer."

"God grant me the serenity to accept the things I cannot change," Kelsey mumbled.

"The courage to change the things I can," Theo said. "Like walking away from her."

They looked at each other and laughed and together finished with, "And the wisdom to know the difference."

"You're a lunkhead." Raylene sank her hands on her hips and gave Noah a look that said she was within inches of coming across the lobby and kicking his ass.

"What did I do?"

"You let Kelsey leave here in tears!"

"Mind your own business." Noah growled.

"She needed your support, but you didn't give her any."

"You don't have a clue what's going on. Butt out."

"I saw that girl's face when she rushed out of here. You hurt her buddy, *big-time*."

Noah chuffed. "Raylene, she hurt *me*."

Raylene cocked her head. "How so?"

"She accused me of getting close to her just to get back at her mother for what she did ten years ago."

"And no part of that is true?"

"Pissing off her mother is a side benefit of our relationship, but I would never use Kelsey in that way. I love her and if she can't see that . . ." He shook his head. "Well, we don't stand a chance of making it."

"I saw that press conference on the nightly news and I agree that her mother is a piece of work, but Noah, Filomena is *still* her mother. You of all people should know how important a mother is."

"That's why I told her to go home and figure her life out."

"By herself?"

"It's not my fight, Raylene."

"The hell it's not."

"What do you mean?"

"You love her, don't you?"

"More than anything."

"Then you're in this up to your neck. You, Noah MacGregor, take the easy way out."

"You think this is easy?"

"It's easier for you than facing the truth."

"Which is?"

"I think, because of losing your own mother, you fear getting trapped in pain and loss. So, you developed this easygoing personality to hide that ten-year-old boy who was so hurt when your mother died."

"What's wrong with that? Easygoing seems to be a much better coping mechanism than a lot of things I could have gotten into."

"For sure, but easygoing has a downside and you need to look at that if you're going to fix things with Kelsey."

Yeah, okay. Taking the easy way out had gotten him into trouble a time or two over the years. He'd lost his career because he hadn't been willing to fight for it, just as Joel had accused him at the casino event. Melissa had said much the same thing when she'd walked out on him.

Noah jammed his hands into his pockets and hunched his shoulders. "What should I have done differently?"

"You should have gone with her. Held her hand. Faced down the dragon with her. Done something to *show* her that you were on her side. But you just sent her off on her own, when she needed your support the most. You're asking her to trust your love, but you didn't show her that she could trust you to be there when the chips were down. She hurt your feelings, and you, who takes the long way around in order to avoid getting hurt, just let her go."

"Is that the way you see me?" Noah gulped.

"That's the way *she* sees you. I guarantee it."

Was Raylene right? Noah already felt bad as hell over the way things had gone down, but to think he'd made things worse for Kelsey was a gut punch.

"Look, you're a good guy, but you got this thing where you always expect life to be smooth and easy. It makes you a joy to be around when things are good, but when the chips are down, you tend to make yourself scarce. You're tall and good-looking and fun. Life comes so easy to you that when you hit a bump, you surrender."

"I don't do that." Noah frowned, an arrow of self-awareness piercing straight to his heart. "Do I?"

"You were a natural basketball player. The NBA rolled right into your lap. But as soon as you hit trouble—bam, you gave up."

"I blew out my knee, Raylene!"

"You didn't even try to come back. You took the doctors at their word and threw in the towel without a fight."

"They said recovery would be long and grueling and not guaranteed!"

"Exactly. You won't ever know, will you, because you didn't fight for it. A comeback was too hard."

He clenched his jaw. "That's not fair. I was taking care of my body."

She shrugged. "That's one way of looking at it. Another way is that you're just too damn lazy."

"I'm not chalking that up to a character flaw."

"Okay, what about your marriage to Melissa?"

"What about it?" He scowled.

"You didn't fight for her either. She left because you stopped trying. Not because you got hurt."

"She found another guy to sleep with, Raylene."

"And you didn't even try to win her back."

"It was done. Over. We were too different. We wanted different things."

"Just like now? With Kelsey?"

"I'm giving her the time and space she needs."

"Okay, whatever you have to do to make things *easier* on you." Raylene shot him a you're-a-lost-cause look.

The way she said "easier" pissed him off. "I tried to fight for Kelsey once and look where it got me. Her mother threatened me. I could have lost my scholarship—"

"Maybe that's where it started," Raylene mused. "Your tendency to give up when the going gets tough."

"I haven't given up on Kelsey."

"Haven't you already mentally signed off? Her mother is a challenge. Kelsey's got some heavy feelings to sort through. You can't just love her when she's perky and optimistic," Raylene said. "You have to allow her to be who she is, and if that means she's not always going to be easy, suck it up, buddy, experience the pain and understand that it's all part of loving her."

"Look at this, dammit," he said, holding up his wrist for her to see his tattoo. *Dare.* "I got this to remind myself of the importance of taking chances. I risked a helluva lot to get where I am. I bought this island and started a B&B when everyone said it wouldn't work—"

"But it *did* work," Raylene said. "It worked so easily because you already had this celebrity status and you are so much fun to be around. You're a natural people person, just like you were a natural basketball player. If this boatel hadn't come together like homemade vanilla ice cream and hot fudge on a sundae, would you still be here? Face it, deep down inside you're terrified of failure, so you only try at things you're automatically good at."

Was that true? Noah stared at Raylene. Then looked down at his wrist.

Dare.

What real risks had he actually taken? Raylene was right. He was a hypocrite and it was tattooed right there on his wrist for him to see.

"Oh shit," he said.

"Yeah." Raylene nodded. "Now you're getting it."

"What do I do?"

"About Kelsey?"

"Yes, yes."

"Follow that damn tattoo. Dare to do something. Grand gesture, baby. Go to her and *show* her you're not the kind of man who takes the easy way out."

CHAPTER 29

Kelsey spent the next four days at her father's condo, trying to figure out how she was going to approach Filomena. She did a lot of self-reflecting and made an appointment with Theo's therapist, who helped her develop a plan of action.

She learned she was enmeshed with her mother, which was typically what happened to the children of parents with Narcissistic Personality Disorder. Kelsey's personal work centered around setting boundaries, letting go of blaming herself for things that weren't her fault, accepting her mother as she was and having no expectations that Filomena would ever change, and to stop putting the wants and needs of others ahead of her own.

Kelsey's central goal was to disentangle her life from her mother's and find out who she was and where she belonged. Meeting Noah again had started her on that inner journey, but she couldn't use him as a crutch.

This was *her* work and she had to do it alone.

With that thought in mind, she did not call or text him. If they were meant to be together, then their relationship would weather this and time away from him would not destroy what they'd started to build.

And if not? Then letting go of him would be part of her journey too.

One thing she discovered was that she did not want to be Lionel Berg's campaign manager. This wasn't to keep from ruffling Filomena's feathers, but because she'd only gone into politics to please her mother.

What she really wanted was to do what she'd studied in college—hospitality. As a child, she'd fantasized about running her own B&B and being at the *Rockabye* had put her back in touch with that long-forgotten dream. She had some savings that could keep her afloat until she found an entry-level job at a hotel. Sure, her finances would take a hit, but Kelsey was frugal by nature and cutting back wouldn't be so hard, especially if it put her in touch with her heart's desire.

And when she called Lionel Berg to turn down his offer, and he upped her salary yet again, one thing held Kelsey solid in her resolve. Tasha's final dare.

Please yourself.

In order to complete her Christmas of Yes, that included saying "no" to things that weren't right for her.

The journey was scary, and she missed Noah so much. At least a dozen times she'd picked up the phone to contact him and had to force herself to put it back down without calling or texting. Every time she resisted, she felt her resolve strengthen. Whatever happened, she *would* get through this and be stronger for it.

On Saturday morning, December 21, two weeks after her failed wedding to Clive, Kelsey understood what she had to do in order to fully move on with her life. She marshaled her courage, bid Theo and Leah farewell as they left on their Christmas cruise, and drove to her mother's house.

She parked at the curb and saw a red Corvette that belonged to her cousin Pamela sitting in the driveway next to Filomena's Town Car.

That threw her for a loop.

She remembered what the therapist had said. "Don't be surprised when she replaces you right away. People with NPD have to get validation from somewhere since they can't self-validate."

The therapist had taught her that this external validation was known as narcissistic supply and the person with NPD was as addicted to the validation as surely as any drug. Kelsey didn't matter to her mother as a person, only as source of her emotional supply.

And if she wasn't plying her mother with attention, she was out of favor, devalued, and discarded.

That tidbit of information had knocked her sideways but strengthened her resolve to extricate herself from her mother's clutches. It looked like Pamela had gotten sucked in.

She blew out her breath and practiced the speech she'd rehearsed with the therapist. This was one of the hardest things she would ever do in her life.

Just as she was about to get out of the car, an Uber pulled up behind Kelsey's Mercedes and Tasha got out. She hadn't heard from her friend since she'd told her good-bye when she'd left Christmas Island and told Tasha she needed to be alone. Her friend had been giving her the space she needed to sort things out.

Instant relief splashed over her. She wouldn't have to do this alone.

Kelsey lowered her window. "What are you doing here?"

"Theo texted and told me you're about to beard the lion in her den." Tasha ran around to the passenger side door and hopped inside Kelsey's car. "How are you doing?"

"Not so good."

Tasha reached to squeeze her hand. "I'm here for you."

"Oh, Tasha." Kelsey swallowed back the tears.

Her best friend leaned across the seat to hug her hard. "Look at it this way. You've always known something was wrong. Now you know it's not you. Now you can start taking care of yourself instead of your mother."

Kelsey nodded. "It's going to be so freeing."

Tasha patted Kelsey's cheek. "You're finally going to get to be *you*."

"I just feel so sorry for her. Her life is miserable, and she can't see how she's creating it."

"You feel sorry for her because you are a kind and loving person." Tasha put a hand to Kelsey's back. "Your mother is not kind or loving. She is not feeling the same tenderness for you that you feel for her. She's broken, and you can't fix her. All you can do is accept the truth."

"I know. That's why I'm tearing up. She'll never be able to see how she's the instrument of her own pain."

"You can't save her. Feeling sorry for her only drags you down," Tasha said. "And if you keep trying to help her, she'll take you down with her."

Kelsey swiped the tears from her eyes. "I know."

"You have to invest your love where it will be reciprocated," Tasha said. "Like me with Sean. I kept trying to make things work with Tag all those years when he clearly did not love me the way I thought I loved him. I kept trying to make something right that wasn't right. It took Sean's steady patience to show me how blind I'd been. Accept that not everyone will love you the way you deserve to be loved and let them go. Love the ones who love you back."

"So, things are good between you two?"

Tasha grinned. "Where do you think I've been for the last five days? I'm still in Twilight."

"In bed with your navy SEAL?"

"Nope. He won me over. We're going to date for quite a while before we get into bed again."

"I am so happy for you, Tasha."

"Hey, be happy for yourself too. You and Noah have got a good thing going on."

Kelsey shook her head. She wasn't sure of that at all. Was it too late to mend fences with Noah? Had things gone too far? Could he forgive her for shoving him away? For accusing him of cooking up a ploy with Tasha to get back at Filomena? She felt so stupid for even letting that thought pop into her head, much less express it to him.

But right now, she couldn't worry about Noah. A monumental task lay in front of her.

"Do you want me to go in with you?" Tasha asked.

Kelsey shook her head. "I have to do this alone."

"I understand. But I'll be here waiting for you."

"Thank you so much. I can't begin to tell you how much you mean to me."

"Prove it," Tasha said. "Consider this your sixth and final dare. Break up with your mother. Get in there and get this thing done!"

When Kelsey rang the doorbell, Pamela answered. Immediately, she shrank back as if she'd encountered a rattlesnake on the front porch.

"It's okay," Kelsey said. "I get it. You're in, I'm out. Good luck."

"Cousin, you have been a terrible daughter—"

She raised a hand. "Look, we don't need to interact. I just need to see my mother."

"Aunt Filomena doesn't want to see *you*."

"That may be, but she's going to see me anyway." Kelsey pushed Pamela aside.

Her cousin's jaw dropped but she scrambled out of the way.

Kelsey walked into the living room to find her mother sitting on the couch with her feet propped on the coffee table, a computer in her lap, piles of folders and papers stacked around her.

"We were having a planning meeting," Pamela mumbled behind Kelsey. Poor dumb Pamela had no idea what she was getting herself into. She'd find out soon enough.

Filomena shot Kelsey a haughty expression, nose turned up, eyes narrowed. How many times had Kelsey seen her pass out such scathing looks to her adversaries? A million? Two million? At least.

"Well, well, look who comes crawling back," her mother mocked, not even removing her feet from the coffee table, much less getting up.

That attitude fortified Kelsey's determination to see this through. "Hello, Mother."

"What do you want?" Filomena waved a hand. "We're busy."

"I came to lodge a complaint."

"You? I should be the one lodging a complaint. *You're* the one who treated me shabbily. Blocking my phone calls."

"I told you I needed some time alone to collect my thoughts. I blocked my phone so that I could have some privacy. It wasn't about you. It was about me and what I needed to heal."

"That's ridiculous. What about *my* needs? I needed you, Kelsey, and you abandoned me." Filomena finally put her feet to the floor and her laptop aside.

The therapist had warned her that the conversation might very well go like this.

"That was unfair of you to fire me publicly."

"You left me no choice," her mother raged, jumping to her feet. "You blocked me. I had to get your attention somehow."

"You tried to have me kidnapped. That got my attention."

"Little good it did me. Both my bodyguard and chauffeur quit over you."

"It wasn't my fault, Mother."

"Nothing ever is, is it? *You* are blameless."

The therapist had also told her to expect Filomena to project her flaws onto Kelsey and warned her not to accuse Filomena of having Narcissistic Personality Disorder. She would only turn things around and say that Kelsey was the narcissist.

"Mother, I'm sorry you feel this way. I understand how much emotional pain you are in."

Filomena's face went blank. "I have no idea what you are talking about. I am absolutely fine. Pamela is with me now. She's all I need."

"You went on television just to tell people you were firing me."

A cunning expression flared in her eyes. "Get over yourself. You're not that important."

You're not that important.

How many times had she heard that over the course of her life? Hundreds. Thousands. All this time, her mother had been telling her exactly who she was, and Kelsey hadn't been able to see it. The blind love a child had for her mother.

But she saw it now. Clear as a windowpane.

"You've kept me tied to your apron strings and that's not healthy for either one of us. It's time I stretch my wings and fly."

There was a flicker in Filomena's eyes and for the briefest of seconds, Kelsey saw past the mask to the injured child her mother had once been. The look on her mother's face hit her like a punch to the throat. She was *terrified* of being alone.

"You cut your hair," Filomena whispered, her voice softening. "You swore you'd never cut it after Chelsea died."

At the mention of her twin's name, Kelsey sank her teeth into her bottom lip to stave off the tears. She couldn't show any weakness. She and her mother had both suffered an impossible loss. Chelsea's death tied them in a way nothing could ever separate.

In a rush of almost unbearable empathy, she saw herself through her mother's eyes. Kelsey looked exactly like the child Filomena had lost. A specter of what might have been. Maybe that was part of why she'd kept Kelsey so close. In her own dysfunctional way, Filomena had been trying to keep Kelsey nearby so that she didn't lose her too.

In that moment, Kelsey's heart just broke, and she knew that while she would set strong boundaries and learn to stop feeding her mother's need for narcissistic supply, she could not go "no contact" as many experts on NPD advised. For better or worse, Filomena was her mother and the only one she would ever have.

She understood now why Theo stayed silent about her mother's condition. Like Kelsey, he too had empathy for Filomena, even if she was unable to feel empathy for them.

"It was time to let go of the past," Kelsey said, brushing her fingers through her hair.

"He's to blame, isn't he? That *boy*." Her mother's lip curled around her teeth. "That Joah." Filomena knew his name. She was mispronouncing it on purpose to belittle him. She did it to other people too, calling Tasha, *Tosha* and Leah, *Lizza*.

"His name is Noah and he told me how you threatened him when he showed up here trying to see me ten years ago."

"I did no such thing." She drew up her spine, peered down her nose at Kelsey. "He made that up. He's a white trash liar."

"I believe him."

Filomena's expression shifted, and she looked even more cunning. "Okay, maybe I did threaten him, but I did nothing wrong. I was trying to protect my daughter. He deserved it."

And there it was in a nutshell. Her mother would never take responsibility for her actions. If anything, the therapist had underestimated how useless facing off with Filomena would be.

"Okay, then." Kelsey nodded. You couldn't get water from a dry well. "That answers all my questions."

Filomena stared her down, eyes cold, unyielding. That tiny flicker of vulnerability over Chelsea was gone.

Her mother was like a hawk—beautiful, powerful, killer instincts. And like a hawk, she was much better viewed from afar than close up. Kelsey could no more change the nature of her mother than she could change a hawk.

Filomena was what she was. Kelsey wished she'd realized all this sooner rather than later. She could have had a much happier life, but she knew better now. She could go forth wiser and guilt free.

It was past time to start living, and the first thing she was going to do was call Noah and ask him to forgive her.

"I'm sorry, Mom, that things are the way they are." She gave Filomena a tender loving smile filled with all the empathy she could muster.

"Don't you dare," her mother yelled. "Don't you dare *smile* at me."

"Excuse me?"

"*You*, acting so smug and superior. Like you're better than me. You're *not* better than me. You will never be better than *me*!"

"I never thought I was better than you." Kelsey felt her defenses go up, but as soon as the words were out of her mouth, she understood what was happening.

Filomena was projecting her feelings of superiority and smugness onto Kelsey.

"You know what? I love you, Mother. I always will, but I'm willing to let you live your life and I will live mine."

"Fine," Filomena chuffed. "Get out of here. I don't need *you*. I've never needed *you*. Your sister was the good one. Why did she have to be taken and you left behind?"

In the past, such a harsh statement would have had Kelsey on her knees begging for Filomena's forgiveness. But no more.

"I know you don't really mean that," Kelsey said softly. "You're just hurting and lashing out."

A hateful look crossed her mother's face, and her hawkish chin jutted into the air. "I *do* mean it."

"I'm leaving now, Mother. I hope you have a Merry Christmas. We'll talk again when you're feeling better."

"Good, fine, go. I don't want you. I never wanted you." Filomena's voice was stone. "Get out of my house. I *dare* you."

CHAPTER 30

On rubber-band legs, Kelsey staggered out of the house, barely able to catch her breath. She'd been braced for this, well prepared, but it didn't lessen the impact of what had happened.

Tasha was sitting in the driver's seat of Kelsey's Mercedes. Gratefully, Kelsey slipped into the passenger seat, trembling all over.

"Sit back, relax, I've got this," Tasha said and drove off.

Kelsey clicked on her seat belt, put the seat back as far as it could go, closed her eyes, and took several long deep breaths. All these years, she'd believed that in order to be loved she had to put the needs of others first.

It was how Filomena had trained her.

What she'd learned from Noah and his friends and family and the quirky community of Twilight was that she was lovable just as she was. There was nothing she needed to do, no specific way she had to act, dress, or talk to deserve love.

With Noah there was no line to toe. She could make mistakes and it would be okay. He didn't hold her to im-

possibly high standards and she never had to worry that
his love would be withdrawn arbitrarily.

She opened one eye. "Where are we going?"

"You leave that to me."

"Twilight?" Kelsey asked hopefully.

"Where else?"

An hour and fifteen minutes later, they arrived on Christmas Island. Kelsey had been napping and jerked awake
as soon as the car stopped in the marina parking lot.

"Oh look," Tasha said. "There's Santa."

"What?"

Sure enough, there was a very tall Santa Claus coming
to open the passenger door. Behind him were a throng of
people looking as if they'd all been waiting for her.

"Is this for the final round of the decorating contest
judging?"

"Yes," Tasha said. "But it's a little more than that."

"What do you mean?" she asked, but Tasha didn't
answer.

The door was thrown open and Santa, with a hearty
"ho, ho, ho" reached for her hand. "Welcome to Christmas Island."

Kelsey looked into those familiar eyes and started
laughing. Santa pulled her into his arms and spun her
around in a wide circle.

Over his shoulder, she saw the contest judges: Flynn
and Jesse; Cash and Paige, who was still very pregnant;
Sean and Raylene and Joel. And oh, there were Theo
and Leah. They were supposed to be on their Christmas
cruise. Why were they here?

Santa set her down on her feet. "Merry Christmas,
Firefly."

Kelsey stared at Noah in that ridiculous Santa suit, and got dizzy because she was holding her breath waiting for him to say something.

That was it? A week without a word from him and he was simply going to wish her Merry Christmas? Thirstily, she drank him in. That silly stocking cap with the white puff ball on the end dangling over his forehead, and that goofy fake beard. The smile was genuine Noah though, but his chocolate brown eyes looked worried.

"It's not Christmas for four more days."

"You forget," he said. "In Twilight, it's *always* Christmas."

"What is everyone doing here?" she asked.

"Well, two things. The contest judges couldn't resist our romantic story." He rubbed her palms where the abrasion burns were almost healed. "And we won the competition!"

"It's the name of the place," Joel called. "The judges are predisposed to call Christmas Island a winner."

"You're just jealous because your twin beat you," Raylene volleyed back to Joel.

"But our love story is what cinched it. So, you see, Firefly," Noah murmured, "I couldn't have done it without you."

"Aww," the crowd sighed in unison.

"The second reason everyone is here," Noah said, "is to celebrate your liberation."

"What?"

"Yep, party in the *Rockabye* dome. Woot. Woot." Tasha pumped her fist in the air and started down the path to the *Rockabye* with Sean.

"You're throwing me a party?"

"We are," Flynn and Jesse said, linking arms and following Tasha and Sean.

Theo and Leah came over and they both hugged Kelsey.

"What are you guys doing here?" she asked. "I thought your cruise left today."

"This is more important," Leah said.

"*You* are more important," Theo added.

"That's so sweet." Kelsey put a hand to her heart that was wide open with love.

"We had just booked the cruise because we figured Filomena would be sucking you into her orbit and you wouldn't have time for us," Leah said. "We didn't count on you breaking free."

"Really?" Kelsey placed two palms over her chest. "You're here for me?"

"We'd much rather spend Christmas with you, sweetheart, than on some silly boat." Her father kissed her forehead. "How did it go today?"

"About how we expected."

"She didn't give an inch."

"It's sad really." Kelsey sighed. "All I can do is love her and keep my boundaries."

"Her dysfunction is not your cross to bear. Just because she gave birth to you doesn't mean you owe her your life." Her father's hug was warm and loving, making up for lost time. "I'm sorry things are the way they are."

"I'm not. Now I know the truth. Now I can set myself free."

"You're amazing, and I love you so much." Theo gave her a final hug and pulled away. "We'll see you up in the dome." He and Leah turned and walked in the direction the others had gone.

The rest of the group peeled away as well, leaving Kelsey standing alone under the mistletoe arch with Noah. She looked at him and felt so much. Much more than words could ever say.

"Cheer up, Firefly," he said, his eyes glistening in the Christmas lights.

"Noah." What she had to say next was hard, but she had to say it. She'd kept quiet too long. No more sweeping things under the rug. "You have to understand something about me."

"What is it?"

"I can't turn my feelings on and off like a switch. I can't be happy, happy, joy, joy all the time like you. While I appreciate your positivity and you certainly make the world a more pleasant place to live in, it's simply not my reality. Not yet anyway."

He took her hand and gave her his full attention.

"I'm striving to be better. I *want* to be upbeat and cheerful most of the time, the way you are, but here's the truth. It may never happen. No matter how hard I try I might never be Miss Merry Sunshine because of the way I was raised. If you can't love me for me, warts and all, then maybe we just aren't meant to be."

"Kelsey," he said. "That's you slapping your fears onto me. I never expected you to be like me."

"Then stop telling me to cheer up. I'm tired of people telling me how I'm supposed to feel. I'm tired of denying my own needs to keep everyone happy but me. The time has come for me to carve out my own happiness and stop worrying about everyone else so much."

"I agree."

"You do?"

"All I've ever wanted, Firefly, is for you to be happy. I made some missteps in this relationship. I admit it. But Raylene pointed something out to me that I hadn't realized about myself."

Her eyes widened. "What's that?"

"I take the easy way out. I don't dig deep. I skim along on the surface. But you don't. You are the deepest person I know. You feel so much. You are so empathetic. It's why your mother held on to you so hard. You have the empathy she lacked. I want this to work out. I want us to work out."

"Oh Noah, that's what I want too."

"For a while, I was afraid that I was falling for you because you were familiar and safe. That maybe I was hanging on to our childish crush and kidding myself that we were fated. But what I feel for you is a mature and solid love."

"How do you know?" she asked.

"Because I'm so much better when I'm with you, and I think you're better with me too. We complement each other, Kels. We're a good mix of similar and opposites. Ultimately, we both have an upbeat outlook on life, even if you've got a darker bent. You're still a glass half-full kind of woman."

"We both prefer to avoid conflict."

"So that we might have to make an effort to pick a fight now and again, so we can have make-up sex." He wriggled his eyebrows.

"We are both people-people." She laughed. "Although I do have more of an introverted side."

"But you're not overly introspective—"

"Otherwise I would have figured things out about Filomena years ago . . ."

"Neither one of us is the broody type," he went on, enumerating why they made a good match.

"We don't stew over failures." She nodded.

"Me by letting things roll right off my back, you by rolling up your sleeves doing the hard work necessary to ensure success."

"We both make the best of whatever circumstances we find ourselves in." She reached for his hand.

He tugged her close. "You make the most mundane things like decorating a gazebo pleasurable."

"And you're funny and lively. You're the talent and I'm the audience."

"I'm always ready to striptease for you, Firefly."

"You give me the energy I need to keep going. You're quick and self-confident and curious and open to new experiences. I love that about you."

"And you bring a sense of steadiness to my sparkle. You're far more sympathetic and soft-hearted than I am."

"This is going to work," she said.

"I've known it from that first day at camp."

"When we got lost together."

His eyes misted at the memory. "I've got something for you."

"A present for me?"

He reached into the pocket of his Santa suit, took out a small black box.

Kelsey gasped. Put a hand to her mouth. She loved Noah with all her heart and soul but she wasn't ready for a ring or marriage. She was just starting to find out who she was and what she wanted. But Noah was definitely on the list.

"Before you say anything," he said. "Please open it."

Fingers trembling, she cracked open the box. It wasn't an engagement ring after all, but it was the most perfect gift.

A tear slid down her cheek.

"Kelsey?"

She fingered the silver firefly necklace that so magically captured the first sweet gift he'd given her, a jar full of fireflies that night at Camp Hope. The romance they'd started so long ago as children had grown and bloomed into a beautiful mature love.

"We're not ready to get married yet," he said. "We need time to get to know each other inside and out. I want to sweep you off your feet. Romance you. Love you. Then when the time is right, I'll ask."

"And I'll say yes."

"At last, you've discovered the real magic of Christmas."

"It's love, isn't it?"

"Yes, Firefly, it is." He nodded and kissed her, and it was the most beautiful kiss right there underneath the Christmas Island arch. It was a rare and beautiful night. One she would treasure forever.

Tasha's Christmas of Yes dares that had started out as a way to push Kelsey out of her comfort zone had landed her right into the most comfortable spot of her life . . .

Noah's loving arms.

EPILOGUE

On Christmas Eve, one year later, Theo James walked his daughter, Kelsey, down the makeshift aisle of the *Rockabye* dome. Filomena had been invited, but she refused to attend, saying she wasn't about to set foot on a hillbilly houseboat.

No one really expected anything else from her. She'd settled right into her mayoral duties and things seemed to be going well. Kelsey was happy for her. Kelsey saw Pamela once at a charity event she was still involved in and her cousin looked miserable. Just before Kelsey left she leaned in and whispered, "It's okay to leave."

Pamela, the poor thing, was still Filomena's aide-de-camp. But Kelsey held out hope for her cousin. A year ago, people hadn't held out much hope for her and now here she was, about to marry the man of her dreams.

Tasha was matron-of-honor of course and couldn't hide the fact that she was five months pregnant. Sean won her over and they'd married at the *Rockabye* on the Fourth of July. Tasha now worked for Noah too, as his executive chef. They'd built a restaurant on Christmas Island, named aptly The Firefly.

Finally using her degree in hospitality, Kelsey had taken over the administrative duties of both the *Rockabye* and The Firefly and she'd doubled their revenue.

"I'm so proud of you," Theo whispered as he passed her over to Noah.

"Thanks, Dad."

She took Noah's hand and looked into the eyes of her best friend, saw the spirit of Christmas brimming there. The holiday she'd once hated was now her favorite time of the year. Of course, they would have a Christmas wedding. She wore the firefly necklace Noah had given her last year as a promise for this day.

A happy smile lit up his dear, easygoing face. "You are the most beautiful thing I've ever seen."

Kelsey's heart skipped a beat, her gaze clinging to her tall, laid-back man who was so much fun and who'd helped define the person she had become. A balanced woman able to freely give and receive love. They complemented each other, both bringing something special to the relationship.

And in the entire year since last Christmas, her eye hadn't twitched once.

When the preacher pronounced them husband and wife and Noah kissed her under the stars shining above the glass dome, she breathed a prayer of gratitude.

This was what she'd been missing all those years. Affection, understanding, love.

So much love. Not just from Noah, but from Theo and Leah, Noah's family and friends, and the community of Twilight as well. There was nowhere else in the world that she would rather be.

As Noah held her in his arms, Kelsey went up on tiptoes, pressed her lips to his ear and whispered, "Wanna slip into a cubbyhole before the photographer starts rounding everyone up for pictures?"

"Why Mrs. MacGregor." He grinned. "Whatever do you mean?"

"You know exactly what I mean, Mr. MacGregor."

"Mrs. MacGregor, are you trying to push me out of my comfort zone?"

She clicked her tongue, gave him a knowing wink, and murmured, "Yes, I am. Find a secret place to have your way with me now . . . I *dare* you."

Keep reading for a look at

TO TAME A WILD COWBOY

**the previous book in Lori Wilde's
Cupid, Texas series**

Available now from Avon Books!

"It takes a village."

Huh?

Rhett Lockhart opened one eye and studied the shapely blonde in the bed next to him. Pouty red lips, which last night had tasted like strawberry gloss, glistened in the bright sunshine pushing against the edges of the light-blocking curtains.

Big smoky brown eyes, circled by smeared mascara, blinked at him. Full perky breasts, which tasted just as delicious in real life as they'd looked in last year's Rodeo Queens of New Mexico pinup calendar, thrust against his arm.

Miss September.

On the calendar, she'd worn spangles, bangles, a pink cowgirl hat, and little else. Much like she was dressed now, minus the hat. She was cute and perky and just the right kind of wrong.

Too bad his head throbbed like a sonofagun.

The culprit, an empty bottle of cinnamon whiskey, lay wedged between his pillow and the headboard. The celebratory hooch she'd brought with her because, as she'd said, he was *red-hot.*

"To get you up, cowboy." She glanced down at his crotch with a knowing smile. "Some bozo's been hammering on your door for a solid five minutes, and I've been calling your name . . ."

Nausea jiggled his stomach. It took him a second to remember where they were. Oh yeah, inside his Featherlite, a horse trailer with living quarters, currently parked on the rodeo fairground's back lot in Albuquerque.

Last night, he'd come in first place, blistering his biggest rival, Brazilian hotshot Claudio Limon. Claiming a solid ninety-two-point ride on Smooth Operator, one of the orneriest bulls bucking. Life didn't get much sweeter than that.

It was only May, but he was jockeying a hot streak. Burning through the circuit, racking up points left and right. This was *his* year. He was on the cusp of earning his lifetime goal and landing the dream he'd been dreaming since he was old enough to strap on chaps.

Come November in Las Vegas, he was finally going to shove Claudio off his lofty perch as a two-time winner of the Professional Bull Riders World Finals Championship and collect the title for himself.

"Rhett?" The blonde snapped her fingers in front of his face. "You with me, hon?"

Quick, what was her name? Carrie . . . Corrie . . . Chrissy . . . no . . . Cassie? Yes, Cassie. That was it. Right? Did he risk calling her Cassie, or just use his old standby?

He flashed her a big smile, winced against the added pressure in his aching temples, and drawled, "Mornin', sweet cheeks."

"It's Carla," she said, her voice flat, and her smile as fragile as iced lace.

Oops, not Cassie after all. But hey, her name started with a *C*. He was in the ballpark. Although the look in her eyes told him she wouldn't find that a plus.

Carla was on her side facing him, hands stacked underneath her cheek, watching him like he was a bug doing the backstroke in her soup.

"I know that," he lied through his teeth. "But those sweet cheeks of yours are drivin' me crazy." He reached to palm her butt.

"You've got a bit of the devil running through your veins, Rhett Lockhart," she breathed out on a wistful sigh. "You ooze temptation with that sexy walk and charmin' talk. How's an honest girl supposed to resist?"

She was right. He couldn't deny it, much as he might want to; he was Duke Lockhart's son. That ornery sonofabitch.

Bam, bam, bam. A firm and urgent knock on his trailer door.

"Shh." Rhett brought a finger to his lips. "Let's pretend we're not here. Maybe they'll leave."

She scooted away, nodded at his mobile phone on the bedside table beside a half-empty box of condoms. "Your cell's been pinging too."

"Ignore it." Rhett walked his fingers up her bare thigh, which was poking out from underneath the covers.

"What if it's an emergency?"

"It's not."

"How do you know?"

"Don't you want to spend the day in bed with me?" he wheedled.

"It's not me. It's the rude dude at the door."

"Maybe it's TMZ wanting an interview." He gave her another wink and a tickle. "I *was* pretty spectacular last night."

Carla laughed. "Yeah, right."

"Pardon me? Are you making fun of my bedroom prowess?"

"Oh, I have no complaints in *that* department," she purred.

Bam, bam, bam.

"It might not be an emergency, but whoever is out there isn't going away. For once in your life, face the music, Lockhart." Carla got out of bed.

Face the music? Not his strong suit.

"Rhett!" his lawyer, Lamar Johnston, called out. "Open the damn door. I know you're in there."

"Want me to get that?" Carla found his black PBR T-shirt draped over the footboard. Pulled the tee down over her head, covering those beautiful boobs.

Darn it.

"It's just Lamar." He reached for her arm and hauled her back onto the mattress beside him. "Ignore him, and he'll leave."

"Who is Lamar?"

"My Texas lawyer."

"Why is your Texas lawyer in New Mexico?"

"I might have been avoiding his calls."

"What have you gotten yourself messed up in?"

"It's nothing." Rhett waved a hand. "People like to sue you when you're in the public eye."

"It doesn't sound like nothing."

Bam, bam, bam.

"Rhett, I'm not going anywhere," Lamar confirmed.

His attorney had crap timing. "You might as well let me the hell in."

Carla rolled out of his arms. Grabbed for the tiny scrap of pink silk that passed for panties lying on the floor and wriggled into them.

Rhett sat up. Shook his head. Wished he had another hour with her. But maybe this was better. Short and sweet.

"This wasn't how I anticipated the day going," she muttered. "I had plans for you."

Yikes, both intriguing and a little frightening.

"Me either," Rhett said as way of an apology. "I'd intended on taking you out to IHOP for breakfast."

"You mean lunch." She nodded at the digital clock on the faux panel walls. One p.m. Was it really that late?

"Rain check?" he asked to be polite.

"If I knew you meant it, I'd say yes." Carla stepped into faded skinny jeans that fit like a second skin. Wriggled and jiggled to get the zipper up.

Rhett licked his lips. He remembered why he'd brought her back to his trailer last night. Besides the pretty face and hot bod, she was an easygoing, no-strings-attached woman.

Just his type.

"But we both know this isn't headed anywhere." She came around to his side of the bed. Kissed him. A light brush of her lips. "I knew you were a good-time Charlie when I crawled into the sack with you. I had no foolish dreams that I was the one girl who could tie you down."

"No?" He gave her his best morning-after grin, relief breaking out all over him. "Giving up that easily? I wouldn't mind if you tried a little harder to lasso me."

She laughed a soft shame-on-you sound. "Do I look stupid? You're a fun guy, Rhett. But let's face it, you're not cut out for the long haul."

"That's it?" he asked, disappointed, and surprised at his disappointment. He liked Carla for sure, but the last thing he wanted was a relationship.

Not now. Not ever.

He wasn't like most people, hell-bent on finding The One, tying the knot, having a passel of kids, growing old, dying . . .

Just the thought of it made him twitchy.

And that spurred another thought. What would his life have been like if he hadn't been born to one of the wealthiest men in the Trans-Pecos, who'd swung through women, leaving a trail of broken hearts in his wake?

He recalled a time when he was seven years old and out to dinner with the family. His mother, that gentle soul, his brothers—two half, one full—and his father. They were at the Barbecue King in Alpine. He recalled the smoky smell of mesquite and the taste of mustard potato salad. One of the waitresses had taken one look at his father, let out a cry of shock, and dropped her tray with a clatter. She'd rushed over to slap Duke hard across the face. Rhett's mother, Lucy, had burst into tears. Duke laughed and rubbed his cheek, which had turned bright red in the shape of a handprint. The restaurant diners gaped. The owner rushed over, fired the waitress, and comped their meal. Ridge punched the old man in the gut. Ranger picked up a book and started reading. Remington threw his arm around their mother and glared at Duke. Rhett crawled underneath the table, stuck his fingers in his ears, and started humming "I Wanna Be a Cowboy."

Ah, family memories. Good times.

"Some people are born to roam the earth alone. That's you to a T." Carla's eyes gentled. She was a kind woman. "Not everyone is meant to find true love and have a family . . . and there's nothing wrong with that."

He agreed. So how come he felt oddly put down?

And a tiny bit sad?

She plunked onto the end of the mattress, tugging on pink rhinestone ankle boots. Stood. Headed for the door. "By the way," she said, her voice as cheerful as Saturday night, "I'm keeping the T-shirt."

"You're welcome to it."

She brought the neckline of the tee up to her nose, inhaled. Sighed. "God, you *do* smell good." Her voice was wistful, but not in a fatalistic way. More like she'd missed out on a sweet deal on a used car.

She picked her cell phone up off the tiny shelf on her side of the bed. Glanced at her messages. "Ah," she said. "It's just as well that we didn't get to spend the day together."

"What is?" Rhett scratched his chest, yawned.

"My ex just texted. He got called into work and I have to go pick up my daughter."

"I didn't know you had a daughter."

"Ivy. She's four." Carla's face was ringed with sudden happiness. "Light of my life. Wanna see a picture?"

He held up a palm. "That's okay. You have to get on the road."

A new look crossed her face, as if she'd dodged a bullet on that used car that turned out to be a clunker.

Yikes.

Carla was the fourth woman he'd dated this past year that had a child. When did everyone start having kids?

Goose bumps sprang up his arms, and his throat tightened. Kids gave him the heebie-jeebies. He had no idea how to relate to them.

She wriggled her fingers and squeezed out of the cramped bedroom loft. He watched her step down to the next level of the trailer, could see only her top half now. She opened the door. "Morning."

"Um . . . hello." Lamar's booming voice filled the trailer.

"Bye," she said.

Rhett heard them pass on the steps, Carla going out, Lamar coming in. The door closed, and he got the oddest feeling. As if something irrevocable had just happened.

Lamar's thick head of curly black hair poked into his doorway. "You're a scoundrel, you know that, right?"

Yawning again, Rhett interlaced his fingers, stretched his arms over his head. "What can I say? I love the ladies, and the ladies love me."

"Have you no shame?"

"Shame? What for? I have rules."

"Like what?"

"No one under twenty-one, and no married women, ever."

Maybe he should start adding "no mothers" to that list too. Kids complicated things. A lot. Last week, he'd spent the night at a woman's house and woke up to find a little boy in Superman Underoos staring at him. Acting as if it were no big deal to find a strange man in Mom's bed, the boy took Rhett by the hand, led him to the kitchen, and asked him to make "boo-berry" Pop-Tarts. Rhett threw Pop-Tarts in the toaster, poured the kid some chocolate milk, and got the hell out of there ASAP. That was the extent of his brush with anything remotely like fatherhood. He barely even saw his brother Ridge's two kids or his eighteen-month-old twin brothers his sixty-year-old father had sired with his third wife, Vivi.

"Oh, what a code of honor." Sarcasm was Lamar's touchstone.

"Hey, I don't make them any promises. The women know right up front where they stand with me."

"And you go through them like Kleenex."

"Why are you here?" Rhett lowered his arms. His mouth was as dry as the Chihuahuan Desert he called home. He needed a gallon of water and a fistful of aspirins for his hangover. But the bed was soft, and he was feeling lazy, so he lazed.

"Get dressed." Lamar turned and moved to the compact kitchenette at the back of the living quarters. Pots and pans clanked. The coffeemaker gurgled to life.

There was something about his lawyer's tone of voice that grabbed Rhett by the short hairs. He threw back the covers.

"Are you fixin' my breakfast?" Rhett called, whisking his Wrangler's from the floor and pulling them on. An uneasy tingling tugged his belly. Something strange was afoot.

Bare-chested, he dropped down off the bedroom platform, landed on the laminate wood flooring with a flat-footed *plop*, and strolled the short space to the kitchen area.

Lamar stood at the gas stove whisking eggs in a bowl. He pointed at a chair with his elbow. "Sit."

Bumfuzzled, Rhett slouched at the table.

Lamar plunked a mug down in front of him. Coffeepot in hand, he leaned over to fill Rhett's mug. "Drink."

"You can cook?"

Fifteen years ago, Lamar had been the star of the
Cupid basketball team; now, he was one of the top civil
law attorneys in the Trans-Pecos. Lamar, as always, was
impeccably dressed, wearing a tailor-made navy blue
pinstripe suit, gold cuff links, a red pocket square, and a
big diamond stud in his left ear. "There's a lot you don't
know about me."

"Yeah, like why you're here cooking me breakfast at
one o'clock in the afternoon?"

"Someone has to make sure you're taken care of since
you seem incapable of doing it yourself." Lamar tsked,
and tossed pepper, salt, and onion powder into the eggs.
Scrambled them with a spatula.

"Hey!"

"Don't act offended. You're the superstar who leaves
the grunt work to us mere mortals." The microwave
dinged. Lamar removed a paper plate with two breakfast
sausages on it. He added the eggs to the plate, sprinkled
cheddar cheese on top, and passed the food to Rhett.
"Eat."

"What's your problem?"

"You got bigger issues than me, buddy."

"Yeah, I don't have a fork."

Lamar rummaged around in a drawer, found a fork,
and shoved it at him, tines first. Nimbly, he sank into the
chair across from Rhett. He looked like a sleek panther
that could easily snap Rhett's neck if he wanted. "We
have to talk."

"What about?"

Lamar reached over for his brown leather briefcase,
took out some legal papers stapled together, and dropped
them in the middle of the table.

"What's this?" Rhett asked.

"Got the test results back."

Rhett stared at the papers in front of him. It was an incomprehensible list of letters and numbers. Oh shit. From the look on Lamar's face, he knew he was in big trouble. The eggs he'd swallowed hung in his throat. He couldn't get them to go either up or down. There they sat, making a giant knot, choking him.

"At last." Lamar chuckled. "You've got nothing to say."

Rhett spat the eggs out into a napkin. "Oh, I got plenty to say. One of these days, you're gonna walk in here and deliver some happy news. General Mills wants to feature me on a box of Wheaties. Claudio is quitting the PBR for good and returning to Brazil. Hollywood is paying big bucks for my life stor—"

"Surprise!" Lamar interrupted. "This time you won the paternity lottery." Lamar thumped the paperwork with a thumb. "Congratulations! You're a father."

The words didn't sink in. Father? Him? No way. He'd been sued for paternity three other times, which was why he had Lamar on retainer, and had always come up in the clear.

"I *can't* be the father." Rhett hopped up and paced the tiny trailer, hand on his forehead. "There has to be some kind of mistake."

"DNA is ninety-nine percent accurate."

"But I never ride bareback." Rhett whacked his hip into the counter, barely even noticed. "*Nev*-er."

"Accidents happen." Lamar shrugged as if he'd been expecting such news for a long time. "The only perfect birth control is abstinence, and the whole world knows you're incapable of that." He pointed to Carla's pink bra hanging from the doorknob. "Case in point."

"I was only with her once."

"Who? The owner of the pink bra or Rhona White?"

"Both."

"Once is enough."

Rhett muttered a curse. "Rhona set me up. She got pregnant on purpose. She just wants money."

"Takes two to tango. Besides, it's not Rhona who's after you, she seems to have disappeared. It's the state of Texas."

No. No. This could *not* be happening. Not at this point in his career. Not when everything was on the line. He shoved his fingers through his hair.

A sharp pinprick of memory pierced the base of his skull. The summer he was seventeen, Brittany Fant, the girl who'd shattered his heart, had ended any stupid beliefs he'd ever had about romantic love. He flashed back to a positive pregnancy test, a rush of intense joy at the thought of being a dad . . . and then the calm announcement by Brittany's mother that she was taking her daughter to a clinic and putting an end to this nonsense. "Is this what you really want?" Rhett had asked, pleading. A pale-faced Brittany nodded in silent agreement. And that had been that.

"I don't know why you're so shocked." Lamar propped his Gucci loafers on the Yeti cooler parked underneath the table. "It's been six weeks since CPS showed up with the swab. You think you'd have braced yourself for the possibility of this outcome."

"I was one of four potential dads. What were the odds it'd be me?"

"Um, twenty-five percent or better."

"How did this happen? It shouldn't have happened."

"You think you're special?" Lamar shot him a look of disdain. "That the laws of nature don't apply to you? You keep having sex with random women, even protected sex, and eventually it's going to catch up with you. Stay away from the casinos when you're in Vegas. Your luck has run out."

"Har, har." Rhett kneaded his brow, felt his stomach flip over. He picked up the papers, reread the part confirming that he was indeed the father of Rhona White's baby.

"Sorry to be the bearer of bad news, but it's time to accept responsibility for your actions, buckaroo."

Panic was a noose around his neck, growing tighter with each breath he took. Rhona had vowed she was on birth control. Assured him that he didn't need to use a condom. He'd insisted anyway. He wasn't dumb. She wouldn't have been the first buckle bunny to get pregnant in order to lasso herself a rodeo hero.

The thing was, he'd liked Rhona. She was cute and had a bubbly personality, and she looked at him as if he'd hung the moon. That was always a nice combo. Although she'd been younger than he liked, just turned twenty-one.

Still, he wished like hell he'd shut the door that night she'd shown up at his trailer, after they'd spent the evening playing darts together at a nearby bar. She'd been holding a bottle of champagne, wearing those hot pink shortshorts and an I-wanna-share-your-bed smile. They'd both gotten drunk, and one thing had led to another . . .

God, he should have known better. Rhett whacked his forehead with the heel of his hand—*stupid, stupid, stupid*.

"There's one major thing you forget in your selfish wallow," Lamar said.

Rhett blinked. "Who? Rhona?"

"The baby, you jackass."

Baby.

Rhett stopped moving, stopped thinking, stopped breathing.

Baby.

The word rolled through him, a freight train of energy. Blasting hot and indigo up his spine. He clenched his teeth and his fist, but his heart loosened, floppy and soft inside his chest.

There was a *real* baby.

He was a dad. He slumped back down into the chair. His jaw dropped, his mouth falling right open of its own accord. "I have a son?"

"No, you have a daughter."

"What?"

Lamar tapped the paper with his index finger. "It's a girl."

"I have a da-da-daughter," Rhett tripped over the word. "Daughter" was so big, carried so many implications. It was too much to absorb. Feelings shot through him like lasers from a ray gun: fear, awe, inadequacy, helplessness, bravery, sheer terror, and, oddly enough, the most prominent feeling of all—joy. Followed by one prevailing thought, *I am not worthy.*

"You do indeed have a daughter."

"Where is she? Do you know?" Rhett gripped the table with his fingers, fear tearing at the seams of his heart. Good God, he was a father. How was he supposed to act? Certainly not like his own father. Oh shit, oh damn, oh hell.

"There were . . . complications," Lamar said.

"Complications?" His heart squeezed down to the size of a pecan. "What do you mean?"

"Your daughter was born four months premature."

"What?" He felt all the blood drain from his face. Cold, sick fear slapped him. He didn't even know the kid and here he was feeling sorry for her. "How is that possible? Can you be born four months early and still live?"

"She was very sick."

Was? His heart popped like a slipping clutch. "What? What? Did she die?" An ugly part of him was secretly relieved that maybe she hadn't made it, but the noble part of him was horrified that he could even think such a thing.

"Relax, she is alive, and finally out of the hospital."

"Oh, thank God." Rhett clasped a hand to his chest, dizzy and disoriented. "Is she okay now? How's Rhona?"

Lamar shook his head as if Rhett was a hopeless case. "No one knows where Rhona is. She abandoned the baby after giving birth at the hospital. She gave the hospital staff the names of potential fathers while she was in labor for fourteen hours. That's why CPS came looking for the dad. To find out if you want the baby. I explained all this when CPS first showed up."

Yeah, he hadn't really been listening, certain that the baby couldn't have been his.

A feeling unlike anything he'd ever experienced crushed Rhett in a powerful grip, flooded his entire system. Big and bad and scary feelings, especially for a man who avoided entanglements.

He had a daughter. A piece of him was out there in the world. Alone.

Thirty minutes ago, he was a cowboy without a worry in the world except winning the PBR championship. Now he was a father, and in one sharp moment, everything had changed.

"Where is my little girl? If Rhona took off, who's looking after her?"

"Relax. She's in good hands. Your daughter is living in El Paso with her foster mother, who, by the way, was also her neonatal nurse."

Whew, well, that was good. Someone competent was looking after her. For a second there, he'd had a crazy image of a little baby tucked in a wicker basket, swaddled in pink, left on a doorstep, coyotes howling in the distance. In much the same way that his older brother Ridge ended up dumped by his mother on their father's doorstep when he was three.

The Lockhart men had complicated histories with women and abandoned babies.

It was going to be okay, he told himself. He could have a kid. Lots of the guys on the circuit did. Yes, many of them were married, but having kids didn't seem to cramp their style. He'd provide for his daughter financially. Of course, that was a given, but it didn't mean he would have to give up his life. It's not like he had to change diapers or anything.

"What's the next step?" he asked his lawyer.

Lamar lifted his shoulders. "That's up to you."

"Meaning?"

"You can file for custody, or . . ." Lamar took a form from his briefcase, spread it on the kitchen table. "Sign over all parental rights so the foster mother can adopt her, and you can walk away with a clear conscience."